*Other Books in The Vintage Library
of Contemporary World Literature*

WE LOVE GLENDA SO MUCH

AND

A CHANGE OF LIGHT

WE LOVE GLENDA SO MUCH

AND

A CHANGE OF LIGHT

JULIO CORTÁZAR

Translated from the Spanish by Gregory Rabassa

AVENTURA

The Vintage Library of Contemporary World Literature

VINTAGE BOOKS   A DIVISION OF RANDOM HOUSE   NEW YORK

CONTENTS

A CHANGE OF LIGHT
AND OTHER STORIES

WE LOVE GLENDA SO MUCH

AND OTHER TALES

I

ORIENTATION OF CATS

To Juan Soriano

When Alana and Osiris look at me I can't complain of the least dissembling, the least duplicity. They look at me straight on, Alana with her blue light and Osiris with his green ray. They also look at one another that way, Alana stroking Osiris's black back as he lifts his mouth from the plate of milk and mews with satisfaction, woman and cat knowing one another on planes that escape me, that my caresses can't reach. For some time now I've renounced all mastery over Osiris, we're good friends across an unbridgeable distance; but Alana is my wife and the distance between us is a different one, something that she doesn't seem to feel but which blocks my happiness when Alana looks at me, when she looks at me straight on just the way Osiris does and smiles at me or speaks to me without the slightest reserve, giving herself in every gesture and everything, just as she gives herself in love, there where her whole body is like her eyes: an absolute surrender, an uninterrupted reciprocity.

It's strange—even though I've renounced entry into Osiris's world, my love for Alana won't accept that simplicity of a thing concluded, of partners forever, of life without secrets. Behind those blue eyes there's more, in the depths of the words and moans and the silences another realm is born, another Alana is breathing. I've never told her so, I love her too much to break this surface of happiness over which so many days have slipped, so many years. In my own way I make a stubborn effort to understand, to discover; I watch her but without spying; I follow her but without mistrust; I love a marvelous mutilated statue, an unfinished text, a fragment of sky inscribed on the window of life.

There was a time when music seemed to me to be the path that would really lead me to Alana; watching her listen to our Bartók, Duke Ellington, and Gal Costa records, a gradual transparency sank me into her, the music undressed her in a different way, turned her more and more Alana, because Alana couldn't be only that woman who had always looked at me straight on without hiding anything from me. Against Alana, beyond Alana, I was looking for her in order to love her better; and if at first the music let me glimpse other Alanas, the day came when facing a Rembrandt print I saw her change even more, as if a set of clouds in the sky had suddenly altered the lights and shadows of a landscape. I felt that the painting was carrying her beyond herself for that only spectator who could measure the instantaneous metamorphosis that was never repeated, the glimpse of Alana in Alana. Involuntary interceders, Keith Jarrett, Beethoven, and Aníbal Troilo had helped me get close, but facing a painting or a print Alana got rid of even more of what she thought she was. For a moment she would enter an imaginary world so that without knowing it she could get out of herself, going from one painting to another, making comments on them or being silent, a deck of cards that each new contemplation shuffled for the one who, stealthy and attentive, a little behind or leading her by the arm, saw coming one after another the queens and the aces, the spades and the clubs—Alana.

What could be done with Osiris? Give him his milk, leave him alone as a satisfied and purring black ball; but Alana I could take to this picture gallery as I did yesterday, go to a theater with mirrors and camera obscuras once more, with sharp images on the canvas facing that other image, gay in blue jeans and a red blouse, who after putting out her cigarette at the entrance would go from picture to picture, stopping at precisely the distance her look required, turning to me from time to time to comment or compare. She had never discovered that I wasn't there for the pictures, that a little to the rear or to the side my way of looking had nothing to do with hers. She probably never realized that her slow and reflective pace from picture to picture was changing her until I had to close my eyes and struggle against squeezing her in my arms and going off into a delirium with her, into a full-fledged bit of madness right out in public. Relaxed, light in her natural way of pleasure and discovery, her pauses and her lingering were inscribed in a different time from mine, alien to the tense expectancy of my thirst.

Until then everything had been a vague omen, Alana in the music, Alana facing Rembrandt. But now my hope was beginning to be unbearably fulfilled; from the moment of our arrival Alana had given herself over to the paintings with the atrocious innocence of a chameleon, going from one state to another without knowing that a spectator in ambush was spying on her posture, the tilt of her head, the movement of her hands or her lips, seeking the inner chromatism that ran through her until it showed her to be another, there where the other one was always Alana adding herself to Alana, the cards piling up until the deck is complete. By her side, going slowly along the walls of the gallery, I was watching her give herself over to each painting, my eyes were multiplying the lightning bolt of a triangle that went from her to the picture and from the picture to me, returning to her and catching the change, the different halo that encircled her for a moment to give way later to a new aura, a tonality that exposed her to the true one, to the ultimate nakedness. It was impossible to foresee how far that osmosis would be repeated, how many new Alanas would finally carry me to the synthesis from which we would both emerge fulfilled, she without knowing it and lighting a new cigarette before asking me to buy her a drink; I knowing that my long search had finally culminated and that from then on my love would take in the visible and the invisible, would accept Alana's clean look without the uncertainty of closed doors, forbidden passageways.

Opposite a solitary boat and a foreground of black rocks, I watched her remain motionless for a long time; an imperceptible fluttering of her hands made her seem to be swimming in the air, going out to sea, a flight from horizons. I was no longer able to be surprised that the other painting, where a spike-topped grating cut off access to the bordering trees, made her step back as if seeking the proper focus. Suddenly it was repulsion, the rejection of an unacceptable limit. Birds, marine monsters, windows opening onto silence or letting a simulacrum of death enter—each new painting was dragging Alana along, despoiling her of her previous color, pulling the modulations of freedom out of her, of flying, of wide-open spaces, affirming her negation facing night and nothingness, her solar anxiety, her almost terrible impulse of a phoenix bird. I remained in back, knowing that it would be impossible for me to bear her look, her interrogative surprise when she saw in my face the bewilderment of confirmation, because that too was I, that was my Project Alana, my Alana life, it had been desired by me and reined in by a present tense of city and parsimony, finally now Alana, finally Alana and I from now on. I would have liked to have held her naked in my arms, love her in such a way that everything would be clear, everything would be spoken forever between us, and that from that endless night of love (as we had already known so many of them) the first dawn of life would be born.

We got to the end of the gallery; I went over to an exit door, still hiding my face, hoping that the air and the street-lights would turn me back into what Alana knew of me. I saw her stop in front of a picture that other visitors had hidden from me, remain motionless for a long time looking at the painting of a window and a cat. One last transformation made her a slow statue neatly separated from the others, from me, who went over indecisively seeking the eyes lost in the canvas. I saw that the cat was identical to Osiris and that it was looking at something in the distance that the sidewall of the window prevented us from seeing. Motionless in his contemplation, he seemed less motionless than Alana's immobility. In some way I felt that the triangle had been broken; when Alana turned her head toward me the triangle no longer existed, she had gone into the picture but she hadn't come back, she was still beside the cat, looking beyond the window where no one could see what they saw, what only Alana and Osiris saw every time they looked at me straight on.

WE LOVE GLENDA SO MUCH

In those days it was hard to know. You go to the movies or the theater and live your night without thinking about the people who have already gone through the same ceremony, choosing the place and the time, getting dressed and telephoning and row eleven or five, the darkness and the music, territory that belongs to nobody and to everybody there where everybody is nobody, the men or women in their seats, maybe a word of apology for arriving late, a murmured comment that someone picks up or ignores, almost always silence, looks pouring onto the stage or the screen, fleeing from what's beside them, from what's on this side. It was really hard to know that there were so many of us—beyond the ads, the endless lines, the posters, and the reviews—so many who loved Glenda.

It took three or four years, and it would not be bold to assert that the nucleus had its start with Irazusta or Diana Rivero; they themselves didn't know how at some moment, over drinks with friends after the movies, things were said or left unsaid that suddenly would form the alliance, what afterward we all called the nucleus and the younger ones the club. There was nothing of a club about it, we simply loved Glenda Garson, and that was enough to set us apart from those who only admired her. Just like them, we admired Glenda too, and also Anouk, Marilyn, Annie, Silvana, and why not Marcello, Yves, Vittorio, or Dirk, but only we loved Glenda so much, and the nucleus was formed because of that and out of that, it was something that only we knew, and we trusted in those who all during our conversations had shown little by little that they loved Glenda too.

Starting with Diana or Irazusta, the nucleus was slowly expanding. In the year of *Snow Fire* there couldn't have been more than six or seven of us; with the premiere of *The Uses of Elegance* the nucleus broadened and we felt that it was growing at an almost unbearable rate and that we were threatened with snobbish imitation or seasonal sentimentality. The first, Irazusta and Diana and two or three more of us, decided to close ranks, not to admit anyone without a test, without an examination disguised under the whiskey and a show of erudition (so Buenos Aires, so London and Mexico, those midnight exams). At the time of the opening of *Fragile Returns,* we had to admit, melancholically triumphant, that there were many of us who loved Glenda. The chance meetings at the movies, the glances exchanged as we came out, that kind of lost look on the women and the painful silence of the men, showed us better than any insignia or password. Mechanics that defied investigation led us to the same downtown café, the isolated tables began to draw closer together, there was the gracious custom of ordering the same cocktail so as to lay aside any useless skirmishing, and finally looking each other in the eyes, there where Glenda's last image in the last scene of the last movie still breathed.

Twenty, maybe thirty, we never knew how many we had come to be, because sometimes Glenda would go on for months at one theater or was in two or three at the same time, and there was also that exceptional moment when she appeared onstage to play the young murderess in *The Lunatics* and her success broke the dikes and created a momentary enthusiasm that we never accepted. By that time we already knew each other; a lot of us would visit each other to talk about Glenda. From the very beginning Irazusta seemed to exercise a tacit command that he had never asked for, and Diana Rivero played her slow chess game of acceptance and rejection that assured us a total authenticity without the risk of infiltrators or boobs. What had begun as a free association was now attaining the structure of a clan, and the casual interrogations of early times had been succeeded by concrete questions, the stumbling scene in *The Uses of Elegance*, the final retort in *Snow Fire*, the second erotic scene in *Fragile Returns*. We loved Glenda so much that we couldn't tolerate parvenus, rowdy lesbians, erudite aestheticians. It was even (we'll never know how) taken for granted that we would go to the café on Fridays when a Glenda movie was playing downtown, and with the reruns in neighborhood theaters we would let a week go by before getting together in order to give everybody the necessary time; like a rigorous regulation, the obligations were defined without error; not respecting them would have meant provoking Irazusta's contemptuous smile or that graciously horrible look with which Diana Rivero denounced and punished treason.

At that time the gatherings were only Glenda, her dazzling presence in every one of us, and we knew nothing of discrepancies or misgivings. Only gradually, at first with a feeling of guilt, did some dare to let partial criticisms slip, disillusion or disappointment with an unfortunate scene, descents into the conventional or the predictable. We knew that Glenda wasn't responsible for the weaknesses that at certain moments clouded the splendid crystal of *The Lash* or the ending of *You Never Know Why*. We found out about other films by the directors, where the stories and the scripts came from, we were implacable with them because we were beginning to feel that our love for Glenda was going beyond the merely artistic terrain and that she alone was saved from what the rest did imperfectly. Diana was the first to talk about a mission; she did it in her tangential way, not stating outright what really counted for her. We saw the joy of a double whiskey, of a satisfied smile in her when we admitted openly that it was true, that we couldn't just stay like that, the movies and the café and loving Glenda so much.

Not even then were clear words spoken; we didn't need them. All that counted was Glenda's happiness in each one of us, and that happiness could only come from perfection. Suddenly the mistakes, the misses, became unbearable for us; we couldn't accept the way *You Never Know Why* ended, or that *Snow Fire* should include the infamous poker scene (in which Glenda didn't take part, but which in some way stained her like vomit—that expression of Nancy Phillips's) and the inadmissible arrival of the repentant son. As almost always, it was up to Irazusta to give a clear definition of the mission that awaited us, and that night we went home as if crushed by the responsibility we had just recognized and assumed, catching a glimpse at the same time of the happiness of a flawless future, of Glenda without blunders or betrayals.

Instinctively, the nucleus closed ranks, the task wouldn't allow for a hazy plurality. Irazusta spoke of the laboratory after it had already been set up in a country house in Recife de Lobos. We divided up the tasks equitably among those who were to collect all the prints of *Fragile Returns*, chosen for its relatively few imperfections. No one had thought to raise the question of money; Irazusta had been Howard Hughes's partner in the Pichincha tin mines, an extremely simple mechanism put the necessary power in our hands, jets and connections and bribes. We didn't even have an office; Hagar Loss's computer programmed the tasks and the stages. Two months after Diana Rivero's remark the laboratory was all set up to replace the ineffective bird scene in *Fragile Returns* with a different one that gave Glenda back the perfect rhythm and the exact feeling of the dramatic action. The film was already several years old and its rerun on international circuits didn't cause the slightest surprise; memory plays with its repositories and makes them accept their own permutations and variants, perhaps Glenda herself wouldn't have noticed the change but would have noticed, because we all had, the marvel of perfect coincidence with a memory washed clean of slag, precisely in tune with desire.

The mission was being accomplished without surcease; as soon as we felt sure that the laboratory was in working order we brought off the rescue of *Snow Fire* and *The Prism*: the other films entered into the process with the exact rhythm foreseen by Hagar Loss's personnel and the people in the laboratory. We had problems with *The Uses of Elegance* because people in the oil-producing emirates owned copies for their personal enjoyment and extraordinary maneuvers and procedures were necessary in order to steal them (there's no reason to use any other word) and to steal them without their owners' noticing. The laboratory was functioning at a level of perfection that had seemed unattainable to us at the start, even though we hadn't dared say so to Irazusta; curiously, the most doubtful one had been Diana; but when Irazusta showed us *You Never Know Why* and we saw the real ending, we saw Glenda, who instead of going back to Romano's house, headed her car toward the cliff and destroyed us with her splendid, necessary fall into the torrent, we knew that there could be perfection in this world and that now it belonged to Glenda, to Glenda for us forever.

The most difficult part was, of course, deciding on the changes, the cuts, the modifications in montage and rhythm; our different ways of feeling Glenda brought on harsh confrontations that calmed down only after long analyses and in some cases the imposition of majority rule in the nucleus. But while some of us, defeated, watched the new version with bitterness over the fact that it wasn't completely up to our dreams, I don't think anyone was disappointed with the finished work, we loved Glenda so much that the results were always justifiable, often beyond what had been foreseen. There were even a few scares, a letter from a reader of the inevitable *Times* of London showing surprise that three scenes in *Snow Fire* had been shown in a different order from how the writer thought he remembered, and also an article in *La Opinión* protesting a supposed cut in *The Prism*, imagining the hand of bureaucratic prudishness. In every case rapid arrangements were made in order to avoid possible follow-ups; it wasn't hard, people are fickle and forget or accept or are in search of what's new, the movie world is ephemeral, like the historical present, except for those of us who love Glenda so much.

Basically more dangerous were the arguments within

the nucleus, risking schism or diaspora. Even though we felt more united than ever because of the mission, there were nights when analytical voices contaminated by political philosophies were raised, bringing up moral problems in the midst of the work, asking if we weren't surrendering to an onanistic hall of mirrors, foolishly carving a piece of baroque madness on an ivory tusk or a grain of rice. It wasn't easy to turn our backs on them because the nucleus had only been able to do its work in the way a heart or an airplane does: by maintaining a perfectly coherent rhythm. It wasn't easy to listen to criticism that accused us of escapism, that suspected a waste of strength that was being turned away from a more pressing reality, one that was more in need of agreement in the times we were living. And yet it wasn't necessary to crush summarily a heresy that was only hinted at, as even its protagonists limited themselves to a partial objection, they and we loved Glenda so much that above and beyond ethical or historical disagreements the feeling that would always unite us remained, the certainty that perfecting Glenda was perfecting us and perfecting the world. We even had splendid recompense in the fact that one of the philosophers re-established the equilibrium after overcoming that period of inane scruples; from his mouth we heard that all partial works are also history, that something as immense as the invention of the printing press had been born of the most individual and particular of desires—to repeat and perpetuate a woman's name.

In that way we came to the day on which we got proof that Glenda's image was now being projected without the slightest weakness; the screens of the world were presenting her in just the way that she herself—we were sure—would have wanted to be presented, and perhaps that was why it didn't surprise us too much to read in the press that she had just announced her retirement from movies and the theater. Glenda's involuntary and marvelous contribution to our work couldn't have been either coincidence or miracle, it was simply that something in her had unknowingly respected our anonymous love, from the depths of her being came the only answer that she could give us, the act of love that included us in one last act of giving, the one that ordinary people would only understand as an absence. We were living the happiness of the seventh day, of the rest after the creation; now we would be able to see every one of Glenda's works without the agonizing threat of a tomorrow plagued by mistakes and blunders; now we could come together with the lightness of angels or birds, in an absolute presence that was like eternity.

Yes, but a poet had said under Glenda's same skies that eternity is in love with the works of time, and it was for Diana to discover and give us the news a year later. Ordinary and human, Glenda was announcing her return to the screen, the usual reasons, the frustration of a professional with nothing to do, a role that was made to order, an imminent filming. No one can have forgotten that night at the café, precisely after seeing *The Uses of Elegance*, which was returning to downtown theaters. It almost wasn't necessary for Irazusta to say what we were all experiencing, a bitter taste of injustice and rebellion. We loved Glenda so much that our discouragement didn't touch her, it was no fault of hers, being an actress and being Glenda, the horror was in the ruptured mechanism, in the reality of figures and awards and Oscars entering our so hard-won heaven like a hidden fissure. When Diana laid her hand on Irazusta's arm and said "Yes, it's the only thing left to do," she was speaking for all of us with no need for consultation. Never had the nucleus had such a fearsome drive, never had it needed fewer words to put it into motion.

We separated, undone, already living what would happen on a day that only one of us would know ahead of time. We were sure we wouldn't meet again at the café, that each of us from then on would hide the solitary perfection of our realm. We knew that Irazusta was going to do what was necessary, nothing simpler for someone like him. We didn't even say good-bye the way we usually did, with the nice security of meeting again after the movies some night with *Fragile Returns* or *The Lash*. It was rather a turning your back, with the pretext that it was late, that you had to leave; we went off separately, each one bearing his or her desire to forget until everything was consummated, and knowing it wouldn't be that way, that we would still have to open the newspaper some morning and read the news, the stupid phrases of professional consternation. We would never talk about that with anybody, we would courteously avoid each other in theaters and on the street; it would be the only way that the nucleus could remain true to its faith, could silently guard the finished work. We loved Glenda so much that we would offer her one last inviolable perfection. On the untouchable heights to which we had raised her in exaltation, we would save her from the fall, her faithful could go on adoring her without any decrease; one does not come down from a cross alive.

STORY WITH
SPIDERS

We arrived at the bungalow at two in the afternoon and half an hour later, true to the telephone appointment, the young agent appears with the keys, starts up the refrigerator, and shows us how the water heater and the air conditioner work. It's understood that we'll stay ten days, paid in advance. We open our bags and take out what we need for the beach; we'll settle in at sundown, the view of the Caribbean sparkling at the base of the hill is too tempting. We go down the sloping path, we even find a shortcut through the brush that gets us there quicker; there are only three hundred feet between the bungalows on the hill and the sea.

.   .   .

Last night, while we were putting our clothes away and lining up the groceries bought in Saint-Pierre, we could hear the voices of the people in the other wing of the bungalow. They speak very softly, not Martinican voices, full of color and laughter. From time to time a few clearer words: American English, tourists no doubt. The first impression is one of displeasure, we don't know why we expected complete solitude when we saw that each bungalow (there are four of them amidst flower beds, banana trees, and coconut palms) is double. Maybe because when we saw them for the first time after a complicated investigation by telephone from the Hotel de Diamant we thought that everything was vacant and at the same time strangely occupied. The open-air restaurant, for example, a hundred feet farther down: abandoned, but with a few bottles, glasses, and place settings at the bar. And in one or two of the bungalows towels, lotion or shampoo bottles, could be glimpsed in the bathrooms through the blinds. The young agent opened up a completely empty one for us, and to a vague question gave just as vague an answer: that the regular manager had gone away and he was taking charge of the bungalows because he was a friend of the owner. Better that way, of course, since we were looking for solitude and beach; but, of course, other people have thought the same thing and two female American voices are murmuring in the adjoining wing of the bungalow. Paper-thin walls, but everything so comfortable, so well set up. We slept interminably, something strange for us. And if we needed anything, that was it.

Friendships: a tame and mendicant female cat, another black one, wilder but just as hungry. The birds here almost land in your hand and the green lizards climb up onto the table in search of flies. We're surrounded by the bleating of goats far off, five cows and a calf are pastured on the highest part of the hill and they moo properly. We can also hear the dogs from the shacks at the end of the valley; the two cats will certainly join the concert tonight.

The beach deserted by European standards. A few boys are swimming and playing, black or cinnamon bodies dance on the sand. In the distance a family—countrymen or Germans, sadly white and blond—is organizing towels, suntan oils, and tote bags. We let the hours pass in the water or on the sand, incapable of anything else, prolonging the rituals of creams and cigarettes. We still haven't felt memories coming to the fore, that need to make an inventory of the past that grows with solitude and boredom. Quite the contrary: shutting out all reference to the preceding weeks, the meetings in Delft, the night at Erik's farm. If that comes back we waft it away like a puff of smoke, the slight movement of a hand that clears the air again.

Two girls go down the hillside path and pick out a distant spot, the shade of a coconut palm. We gather that they are our neighbors in the bungalow, we imagine them to be secretaries or elementary school teachers from Detroit, from Nebraska. We watch them go into the sea together, go off sportingly, return slowly, savoring the hot and transparent water, a beauty that becomes a topic only when it is described, the eternal matter of postcards. There are two sailboats on the horizon, a motorboat leaves Saint-Pierre with a woman on water skis who meritoriously gets up after every fall, and there are a lot of them.

At dusk, we've come back to the beach after a siesta, the day declines through great white clouds—we tell ourselves that this Christmas will be the perfect answer to our wishes: solitude, the assurance that no one knows where we are, being out of reach of any possible difficulties and at the same time far from the stupid gatherings that come at the end of the year and from conditioned memories, an agreeable freedom to open canned goods and mix a white rum punch made with cane sugar syrup and limes. We dine on the veranda, separated by a bamboo screen from the symmetrically placed terrace where, late now, we hear the barely murmuring voices again. We are a reciprocal marvel as neighbors, we respect each other in an almost exaggerated way. If the girls on the beach are really the occupants of the bungalow, maybe they're wondering if the two people they saw on the sand are the ones living in the other wing. Civilization does have its advantages, we recognize between drinks: no shouting, no transistors, no cheap humming. Oh, if only they'll stay here for the ten days instead of being replaced by a couple with children. Christ has been born again; for our part we can sleep.

We get up with the sun, guava juice and mugs of coffee. The night has been long, with gusts of rain confessedly tropical, quick floods that suddenly and shamedly cease. The dogs barked from every direction, although there was no moon; frogs and birds, sounds that the citified ear can't recognize but that perhaps explain the dreams that we now recall with the first cigarettes. *Aegri somnia*. Where is that from? Charles Nodier, or Nerval, sometimes we can't resist that past of libraries that other vocations have almost erased. We tell each other about dreams where larvae, uncertain threats, and unwelcome but predictable exhumations spin their webs or make us spin them. Nothing surprising after Delft (but we've decided not to bring back recent memories, there'll be time, as always. Curiously, it doesn't affect us to think about Michael, about the well on Erik's farm, things all closed up now; we almost never talk about them or about what preceded them even though we know they can be mentioned without doing us any harm. After all, pleasure and delight came from them, and the night on the farm was worth the price we're paying, but at the same time we feel all that is still too close, the details. Michael naked in the moonlight, things that we would have liked to avoid beyond the inevitable dreams; better this blocking out, then, *other voices, other rooms*: literature and airplanes, what splendid drugs).

The sea at nine in the morning carries off night's last drivel, sun and salt and sand bathe the skin with a hot touch. When we see the girls going down the path we all become aware at the same time, we look at each other. We had made only one comment, almost on the edge of sleep, late at night: at some moment the voices from the other side of the bungalow had gone from whispering to a few clearly audible phrases, even if their meaning escaped us. But it wasn't the meaning that attracted us in that exchange of words that ceased almost at once and returned to a monotone, a discreet murmur, but that one of the voices was that of a man.

At siesta time the muffled sound of conversation on the other veranda reaches us again. Without knowing why, we insist on making the two girls on the beach match the voices in the bungalow, and now that nothing makes one think of a man near them, the memory of last night is unsketched, joined to the other sounds that have aroused us, the dogs, the sudden gusts of wind and rain, the creaking on the roof. City people, people very impressionable away from their own sounds, their mannerly rainstorms.

Besides, what do we care what goes on in the bungalow

next door? The reason we're here is that we had to get away from the other thing, from other people. It's not easy to give up habits, conditioned reflexes, of course; without admitting it to ourselves, we pay attention to what's softly coming through the wall, the dialogue that we imagine to be placid and anodyne, the purring of pure routine. It's impossible to recognize words, even voices, so similar in their register that for moments one might even think it the broken parts of a monologue. That's the way they must have heard us too, but they're not listening to us, of course; to do that they'd have to be silent, they'd have to be here for reasons similar to ours, crouching vigilantly in wait like the black cat that's stalking a lizard on the veranda. But we don't interest them at all: so much the better for them. The two voices alternate, cease, start up again. And there's no man's voice, even if it were speaking that softly we would have recognized it.

As always in the tropics, night falls fast, the bungalow is poorly lighted but that doesn't bother us; we do almost no cooking, the only thing hot is the coffee. We have nothing to say to each other and maybe that's why we seek distraction in listening to the murmuring of the girls, without admitting it openly we're lying in wait for the man's voice, even though we know that no car has come up the hill and that the other bungalows are still empty. We rock in the rocking chairs and smoke in the darkness; there aren't any mosquitoes, the murmurs come from holes of silence, become still, return. If they could imagine us they wouldn't like it; it's not that we're spying on them, but they would certainly look upon us as two spiders in the darkness. After all, it doesn't upset us that the other side of the bungalow is occupied. We were looking for solitude but now we're thinking about what night would be like here if there really weren't anybody on the other side, impossible to deny that the farm, Michael, are still so close.

Having to look at each other, talk, take out the cards or the dice again. It's better like that, in the sling chairs, listening to the rather catlike murmurs until it's time to sleep.

Until it's time to sleep, but here the nights don't bring us what we'd hoped for, a no-man's-land where finally—or for a time, there's no need to pretend what's not possible— we'd be under cover of everything that begins beyond the windows. In our case too, foolishness hasn't been the strong point; we've never reached a destination without foreseeing the next one or the next ones. Sometimes it would seem that we're playing at fencing ourselves in as now on an insignificant island where anything can be easily located; but that's part of an infinitely more complex chess game in which the modest movement of a pawn conceals more important plays. The famous story of the purloined letter is objectively absurd. Objectively; the truth runs underneath, and the Puerto Ricans who for years cultivated marijuana on their New York fire escapes or smack in the middle of Central Park knew more about that than a lot of police. In any case, we're in control of immediate possibilities, ships and planes: Venezuela and Trinidad are a stone's throw away, two choices among six or seven; our passports are the kind that slip through airports with no trouble whatsoever. This innocent hill, this bungalow for petty bourgeois tourists: beautiful loaded dice that we've always known how to use at the proper moment. Delft is far, far away, Erik's farm is beginning to recede in our memories, being erased in the same way that the well and Michael fleeing in the moonlight are being erased, Michael, so white and naked in the moonlight.

. . .

The dogs howled again intermittently, from one of the shacks in the dell the shouts of a woman suddenly cut off at their highest point, the silence next door let a murmur of confused alarm pass in the dozing of tourist women too fatigued and out of it to be really interested in what surrounded them. We stayed listening, far removed from sleep. After all, what's the use of sleeping if later on it could be the roar of a cloudburst on the roof or the shrill lovemaking of cats, the preludes to nightmares, dawn, when heads finally flatten pillows and then nothing can get into them until the sun climbs up the palm trees and you have to go back to living.

On the beach, after taking a long swim out to sea, we wondered again about the abandonment of the bungalows. The restaurant hut with its glasses and bottles brings out the memory of the mystery of the *Mary Celeste* (so well known and so well read about, but that obsessive recurrence of the unexplained, the sailors boarding the ship drifting along at full sail and with nobody on board, the ashes still warm in the cook stoves, the cabins with no signs of mutiny or plague. A collective suicide? We looked at each other ironically, it's not an idea that can open a path in our way of seeing things. We wouldn't be here if we'd accepted it at one time).

The girls go down to the beach late, they sun themselves for a long time before swimming. There too, we notice without commenting, they talk to each other in low voices, and if we'd been closer we would have been reached by the same confidential murmur, the polite fear of intruding in the life of others. If at some moment they would come over to ask for a light, to find out the time . . . But the bamboo screen seems to have been extended down to the beach, we know that they won't bother us.

Siesta time is long, we don't feel like going back to the

beach nor do they, we can hear them talking in the room and then on the veranda. Alone, of course. But why of course? Night can be different and we wait for it without saying so, busying ourselves with nothing, lingering in rocking chairs and with cigarettes and drinks, leaving only one light burning on the veranda; the blinds of the living room filter it through in thin strips that don't drive off the shadows of the air, the silence of waiting. We're not waiting for anything, of course. Why of course? Why lie to ourselves if the only thing we're doing is waiting, as in Delft, as in so many other places? A person can wait for nothing or for a murmur from the other side of the thin wall, a change in the voices. Later a creaking of a bed will be heard, the silence will begin full of dogs, of foliage moved by the gusts of wind. It's not going to rain tonight.

They're leaving; at eight o'clock in the morning a taxi comes to pick them up, the black chauffeur laughs and jokes, taking out their suitcases, their beach bags, large straw hats, tennis rackets. From the veranda you can see the path, the white taxi; they can't make us out among the plants, nor do they even look in our direction.

The beach is peopled with fishermen's children who play ball before swimming, but today it seems even more empty to us now that they won't be back to swim. On the way back we take a roundabout path without realizing it, in any case, without expressly deciding upon it, and we pass in front of the other wing of the bungalow which we had always avoided. Now everything is really abandoned except for our wing. We try the door, it opens noiselessly, the girls have left the key on the inside, no doubt by agreement with the agent who will or will not come by later to clean the bungalow. It no longer surprises us that things are exposed to the whims of anyone, like the glasses and the plates from the restaurant; we see wrinkled sheets, damp towels, empty bottles, insecticides, Coca-Cola bottles and glasses, magazines in English, bars of soap. Everything is so alone, so left behind. They slept there, in the big bed with sheets with yellow flowers. The two of them. And they talked, they talked before going to sleep. They talked so much before sleeping.

The siesta hangs heavy, interminable because we don't feel like going to the beach until the sun is lower in the sky. While making coffee or washing the dishes we catch ourselves in the same position of listening, our ears intent on the wall. We should have laughed but we didn't. Not now, now that finally and really we have the solitude so sought after and so necessary, now we don't laugh.

Preparing dinner takes time, we deliberately complicate the simplest things so that everything will last and night will close in over the hill before we've finished eating. From time to time we catch ourselves looking toward the wall again, waiting for what is already so far away, a murmur that is probably continuing on an airplane or in the cabin of a ship. The agent hasn't come, we know that the bungalow is vacant and open, that it still smells of cologne and youthful skin. It suddenly gets warmer, the silence accentuates it or digestion or boredom because we sit without moving out of the rocking chairs, just barely swaying in the darkness, smoking and waiting. We won't admit it, of course, but we know that we're waiting. The sounds of the night slowly grow, faithful to the rhythm of things and stars; as if the same birds and the same frogs from last night had taken up position and begun their song at the same moment. The chorus of dogs too (*a horizon of dogs*, impossible not to recall the poem), and in the underbrush the lovemaking of the cats tears the air. All that's missing is the murmur of the two voices in the bungalow next door, and that really is silence, silence itself. Everything else slips through the ears that are absurdly concentrated on the wall as if expecting. We don't even talk, fearing that we'll crush the impossible murmurs with our voices. It's already quite late but we don't feel sleepy, the heat keeps on rising in the living room but it doesn't occur to us to open the two doors. We don't do anything but smoke and hope for the hopeless; it doesn't even occur to us, as in the beginning, that the girls might imagine us as spiders lying in wait; they're no longer there for us to attribute our own imaginations to, to turn them into mirrors of this thing taking place in the darkness, of this that unbearably isn't taking place.

Because we can't lie to ourselves, each creak of the rocking chairs replaces a dialogue but at the same time keeps it alive. Now we know that everything was useless, the running away, the trip, the hope of still finding a dark hollow without witnesses, a favorable refuge for beginning again (because repentance doesn't enter our nature, what we did is done and we'll start all over again as soon as we know we're safe from reprisals). It's as if suddenly the whole veteranship of the past has ceased to operate, has abandoned us the way the gods abandon Antony in Cavafy's poem. If we still think about the strategy that guaranteed our arrival on the island, if we imagine for a moment the possible timetables, the efficient telephones in other ports and cities, we do it with the same abstract indifference with which we so frequently quote poems while playing the infinite caroms of mental association. The worst part is that, we don't know why, the change has taken place since our arrival, since the first murmurs from the other side of the wall that we considered a mere barrier, also abstract, for solitude and rest. That another unexpected voice should be joined to the whispers was no reason to go beyond a banal summer enigma, the mystery of the room next door like that of the *Mary Celeste*, frivolous food for siestas and strolls. Nor did we give it any special importance, we've never mentioned it; we only know that it's now impossible to cease paying attention, to cease orienting all activity, all relaxation, toward the wall.

Maybe that's why late at night while we pretend to sleep, we're not disconcerted too much by the short, dry cough that comes from the other side of the bungalow, its tone unmistakably masculine. It almost isn't a cough, rather an involuntary signal, at the same time discreet and penetrating as the girls' murmurs were, but now it's a signal, now it's a summons, after so much alien chatter. We get up without speaking, silence has fallen over the living room again, only one dog is baying and baying far away. We wait for a length of time that's impossible to measure; the visitor in the bungalow is silent too, maybe he's also waiting or has gone to sleep among the yellow flowers on the sheets. It doesn't matter, now there's an agreement that has nothing to do with will, there's an ending that has no need for form or formulas; at some moment we come closer together without consulting each other, without even trying to look at each other, we know that we're thinking about Michael, about how Michael too went back to Erik's farm, went back with no apparent reason, even though the farmhouse for him was as empty as the wing of the bungalow next door, came back just as the girls' visitor has come back, just like Michael and the others, coming back like flies, coming back without knowing that they're expected, that this time they're coming to a different appointment.

At bedtime we'd put on our nightshirts as usual; now we let them drop like white, gelatinous splotches onto the floor, naked, we go toward the door and out into the garden. It's simply a matter of going around the hedge that extends the separation of the two wings of the bungalow; the door is still closed but we know that it isn't locked, that all we have to do is lift the latch. There's no light inside when we go in together; it's the first time in a long while that we lean on each other in order to walk.

II

GRAFFITI

To Antoni Tàpies

So many things begin and perhaps end as a game, I suppose that it amused you to find the sketch beside yours, you attributed it to chance or a whim and only the second time did you realize that it was intentional and then you looked at it slowly, you even came back later to look at it again, taking the usual precautions: the street at its most solitary moment, no patrol wagon on neighboring corners, approaching with indifference and never looking at the graffiti face-on but from the other sidewalk or diagonally, feigning interest in the shop window alongside, going away immediately.

Your own game had begun out of boredom, it wasn't really a protest against the state of things in the city, the curfew, the menacing prohibition against putting up posters or writing on walls. It simply amused you to make sketches with colored chalk (you didn't like the term graffiti, so art critic–like) and from time to time to come and look at them and even, with a little luck, to be a spectator to the arrival of the municipal truck and the useless insults of the workers as they erased the sketches. It didn't matter to them that they weren't political sketches, the prohibition covered everything, and if some child had dared draw a house or a dog it would have been erased in just the same way in the midst of curses and threats. In the city people no longer knew too well which side fear was really on; maybe that's why you overcame yours and every so often picked the time and place just right for making a sketch.

You never ran any risk because you knew how to choose well, and in the time that passed until the cleaning trucks arrived something opened up for you like a very clean space where there was almost room for hope. Looking at your sketch from a distance you could see people casting a glance at it as they passed, no one stopped, of course, but no one failed to look at the sketch, sometimes a quick abstract composition in two colors, the profile of a bird or two entwined figures. Just one time you wrote a phrase, in black chalk: *It hurts me too*. It didn't last two hours, and that time the police themselves made it disappear. Afterward you went on only making sketches.

When the other one appeared next to yours you were almost afraid, suddenly the danger had become double, someone like you had been moved to have some fun on the brink of imprisonment or something worse, and that someone, as if it were of no small importance, was a woman. You couldn't prove it yourself, but there was something different and better than the most obvious proofs: a trace, a predilection for warm colors, an aura. Probably since you walked alone you were imagining it out of compensation; you admired her, you were afraid for her, you hoped it was the only time, you almost gave yourself away when she drew a sketch alongside another one of yours, an urge to laugh, to stay right there as if the police were blind or idiots.

A different time began, at once stealthier, more beautiful and more threatening. Shirking your job you would go out at odd moments in hopes of surprising her. For your sketches you chose those streets that you could cover in a single quick passage; you came back at dawn, at dusk, at three o'clock in the morning. It was a time of unbearable contradiction, the deception of finding a new sketch of hers beside one of yours and the street empty, and that of not finding anything and feeling the street even more empty. One night you saw her first sketch all by itself; she'd done it in red and blue chalk on a garage door, taking advantage of the worm-eaten wood and the nail heads. It was more than ever she—the design, the colors—but you also felt that that sketch had meaning as an appeal or question, a way of calling you. You came back at dawn, after the patrols had thinned out in their mute sweep, and on the rest of the door you sketched a quick seascape with sails and breakwaters; if he didn't look at it closely a person might have said it was a play of random lines, but she would know how to look at it. That night you barely escaped a pair of policemen, in your apartment you drank glass after glass of gin and you talked to her, you told her everything that came into your mouth, like a different sketch made with sound, another harbor with sails, you pictured her as dark and silent, you chose lips and breasts for her, you loved her a little.

Almost immediately it occurred to you that she would be looking for an answer, that she would return to her sketch the way you were returning now to yours, and even though the danger had become so much greater since the attacks at the market, you dared go up to the garage, walk around the block, drink endless beers at the café on the corner. It was absurd because she wouldn't stop after seeing your sketch, any one of the many women coming and going might be her. At dawn on the second day you chose a gray wall and sketched a white triangle surrounded by splotches like oak leaves; from the same café on the corner you could see the wall (they'd already cleaned off the garage door and a patrol, furious, kept coming back), at dusk you withdrew a little, but choosing different lookout points, moving from one place to another, making small purchases in the shops so as not to draw too much attention. It was already dark night when you heard the sirens and the spotlights swept your eyes. There was a confused crowding by the wall, you ran, in the face of all good sense, and all that helped you was the good luck to have a car turn the corner and put on its brakes when the driver saw the patrol wagon, its bulk protected you and you saw the struggle, black hair pulled by gloved hands, the kicks and the screams, the cut-off glimpse of blue slacks before they threw her into the wagon and took her away.

Much later (it was horrible trembling like that, it was horrible to think that it had happened because of your sketch on the gray wall) you mingled with other people and managed to see an outline in blue, the traces of that orange color that was like her name or her mouth, her there in that truncated sketch that the police had erased before taking her away, enough remained to understand that she had tried to answer your triangle with another figure, a circle or maybe a spiral, a form full and beautiful, something like a yes or an always or a now.

You knew it quite well, you'd had more than enough time to imagine the details of what was happening at the main barracks; in the city everything like that oozed out little by little, people were aware of the fate of prisoners, and if sometimes they got to see one or another of them again, they would have preferred not seeing them, just as the majority were lost in the silence that no one dared break. You knew it only too well, that night the gin wouldn't help you except to make you bite your hands with impotence, cry, crush the pieces of colored chalk with your feet before submerging yourself in drunkenness.

Yes, but the days passed and you no longer knew how to live in any other way. You began to leave your work again to walk about the streets, to look fleetingly at the walls and the doors where you and she had sketched. Everything clean, everything clear; nothing, not even a flower sketched by the innocence of a schoolboy who steals a piece of chalk in class and can't resist the pleasure of using it. Nor could you resist, and a month later you got up at dawn and went back to the street with the garage. There were no patrols, the walls were perfectly clean; a cat looked at you cautiously from a doorway when you took out your chalk and in the same place, there where she had left her sketch, you filled the boards with a green shout, a red flame of recognition and love, you wrapped your sketch in an oval that was also your mouth and hers and hope. The footsteps at the corner threw you into a felt-footed run, to the refuge of a pile of empty boxes; a staggering drunk approached humming, he tried to kick the cat and fell face down at the foot of the sketch. You went away slowly, safe now, and with the first sun you slept as you hadn't slept for a long time.

That same morning you looked from a distance: they hadn't erased it yet. You went back at noon: almost inconceivably it was still there. The agitation in the suburbs (you'd heard the news reports) had taken the urban patrols away from their routine; at dusk you went back to see that a lot of people had been seeing it all through the day. You waited until three in the morning to go back, the street was empty and dark. From a distance you made out the other sketch, only you could have distinguished it, so small, above and to the left of yours. You went over with a feeling that was thirst and horror at the same time; you saw the orange oval and the violet splotches where a swollen face seemed to leap out, a hanging eye, a mouth smashed with fists. I know, I know, but what else could I have sketched for you? What message would have made any sense now? In some way I had to say farewell to you and at the same time ask you to continue. I had to leave you something before going back to my refuge where there was no mirror anymore, only a hollow to hide in until the end in the most complete darkness, remembering so many things and sometimes, as I had imagined your life, imagining that you were making other sketches, that you were going out at night to make other sketches.

CLONE

CLONE *(klōn)*, n. Biol. *a group of organisms
derived from a single individual by various
types of asexual reproduction.*

Random House Dictionary
of the English Language

Everything seems to revolve around Gesualdo: whether he
had the right to do what he did or whether he took revenge on
his wife for something he should have taken revenge on himself for. Between rehearsals, taking a break in the hotel bar,
Paola argues with Lucho and Roberto, the others play canasta
or go up to their rooms. He was right then, Roberto insists,
and today it's the same thing, his wife cheated on him and he
killed her, just another tango, Paolita. Your macho nonsense,
Paola says, tangos, sure, but there are women writing tangos
now and they're not always singing the same tune. You have
to look deeper, timid Lucho suggests, it's not so easy to know
why people cheat and why they kill. Maybe in Chile, Roberto

says, you people are so refined, but those of us who come from
La Rioja shove in a shiv and that's that. They laugh, Paola
orders a gin and tonic, it's true that you have to look deeper,
for what's behind it, Carlo Gesualdo found his wife in bed
with another man and killed them or had them killed—that's
the police report on the twelve-thirty news—everything else
(and certainly the real news is hiding in everything else)
would have to be looked into and that's not so easy after four
centuries. There's a lot of bibliography on Gesualdo, Lucho
reminds them, if you're so interested go check it out when we
get back to Rome in March. A good idea, Paola admits, what
remains to be seen is whether or not we'll get back to Rome.

Roberto looks at her without speaking, Lucho lowers his
head and then calls the waiter to order another round. Are you
referring to Sandro? Roberto asks when he sees that Paola's
lost again in Gesualdo or in the fly that's buzzing near the
ceiling. Not concretely, Paola says, but you can see that things
aren't going so easy now. It'll pass, Lucho says, it's nothing
but a whim and a tantrum at the same time, Sandro won't go
beyond that. Yes, Roberto admits, but in the meantime the
group has to pay for the broken china, we're rehearsing badly
and not very much and that's going to be noticed in the end.
True, Lucho says, we're singing clenched, we're afraid of
making a mistake. We already did in Caracas, Paola says. At
least the audience doesn't know Gesualdo very well, Mario's
slip was taken as another harmonic audacity by them. The
worst thing will be if one of these days it happens with a
Monteverdi, Roberto mutters, him they know by heart, damn it.

It continued to be extraordinary that the only stable
couple in the group was Franca and Mario. Looking from a
distance at Mario who was talking to Sandro over a score and

two beers, Paola said to herself that ephemeral alliances, pairing for a brief good time, hadn't been too common in the group: some weekend for Karen and Lucho (or Karen and Lily, because Karen, you know, and Lily probably out of sheer goodness or to find out what it was like even though Lily and Sandro, the generous breadth of Karen and Lily, in the end). Yes, you had to recognize the fact that the only stable couple and the one that deserved the name was Franca and Mario, with a ring on the finger and all the rest. As for herself, once in Bergamo she'd given in to a hotel room, if that meant anything, all curtains and lace, with Roberto in a bed that looked like a swan, a quick interlude with no tomorrow, as good friends as ever, things like that between two concerts, almost between two madrigals, Karen and Lucho, Karen and Lily, Sandro and Lily. And all such good friends, because, as a matter of fact, real couples were brought together at the end of a tour, in Buenos Aires and Montevideo, waiting there were wives and husbands and children and homes and dogs until the next tour, a sailor's life with the inevitable sailor's parentheses, nothing important, modern people. Until. Because now something had changed ever since. I don't know how to think, thought Paola, loose pieces of things come out of me. We're all too tense, damn it. All of a sudden just like that, looking at Mario and Sandro differently as they argued about music, as if underneath she were imagining a different argument. But no, they weren't talking about that, it was most certain they weren't talking about that. Finally, the fact remained that the only real couple was Mario and Franca even though, of course, it wasn't that that Mario and Sandro were discussing. Although probably underneath, always underneath.

. . .

The three of them are going to the beach at Ipanema, at night the group is going to sing in Rio and they have to take advantage. Franca likes to stroll with Lucho, they have the same way of looking at things, as if they only brushed them with the fingers of their eyes, they have such fun. Roberto will tag along at the last minute, a pity, because he sees everything seriously and tries to be an audience, they'll leave him in the shade reading the *Times* and will play ball on the sand, swim, and talk—while Roberto is lost in a half sleep in which Sandro reappears—about Sandro's imperceptible loss of contact with the group, his muffled stubbornness that's making things so bad for everyone. Now Franca will throw the red and white ball, Lucho will leap to catch it, they'll laugh like lunatics with every throw, it's hard to concentrate on the *Times*, it's hard to keep your cohesion when a conductor loses contact the way Sandro has and not through any fault of Franca's, it isn't her fault of course, any more than it's Franca's fault that the ball now falls among the glasses of people drinking beer under an umbrella and she has to run and apologize. Folding the *Times*, Roberto will remember his chat with Paola and Lucho at the bar; if Mario doesn't decide to do something, if he doesn't tell Sandro that Franca will never enter any other game but his, everything will go to hell, Sandro isn't just conducting the rehearsals poorly, he's even singing badly, he's losing the concentration that in its time had also concentrated the group and given it the unity and tonal color that the critics talked so much about. Ball in the water, double chase. Lucho first, Franca diving into a wave. Yes, Mario should have realized (it can't be that he hasn't realized yet), the group is going straight to hell unless Mario decides to settle the matter. But where does the matter begin, where should it be settled, since nothing has happened, since no one can say that anything has happened?

. . .

They're starting to suspect, I know it and what can I do, since it's like an illness, since I can't look at her, give her a cue without that pain and that delight at the same time again, without everything's trembling and sliding like sand, a wind on the stage, a river under my feet. Oh, if somebody else would only lead, if Karen or Roberto would lead so I could blend into the group, a simple tenor among the other voices, maybe then, maybe finally. There the way you see him is how he is now, says Paola, there you have him daydreaming right in the middle of the most fucked-up part of Gesualdo, when you have to measure inch by inch in order not to fuck up, precisely then you're stuck with him as if he were up in the air, God damn it. Child, child, Lucho says, proper women don't say fuck. But what pretext for making the change, talking to Karen or Roberto, without counting on the fact that it isn't certain they'll accept, I've led them for such a long time and it can't be changed just like that, technique apart. Last night was so rough, for a minute I thought one of them was going to tell me during intermission, it's obvious they can't take it anymore. Underneath it all you've got good reason to curse, Lucho says. Underneath it all, yes, but it's idiotic, says Paola, Sandro is more musician than any of us, without him we wouldn't be what we are. What we were, Lucho mutters.

There are nights now when everything seems to stretch out interminably, the old celebration—a little crimped before getting lost in the jubilation of each melody—replaced more and more by a dutiful fulfillment of our trade, trembling while putting on the gloves, Roberto says hoarsely, climbing into the ring and foreseeing that you're going to get clobbered.

Such delicate images, Lucho comments to Paola. He's right, what the fuck, Paola says, for me singing used to be like making love and now it's like jerking off. Look at you, talking about images, Roberto laughs, but it's true, we used to be different people, look, the other day, reading some science fiction, I found the exact word: we were a clone. A what? (Paola). I understand you, Lucho sighs, it's true, it's true, singing and living and even thinking were all one single thing in eight bodies. Like the three musketeers, Paola asks, all for one and one for all? That's it, girl, Roberto concedes, but nowadays they call it clone, which is more chic. And we used to sing and live like a single being, Lucho murmurs, not this dragging off now to rehearsals and concerts, programs that never end, neverever. Endless fear, Paola says, every time I think that somebody is going to goof again, I look at Sandro as if he were a lifeguard and the big idiot is there hanging on Franca's eyes, and to make matters worse every time she can she's looking at Mario. She's doing the right thing, Lucho says, he's the one she should look at. Of course she's doing the right thing but everything's going to hell. So gradually that it's almost worse, a shipwreck in slow motion, Roberto says.

Almost a mania, Gesualdo. Because they loved him, of course, and singing his sometimes almost unsingable madrigals called for an effort that was prolonged in the study of the texts, looking for the best way to link the poems to the melody as the Prince of Venosa had done in his obscure genius way. Each voice, each accent, had to find that elusive center from which the reality of the madrigal was to rise, and not one of the so many mechanical versions that they listened to on records sometimes for comparison had it as they tried to compare, in order to learn, to be a bit Gesualdo, assassin prince, lord of music.

Then the arguments would break out, almost always Roberto and Paola, Lucho more moderate, but hitting the mark, each one in his or her way of feeling Gesualdo, the difficulty of clinging to a different version even though there was a minimal difference from the one desired. Roberto had been right, the clone was breaking up and day by day individuals appeared with their discrepancies, their resistance; finally Sandro, as always, overcame the problem, no one disputed his way of feeling Gesualdo except Karen and sometimes Mario, during rehearsals they were always the ones who suggested changes and found defects, Karen almost poisonously against Sandro (it was an old love that had failed, Paola's theory) and Mario resplendent with musical comparisons, examples, and juridical decisions. As in an ascending modulation the conflicts went on for hours until the compromise or momentary agreement. Every Gesualdo madrigal that they added to the repertory meant a new confrontation, the recurrence, perhaps, of the night the prince had unsheathed his dagger as he looked at the naked, sleeping lovers.

Lily and Roberto listening to Sandro and Lucho who are flexing their intellects after two Scotches. There's talk of Britten and Webern and always, finally, the man from Venosa, today it's an accent that would have to be heavier in "O voi, troppo felici" (Sandro) or letting the melody flow in all of its Gesualdic ambiguity (Lucho). Yes, no, this is how it is, Ping-Pong for the pleasure of the effective shots, barbed answers. You'll see when we rehearse (Sandro), maybe that won't be a good test (Lucho), I'd like to know why, and Lucho, fed up, opening his mouth to say what Roberto and Lily would have said too if Roberto hadn't cut in, mercifully squelching Lucho's words, proposing another drink and Lily yes, the others indeed, with plenty of ice.

But it's getting to be an obsession, a kind of cantus firmus around which the life of the group revolves. Sandro is the first to feel it, formerly that center was the music and around it the lights of eight lives, eight sets, the eight small planets of the Monteverdi sun, the Josquin des Prés sun, the Gesualdo sun. Then Franca gradually ascending in a sound sky, her green eyes intent on the cues, the barely perceptible rhythmic indications, altering without knowing it, dislocating without wanting to, the cohesion of the clone, Roberto and Lily think that in unison while Lucho and Sandro return, calm now, to the problem of "O voi, troppo felici," seek the path with the great intelligence that never fails after the third Scotch of the evening.

Why did he kill her? The usual thing, Roberto tells Lily, he found her in the hideout and in other arms, like Rivero's tango, right then and there the man from Venosa stabbed them in person or maybe his executioners, before fleeing the vengeance of the dead woman's brothers and shutting himself up in castles where over the years the delicate webs of the madrigals could be woven. Roberto and Lily have fun fabricating dramatic and erotic variants because they're fed up with the problem of "O voi, troppo felici" that continues its know-it-all debate on the sofa next to them. You can feel in the air that Sandro has understood what Lucho was going to tell him, if the rehearsals go on being what they are now, everything will get more and more mechanical, will be impeccably glued to the score and the text, will be Carlo Gesualdo without love and without jealousy, Carlo Gesualdo without dagger or vengeance, in short, an assigned madrigalist among all the others.

"Let's try it with you," Sandro will propose the next morning. "It really would be better if you led from now on, Lucho."

"Don't be an asshole," Roberto will say.

"That's right," Lily will say.

"Yes, let's try with you and see what happens, and if the others agree, you'll keep on leading."

"No," Lucho, who has blushed and hates himself for blushing, will say.

"Changing conductors isn't what we need," Roberto will say. "Really," Lily will say.

"It could be, yes," Sandro will say, "it could be good for all of us."

"In any case, not me," Lucho will say. "I can't see myself, what do you expect? I've got my ideas like everybody, but I know my own incapacities."

"This Chilean is a delight," Roberto will say. "Really," Lily will say.

"You people decide," Sandro will say. "I'm going to bed."

"Inspiration comes while you're sleeping," Roberto will say. "Really," Lily will say.

. . .

He looked for him after the concert, not that things had gone badly, but once more that tightness like a latent threat of danger, of error, Karen and Paola singing without spirit, Lily pale, Franca almost never looking at him, the men concentrating and seeming to be absent at the same time; he himself with voice problems, leading coldly but fearful as the program went along, an enthusiastic Honduran audience that wasn't enough to erase that bad taste in his mouth, that's why he looked for Lucho after the concert and there in the hotel bar with Karen, Mario, Roberto, and Lily, drinking almost without speaking, waiting for bedtime in the midst of listless anecdotes, Karen and Mario went off right away, but Lucho didn't seem to want to break away from Lily and Roberto, he had to stay on unwillingly, with the one for the road stretching out in silence. After all, it would be better if we were what we were the other night again, Sandro said, diving into the water, I was looking for you so I could repeat what I said to you then. Oh, Lucho said, but I'll give you the same answer I gave you then. Roberto and Lily once more to the defense, there are all kinds of possibilities, hey, why insist only on Lucho. Whatever you want, it's all the same to me, Sandro said, drinking down his whiskey in one swig, talk it over among yourselves, let me know what you decide. I vote for Lucho. I'm for Mario, Lucho said. It's not a question of voting now, God damn it (Roberto exasperated and Lily of course not). Okay, we've got time, the next concert is in Buenos Aires in two weeks. I'm going to run up to La Rioja to see the old lady (Roberto, and Lily I've got to buy a handbag). You looked for me to tell me this, Lucho said, that's fine, but something like this has to be explained, everybody here has got his or her theory and you too, naturally, it's time to lay them on the table. In any case, not tonight, Roberto decreed (and Lily of course not, I'm falling asleep on my feet, and Sandro pale, looking at the empty glass without seeing it).

It really fell apart this time, Paola thought after erratic dialogues and consultations with Karen, Roberto, and someone or other else. We won't get beyond the next concert, all the more since it's in Buenos Aires and I know my world. Down there they're going to lay their cards on the table, in the end there's family support and if worse comes to worst I'll go live with Mama and my sister while I wait for another chance.

Everybody's got his or her idea, thought Lucho, who, without talking too much, had been taking soundings on all sides. They'll all arrange things to suit themselves if there's no clone understanding as Roberto would say, but instinct tells me we won't get beyond Buenos Aires without squalls. This time it was too much.

Cherchez la femme. La femme? Roberto knows that it's better to look for the husband when it's a question of finding something solid and certain, Franca as always will be evasive with the movements of a fish wiggling in its fishbowl, great innocent green glances, when all's said and done she doesn't seem to be to blame for anything, so look for Mario and find him. Behind the smoke from his cigar, Mario almost smiling, an old friend has every right, but of course that's it, it started in Brussels six months back, Franca told me right after. What about you? Roberto from La Rioja shove in the shiv. Bah, me, Mario the quiet one, the wise one who enjoys tropical tobacco and great green eyes, I can't do anything old man, if he's involved, he's involved. But her, Roberto wants to say and doesn't.

Paola on the other hand yes, who was going to hobble Paola at the moment of truth. She looked for Mario too (they'd arrived in Buenos Aires the night before, the recital was a week away, the first rehearsal after a rest had been pure routine with no great desire, Jannequin and Gesualdo coming out almost the same, disgusting). Do something, Mario, I don't know what, but do something. The only thing that can be done is not doing anything, Mario said, if Lucho refuses to lead I don't see who's capable of replacing Sandro. You, God damn it. Yes, but no. Then we've got to think you're doing it on purpose, Paola shouted, you're not only letting things slip away right under your nose but on top of that you're leaving us in the lurch. You don't have to raise your voice, Mario said, I can hear you quite well, believe me.

It was just the way I'm telling you now, I shouted at him right in his face and you see how he answers me, the big . . . Shh, girl, Roberto says, cuckold is a dirty word, if you ever use it where I come from you'll have a fight on your hands. I didn't mean to say it, Paola has regrets, nobody knows whether or not they're going to bed together and, after all, what difference does it make if they do go to bed or look at each other as if they were in bed together right in the middle of the concert, that isn't the question. That isn't fair, Roberto says, the one who's looking, the one who's falling apart inside, the one who's acting like a moth around a lamp, the idiot who is tainted is Sandro, no one can reproach Franca, she gave him back that kind of leech he puts on her every time he has

her in front of him. But Mario, Paola insists, how can he
stand it? I suppose he trusts her, Roberto says, and he
certainly is in love with her with no need for leeches or
languid faces. Maybe so, Paola accepts, but why does he
refuse to lead us when Sandro is the first one to agree, when
Lucho himself has asked him and we've all asked him?

Because if vengeance is an art, its forms will of necessity
seek the circumvolutions that render it more subtly beautiful.
It's curious, Mario thinks, that someone capable of conceiving
the universe of sound that rises up from his madrigals should
avenge himself so crudely, so much in the manner of the
cheap thug, when it had been given him to spin the perfect
web, watch his prey fall into it, bleed them gradually,
madrigalize a torture of weeks or months. He looks at Paola,
who is working on and repeating a passage from "Poichè
l'avida sete," smiles at her in a friendly way. He knows very
well why Paola has returned to Gesualdo, why almost all of
them look at him when the talk is about Gesualdo and lower
their eyes and change the subject. "Sete," he tells her, don't
stress "sete" so much, Paolita, you feel the thirst more
strongly if you say the word softly. Don't forget the period,
that way of saying so many things in a quiet way, and even
doing them that way.

They saw them coming out of the hotel together, Mario
was holding Franca by the arm, Lucho and Roberto from the
bar could follow them as they went off slowly, arm in arm,
Franca's hand going around Mario's waist as he turned his
head a little to talk to her. They got into a cab, the downtown
traffic sucked them up into its slow serpent.

"I don't get it, old man," Roberto said to Lucho, "I swear, I don't get it at all."

"You're telling me, bub."

"It's never been clearer than this morning, everything leaped into sight, because it's a question of sight, Sandro's useless fakery as he remembers to fake it too late, the damned fool, and she, just the opposite, singing for him and only for him for the first time."

"Karen put me onto it, you're right, she was looking at him this time, she was the one who was burning him with her eyes, and what those eyes can do when they want to!"

"So there you see," Roberto said, "on one side the worst breakdown we've had since we started, and six hours before the concert, and what a concert, they don't let you get away with it here, you know, on the one hand it's the very evidence that the thing has been done, it's something you feel with your blood or your prostate, I've always been aware of that."

"Almost the exact words of Karen and Paola except for the part about the prostate," Lucho said. "I must be less sexy than you people, but it's transparent for me too this time."

"And on the other side you've got Mario, so happy to go out shopping or have a drink with her, the perfect married couple."

"He must know by now."

"And he lets her give that cheap whore come-on."

"Come off it, Roberto."

"Shit, Chile boy, at least let me let it all hang out."

"You're doing fine," Lucho said, "just what we need before the concert."

"The concert," Roberto said. "I wonder if."

They looked at each other, as was customary they shrugged their shoulders and took out their cigarettes.

.   .   .

No one probably sees them but just the same they must feel uncomfortable crossing the lobby, Lily will look at Sandro as if she wanted to tell him something and will hesitate, she'll stop beside a display window and Sandro, with a vague wave, will turn toward the cigarette stand and ask for a pack of Camels, will feel Lily's look on the back of his neck, will pay and start walking toward the elevators while Lily will break away from the show window and pass by him as in other times, as in another fleeting encounter that's revived now and hurts. Sandro will murmur a "hi," will lower his eyes while he opens the pack of cigarettes. From the elevator door he'll see her stop at the entrance to the bar, turn toward him. He'll carefully light the cigarette and go up to get dressed for the concert, Lily will go to the bar and ask for a cognac, which isn't good at that time any more than smoking two Camels in a row is good when there are fifteen madrigals waiting.

As always in Buenos Aires the friends are there and not just in the audience but looking for them in the dressing rooms and backstage, meetings and greetings and pats on the back, home at last, brother, but look how pretty you are Paolita, let me introduce you to my fiancé's mother, hey Roberto you're getting too fat, well hello Sandro, I've been reading the Mexican critics, great, the sound of a full house, Mario greeting an old friend who asks for Franca, she must be around here somewhere, the audience beginning to get restless, ten minutes to go, Sandro making a calm sign for them to come together, Lucho getting away from two Chilean women with autograph albums, Lily almost running, they're

so adorable but you can't talk to all of them, Lucho beside
Roberto taking a quick look and suddenly talking to Roberto,
in less than a second Karen and Paola at the same time
where's Franca, the group is onstage but where in the world
is Franca, Roberto to Mario and Mario how should I know,
I left her downtown at seven o'clock, Paola where's Franca,
and Lily and Karen, Sandro looking at Mario, I told you so,
she was coming back on her own, she'd make it in time, five
minutes, Sandro going over to Mario with Roberto crossing
over quietly, you must know what's going on and Mario I
told you I didn't, pale, looking into the air, a stagehand
talking to Sandro and Lucho, running backstage, she's not
there, sir, they haven't seen her come in, Paola covering her
face and doubling over as if she were going to vomit, Karen
grabbing her and Lucho please, Paola, control yourself, two
minutes, Roberto looking at Mario, silent and pale as silent
and pale perhaps as Carlo Gesualdo leaving the bedroom,
five of his madrigals on the program, impatient clapping and
the curtain still down, she's not there, sir, we've looked
everywhere, she hasn't arrived at the theater, Roberto crossing
over between Sandro and Mario, you did it, where's Franca,
shouting, the murmur of surprise from the other side, the
manager trembling, going to the curtain, ladies and gentlemen,
we ask your indulgence for a moment, Paola's hysterical
shriek, Lucho struggling to hold her back and Karen turning,
going off step by step, Sandro falling apart in the arms of
Roberto who holds him like a dummy, looking at Mario, pale
and motionless, Roberto understanding that it had to be there,
there in Buenos Aires, there Mario, there'll be no concert,
there'll never be another concert, they're singing their last
madrigal for nothingness, without Franca they're singing it
for an audience that can't hear them, that, disconcerted, is
beginning to leave.

NOTE ON THE THEME OF A KING AND
THE VENGEANCE OF A PRINCE

When the moment arrives it's natural for me to write as if someone were dictating to me; that's why I impose strict rules on myself from time to time as a variant of something that might end up being monotonous. In this tale the "catch" consisted in adjusting a still nonexistent narrative to the mold of *A Musical Offering* by Johann Sebastian Bach.

It is well known that the theme of this series of variations in the form of a canon and fugue was given to Bach by Frederick the Great, and that after improvising in his presence a fugue based on that theme—unpleasant and thorny—the master wrote *A Musical Offering*, where the initial theme is reprised in a more diverse and complex way. Bach didn't indicate the instruments to be used with the exception of the trio sonata for flute, violin, and clavichord; ever since even the order of the parts has depended on the will of the musicians performing the work. In this case I have made use of the arrangement for eight instruments contemporary to Bach by Millicent Silver, which allows one to follow the elaboration of each passage in all its details and was recorded by the London Harpsichord Ensemble on Saga XID 5237.

Once I had chosen this version (or after she had chosen it, for it was listening to her that I got the idea of a tale that would follow its course) I let time pass; nothing can be hurried in writing, and apparent forgetfulness, distraction, dreams, and chance all imperceptibly weave their future carpet. I made a trip to the beach carrying a photocopy of the jacket of the record where Frederick Youens analyzes the elements of *A Musical Offering*; I vaguely imagined a tale that immediately seemed too intellectual to me. The rules of the game were threatening: eight instruments had to be transfigured into eight characters, eight musical sketches, responding, alternating, or opposing one another, had to find their correlation in the feelings, behavior, and relationships of eight people. Conceiving a literary double of the London Harpsichord Ensemble seemed foolish to me in the degree that a violinist or flautist does not in his private life cleave to the musical themes he performs; but, at the same time, the notion of a body, a group, had to exist in some way from the beginning, since the short scope of a story wouldn't permit the effective integration of eight people who had no relationship or contact previous to the narration. A casual conversation brought back to me the recollection of Carlo Gesualdo, a genius for madrigals and the murderer of his wife; everything fell into place immediately, and the eight instruments were seen as the component parts of a vocal group; from the first sentence on, that was how the cohesion of a group could exist, all of them would know and love or hate each other *since before*; and furthermore, naturally, they would sing Gesualdo's madrigals, noblesse oblige. Conceiving a dramatic action in that context wasn't hard; attaching it to the successive movements of *A Musical Offering* held the challenge, I mean the pleasure the writer proposed before anything else.

That was the necessary literary stew, then; the web in the depths would have to be shown at its moment, as almost always happens. To begin, the instrumental distribution by Millicent Silver found its equivalent in eight singers whose vocal register kept an analogous relation to the instruments. This gave:

Flute: Sandro, tenor
Violin: Lucho, tenor
Oboe: Franca, soprano

English horn: Karen, mezzo-soprano
Viola: Paola, contralto
Cello: Roberto, baritone
Bassoon: Mario, bass
Clavichord: Lily, soprano

I saw the characters as Latin Americans, with their home base in Buenos Aires, where they would offer the last recital of a long tour that had taken them to different countries. I saw them at the start of a crisis that was still vague (more for me than for them), where the only thing clear was the fissure that was beginning to work on the very cohesion of a group of madrigalists. I had written the first passages feeling my way along—I haven't changed them, I don't think I've ever changed the uncertain beginning of a lot of stories of mine because I feel it would be the worst kind of betrayal of my writing—when I came to understand that it was impossible to adjust the tale to *A Musical Offering* without knowing in detail what instruments—that is, what characters—would figure in each passage until the end. Then, with a touch of wonderment that luckily is still with me when I write, I saw that the final fragment would have to include all of the characters *minus one*. And that one, from the first pages already written, had been the still-uncertain cause of the fissure that was growing in the group, in what another character would describe as a clone. In the same moment Franca's necessary absence and the story of Carlo Gesualdo, which had underlain the whole process of imagination, were the fly and the spider in the web. Now I could go ahead, everything had been consummated since before.

About the writing itself: Each fragment corresponds to the order which is given in the version of *A Musical Offering* done by Millicent Silver; on one side the development of each passage tries to resemble the musical form (canon, trio sonata, canonical fugue, etc.) and contains exclusively the characters who replace the instruments according to the table above. Therefore it will be useful (useful for curious people, but all curious people tend to be useful) to indicate here the sequence as Frederick Youens lays it out, with the instruments chosen by Mrs. Silver:

Ricercar in three voices: Violin, viola, and cello
Perpetual canon: Flute, viola, and bassoon
Canon in unison: Violin, oboe, and cello
Canon in contrary movement: Flute, violin, and viola
Canon in increasing and contrary movement: Violin, viola, and cello
Canon in ascending modulation: Flute, English horn, bassoon, violin, viola, and cello
Trio sonata: Flute, violin, and continuo (cello and clavichord)
    1. Largo
    2. Allegro
    3. Andante
    4. Allegro
Perpetual canon: Flute, violin, and continuo
"Crab" canon: Violin and viola
"Enigma" canon:
    a. Bassoon and cello
    b. Viola and bassoon
    c. Viola and cello
    d. Viola and bassoon
Canon in four voices: Violin, oboe, cello, and bassoon
Canonical fugue: Flute and clavichord
Ricercar in six voices: Flute, English horn, bassoon,

violin, viola, and cello, with continuo of clavichord
(In the final fragment announced as "for six
voices," the clavichord continuo adds the seventh
performer.)

Since this note is already as long as the story, I have no
scruples about making it a little longer still. My ignorance in
matters of vocal groups is complete, and professionals in the
genre will find ample reasons for merriment here. In fact,
almost everything I know about music and musicians comes
to me from record jackets, which I read with great care and
benefit. This also goes for the references to Gesualdo, whose
madrigals have been with me for a long time. That he killed
his wife is certain; the rest, other possible agreements with
my text, would have to be asked of Mario.

RETURN TRIP TANGO

*Le hasard meurtrier se dresse au coin
de la première rue.
Au retour l'heure-couteau attend.*

Marcel Bélanger, *Nu et noir*

One goes along recounting things ever so slowly, imagining them at first on the basis of Flora or a door opening or a boy who cries out, then that baroque necessity of the intelligence that leads it to fill every hollow until its perfect web has been spun and it can go on to something new. But how can we not say that perhaps, at some time or another, the mental web adjusts itself, thread by thread, to that of life, even though we might be saying so purely out of fear, because if we didn't believe in it a little, we couldn't keep on doing it in the face of outside webs. Flora, then, and she told me everything little by little when we got together, no longer worked at Miss Matilde's (she still called her that even though she didn't have any reason now to continue giving her that title of respect from a maid of all work). I enjoyed having her reminisce about her past as a country girl from La Rioja who'd come down to the capital with great frightened eyes and little breasts that in the end would be worth more in life for her than any feather duster or good manners. I like to write for myself, I've got notebooks and notebooks, poetry, and even a novel, but what I like to do is write, and when I finish it's like a fellow's slipping aside after the pleasure, sleep comes, and the next day there are other things rapping on your window, that's what writing is, opening the shutters and letting them in, one notebook after another: I work in a hospital, I'm not interested in people reading what I write, Flora or anybody else; I like it when I finish a notebook, because it's as if I'd already published it, but I haven't thought about publishing it, something raps on the window and we're off again on a new notebook the way you would call an ambulance. That's why Flora told me so many things about her life without imagining that later on I would go over them slowly, between dreams, and would put some into a notebook. Emilio and Matilde went into the notebook because it couldn't remain just Flora's tears and scraps of memory. She never spoke to me about Emilio and Matilde without crying at the end. After that I didn't ask her about it for a few days, even steered her to other memories, and one beautiful morning I led her gently back to that story again, and Flora rushed into it again as if she'd already forgotten everything she'd told me, began all over, and I let her because more than once her memory brought back things she hadn't mentioned before, little bits that fitted into other little bits, and, for my part, I was watching the stitches of the suture appear little by little, the coming together of so many scattered or presumed things, puzzles during insomnia or maté time. The day came when it would have been impossible for me to distinguish between what Flora was telling me and what she and I myself had been putting together, because both of us, each in his or her own way, needed, like everybody, to have that business finished, for the last hole finally to receive the piece, the color, the end of a line coming from a leg or a word or a staircase.

Since I'm very conventional, I prefer to grab things from the beginning, and, besides, when I write I see what I'm writing, I really see it, I'm seeing Emilio Díaz on the morning he arrived at Ezeiza airport from Mexico and went down to a hotel on the Calle Cangallo, spent two or three days wandering about among districts and cafés and friends from other days, avoiding certain encounters but not hiding too much either, because at that moment he had nothing to reproach himself for. He was probably slowly studying the terrain in Villa del Parque, walking along Melincué and General Artigas, looking for a cheap hotel or boardinghouse, settling in unhurriedly, drinking maté in his room, and going out to a bistro or the movies at night. There was nothing of the ghost about him, but he didn't speak much and not to many people, he walked on crepe soles and wore a black Windbreaker and brown pants, his eyes quick for the get-up-and-go, something that the landlady of the boardinghouse would have called sneakiness; he wasn't a ghost but he looked like one from the distance, solitude surrounded him like another silence, like the white bandana around his neck, the smoke of his butt, never too far away from those almost too thin lips.

Matilde saw him for the first time—for this second first time—from the window of the bedroom on the second floor. Flora was out shopping and had taken Carlitos along so he wouldn't whimper with boredom at siesta time, it was the thick heat of January and Matilde was looking for some air by the window, painting her nails the way Germán liked them, although Germán was traveling in Catamarca and had taken the car and Matilde was bored without the car to go downtown or to Belgrano, she was already used to Germán's absence, but she missed the car when he took it. He'd promised her another one all for herself when the firms merged, she didn't understand those business matters, but evidently they still hadn't merged, at night she would go to the movies with Perla, would hire a rental car, they'd dine downtown, afterward the garage would pass the bill for the car on to Germán, Carlitos had a rash on his legs and she'd have to take him to the pediatrician, just the idea made him even hotter, Carlitos throwing a tantrum, taking advantage of his father's absence to give her a hard time, incredible how that kid blackmailed her when Germán was away, only Flora, with affection and ice cream, Perla and she would have ice cream too after the movies. She saw him beside a tree, the streets were empty at that time, under the double shadow of the foliage that came together up above; the figure stood out beside a tree trunk, a wisp of smoke rising up along his face. Matilde drew back, bumping into an easy chair, muffling a shriek with her hands that smelled of pink nail polish, taking refuge against the back wall of the room.

Milo, she thought, if that was thinking, that instantaneous vomiting of time and images. It's Milo. When she was able to look out from another window no one was on the corner across the way anymore, two children were coming along in the distance playing with a black dog. He saw me, Matilde thought. If it was he, he'd seen her, he was there in order to see her, he was there and not on any other corner, leaning on any other tree. Of course he'd seen her, because if he was there it was because he knew where the house was. And the fact that he'd gone away the instant he was recognized, seeing her draw back, cover her mouth, was even worse, the corner was filled with an emptiness where doubt was of no use at all, where everything was certainty and threat, the tree all alone, the wind in its leaves.

She saw him again at sundown, Carlitos was playing with his electric train and Flora was humming *bagualas* on the ground floor, the house, inhabited once more, seemed to be protecting her, helping her doubt, tell herself that Milo was taller and more robust, that maybe the siesta-time drowsiness, the blinding light . . . Every so often she would leave the television set and from as far away as possible look out a window, never the same one but always on the upper floor because at street level she would have been more afraid. When she saw him again he was in almost the same place but on the other side of the tree trunk. Night was coming on and his silhouette stood out against the other people passing by, talking and laughing; Villa del Parque coming out of its lethargy and going to cafés and movies, the neighborhood night slowly beginning. It was he, there was no denying it, that unchanged body, the gesture of the hand lifting the cigarette to his mouth, the edges of the white bandana, it was Milo, whom she'd killed five years before after escaping from Mexico, Milo, whom she'd killed with papers put together with bribes and accomplices in a studio in Lomas de Zamora where she had a childhood friend left who would do anything for money and maybe for friendship too, Milo, whom she'd killed with a heart attack in Mexico for Germán, because Germán wasn't a man to accept anything else, Germán and his career, his colleagues and his club and his parents, Germán to get married and set up a family, the chalet and Carlitos and Flora and the car and the country place in Manzanares, Germán and so much money, security, then deciding, almost without thinking about it, sick of misery and waiting, after the second meeting with Germán at the Recanatis', the trip to Lomas de Zamora to entrust herself to the one who had said no at first, that it was an outrage, that it couldn't be done, that it would take a lot of pesos, that all right, that in two weeks, that agreed, Emilio Díaz dead in Mexico of a heart attack, almost the truth because she and Milo had lived like dead people during those last months in Coyoacán, until the plane that brought her back to what was hers in Buenos Aires, to everything that had belonged to Milo before going to Mexico together and falling apart together in a war of silences and deceptions and stupid reconciliations that weren't worth anything, the curtain ready for the new act, for a new night of long knives.

The cigarette was still burning slowly in Milo's mouth as he leaned against the tree, looking unhurriedly at the windows of the house. How could he have found out? Matilde thought, still clinging to that absurdity of thinking something was there, but outside or ahead of any thought. Of course he'd ended up finding out about it, discovering in Buenos Aires that he was dead because in Buenos Aires he was dead in Mexico, finding out had probably humiliated him and lashed him down to the first gust of rage that whipped his face, pulling him into a return flight, guiding him through a maze of foreseeable inquiries, maybe Cholo or Marina, maybe the Recanatis' mother, the old hangouts, the cafés where the gang gathered, the hunches, and thereabouts the definite news, that she'd married Germán Morales, man, but just tell me how can that be, I tell you she got married in church and everything, the Moraleses, you know, textiles and dough, respectability, old man, respectability, but just tell me how can that be since she said, but we thought that you, it can't be, brother. Of course it couldn't be and that's why it was all the more so, it was Matilde behind the curtain spying on him, time immobilized in a present that contained everything, Mexico and Buenos Aires and the heat of siesta time and the cigarette that kept going up to his mouth, at some moment nothingness again, the empty corner, Flora calling her because Carlitos wouldn't take his bath, the telephone with Perla, restless, not tonight Perla, it must be my stomach, you go by yourself or with Negra, it's quite painful, I'd better go to bed, I'll call you tomorrow, and all the time no, it can't be like that, how come they haven't told Germán by now if they knew, he didn't find the house through them, it couldn't have been through them, the Recanatis' mother would have called Germán immediately just for the scene it would cause, to be the first to tell him because she'd never accepted her as Germán's wife, think of the horror, bigamy, I always said she wasn't to be trusted, but nobody had called Germán or maybe they had but at the office and Germán was now far away on a trip, the Recanatis' mother is certainly waiting for him to tell him in person, so she won't lose anything, she or somebody else, Milo had found where Germán lived from somebody, he couldn't have found the chalet by chance, he couldn't be there smoking against the tree by chance. And if he wasn't there now it didn't matter, and double-locking the doors didn't matter, although Flora was a little surprised, the only thing for sure was the bottle of sleeping pills, so that after hours and hours she'd stop thinking and lose herself in a drowsiness broken by dreams where Milo never . . . but in the morning now the shriek when she felt a hand, Carlitos, who wanted to surprise her, the sobbing of Carlitos, offended, and Flora taking him out for a walk, lock the door, Flora. Getting up and seeing him again, there, looking directly at the window without the slightest gesture, drawing back and spying later from the kitchen and nothing, beginning to realize that she was locked up in the house and that it couldn't go on like that, that sooner or later she'd have to go out to take Carlitos to the pediatrician or get together with Perla who was phoning every day and getting impatient and didn't understand. In the orange and asphyxiating afternoon, Milo leaning against the tree, the black Windbreaker in all that heat, the smoke rising up and floating away. Or just the tree, but Milo all the same, Milo all the same, being erased only a little by the pills and the television until the last program.

On the third day Perla arrived unannounced, tea and scones and Carlitos, Flora taking advantage of a moment alone to tell Perla that it couldn't go on like that, Miss Matilde needs distraction, she spends her days locked up, I don't understand, Miss Perla, I'm telling you even if it's not my place to, and Perla smiling at her in the study, you did the right thing, child, I know that you love Matilde and Carlitos very much, I think it's Germán's being away that's depressing her, and Flora without a word lowering her head, the mistress needs distraction, I'm only telling you even if it's not my place to. Tea and the usual gossip, nothing about Perla that made her suspect, but then how had Milo been able, impossible to imagine that the Recanatis' mother would have been silent so long if she knew, not even for the pleasure of waiting for Germán and telling him for the sake of the Lord Jesus or something like that, she tricked you so you'd lead her down the aisle, that's exactly what that old witch would say and Germán falling down out of the clouds, it can't be, it can't be. But, yes, it could be, except that now she didn't even have the confirmation that she hadn't been dreaming, that all she had to do was go to the window, but not with Perla there, another cup of tea, tomorrow we'll go to the movies, I promise, come pick me up in your car, I don't know what's got into me these days, come in your car and we'll go to the movies, the window there beside the easy chair, but not with Perla there, waiting for Perla to leave and then Milo on the corner, peaceful against the wall as if waiting for a bus, the black Windbreaker and the bandana around his neck and then nothing until Milo again.

On the fifth day she saw him follow Flora, who was going to the store, and everything became future, something like the pages remaining in that novel left face down on a sofa, something already written and which it wasn't even necessary to read because it had already happened before being read, had already happened before happening in the reading. She saw them coming back chatting, Flora timid and somewhat mistrustful, saying good-bye on the corner and crossing rapidly. Perla came in her car to pick her up, Milo wasn't there and he wasn't there when they got back late at night either, but in the morning she saw him waiting for Flora, who was going to the market, now he went directly over to her and Flora shook hands with him, they laughed and he took the basket and afterward carried it back filled with the fruit and vegetables, accompanied her to the door, Matilde no longer saw them because the balcony jutted out over the sidewalk, but Flora was taking a long time to come in, they were standing there a while chatting by the door. The next day Flora took Carlitos shopping with her and she saw the three of them laughing and Milo stroked Carlitos on the head, on his return Carlitos was carrying a plush lion and said that Flora's boyfriend had given it to him. So you have a boyfriend, Flora, the two of them alone in the living room. I don't know, ma'am, he's so nice, we met all of a sudden, he went shopping with me, he's so good with Carlitos, you don't really mind, do you, ma'am? Telling her no, that was her business, but she should be careful, a young girl like her, and Flora lowering her eyes and of course, ma'am, he just goes with me and we talk, he owns a restaurant in Almagro, his name is Simón. And Carlitos with a magazine in colors, Simón bought it for me, Mama, that's Flora's boyfriend.

Germán telephoned from Salta announcing that he'd be back in about ten days, love, everything fine. The dictionary said: bigamy, marriage contracted after widowhood by the surviving spouse. It said: status of a man married to two women or of a woman married to two men. It said: interpretative bigamy, according to canon law, that acquired by a marriage contracted with a woman who has lost her virginity through having prostituted herself or through having declared her first marriage null and void. It said: bigamist, one who marries for a second time without the death of the first spouse. She'd opened the dictionary without knowing why, as if that could change anything, she knew it was impossible to change anything, impossible to go out onto the street and talk to Milo, impossible to appear at the window and summon him with a gesture, impossible to tell Flora that Simón wasn't Simón, impossible to take the plush lion and the magazine away from Carlitos, impossible to confide in Perla, just being there, seeing him, knowing that the novel thrown onto the sofa was written down to the words The End, that she couldn't change anything, whether she read it or not, even if she burned it or hid it in the back of Germán's library. Ten days and then yes, but what, Germán returning to office and friends, the Recanatis' mother or Cholo, any one of Milo's friends who'd given him the address of the house, I've got to talk to you Germán, it's something very serious, old man, things would be happening one after the other, first Flora with her cheeks flushed, would you mind, ma'am, if Simón came to have coffee in the kitchen with me, just for a little while? Of course she wouldn't mind, how could she mind since it was broad daylight and just for a little while, Flora had every right to receive him in the kitchen and give him a cup of coffee, and Carlitos had every right to come down and play with Simón, who'd brought him a wind-up duck that walked and everything. Staying upstairs until she heard the knock on the door, Carlitos coming up with the duck and Simón told me he's for the River team, that's too bad, Mama, I'm for San Lorenzo, look what he gave me, look how it walks, but look, Mama, it looks like a real duck, Simón gave it to me, he's Flora's boyfriend, why didn't you come down to meet him?

Now she could look out the windows without the slow useless precautions, Milo no longer standing by the tree, every afternoon he would come at five and spend half an hour in the kitchen with Flora and almost always with Carlitos, sometimes Carlitos would come up before he left and Matilde knew why, knew that in those few minutes when they were alone what had to happen was being prepared, what was already there as in the novel open on the sofa was being prepared in the kitchen, in the house of somebody who could be anybody at all, the Recanatis' mother or Cholo, a week had passed and Germán telephoned from Córdoba to confirm his return, announcing almond paste for Carlitos and a surprise for Matilde, he would stay home and rest up for five days, they would go out, go to restaurants, go horseback riding at the Manzanares place. That night she telephoned Perla just to hear her talk, hanging on to her voice for an hour until she couldn't anymore because Perla was beginning to realize that all that was artificial, that something was going on with Matilde, you should go see Graciela's analyst, you're acting strange, Matilde, believe me. When she hung up she couldn't even go to the window, she knew that it was already useless that night, that she wouldn't see Milo on the corner which was dark now. She went down to be with Carlitos while Flora served him his dinner, she listened to him complain about the soup even though Flora looked at her, expecting her to intervene, to help her before she put him to bed, while Carlitos resisted and insisted on staying up in the living room playing with the duck and watching television. The whole ground floor was like a different zone; she'd never understood too well why Germán had insisted on putting Carlitos's bedroom next door to the living room, so far from them upstairs, but Germán couldn't stand any noise in the morning, so Flora could get Carlitos ready for school and Carlitos could shout and sing, she kissed him by the bedroom door and went back to the kitchen, although she no longer had anything to do there, looked at the door to Flora's room, went over and touched the knob, opened it a little and saw Flora's bed, the bureau with photographs of rock bands and the singer Mercedes Sosa, she thought she heard Flora coming out of Carlitos's bedroom and she closed it quietly and started to look in the refrigerator. I made mushrooms the way you like them, Miss Matilde, I'll bring up your dinner in half an hour since you're not going out; I've also got a pumpkin dessert that turned out very good, just like in my village, Miss Matilde.

The stairway was poorly lighted but the steps were few and wide, she went up almost without looking, the bedroom door ajar with a beam of light breaking on the waxed landing. She'd been eating at the little table beside the window for several days now, the dining room downstairs was so solemn without Germán, everything fit on a tray and Flora, agile, almost enjoying the fact that Miss Matilde was eating upstairs now that the master was away, stayed with her and they talked for a while and Matilde would have liked Flora to have eaten with her, but Carlitos would have told Germán and Germán the discourse on distance and respect, Flora herself would have been afraid because Carlitos always ended up finding out everything and would have told Germán. And now what could she talk about to Flora when the only thing possible was to get the bottle she'd hidden behind the books and drink half a glass of whiskey in one swig, choke and pant and pour herself another drink, almost beside the window opening onto the night, onto the nothingness there outside where nothing was going to happen, not even the repetition of the shadow beside the tree, the glow of the cigarette going up and down like an indecipherable signal, perfectly clear.

She threw the mushrooms out the window while Flora prepared the tray with the dessert, she heard her coming up with that rhythm like a sleigh or a runaway colt that Flora had when she came up the stairs, told her that the mushrooms were delicious, praised the color of the pumpkin dessert, asked for a double cup of strong coffee, and for her to bring her up another pack of cigarettes from the living room. It's hot tonight, Miss Matilde, we'll have to leave the windows open wide, I'll spray some insecticide before we go to bed, I've already put Carlitos in, he went right to sleep and you saw how he was complaining, he misses his daddy, poor thing, and then Simón was telling him stories this afternoon. Tell me if you need anything, Miss Matilde, I'd like to go to bed early if you don't mind. Of course she didn't mind even though Flora had never said anything like that before, she would finish her work and shut herself up in her room to listen to the radio or knit, she looked at her for a moment and Flora smiled at her, content, she was carrying the tray with the coffee and she went down to get the insecticide, I'd best leave it here on the dresser, Miss Matilde, you can spray it yourself before you go to bed, because no matter what they say, it does have a bad smell, it's best when you're getting ready to go to bed. She closed the door, the colt tripped lightly down the stairs, one last sound of dishes; the night began in exactly that second when Matilde went into the library to get the bottle and bring it over beside the easy chair.

The low light from the lamp barely reached the bed at the back of the room, vaguely visible were one of the night tables and the sofa where the novel had been left, but it wasn't there anymore, after so many days Flora must have decided to put it on the empty shelf in the library. With the second whiskey Matilde heard ten o'clock strike in some distant belfry, she thought that she'd never heard that bell before, counted each ring and looked at the telephone, maybe Perla, but no, not Perla at that hour, she always got annoyed or she wasn't in. Or Alcira, calling Alcira and telling her, just telling her that she was afraid, that it was stupid but maybe if Mario hadn't gone out with the car, something like that. She didn't hear the street door open but it didn't matter, it was absolutely clear that the main door was being opened or was going to be opened and nothing could be done, she couldn't go out to the landing, lighting it with the lamp from the bedroom and looking down into the living room, she couldn't ring the bell for Flora to come, the insecticide was there, the water too for medicine and thirst, the turned-down bed waiting. She went to the window and saw the empty corner; maybe if she'd looked out before she would have seen Milo approaching, crossing the street, and disappearing under the balcony, but it would have been even worse, what could she have shouted to Milo, how could she have stopped him since he was going to come into the house, since Flora was going to open the door and receive him in her room, Flora even worse than Milo at that moment, Flora who would have learned everything, who would have her revenge on Milo by having revenge on her, dragging her down into the mud, on Germán, involving her in a scandal. There wasn't the slightest possibility for anything left, but neither could it have been she who'd cried out the truth, completely impossible was an absurd hope that Milo was only coming for Flora, that some incredible turn of fate had shown him Flora completely separate from the other business, that the corner there had been just any corner for Milo back in Buenos Aires, that Milo didn't know it was Germán's house, didn't know he was dead back there in Mexico, that Milo wasn't looking for her through Flora's body. Staggering drunkenly over to the bed, she pulled off the clothing that clung to her body; naked, she rolled onto her side on the bed and looked for the bottle of pills, the final pink or green port within reach of her hand. It was hard to get the pills out and Matilde piled them up on the night table without looking at them, her eyes lost on the shelves where the novel was, she could see it very clearly, open and face down on the one empty shelf where Flora had put it, she saw the Malayan knife that Cholo had given Germán, the crystal ball on the base of red velvet. She was sure that the door had opened downstairs, that Milo had come into the house, into

Flora's room, was probably talking to Flora or had already begun to undress her, because for Flora that had to be the only reason Milo was there, gaining access to her room in order to undress her and undress himself, kissing her, let me, let me stroke you like this, and Flora resisting and not today, Simón, I'm afraid, let me, but Simón in no hurry, little by little he'd laid her crosswise on the bed and was kissing her hair, looking for her breasts under her blouse, resting a leg on her thighs and taking off her shoes as if playing, talking into her ear and kissing her closer and closer to her mouth, I want you, my love, let me undress you, let me see you, you're so beautiful, moving away the lamp and enwrapping her in shadows and caresses, Flora giving in with a first whimper, the fear that something will be heard upstairs, that Miss Matilde or Carlitos, but no, speak low, leave me like this now, the clothes falling just anywhere, the tongues finding each other, the moans, Simón, please don't hurt me, it's the first time, Simón, I know, stay just like that, be quiet now, don't cry out, love, don't cry out.

She cried out but into Simón's mouth as he knew the moment, holding her tongue between his teeth and sinking his fingers into her hair, she cried out and then she wept under Simón's hands as he covered her face, caressing it, she went limp with a final Mama, Mama, a whimper that passed into a panting and a sweet and soft sob, a my love, love, the bland season of blended bodies, of the hot breath of night. Much later, after two cigarettes against a backrest of pillows, towels between guilt-ridden thighs, the words, the plans that Flora babbled out as in a dream, the hope that Simón was listening, smiling at her, kissing her breasts, moving a slow spider of fingers across her stomach, letting himself go, drowsing, doze off a bit, I'm going to the bathroom and

I'll be right back, I don't need any light, I'm like a night cat, I know where it is, and Flora no, they might hear you, Simón don't be silly, I told you I'm like a cat and I know where the door is, doze off a bit, I'll be right back, that's it, nice and quiet.

He closed the door as if to add a bit more silence to the house, naked, he crossed the kitchen and the dining room, faced the stairs and put his foot on the first step, feeling around for it. Good wood, a good house Germán Morales has. On the third step he saw the mark of the beam of light from under the bedroom door; he went up the other four steps and put his hand on the knob, opened the door with one push. The blow against the dresser reached Carlitos in his restless sleep, he sat up in bed and cried out, he cried out a lot at night and Flora would get up to calm him, give him some water before Germán could get angry. She knew she had to quiet Carlitos because Simón hadn't come back yet, she had to calm him down before Miss Matilde got worried, she wrapped herself in the sheet and ran to Carlitos's room, found him sitting at the foot of the bed staring into space, shouting with fear, she picked him up in her arms, talking to him, telling him no, no, she was there, she'd bring him some chocolate, she'd leave the light on, she heard the incomprehensible cry and went into the living room with Carlitos in her arms, the stairway was illumined by the light from above, she reached the foot of the stairs and saw them in the doorway, staggering, the naked bodies wrapped in a single mass that fell slowly onto the landing, that slipped down the steps, that without breaking apart rolled downstairs in a confused tangle until it stopped motionless on the living room rug, the knife planted in Simón's chest as he spread out on his back, and Matilde—but that only the autopsy would show afterward—that she had taken enough sleeping pills to kill her two hours later, when I arrived with the ambulance and was giving Flora an injection to bring her out of her hysteria, giving Carlitos a sedative, and asking the nurse to stay until relatives or friends got there.

III

PRESS CLIPPINGS

Although I don't think it's really necessary to say so, the first clipping is real and the second one imaginary.

The sculptor lives on the Rue Riquet, which doesn't seem like a good idea to me, but in Paris you haven't got much choice if you're an Argentine and a sculptor, generally two difficult ways of living in this city. We really don't know each other too well, through snippets of time that stretch back twenty years; when he called me to talk about a book with prints of his most recent work and asked me to do a text to accompany it, I said what it's always best to say in such cases, that he should show me some of his sculptures and then we'd see, or, rather, we'd see then.

I went to his apartment at night and first there was coffee and some friendly sparring, both of us feeling what is inevitably felt when someone shows his work to another person and that fearful moment comes when bonfires will be lighted or a person has to admit, covering it with words, that the wood was wet and gave off more smoke than heat. And before that, on the telephone, he'd told me about his work, a series of small pieces whose theme was the violence in all the political and geographical latitudes that man inhabits as a man/wolf. We knew something about that, two Argentines, letting the nausea of memories rise up once more, the daily accumulation of fright through cables, letters, sudden silences. While we were talking he was clearing a table; he sat me down in a chair that was just right and began to bring out the pieces, putting them under a carefully placed light, and letting me look at them slowly, and then he turned them gradually; we said practically nothing now, because they had the word and that word was still ours. One after another, until there were ten or so of them, small and filiform, clayish or plaster, born out of wires or bottles patiently wrapped by the work of fingers and spatula, growing out of empty cans and objects underneath that only the sculptor's skill showed me as bodies and heads, arms and hands. It was late at night, all that reached us from the street was the rumble of heavy trucks, the siren of an ambulance.

I was glad that there wasn't anything systematic or too explicative in the sculptor's work, that each piece had something of an enigma about it and that sometimes one had to look for a long time in order to understand the modality that violence assumed there; at the same time, the sculptures seemed to me to be at the same time naive and subtle, in any case without any sense of dread or sentimental exaggeration. Even torture, that last form in which violence takes the place of the horror of immobility and isolation, had not been shown with the doubtful trifle of so many posters and texts and movies that returned to my memory, also doubtful, also ready to hold the images and give them back for who knows what kind of obscure pleasure. I said to myself that if I wrote the text the sculptor had asked me to, if I write the text you ask me to, I told him, it will be a text like these pieces, I'll never let myself be carried along by the facility that all too often abounds in this field.

"That's up to you, Noemí," he said to me. "I know it's not easy, we carry so much blood in our memories that sometimes you feel guilty when you put a limit on it, channel it so it doesn't flood us out completely."

"You're talking to the right person. Look at this clipping, I know the woman who signed it, and I learned other things from what friends told me. It happened three years ago, just as it could have happened last night and can be happening at this very moment in Buenos Aires or Montevideo. Just before leaving to come here I opened a letter from a friend and he'd sent me the clipping. Let me have another cup of coffee while you read it, you really don't have to read it after what you've shown me, but, I don't know, I'd feel better if you read it too."

What he read was this:

The undersigned, Laura Beatriz Bonaparte Bruschtein, domiciled at No. 26 Atoyac, District 10, Colonia Cuauhtémoc, Mexico 5, D. F., wishes to pass the following testimony on to public opinion:

1. Aída Leonora Bruschtein Bonaparte, born May 21, 1951, in Buenos Aires, Argentina, profession, teacher in literacy program.

Fact: At ten o'clock in the morning of December 24, 1975, she was kidnapped by personnel of the Argentine army (601st Battalion) at her place of employment in the Monte Chingolo slum, near the federal capital.

The previous day that place had been the scene of a battle that had left a toll of one hundred dead, including inhabitants of the area. My daughter, after being kidnapped, was taken to the military headquarters of the 601st Battalion.

There she was brutally tortured, the same as other women. Those who survived were shot that same Christmas night. Among them was my daughter.

The burial of those killed in the fighting and of the civilians kidnapped, as was the case of my daughter, was delayed for about five days. All the bodies, including hers, were transferred in mechanical shovels from the battalion to the Lanús police station, from there to the Avellaneda cemetery, where they were buried in a common grave.

I kept on looking at the last sculpture that had remained on the table, I refused to cast my eyes on the sculptor who was reading in silence. For the first time I heard the ticking of a clock on the wall, it was coming from the vestibule and was the only thing audible at that moment in which the street was becoming more and more deserted; the soft sound reached me like a nighttime metronome, an attempt to keep time alive inside that hole where the two of us were stuck in a way, the duration that took in a flat in Paris and a miserable slum in Buenos Aires, that abolished calendars and left us face to face with that, what we could only call that, all epithets exhausted, all expressions of horror fatigued and filthy.

" 'Those who survived were shot that same Christmas night,' " the sculptor read aloud. "They probably gave them sweet rolls and cider, remember that in Auschwitz they passed out candy to the children before sending them into the gas chambers."

He must have seen something in my face, he made a

gesture of apology, and I lowered my eyes and looked for another cigarette.

> I received official notice of my daughter's murder in Court No. 8 in the city of La Plata, January 8, 1976. Then I was conducted to the Lanús police station, where, after three hours of interrogation, they told me where the grave was located. All they would show me of my daughter were the hands cut off her body and placed in a jar that carried the number 24. What remained of her body could not be turned over because it was a military secret. The following day I went to the Avellaneda cemetery, looking for stake number 28. The inspector had told me that there I would find "what remained of her because one couldn't call what had been turned over to them bodies." The grave was a patch of recently turned ground, twenty feet by twenty, more or less at the rear of the cemetery. I knew how to locate the grave. It was terrible when I realized how more than a hundred people had been murdered and buried, among them my daughter.
>
> 2. In view of this infamous situation and one of such indescribable cruelty, in January 1976 I, domiciled on 730 Calle Lavalle, fifth floor, district nine, in the federal capital, bring charges of murder against the Argentine army. I do it in the same tribunal of La Plata, number 8, civil court.

"You can see, all this is worth nothing," the sculptor said, sweeping his arm through the air. "Worth nothing, Noemí, I've spent months making this shit, you write books, that woman denounces atrocities, we attend congresses and round tables to protest, we almost come to believe that things are changing, and then all you need is two minutes of reading to understand the truth again, to—"

"Shh, I'm thinking things like that right now too," I said with a rage at having to say it. "But if I accepted them it would be like sending them a telegram of support, and, besides, you know very well that tomorrow you'll get up and in a while you'll be shaping another sculpture and you'll know that I'm at my typewriter and you'll think that we're many, even though we're so few, and that difference in strength isn't and never will be any reason to be silent. End of sermon. Did you finish reading? Hey, I've got to go."

He shook his head negatively, pointed to the coffeepot.

As a consequence to this legal recourse of mine, the following things happened:

3. In March of 1976, Adrián Saidón, Argentine, twenty-four years old, employed, my daughter's fiancé, was murdered on a street in the city of Buenos Aires by the police, who informed his father.

His body was not returned to his father, Dr. Abraham Saidón, because it was a military secret.

4. Santiago Bruschtein, Argentine, born December 25, 1918, father of my murdered daughter, mentioned previously, doctor of biochemistry by profession, with a laboratory in the city of Morón.

Fact: on June 11, 1976, at 12 noon, a group of military men in civilian clothes came to his apartment at 730 Calle Lavalle, Apt. 9. My husband, attended by a nurse, was in bed, on the verge of death because of a heart attack and with a prognostication of three months to live. The military men questioned him about me and our children, and added that "*like the Jew bastard you are, you're capable of bringing charges of murder against the Argentine army.*" Then they made him get out of bed, and, *beating him*, put him into a car, without letting him bring along his medicine.

Eyewitnesses have affirmed that the army and the police used around twenty cars for the arrest. We have not heard anything more about him since. Through unofficial sources, we were informed that he died suddenly at the beginning of his torture session.

"And here I am thousands of miles away arguing with a publisher about what kind of paper the photographs should have, the format, and the jacket."

"Bah, pal, just now I've been writing a story where I talk, no less, about the psy-cho-log-i-cal problems of a girl at the moment of puberty. Don't start up with autotorture, the real kind is quite enough, I think."

"I know, Noemí, I know, God damn it. But it's always the same thing, we always have to recognize that all this happened in another space, another time. We never were and never will be there, where maybe . . ."

(I remembered something I'd read when I was a girl, in Augustin Thierry, perhaps, a story about how a saint, God knows what his name was, had converted Clovis and his nation to Christianity and was describing the scourging and crucifixion of Jesus, and the king rose up on his throne, shaking his spear and shouting: "Oh, if only I could have been there with my Franks!"—the miracle of an impossible wish, the same impotent rage of the sculptor, lost in his reading.)

5. Patricia Villa, Argentine, born in Buenos Aires in 1952, journalist, worked at the Inter-Press Service, and is my daughter-in-law's sister.

Fact: Along with her fiancé, Eduardo Suárez, also a journalist, she was arrested in September 1976, and they were taken as prisoners to the general headquarters of the federal police of Buenos Aires. A week after their seizure, her mother, who had taken legal action in the case, was informed that unfortunately it had been a mistake. Their bodies have not been returned to their families.

6. Irene Mónica Bruschtein Bonaparte de Ginzberg, twenty-two years old, artist by profession, married to Mario Ginzberg, construction foreman, twenty-four years old.

Fact: On March 11, 1977, at six in the morning, a joint force of army and police came to the apartment where they lived, taking the couple away and leaving behind their small children: Victoria, two years, six months old, and Hugo Roberto, one year, six months, abandoned at the door of the building. We immediately asked for a writ of habeas corpus, I at the consulate in Mexico City and Mario's father in the federal capital.

I have inquired about my daughter Irene and Mario, denouncing that horrendous sequence of events to the United Nations, the OAS, Amnesty International, the European Parliament, the Red Cross, etc.

Up to this time, however, I have received no news as to their place of detention. I have a firm hope that they are still alive.

As a mother, unable to return to Argentina because of the situation of family persecution that I have described, and since legal recourses have been annulled, I ask the institutions and people who fight for the defense of human rights to begin the necessary procedures to return my daughter Irene and her husband, Mario, to me and thus safeguard their lives and liberty. Signed, Laura Beatriz Bonaparte Bruschtein (from *El País*, October 1978, reprinted in *Denuncia*, December 1978).

The sculptor gave me back the clipping, we didn't say very much because we were dropping from lack of sleep, I sensed that he was glad I had agreed to go along with him on his book, and only then did I realize that he had been doubtful up to the last because I'm known to be very busy, maybe selfish, in any case, a writer deeply involved in her own pursuits. I asked him if there was a taxi stand nearby and I went out onto the street that was deserted and cold and too broad, to my taste, for Paris. A gust of wind made me turn up my coat collar, I could hear my heels clicking in the silence, marking out a rhythm in which fatigue and obsessions so often insert a melody that keeps coming back, or a line from a poem, but which only let me see her hands cut off her body and put into a bottle that bears the number twenty-four, only let me see her hands cut off her body, I recovered quickly rejecting the recurrent nausea, forcing myself to take a deep breath, to think about tomorrow's work; I never knew why I crossed to the opposite sidewalk, there was no need to since the street opened onto the Place de la Chapelle, where I might be able to get a cab. It made no difference which sidewalk I went along, I crossed because I crossed, because I didn't even have enough strength left to ask myself why I crossed over.

The little girl was sitting on the steps of a porch that was almost lost among the other porches of the tall and narrow houses barely distinguishable from each other in that particularly dark block. That there should be a child on the edge of a step at that hour of the night and in that loneliness didn't surprise me as much as her position, a little whitish splotch with legs tight together and hands covering her face, something that could also have been a dog or some garbage forgotten at the entrance to the house. I looked vaguely around; a truck was pulling away with its weak lights yellow, on the sidewalk opposite a man was walking hunched over, his head sunk in the raised collar of his overcoat and his hands in his pockets. I stopped, took a close look, the child had thin hair, a white skirt, a pink sweater, and when she removed her hands from her face I saw her eyes and her cheeks and not even the half-darkness could hide the tears, the glow that trickled down to her mouth.

"What's wrong? What are you doing there?"

I heard her breathe deeply, swallow tears and mucus, a hiccup or a pout, I saw her face fully lifted toward me, her tiny red nose, the curve of a mouth that was trembling. I repeated the questions, who knows what I said to her, crouching until I felt her very close.

"My mama," the little girl said, speaking between gasps. "My papa is doing things to my mama."

Maybe she was going to say more, but her arms reached out and I felt her cling to me, weeping desperately against my neck; she smelled dirty, of wet underpants. I tried to take her in my arms and get up, but she drew away from me, looking into the darkness of the hallway. She pointed at something, she started forward, and I followed her, barely glimpsing a stone arch and behind the half-darkness the beginning of a garden. Silently she came out into the open air, it wasn't a flower garden but rather a vegetable patch with low wire fences that marked off planted sections, there was enough light to see the skimpy mastic trees, the poles that supported climbing plants, rags to scare off the birds; toward the center you could make out a low hut patched with zinc and tin cans, from whose small window a greenish light came. There was no lighted lamp in any of the windows of the buildings around the plot, the black walls went up five stories until they merged with a low and cloudy sky.

The little girl had gone directly to the narrow passage-way between two vegetable patches that led to the door of the hut; she turned a little to make sure I was following her and went into the shack. I know that I must have stopped there and half-turned, telling myself that the girl had had a bad dream and was going back to bed, every reason that reason could produce telling me at that moment how absurd and perhaps risky it was to go into a strange house at that hour of the night; maybe I was still telling myself these things when I went through the half-open door and saw the little girl waiting for me in a vague entrance full of old furniture and garden tools. A ray of light filtered through under the door at the back, and the girl pointed to it and almost jumping over the rest of the entrance began almost imperceptibly opening the door. Just beside her, face full in the yellowish ray of the opening that was slowly growing larger, I smelled burning, I heard a kind of muffled shriek which was repeated over and over, interrupted then taken up again; my hand pushed on the door and I took in the foul room—the broken stools and beer and wine bottles on the table, the glasses, and the table covering of old newspapers, beyond that the bed and the naked body gagged with a dirty towel, her hands and feet tied to the iron bedstead. His back to me, sitting on a bench, the girl's papa was doing things to her mama; he was taking his time, slowly lifting his cigarette to his mouth, letting the smoke out of his nose slowly while the lighted end came down to rest on one of the mama's breasts, remained there for the duration of the gagged shrieks under the towel wrapped around her mouth and face except for the eyes. Before under-standing, accepting being part of that, there was time for the papa to withdraw the cigarette and bring it up to his mouth again, time to enliven the lighted end and savor the excellent French tobacco, time for me to see the body burned from the stomach to the neck, the purple or red splotches that went up from the thighs and the sex to the breasts where now the lighted end rested again with a careful delicacy, seeking an unscarred spot on the skin. The shriek and the shudder of the body on the bed that creaked under the spasm were mixed with things, with acts that I didn't choose and which I will never be able to explain to myself. Between the man with his back to me and myself there was a broken-down stool, I saw it rise up in the air and fall at an angle onto the papa's head; his body and the stool rolled onto the floor almost at the same second. I had to jump back not to fall too. I had put all my strength into the motion of raising the stool and hitting him; that strength immediately abandoned me, leaving me a stagger- ing simpleton. I know that I looked for support without finding it, that I looked vaguely behind and saw the door half-open, the little girl no longer there and the man on the floor a confused splotch, a wrinkled rag. What came afterward I could have seen in a movie or read in a book, I was there as if not being there, but I was there with an agility and an intent that in a very brief time—if it happened in time—led me to find a knife on the table, cut the bonds that held the woman, pull the towel from her face, and see her get up silently, perfectly silent now as if that were necessary and even essential, look at the body on the floor as it began to contract from an unconsciousness that wasn't going to last, look at me wordlessly, go to the body and grab it by the arms while I held its feet. With a double lift we laid it out on the bed, tied it with the same cords, quickly reset and knotted, tied him and gagged him in that silence where something seemed to vibrate and tremble with an ultrasonic sound. What follows I don't know, I see the woman still naked, her hands pulling off pieces of clothing, unbuttoning pants and lowering them into wrinkles at the feet, I see her eyes on mine, a single pair of wide-open eyes, and four hands pulling and tearing and undressing, vest and shirt and shorts, now that I have to remember it and have to write it, my cursed state and my harsh memory bring me something else indescribably lived but not seen, a passage from a story by Jack London where a trapper in the north struggles to win a clean death while beside him, turned into a bloody thing that still holds a glimmer of consciousness, his comrade in adventures howls and twists, tortured by the women of the tribe who horribly prolong his life in spasms and shrieks, killing him without killing him, exquisitely refined in each new variant, never described but there, like us there, never described and doing what we must, what we had to do. It's useless to wonder now why I was involved in that, what was my right and my part in what was going on under my eyes that without doubt saw, that without doubt remember how London's imagination must have seen and remembered what his hand was incapable of writing. I only know that the little girl wasn't with us after my entry into the room, and that now the mama was doing things to the papa, but who knows whether only the mama or whether once more they were gusts of night, pieces of images coming back out of a newspaper clipping, the hands cut off her body and put in a bottle that bore the number twenty-four, through unofficial sources we found out that he died suddenly at the beginning of the torture session, the towel over her mouth, the lighted cigarettes, and Victoria, two years and six months old, and Hugo Roberto, one year and six months, abandoned at the door of the building. How could I know how long it lasted, how could I understand that I too, I too even though I thought I was on the right side, I too, how could I accept that I too there on the other side from the cut-off hands and the common graves, I too on the other side from the girls tortured and shot that same Christmas night, the rest is turning my back, crossing the garden patch, bumping against a wire fence and scratching my knee, going out onto the freezing and deserted street and getting to La Chapelle and almost immediately finding the taxi that took me to glass after glass of vodka and a sleep from which I awoke at noon, lying across the bed and fully clothed, with my knee bleeding and that perhaps providential headache that straight vodka brings on when it passes from bottleneck to throat.

I worked all afternoon, it seemed inevitable and frightening to me that I was capable of concentrating to such a degree; at dusk I phoned the sculptor, who seemed surprised at my early reappearance, I told him what had happened to me, I spat it out in a single flow of words that he respected, although at times I could hear him coughing or trying to get a question in.

"So you see," I told him, "you see I haven't taken too much time to give you what I promised."

"I don't understand," the sculptor said. "If you mean the text about—"

"Yes, that's what I mean. I just read it to you, that's the text. I'll send it to you as soon as I make a clean copy, I don't want it around anymore."

After two or three days that had been lived in a haze of pills and drinks and records, anything that could be a barrier, I went out to buy some food, the refrigerator was empty and Cuddles was mewing at the foot of my bed. I found a letter in the mailbox, the sculptor's thick handwriting on the envelope. There was a sheet of paper and a newspaper clipping, I began to read while I walked toward the market and only afterward did I realize that when I had opened the envelope I had torn and lost a piece of the clipping. The sculptor was thanking me for the text to his album, unusual but to all appearances very much like me, far removed from the usual things in albums, although that didn't bother him any more than it bothered me. There was a postscript: "A great dramatic actress has been lost in you, although luckily an excellent writer has been saved. The other afternoon I thought you were telling me something that had really happened to you, then by chance I read *France-Soir*, from which I have taken the liberty of clipping the source of your remarkable personal experience. It's true that a writer can argue that if his inspiration comes from reality, and even from the crime news, what he is capable of doing with it raises it to another dimension, gives it a different value. In any case, my dear Noemí, we're too good friends for you to have felt it necessary to prepare me in advance for your text and unfold your dramatic talents on the telephone. But let's leave it at that, you know how much I appreciate your collaboration and I'm very glad that . . ."

I looked at the clipping and saw that I had inadvertently torn it, the envelope and the piece stuck to it were thrown away somewhere. The news item was worthy of *France-Soir* and its style: an atrocious drama in a suburb of Marseilles, the macabre discovery of a sadistic crime, ex-plumber bound and gagged on a cot, the corpse, et cetera, neighbors furtively aware of repeated scenes of violence, small daughter missing for several days, neighbors suspecting abandonment, police looking for mistress, horrendous spectacle offered to the—the clipping broke off there, when the sculptor had licked the envelope too abundantly he had done the same thing as Jack London, the same as Jack London and as my memory; but the photograph of the shack was intact and it was the shack in the vegetable patch, the wire and the zinc sheeting, the high walls surrounding it with their blind eyes, neighbors furtively aware, neighbors suspecting abandonment, everything there slapping me in the face from the bits of the news item.

I caught a cab and got out on the Rue Riquet, knowing that it was stupid and doing it because that's how stupid things get done. In broad daylight it had nothing that matched my memory and even though I walked along looking at every house and crossed over to the opposite sidewalk as I remembered having done, I couldn't recognize any entranceway that looked like the one from that night, the light fell onto things like an infinite mask, porches but not that porch, no access to an inner garden, simply because that garden was in the suburbs of Marseilles. But the little girl was there, sitting on the steps of some entrance or other, she was playing with a rag doll. When I spoke to her she ran off to the first door, a concierge came out before I could call to her. She wanted to know if I was a social worker, certain that I had come for the little girl whom she had found lost in the street, that very morning some gentlemen had been there to identify her, a social worker would come to get her. Although I already knew it, before leaving I asked what her last name was, then I went into a café and on the back of the sculptor's letter I wrote the end to the text and went to slip it under his door, it was proper that he should know the ending, so that the text accompanying his sculptures would be complete.

TEXT IN A NOTEBOOK

The matter of a passenger survey came up—it must be said —while we were talking about indetermination and analytic residues. Jorge García Bouza had made some allusions to the Montreal subway before concretely mentioning the Anglo line in Buenos Aires. He didn't tell me so, but I suspect he had had something to do with technical studies by the system— since it was the system itself that organized the survey. With special procedures that my ignorance categorizes as such (although García Bouza insisted on their effective simplicity) an exact count had been made of passengers using the subway every day during a certain week. Since he was also interested in finding out the percentage of inflow at the various stations on the line, as well as trips from one end to the other or between intermediate stations, the survey was made with the tightest control possible at all entrances and exits from Primera Junta to Plaza de Mayo. In those days, I'm talking about the forties, the Anglo line still hadn't been connected to the newer underground networks, which made the survey easier.

On Monday of the chosen week a basic total figure was obtained; on Tuesday the figure was approximately the same: on Wednesday, with an analogous total, the unexpected was produced: as against 113,987 people entering, the figure of those who had returned to the surface was 113,983. Common sense called for four errors in calculation, and those responsible for the operation went over the survey positions looking for possible negligence. Chief Inspector Montesano (I'm speaking now from data that García Bouza didn't know about and that I got hold of later) even went so far as to increase the personnel assigned to the survey. Being ever so scrupulous, he had the subway dragged from one end to the other, and workers and train personnel had to show their ID cards as they left. This all makes me see now that Chief Inspector Montesano had vague suspicions at the start of what concerns both of us now. Let me add unnecessarily that no one found the supposed error, which ended up suggesting (and at the same time eliminating) four passengers who were impossible to find.

On Thursday everything went fine; 107,328 inhabitants of Buenos Aires reappeared obediently after their episodic underground immersion. On Friday (after the preceding operations the survey could now be considered perfect), the figure of those who came out again was one greater than that of those tabulated upon entry. On Saturday equal figures were obtained and the system considered the task completed. The anomalous results weren't made public, and except for Chief

Inspector Montesano and the technicians running the adding machines at the Once station, I think few people were aware of what had happened. I also think that those few (I continue to make an exception of the chief inspector) reasonably forgot by the simple attribution of error to the machines or their operators.

This took place in 1946 or early in 1947. During the months that followed I had occasion to use the Anglo line a lot; from time to time, because the trip was long, the memory of that chat with García Bouza would come back to me, and I was ironically puzzled as I looked at the people around me on the seats or hanging from the straps like sides of beef on a hook. Twice, at the José María Moreno station, it seemed to me, unreasonably, that some of the people (a man, later on two old women) weren't ordinary passengers like the others. One Thursday night at the Medrano station, after going to the fights and seeing Jacinto Llanes win on points, it seemed to me that the girl half-asleep on the second bench on the platform wasn't there waiting for the uptown train. She did in fact get on the same car as I did but only to get off at the Río de Janeiro station and stay on the platform as if she were doubtful about something, as if she were terribly tired or bored.

I'm saying all this now that there's nothing left for me to know anymore; in the same way too that after a robbery you remember some suspicious-looking guys walking around the block. And yet, from the beginning, there was something about these fantasies woven in distraction that went farther and left behind a kind of sediment of suspicion; that's why on the night that García Bouza mentioned the results of the survey as a curious detail, the two things became immediately associated and I felt that something was coming together in strangeness, almost in fear. Maybe, of those on the outside, I was the first to know.

This was followed by a confused period where there was a mixture of a growing desire to verify suspicions, a dinner at El Pescadito that brought me close to Montesano and his recollections, and a progressive and cautious descent into the subway understood as something else, as a slow and different breathing, a pulse that in some unthinkable way wasn't beating along with the city, wasn't just another means of transportation in the city anymore. But before I really began descending (I'm not referring to the trivial fact of circulating through the subway like everybody else) there was a time of reflection and analysis. For three months, during which time I preferred taking streetcar number 86 so as to avoid verifications or deceptive coincidences, I was kept up on the surface by a theory of Luis M. Baudizzone that merits attention. Since I had mentioned—almost as a joke—García Bouza's information to him, he thought it was possible to explain the phenomenon by a kind of atomic attrition that is predictable in large multitudes. No one has ever counted the people leaving the River Plate stadium after a championship game on Sunday, no one has compared that figure with those of the box office. Does a herd of five thousand buffalo running through a draw have the same count coming out as going in? The rubbing together of people on the Calle Florida subtly erodes coat sleeves, the backs of gloves. The contact among 113,987 passengers on crowded trains that shake them and rub them against each other at every curve and stop can have, as a result (through the nullification of individuality and the action of erosion on the crowd-creature), the nullification of four units by the end of twenty hours. For the second anomaly, I mean that Friday when there was one passenger extra,

Baudizzone could only agree with Montesano and attribute it to some mistake in arithmetic. At the end of these rather literary conjectures, I felt myself very much alone again—I, who didn't have any conjectures of my own and, in fact, a slow cramp in the stomach every time I came to a subway entrance. That's why on my own I followed a spiral path that was slowly getting closer and closer to the truth. That's why I used the streetcar so much before I felt myself capable of going back to the Anglo line, of really descending, not just going down to take the subway.

It must be said here that I haven't had the slightest bit of help from them, quite the contrary; expecting it or seeking it would have been foolish. They're there and they don't even know that their written history begins with this very paragraph. For my part, I wouldn't like to give them away, and, in any case, I won't mention the few names I got to know during those weeks when I was in their world; if I've done all this, if I'm writing this report, I think my reasons were good, I wanted to help the people of Buenos Aires, always afflicted by transportation problems. Not even that matters now, I'm afraid now, I no longer feel like going down there now, but it's not fair to have to travel slowly and uncomfortably on the streetcar when the subway that everybody else takes because no one is afraid is only two steps away. I'm honest enough to recognize that if they're expelled—without any uproar, without anyone learning too much—I'll feel a lot more comfortable. And not just because my life was obviously in danger while I was down there, but I didn't feel safe either while I went ahead with my investigation that took up so many nights (everything there happens at night, there's nothing falser or more theatrical than the sunlight pouring through the gratings between two stations or rolling down the stairs that lead to the stations); it's quite possible that something has finally given me away and they already know why I spend so many hours in the subway in the same way that I can immediately spot them among the crowds all jammed together in the stations. They're so pale, they proceed with such manifest efficiency; they're so pale and so sad, almost all of them are so sad.

Curiously, what has bothered me most from the start has been finding out how they lived, without any reason for that life to be of the least importance to me. Almost immediately I rejected the idea of sidings or abandoned tunnels; the existence of all of them was manifest and coincided with the coming and going of the passengers between stations. It's true that between Loria and Plaza Once you can catch sight of a vague kind of Hades full of forges, sidings, piles of materials, and strange little huts with blackened windows. That kind of Nibelheim is glimpsed for a few seconds as the train shakes us almost brutally on the curves at the entrance to the station that's so bright in contrast. But it was enough for me to think of all the workers and foremen who share those dirty galleries to dismiss them as a usable redoubt; they wouldn't have exposed themselves there, not during the early days at least. I needed only a few observation trips to realize that nowhere, outside of the line itself—I mean the stations and their platforms and the trains in almost permanent motion—was there a place or conditions that could lend themselves to their life. I went along eliminating sidings, switch-offs, and storerooms until I arrived at the clear and horrible truth through what was of necessity left behind, residual, there in that twilight realm where the idea of being left behind kept returning time and time again. The existence that I am sketching out (some are probably saying that I'm proposing it) appeared to me to be conditioned by the most brutal and implacable necessity; out of the successive rejections of possibilities the only possible solution left was emerging. They, it had become only too clear now, aren't localized anywhere; they live on the subway, on the trains of the subway, moving continually. Their existence and their circulation like leukocytes—they're so pale!—favors the anonymity that has protected them so far.

Having reached this conclusion, I found the rest obvious. Except at dawn and very late at night, the Anglo trains are never empty because Buenos Aires people are night owls and there are always a few passengers coming and going before the station gates are closed. One might imagine now a last useless train that runs along following its schedule even though no one is getting on any longer, but I never got to see that. Or rather, yes, I did get to see it a few times but it was empty really only for me; the few passengers belonged to them, continuing their night through the fulfillment of inflexible instructions. I was never able to locate the nature of their necessary refuge during the three idle hours when the Anglo branch shuts down, from two to five in the morning. Either they stay on a train that's going onto a siding (and in that case the motorman has to be one of them) or they mingle episodically with the nocturnal cleaning people. This last is the least probable, for reasons of dress and personal relationships, and I prefer to suspect the use of the tunnel, unknown to regular passengers, that connects the Once station with the docks. Besides, why is the room with the sign No Admittance at the José María Moreno station full of rolls of toilet paper, not to mention a strange large chest where things can be stored? The visible fragility of that door lends itself to the worst of suspicions; but all in all, even though it might not be too reasonable, my impression is that in some way they continue the existence that has already been described without leaving the trains or the station platforms; an aesthetic necessity underneath it all gives me the certainty, perhaps the reason. There don't seem to be any valid residues in that permanent circulation that carries them back and forth between the two terminals.

I've mentioned aesthetic necessities, but maybe the reasons are only pragmatic. The plan demands a great simplicity so that each one of them can react mechanically and without any mistakes to the successive moments that comprise their permanent life underground. For example, as I was able to verify after much patience, each one knows that he or she mustn't make more than one trip in the same car so as not to draw attention; on the other hand, at the Plaza de Mayo terminal it's all right for them to stay in their seats, since the congestion causes a lot of people to get on the train at Florida in order to get a seat and get the jump on those waiting at the terminal. At Primera Junta the operation is different, all they have to do is get off, walk a few feet, and mingle with the passengers getting on the train across the platform. In every case they have the advantage that the enormous majority of passengers aren't going the whole way. Since they'll only take the subway again much later, within thirty minutes if they're going on a short errand and eight hours if they're office or factory workers, it's unlikely that they'll recognize the ones who stay down there, particularly since they're continually changing cars and trains. This last change, which was hard for me to verify, is much more subtle and is in response to an inflexible pattern destined to prevent possible visual imprints on trainmen or passengers who coincide with them (two times in five, depending on the time and crowding of the public) on the same trains. I know now, for example, that the girl who was waiting at Medrano that night had gotten off the train before mine and had gotten on the one behind us after traveling as far as Río de Janeiro; like all of them, she had precise instructions that went through the end of the week.

Practice has taught them how to sleep in their seats, but only for periods of a quarter of an hour maximum. Even those of us who travel episodically on the Anglo end up having a tactile memory of the itinerary, entry into the few curves on the line infallibly tells us whether we're leaving Congreso in the direction of Sáenz Peña or going up toward Loria. With them the habit is such that they awake at the precise moment to get off and change cars or trains. They sleep with dignity, erect, their heads inclined slightly over their chests. Twenty quarter-hour periods are sufficient to give them rest and, in addition, in their favor they have those three hours forbidden to my knowledge when the Anglo is closed to the public. The day I came to know that they were in possession of at least one train, which confirmed, perhaps, my hypothesis about the siding during closing time, I said to myself that their life must have taken on an almost agreeable community value if it had been given them to travel all together on that train. Quick but delicious collective meals between stations, uninterrupted sleep on a trip from terminal to terminal, even the joy of dialogue and contacts among friends and—why not?—relatives. But I came to ascertain that they strictly abstained from getting together on their train (if it's only one, since their number is doubtless gradually growing); they know only too well that any identification would be fatal for them, and that memory records three faces together at one time, as certain pleonasts say, more easily than mere isolated individuals.

Their train affords them a fleeting clandestine council when they need to receive and hand out the new weekly tabulation that Number One, the first of them, prepares on the pages of a small notebook and distributes every Sunday to the group chiefs; there they also receive money for the week's food, and one of Number One's emissaries (the train's motorman no doubt) listens to what each one has to tell him in matters of clothing, messages to the outside, and state of health. The schedule consists of such an alteration of trains and cars that any meeting is practically impossible and their lives are far apart again until the end of the week. I presume —I've come to understand all this after tense mental projections, imagining myself to be them and suffering or enjoying as they do—that they look forward to each Sunday as we up here look forward to the peace of ours. That Number One had chosen that day is not in response to any traditional respect, which would have surprised me in them; he simply knows that on Sundays there is a different type of passenger on the subway and therefore trains are more anonymous than on a Monday or Friday.

By delicately putting together so many pieces of the mosaic, I was able to understand the initial phase of the operation and the taking of the train. The first four, as the survey figures verify, went down one Tuesday. That afternoon, on the Sáenz Peña platform, they studied the caged faces of the passing motormen. Number One made a sign, and they boarded a train. They had to wait until they left Plaza de Mayo, making use of thirteen stops along the way, and having the conductor in another car. The hardest part was finding a moment when they were alone; a chivalrous arrangement by the Transportation Corporation of the City of Buenos Aires helped them by reserving the first car for women and children along with a Buenos Aires mannerism that consists of an obvious disdain for said car. At Perú two ladies were riding along talking about the sale at the Casa Lamota (which dresses Carlota) and a boy was sunk in the inadequate reading of *Rojo y Negro* (the magazine, not Stendhal). The conductor was down toward the middle of the train when Number One went into the car for ladies and knocked discreetly on the door to the motorman's cabin. The latter opened it with surprise but not suspecting anything, and the train was already on its way up to Piedras. They went through Lima, Sáenz Peña, and Congreso without incident. At Pasco there was a slight delay in leaving, but the conductor was at the other end of the train and not concerned. Forty-eight hours later a motorman in civilian clothes that were a little large on him mingled with the people coming out at Medrano and gave Chief Inspector Montesano the displeasure of having the Friday figure raised by one unit. Number One was already driving his train, with the other three furtively practicing in order to replace him when the time came. I needn't mention that little by little they did the same with the conductors on the trains they were taking.

Masters of more than one train, they have at their disposal a mobile territory where they can operate with some security. I will probably never know why the Anglo motormen gave in to Number One's extortion or bribery, or how the latter avoids his possible identification when he comes face to face with other employees, collects his pay, or fills out forms. I can only proceed peripherally, uncovering one by one the immediate mechanisms of the vegetative life, the external conduct. It was hard for me to admit that they fed themselves almost exclusively on the products sold in the kiosks in the stations, until I was persuaded that the most extreme rigor governs this existence without gratifications. They buy chocolate bars and almond paste, coconut and sweet-milk candy, nutritive nougats and caramels. They eat them with the indifferent air of one who is treating himself to a tidbit, but when they're traveling on one of their own trains couples dare buy one of those big crepes covered with milk paste and sprinkles, and they eat it shamefacedly, in little pieces, with the joy of a real meal. They've never been able to solve the problem of ordinary eating in a satisfactory way; how many times must they have been hungry, with the candy becoming repugnant to them and the memory of salt, like the blow of a heavy wave on the mouth, will fill them with horrible delight, and with the salt the taste of the unattainable roast, the soup smelling of parsley and celery! (Around those times a grill had been opened at the Once station and sometimes the smoky smell of sausages and loin sandwiches reached the subway platform. But they couldn't make use of it because it was on the other side of the turnstiles, on the platform of the train to Moreno.)

Another difficult part of their lives is clothing. Pants, skirts, and petticoats wear out. They don't damage jackets and blouses very much, but after a time they have to be changed, for security reasons as well. One morning when I was following one of them, trying to learn more about their customs, I discovered the relations they have with the surface. This is how it is: They get out singly at the indicated station on the indicated day and at the indicated time. Someone comes from the surface with a change of clothing (I ascertained afterward that it was a complete set: clean underwear in every case, and a suit or dress ironed occasionally), and the two get on the same car of the next train. There they can talk, the package is passed, and at the following station they change —that's the most painful part—in the always filthy toilets. One station beyond, the same agent is waiting for them on the platform; they ride together to the next station, and the agent returns to the surface with the package of dirty clothes.

By pure chance and after having convinced myself that I now knew almost all of their possibilities in that terrain, I discovered that along with the periodic exchanges of clothing they have a storeroom where they precariously keep a few articles and objects for cases of emergency, perhaps to cover the prime necessities when new ones arrive, the numbers of whom I can't calculate, but which I imagine to be large. A friend had introduced me on the street to an old man who is struggling along as a *bouquiniste* in the stalls of the Cabildo. I was looking for a back number of *Sur*; to my surprise and leading me perhaps to the inevitable, the book dealer took me down into the Perú station and to the left side of the platform where a well-used passageway begins that doesn't have much of a subway look about it. That's where he had his cache of confused piles of books and magazines. I didn't find *Sur*, but on the other hand there was a small door ajar that opened into another room; I saw the back of someone with that ever-so-white neck they all have; at his feet I managed to glimpse a pile of coats, some handkerchiefs, a red scarf. The book dealer thought he was a retailer or concessionaire like himself; I let him think so and I bought a handsome edition of *Trilce*. But in that matter of clothing some horrible things already had been revealed to me. Since they have more money than they can use and aim to spend it (I imagine it must be the same in minimum security prisons) they satisfy inoffensive whims with a vigor that is touching. At that time I was following a blond boy, I always saw him in the same brown suit; he only changed his tie; two or three times a day he would go into the lavatories to do it. One noon he got off at Lima to buy a necktie at the stand on the platform; he took a long time choosing, unable to decide; it was his great escapade, his Saturday spree. In the pockets of his jacket I could see the bulge of his other ties, and I felt something that wasn't far removed from horror.

The women buy themselves handkerchiefs, knickknacks, key chains, everything there's room for in kiosks and purses. Sometimes they get off at Lima or Perú and stand looking into the show windows on the platform where furniture is on display, they look for a long time at bureaus and beds, they look at the furniture with a humble and contained desire, and when they buy the newspaper or *Maribel* they linger in absorption over the ads for sales, perfumes, figurines, gloves. They're also on the point of forgetting their instructions for indifference and coolness when they see mothers taking their children for an outing get on. Two of them, I saw them only a few days apart, left their seats to ride standing near the children, almost rubbing against them; I wouldn't have been too surprised if they'd stroked their hair or given them candy, things that aren't done on the Buenos Aires subway or probably on any subway.

For a long time I wondered why Number One had chosen precisely one of the survey days to bring the other three down. Knowing his methods, although not him yet, I thought it a mistake to attribute it to arrogance, to the desire to create a stir if the difference between the figures was published. More in accord with his reflective wisdom was to suspect that during those days the attention of the Anglo personnel was centered, directly or indirectly, on the survey operations. The taking of the train, therefore, turned out more feasible; even the return to the surface by the replaced motorman wouldn't bring him any dangerous consequences. Only three months later the chance meeting in the Parque Lezama of the ex-motorman and Chief Inspector Montesano, and the latter's taciturn inferences, managed to bring him and bring me to the truth.

At that time—I'm speaking almost of the present—they had three trains in their possession and I think, without being sure, a position in the control booth at Primera Junta. A suicide shortened my last doubts. That afternoon I'd followed one of the women and saw her go into the telephone booth at the José María Moreno station. The platform was almost deserted and I leaned my face against the side panel, feigning the fatigue of people coming home from work. It was the first time I'd seen one of them in a phone booth, and I hadn't been surprised by the girl's furtive and somewhat frightened manner, her moment of hesitation before looking around and going into the booth. I couldn't hear much, some weeping, the sound of a purse opening, blowing her nose, and then, "But the canary, you're taking care of him, aren't you? Are you giving him birdseed every morning, and the little piece of vanilla?" I was surprised at that banality because the voice wasn't a voice sending a message based on any code, tears were wetting that voice, smothering it. I got on a train before she could discover me and I made the whole circuit, continuing a survey of time schedules and changes of clothing. When we got into José María Moreno again she jumped, after crossing herself (they say); I recognized her by the red shoes and the light-colored purse. There was an enormous crowd, with a lot of people surrounding the motorman and the conductor waiting for the police. I saw that they both belonged to them (they're so pale) and I thought that what had happened would test then and there how solid Number One's plans were, because it's one thing to replace someone in the depths and quite another to bear up under a police interrogation. A week passed without anything new, without the least follow-up of a banal and almost everyday suicide; then I began to be afraid to go down.

I know now that there are still many things I don't know, even the most important, but the fear is stronger than I am. During these days I only manage to get to the entrance at Lima, which is my station, I get that hot smell, that Anglo smell, which comes up to the street; I hear the trains pass. I go into a café and consider myself an imbecile, I ask myself how can I quit when I'm so few steps away from the complete revelation. I know so many things, it might be useful to society to reveal what's going on. I know that over the last few weeks they already have eight trains, and that their number is increasing rapidly. The new ones are still unrecognizable because the fading of the skin is very slow and they're doubtless extreme in their precautions; Number One's plans don't seem to have any error, and the result is that it's impossible for me to calculate their numbers. Only instinct told me, when I still had the courage to go down and follow them, that most of the trains are already full of them, that the regular passengers are finding it more and more difficult to travel all the time; and it doesn't surprise me that the newspapers are asking for new lines, more trains, emergency measures.

I saw Montesano, I told him a few things and I hoped he would guess others. He seemed to mistrust me, to follow any track on his own or, rather, simply to prefer not understanding something that was beyond his imagination, not to mention that of his superiors. I understood that it was useless to talk to him again, that he might accuse me of complicating his life with fantasies that were probably paranoid, especially when he told me, patting me on the back: "You're tired, you should take a trip."

But the trip I should take is on the Anglo branch. I'm a bit surprised that Montesano hasn't decided to take any measures, at least against Number One and the other three, cutting off at the crown the tree that's sinking its roots deeper and deeper into the asphalt and the earth. There's that penned-in smell, you can hear the brakes on a train, and then the gust of people climbing the stairs with the bovine look of those who've traveled standing up, crammed together in cars that are always full. I should go over, take them aside one by one and explain; then I hear another train coming in and my fear returns. When I recognize one of the agents going down or coming up with the package of clothing, I hide in the café and don't dare go out for a long time. I think, over two glasses of gin, that as soon as I get my courage back I'll go down and check on their numbers. I believe that they've got all the trains now, the administration of many stations, and a part of the repair shops. Yesterday I thought that the saleslady at the candy kiosk at Lima might inform me indirectly about the recent increase in her sales. With an effort that barely overcame the cramps clutching at my stomach, I managed to go down to the platform, repeating to myself that it wasn't a matter of getting on a train, mingling with them; just two questions and going back up to the surface, safe again. I put the coin in the turnstile and went over to the kiosk; I was going to buy a Milkibar when I saw that the saleslady was staring at me. Pretty, but so pale, so pale. I ran desperately toward the stairs, stumbled up. Now I know that I can't go back down; they know me, they've finally gotten to know me.

I've spent an hour in the café without having decided to take the first step onto the stairway again, standing there among the people going up and down, ignoring those who look at me out of the corners of their eyes without understanding that I can't make up my mind to move in a zone where everybody is moving. It seems almost inconceivable to me to have come to the end of the analysis of their general methods and be incapable of taking the final step that will allow me the revelation of their identities and their aims. I refuse to accept the fear that tightens my chest like this. Maybe I'll make up my mind, maybe the best thing would be to hang on to the railing of the stairs and shout out what I know about their plan, what I think I know about Number One (I'll say it even if Montesano is displeased that it's upsetting his own investigation), and, above all, the consequences of all that for the people of Buenos Aires. Up till now I've been writing in the café, the peacefulness of being on the surface and in a neutral place fills me with a calm that I didn't have when I went down to the kiosk. I feel that in some way or other I'm going back down, that I'll make myself, step by step, go down the stairs, but in the meantime the best thing would be to finish my report, send it to the commissioner or chief of police, with a copy to Montesano, and then I'll pay my check and will certainly go down, of that I'm sure, even though I don't know how I'm going to do it, where I'm going to get the strength to go down step by step now that they know who I am, now that they've finally ended up knowing who I am, but that doesn't matter anymore, before I go down I'll have the rough draft ready, I'll say Dear Mr. Commissioner or Dear Mr. Chief of Police, there's someone walking around down there, someone who goes along the platforms and when no one notices, when only I can know and listen, shuts herself up in a dimly lighted booth and opens her purse. Then she weeps, first she weeps a little, and then, Mr. Commissioner, she says, "But the canary, you're taking care of him, aren't you? Are you giving him birdseed every morning, and the little piece of vanilla?"

STORIES I TELL
MYSELF

I tell myself stories when I sleep alone, when the bed seems larger than it is and colder, but I also tell them to myself when Niágara is there and falls asleep in the midst of pleasant murmurs, almost as if she too were telling a story. More than once I wanted to wake her up to find out what her story was about (there's been only one murmur so far, and that's not enough for a story), but Niágara always comes back so tired from work that it wouldn't be fair or nice to wake her up when she's just fallen asleep and seems sunken, lost in her perfumed and murmuring little snail shell, so I let her sleep and tell myself stories, the same as on days when she has the night shift and I sleep alone in that suddenly enormous bed.

The stories I tell myself can be anything, but almost always with myself in the main role, a kind of Buenos Aires Walter Mitty who imagines himself in anomalous or silly situations or ones that are intensely dramatic and exaggerated so that the person following the story will enjoy the melodrama or the banality or the humor that the person telling it puts in. Because Walter Mitty also has his Jekyll-and-Hyde side, Anglo-Saxon literature has of course made inroads on his unconscious and the stories are almost always born to him in a bookish way and as if all ready for an equally imaginary press. The very idea of writing down the stories I tell myself before falling asleep seems inconceivable in the morning, and, besides, a man has to have his secret luxuries, his quiet extravagances, things that others would take advantage of down to the last crumb. And there's also superstition. I've always told myself that if I put any of the stories that I tell myself into writing, that story would be my last, for a reason that escapes me but has something to do perhaps with notions of transgression or punishment; no, it's impossible to imagine myself waiting for sleep, alongside Niágara or alone, but unable to tell myself a story, having to count sheep in an imbecilic way or, even worse, to remember my not very memorable daily activities.

Everything depends on the mood of the moment, because it would never occur to me to choose a certain type of story when I or we turn out the light and I enter that second and beautiful cover of darkness that my eyelids bring, the story is there, an almost always stimulating beginning of a story, it might be an empty street with a car coming from way far off, or Marcelo Macía's face when he finds out he's been promoted, something inconceivable until that moment, given his incompetence, or simply a word or sound that's repeated five or six times and out of which the first image of the story begins to emerge. Sometimes I'm surprised that after an episode that could be classified as bureaucratic, the next night the story is erotic or connected to sports; I do have an imagination, no doubt about it, even if it's only evident before I fall asleep, but such an unpredictably varied and rich repertory never ceases to surprise me. Dilia, for example—why did Dilia have to appear in that story and precisely in that story, when Dilia wasn't a woman who lent herself in any way to such a story? Why Dilia?

A long time ago, however, I decided not to ask myself why Dilia or the Trans-Siberian or Muhammad Ali or any of the settings where the stories I tell myself are staged. If I remember Dilia at this moment out of the story now it's for other reasons that were and are also out of it, because of something that isn't the story anymore, and maybe that's why I'm obliged to do what I wouldn't have wanted to do or couldn't have done with the stories I tell myself. In that story (alone in bed; Niágara wouldn't be back from the hospital until eight in the morning) there was a mountain scene and a road that engendered fear, made you drive carefully, the headlights sweeping away the always possible visual traps at every curve, alone and at midnight in that huge truck that was difficult to drive on a road that was like a cornice. Being a truck driver had always seemed to be an enviable occupation to me because I imagine it to be one of the simplest forms of freedom, going from one place to another in a truck, which at the same time is a home with a mattress where you can spend the night on a tree-lined road, a lantern to read by, and cans of food and beer, a transistor to listen to jazz with surrounded by perfect silence, and also that sense of knowing that you're being ignored by the rest of the world, that no one is aware of the fact that you've taken that route and not another, so many possibilities of towns and adventures on the trip, including holdups and accidents where I always come out on top like Walter Mitty.

Sometimes I've wondered why a truck driver and not an airplane pilot or captain of an ocean liner, knowing at the same time that it fits my simple and earthy side that I've had to hide more and more during the day. Being a truck driver is people who talk to truck drivers, places where a truck driver moves about, so when I tell myself a story about freedom it frequently starts in that truck crossing the pampa or going through an imaginary landscape like the one now, the Andes or the Rocky Mountains, in any case, on that night a difficult road I was climbing along when I saw Dilia's fragile figure at the base of the rocks, violently pulled out of nothingness by the beam of the headlights, the purple walls making the image of Dilia even smaller and more forlorn as she gave me the gesture used by people asking for help, after having walked so long with a knapsack on her back.

Since being a truck driver is a story I've told myself many times, it's not hard to find women asking for a lift as Dilia was doing, although, of course, I'd put them there because those stories almost always capped a fantasy in which night, truck, and solitude were the perfect accessories for a brief moment of happiness at the end of the period. Sometimes not, sometimes it was only an avalanche from which I escaped. God knows how, or the brakes that gave out on the downgrade so that everything ended in a whirlwind of changing visions that made me open my eyes and refuse to go on, seeking sleep or Niágara's warm waist with the relief of having escaped the worst. When the story put a woman beside the road, that woman was always a stranger, the whims of the stories opting for a redhead or a mulatto girl, seen perhaps in a movie or a magazine picture and forgotten on the surface of the day until the story brought her out without my recognizing her. Seeing Dilia was more than a surprise therefore, almost a scandal, because Dilia had nothing to do with that route and in some way she was ruining the story with her expression—somewhere between imploring and undermining. Dilia and Alfonso are friends that Niágara and I see from time to time, they live in a different orbit and the only things that bring us together are a faithful friendship since university days, common tastes, a dinner from time to time at their place or here; we keep track of them from a distance as a couple with a baby and a bit of money. What in the devil did Dilia have to do here where the story was happening in a way in which any imaginary girl yes but not Dilia, because if there was anything clear in the story it was that this time I would meet a girl on the way and out of it would come some of the many things that can happen when you reach the flats and make a stop after the long tension of the crossing; everything so clear from the first image, dinner with other truck drivers at the lunch room in the town before the mountains, a story no longer original at all but always pleasing because of its variants and unknown women, except that now the unknown woman was different, it was Dilia, who made no sense whatever on that curve in the road.

It might be that if Niágara had been there murmuring and softly snorting in her sleep I would have preferred not bringing Dilia up, erasing her and the truck and the story by just opening my eyes and saying to Niágara, "That's funny, I was on the point of going to bed with a woman and it was Dilia," so that maybe Niágara would open her eyes in turn and kiss me on the cheek, calling me silly or getting Freud into the act or asking me if I'd ever wanted Dilia sometime, in order to hear me tell the truth, but never in this rotten life, although then Freud again or something like that. But feeling myself so alone in the story, as alone as I was, a truck driver in the midst of crossing the mountains at midnight, I wasn't capable of passing by: I slowly braked, opened the door, and let Dilia get in as she scarcely murmured a "thanks" full of fatigue and sleep and stretched out on the seat with her pack by her feet.

The rules of the game are observed from the first moment in the stories I tell myself. Dilia was Dilia but in the story I was a truck driver and only that for Dilia, it never would have occurred to me to ask her what she was doing there in the middle of the night or call her by her name. I think that in the story the exceptional thing was that that girl should contain the person of Dilia, her straight blond hair, her blue eyes, and her legs almost conventionally evoking those of a colt, too long for her figure; outside of that, the story treated her like any other girl, without any name or previous connection, a perfect fateful meeting. We exchanged two or three phrases, I gave her a cigarette and lighted another, we began going downhill as a heavily loaded truck should, while Dilia stretched out even more, smoking with an abandonment and drowsiness that washed away all her hours of walking and maybe fear on the mountain.

I thought she was going to fall asleep right away and that it was pleasant to imagine her like that until reaching the flats there below us. I thought that maybe it would be a friendly gesture to invite her to get into the back of the truck and stretch out on a real bed, but never in a story have things allowed me to do that, because any of the girls would have looked at me with that expression that was somewhere between bitter and desperate out of which she imagines the immediate intentions, almost always looking for the door handle, the necessary flight. In the stories just as in the presumptive reality of any truck driver things couldn't happen that way, you'd have to talk, smoke, make friends, get out of all that the almost always silent acceptance of a stop in the woods or a rest area, the acquiescence for what would come later but which was no longer bitterness or anger, simply sharing what was already being shared since the talk, the cigarettes, and the first beer drunk out of the bottle between two curves.

I let her sleep, then, the story had that development, which I've always liked in the stories I tell myself, the minute description of every thing and every act, a film in very slow motion for a pleasure that goes progressively along, climbing up through body and words and silences. I still wondered why Dilia that night but I immediately stopped wondering, it seemed so natural to me now—Dilia there half-asleep beside me, accepting another cigarette from time to time or murmuring an explanation of why there in the middle of the mountains—that the story got embroiled between yawns and broken phrases since nothing could have explained why Dilia was there in the loneliest spot on that road at midnight. At some moment she stopped talking and looked at me, smiling, that girl's smile that Alfonso described as a shopper's smile, and I gave her my truck driver's name, always Oscar in any of the stories, and she said Dilia and added as she always added that it was an idiotic name, the fault of an aunt who read gooey novels, and almost incredibly I thought that she didn't recognize me, that in the story I was Oscar and that she didn't recognize me.

Afterward came all that the stories tell me but I can't

tell it the way they do, only uncertain fragments, threads that might be false, the lantern lighting up the folding table in the back of the truck parked among the trees at a rest stop, the sputter of fried eggs, then the cheese and sweets, Dilia looking at me as if she were going to say something and deciding that she wouldn't say anything, that it wasn't necessary to explain anything, to get out of the truck and disappear under the trees, I making things easier with the coffee almost ready and even a shot of grappa, Dilia's eyes as they would close between drink and phrase, my careless way of moving the lamp to the little table beside the mattress, adding a blanket in case later on the cold, telling her I was going up front to lock the doors just in case, you never knew on those deserted stretches and she lowering her eyes and saying, you know, don't stay there and go to sleep on the seat, it would be idiotic, and I turning my back so she wouldn't see my face where there was probably a vague surprise at what Dilia was saying although of course it always happened that way in one form or another, sometimes the little Indian girl would talk about sleeping on the ground or the gypsy would take refuge in the cab and I would have to take her by the waist and lead her inside, carry her to the bed even though she cried or struggled, but not Dilia, Dilia slowly moving from the table to the bed with one hand already searching for the zipper on her jeans, those movements that I could see in the story even though my back was turned and I was going into the cab to give her time, to tell myself yes, that everything would be the way it had to be one more time, an uninterrupted and perfumed sequence, the very slow dolly shot of the motionless figure in the headlights at the curve in the mountain to Dilia now almost invisible under the wool blankets, and the cut as always, putting out the lantern so that all that was left was the vague ember of the night coming in through the rear window with the occasional plaint of a nearby bird.

That time the story lasted interminably because neither Dilia nor I wanted it to end, there are stories that I would like to prolong, but the little Japanese girl or the cold, condescending Norwegian tourist won't let them go on, and in spite of the fact that I'm the one who decides in the story, a moment comes when I haven't got the strength or even the desire to make something last after the pleasure begins to slip into insignificance, there where you would have to invent alternatives or unexpected incidents for the story to stay alive instead of carrying me off to sleep with a last distracted kiss or the remains of an almost useless moan. But Dilia didn't want the story to end. From her first gesture when I slipped in beside her, instead of the expected I felt her searching for me; from the first double caress I knew that the story had only just begun, that the night of the story would be as long as the night in which I was telling the story. Only now there's nothing left but this, words talking about the story; words like matches, moans, cigarettes, laughter, entreaties, and demands, coffee at daybreak and a dream of heavy waters, of night dew and returns and abandonments, and a first timid tongue of sun coming through the window to lick Dilia on the shoulder as she lay stretched out on top of me, blinding me while I held her tightly and felt her open up once more amidst cries and caresses.

The story ends there, without any conventional good-byes in the first town on the way as would have been almost inevitable, from the story I passed into sleep with nothing but the weight of Dilia's body as she fell asleep in turn after one last murmur, when I woke up Niágara was talking to me about breakfast and a date we had for that evening. I know that I was on the point of telling her and something held me back, something that might have been Dilia's hand returning me to the night and forbidding me words that would have soiled everything. Yes, I'd slept quite well; of course, at six o'clock we would meet on the corner of the square and go see the Marinis.

Around that time Alfonso had told us that Dilia's mother was quite ill and that Dilia was going to Necoches to be with her, Alfonso had to take care of the baby, who was giving him a lot of trouble, how about our visiting them when Dilia got back. The sick woman died a few days later and Dilia didn't want to see anybody until two months later; we went to dinner, bringing them some cognac and a rattle for the baby and everything was fine now, Dilia finishing a duck à l'orange and Alfonso with the table set up to play canasta. The dinner rolled along pleasantly as it should have because Alfonso and Dilia are people who know how to live and they began by talking about the most painful thing, quickly exhausting the theme of Dilia's mother, then it was like softly drawing a curtain so as to return to the immediate present, our usual games, the key words and codes of the humor that made it so agreeable to spend the evening with them. It was already late and cognac when Dilia mentioned a trip to San Juan, the need to forget her mother's last days and the problem with those relatives who complicate everything. It seemed to me she was talking to Alfonso, although Alfonso must have known the story already because he was smiling pleasantly while he served us another cognac, the breakdown of the car in the middle of the mountains, the empty night and the interminable wait by the side of the road where every night bird was a menace, the inevitable return of so many childhood ghosts, the lights of a truck, the fear that maybe the driver would also be afraid and pass her by, the blinding from the lights striking the stone walls, then the wonderful squeal of the brakes, the warm cab, the descent with unnecessary dialogues but which did so much to make her feel better.

"She's been traumatized," Alfonso said. "You already told me, sweetheart, each time I learn more details about that rescue, about your Saint George in coveralls saving you from the wicked dragon of the night."

"It's not easy to forget," Dilia said, "it's something that keeps coming back, I don't know why."

Maybe she didn't, maybe Dilia didn't know why but I did, why I had to drink the cognac down in one gulp and pour myself another while Alfonso raised his eyebrows, surprised at a brusqueness he didn't recognize in me. His jokes, on the other hand, were more than predictable, telling Dilia that sometime she should decide to finish the story, he knew the first part only too well, but was sure that it had a second part, there was so much ravine, so much truck in the night, so much everything that's so much in this life.

I went to the bathroom and stayed awhile trying not to look at myself in the mirror, not to find there too and horribly the thing I'd been while I was telling myself the story and which I felt again now but here, now, tonight, the thing that was slowly beginning to take over my body, the thing I had never imagined possible all through so many years of Dilia and Alfonso, our friendly double pairing at parties and movies and kisses on the cheek. Now it was the other thing, it was Dilia afterward, the desire again but on this side, Dilia's voice reaching me from the parlor, laughter from Dilia and Niágara who must have been teasing Alfonso about his stereotyped jealousy. It was late now, we drank still more cognac

and had one last coffee, the baby's crying came from upstairs
and Dilia ran up, brought him down in her arms, he was all
wet the little pig, I'm going to change him in the bathroom,
Alfonso enchanted because that gave him another half hour
to argue with Niágara about the possibilities of Vilas versus
Borg, another cognac, girl, after all, we're all immune now.

Not me, I went to the bathroom to keep Dilia company
as she laid her son out on a little table and looked for things
in a cupboard. And it was as if she knew in some way when
I said to her Dilia, I know that second part, when I told her
I now know it can't be but you see, I know it, and Dilia turned
her back to me to start undressing the baby and I saw her
lean over not only to undo the safety pins and take off the
diaper but also as if she were suddenly overwhelmed by a
weight that she had to free herself from, from which she was
already freeing herself when she turned, looking me in the
eyes and said yes, it's true, it's idiotic and it has no importance but it's true, I went to bed with the truck driver, tell
Alfonso if you want, in any case he's convinced in his own
way, he doesn't believe it but he's so sure.

That's how it was, I wouldn't say anything and she
wouldn't understand why she was saying that to me, why to
me, who hadn't asked her anything and, on the other hand,
had told her what she couldn't understand on this side of the
story. I felt my eyes going down across her mouth, her throat
like fingers, seeking her breasts under the black blouse, I
sketched again how my hands had sketched all that night, all
that story. Desire was a crouching leap, an absolute right to
look for her breasts under the blouse and enwrap her in the
first embrace. I saw her spin, lean over again but now light,
freed from the silence; she deftly removed the diaper, the
smell of the baby who'd peed and pooed reached me along

with Dilia's murmuring, calming him so he wouldn't cry, I saw her hands as they picked up the cotton and put it between the baby's uplifted legs, I saw her hands cleaning the baby instead of coming to me as they had come in the darkness of that truck that has served me so well so many times in the stories I tell myself.

MOEBIUS STRIP

In memoriam J. M. and R. A.

Impossible to explain. She was leaving that zone where things have a fixed form and edges, where everything has a solid and immutable name. She was sinking deeper and deeper into the liquid, quiet, and unfathomable region where vague and cool mists like those of morning hovered.

Clarice Lispector
Close to the Savage Heart

Why not, maybe it would have been enough just to try as she would try eagerly later on and she would be seen, she would be felt, with the same clarity that she was seen and felt pedaling into the woods in the still cool morning, following paths wrapped in the shadow of ferns, in some place in Dordogne that the newspapers and radio would later fill with a fleeting infamous celebrity until quick oblivion, the vegetable silence of that perpetual half-light through which Janet passed like a blond splotch, a tinkle of metal (her canteen poorly fastened onto the aluminum crossbar), her long hair offered to the air that her body broke and altered, a lightweight figurehead sinking her feet into the soft alternation of the pedals, receiving on her blouse the hand of the breeze grasping her breasts, a double caress with the double defile of tree trunks and ferns in a tunnel-green translucence, a smell of mushrooms and bark and moss, vacation time.

And the other woods too, even if they were the same woods, but not for Robert, turned away at farms, dirty from a night face down on a poor mattress of dry leaves, a ray of sunlight that filtered through the cedars, stroking his face, vaguely wondering if it was worth the trouble to stay in the region or go to the flatlands where maybe a pitcher of milk and a little work was awaiting him before going back to the highways or getting lost in the nameless woods, always the same woods, with hunger and that useless rage that twisted his mouth.

At the narrow crossroads Janet put on the brakes indecisively, right or left or straight ahead, all equally green and cool, held out like the fingers of a great earthen hand. She'd left the youth hostel at daybreak because the dormitory was full of heavy breathing, fragments of others' nightmares, the smell of people scarcely washed, the merry groups that had roasted corn and sung until midnight before lying down on the canvas cots with their clothes on, the girls on one side and the boys farther off, vaguely offended by so many idiotic regulations, half-asleep already despite their useless sarcastic comments. In the open countryside before the woods she'd drunk the milk in the canteen, never again to meet the people of the night before, she too had her idiotic regulations, to cover France while her money and time lasted, to take pictures, to fill her orange-colored notebook, nineteen English years old already with lots of notebooks and pedaled miles, a predilection for open spaces, her eyes dutifully blue and her hair blond, tall and athletic and a kindergarten teacher whose Kinder were happily scattered over beaches and villages in her happily distant homeland. To the left, maybe, there was a slight slope in the shadows, letting herself coast after a simple push on the pedal. It was starting to get hot, the bicycle seat was receiving her heavily, with a first dampness that would later oblige her to get off, unstick her panties from her skin and lift up her arms so that the cool breeze could get under her blouse. It was only ten o'clock, the woods were revealing themselves, slow and deep; perhaps before reaching the road on the opposite side it would be nice to settle down under an oak tree and eat the sandwiches, listen to the pocket radio or add another entry to her travel diary, interrupted so many times by the start of poems and not always happy thoughts that the pencil wrote and then, with embarrassment, with difficulty, scratched out.

It wasn't easily seen from the path. Without knowing it, he'd slept sixty feet away from an abandoned shed, and now it seemed to him stupid to have slept on the damp ground when behind the pine boards full of holes he saw a floor of dry straw under an almost intact roof. He was no longer sleepy and it was a pity; motionless, he looked at the shed and wasn't surprised that the woman on the bicycle had come along the path and stopped, she was the one who was disconcerted by the structure that rose up among the trees. Before Janet saw him he already knew everything, everything about her and about him in one single wordless wave, taking off from an immobility that was like a future crouching in wait. Now she was turning her head, the bicycle tilted, and one foot on the ground, and she found his eyes. They both blinked at the same time.

There was only one thing that could be done in cases like that, infrequent but always probable: say bonjour and leave without excessive haste. Janet said bonjour and pushed the bicycle to give it a half turn; her foot was lifted from the ground to give the pedal its first push when Robert cut off her way and grabbed the handlebars with a hand that had black nails. Everything was quite clear and confused at the same time, the bicycle tipping over and the first cry of panic and protest, the feet looking for a useless support in the air, the strength of the arms encircling her, the pace—almost a run—through the broken boards of the shed, a smell both young and savage at the same time of leather and sweat, a dark three-day beard, a mouth burning her throat.

He never wanted to hurt her, he'd never hurt anyone to possess the little that had been given him in the inevitable reformatories, it was only like that, twenty-five years and like that, all at the same time, slow, as when he had to write his name, Robert letter by letter, then the last name even slower, and quick, like the movement that was sometimes worth a bottle of milk or a pair of pants laid out to dry on the grass in a garden, everything could be slow and instantaneous at the same time, a decision followed by a desire for everything to last for a long time, for that girl not to fight absurdly, since he didn't want to hurt her, for her to understand the impossibility of escape or of being rescued and to submit quietly, not even submitting, letting herself go as he was letting himself go, laying her down on the straw and shouting into her ear for her to shut up, not be a fool, to wait while he looked for buttons and fasteners without finding anything but convulsions of resistance, gusts of words in a different language, shouts, shouts that someone would end up hearing.

It hadn't been exactly like that, there was the horror and the revulsion at the attack by the beast, Janet had struggled to get away and run off and now it was no longer possible and the horror didn't come only from the bearded beast, because he wasn't a beast, his way of speaking into her ear and holding her down without sinking his hands into her flesh, his kisses that fell onto her face and neck with the prickle of the stubble, but kisses, the revulsion came from submitting to that man who wasn't a hairy beast but a man, the revulsion that had always been lying in wait, ever since her first bleeding one afternoon at school, Mrs. Murphy and her warnings to the class in her Cornish accent, the crime news in the paper always commented on secretly at the boarding school, the forbidden books where that wasn't what was hinted at rosily in the books recommended by Mrs. Murphy with or without Mendelssohn and showers of rice, the clandestine comments about the episode of the first night in *Fanny Hill*, the long silence of her best friend back from her honeymoon and then the sudden weeping, clinging to her, it was horrible, Janet, although later with the joy of the first child, the vague evocation of the past one afternoon on a walk together, I was wrong to exaggerate so much, Janet, you'll see one day, but too late now, the idée fixe, so horrible, Janet, another birthday, the bicycle and the plan to travel alone until maybe, maybe little by little, nineteen years old and the second vacation trip to France, Dordogne in August.

Someone would end up hearing her, he shouted into her face although he already knew that she was incapable of understanding, she looked at him rolling her eyes and begging something in another language, fighting to get her legs free, to stand up, for a moment it seemed to him that she was trying to tell him something that wasn't just shouts or pleas or insults in her language, he unbuttoned her blouse blindly looking for the fasteners farther down, holding her onto the straw bedding with his whole body crossed over hers, asking her not to shout anymore, that it wasn't possible for her to go on shouting, somebody was going to come, let me, don't shout anymore, just let me, please, don't shout.

How to stop struggling if he didn't understand, if the words she had tried to tell him in his language came out in pieces, got mixed up with his babbling and his kisses and he couldn't understand that it wasn't a question of that, that horrible as what he was trying to do to her, what he was going to do to her, was, it wasn't that, how to explain to him that up until then never, that *Fanny Hill*, that at least he should wait, that in her bag there was facial cream, that it mustn't be like that, it mustn't be without what she'd seen in the eyes of her friend, the nausea of something unbearable, it was horrible, Janet, it was so horrible. She felt her skirt give way, the hand that ran under her panties and pulled them down, she contracted with a last shriek of anguish and fought to explain, to stop him at the brink so that it would be different, she felt him against her and the attack between her open thighs, a sharp pain that grew until the red and the fire, she howled from horror more than from suffering, as if that couldn't be everything and only the beginning of the torture, she felt his hands on her face covering her mouth and slipping down below, the second attack against the one who could no longer struggle, against which there were no longer shouts or tears.

Plunged in her in a sudden end of struggling, taken in
without that desperate resistance that he had had to
beat down by impaling her time and time again until he
reached the deepest part and felt all her skin against
his, the pleasure came like a lash and he dissolved in a
thankful babbling, in a blind, interminable embrace.
Taking his face out of the hollow of Janet's shoulder,
he sought her eyes to tell her so, to thank her for being
quiet at last; he couldn't suspect other reasons for that
savage resistance, that struggle that had obliged him to
rape her without pity, but neither did he understand
her surrender, the sudden silence. Janet was looking at
him, one of her legs had slowly slipped to the side.
Robert began to draw away, come out of her, looking
into her eyes. He understood that Janet didn't see him.

Neither tears nor breath, the breath had stopped suddenly, from the depths of her skull a wave had covered her
eyes, she no longer had a body, the last thing had been the
pain time and again and then halfway through a shriek her
breath had suddenly given out, expired without coming in
again, replaced by the red veil like blood eyelids, a sticky
silence, something that lasted without being, something that
was in a different way where everything was still there but in
a different way, this side of sense and memory.

She didn't see him, the dilated eyes passed right
through his face. Getting free of her he kneeled at her
side, talking to her while his hands somehow or other
adjusted his pants and he looked for the glittering
closing as if working independently, smoothing his
shirt and tucking it in. He saw the half-open, twisted
mouth, the thread of pink drool slipping down over
her chin, the arms crossed with the hands clenched,

the fingers motionless and shiny with blood slipping slowly down the half-open thighs. When he shouted, leaping up, he thought for a second that the shout had come from Janet, but from up above, standing like a swaying doll, he saw the marks on her throat, the unacceptable twisting of the neck that turned Janet's head to one side, made something of it that was mocking him with the look of a fallen marionette, all its strings cut.

Different, perhaps from the very beginning, in any case not there, becoming like something diaphanous, a translucent medium in which nothing had a body and where what had been her wasn't located through thoughts or objects, to be wind while being Janet or Janet being wind or water or space but always clear, the silence was light or the opposite or both things, time was illuminated and that was to be Janet, something without a handle, without the slightest shadow of memory to interrupt and fix that course as among crystals, a bubble inside a mass of Plexiglas, the orbit of a transparent fish in a limitless lighted aquarium.

The woodcutter's son found the bicycle on the path and through the boards of the shed he glimpsed the body face up. The police verified that the murderer had not touched Janet's overnight case or purse.

To drift in the immobile with no before or after, a hyaline now without contact or references, a state in which the container and the contained were undifferentiated, water flowing in water, until without transition it was the impetus, a violent rushing projecting her, drawing her along unable to grasp the change in any way except in the dizzy rush on the horizontal or the vertical of a space that shuddered in its velocity. Sometimes it would come out of the shapeless and accede to a rigorous fixedness also separated from all reference and nevertheless tangible, there was that moment when Janet ceased to be water of water or wind of wind, for the first time she felt, felt herself closed in and limited, cube of a cube, motionless cubeness. In that cube state outside the translucent and the hurricaned, something like a duration was being installed, not a before or an after but a more tangible now, a beginning of time reduced to a thick and manifest present, cube in time. If she had been able to choose she would have preferred the cube state without knowing why, perhaps in the continuous changes it was the only condition where nothing changed as if there she were inside given limits, in the certainty of a constant cubeness, of a present that hinted at a presence, almost a tangibility, a present that contained something that perhaps was time, perhaps an immobile space where every displacement remained as drawn. But the cube state could give way to other vertigos and before and after or during you were in another medium, you were once more a thunderous sliding through an ocean of crystals or diaphanous rocks, a flowing without direction toward anything, a tornado suction with whirlwinds, something like sliding along through the entire foliage of a jungle, held up from leaf to leaf by a weightlessness of devil's drool and now—now without a before, a dry and given now there—perhaps again the cube state coming closer and stopping, limits in the now and the there that in some way were rest.

The trial opened in Poitiers toward the end of July 1956. Robert was defended by Maître Rolland; the jury would not admit the extenuating circumstances of early orphanhood, reformatories, and unemployment.

> The accused listened to the sentence of death in a
> peaceful stupor, the applause of an audience among
> which there were a great number of British tourists.

Little by little (little by little in a condition outside of
time? a manner of speaking) other states were presenting
themselves, had perhaps already been presented, although
already would mean before and there was no before; now (or
any now either) a wind state prevailed and now a crawling
state in which each now was painful, the complete opposite
of the wind state because it was only presented as a dragging,
a progression to nowhere; if she had been able to think, Janet
would have passed to the image of the caterpillar crawling
over a leaf suspended in the air, passing over its faces and
passing again without the slightest sight or touch or limit,
infinite Moebius strip reptation to the edge of a face to arrive
at or already to be on the opposite side and to return cease-
lessly from one side to the other, a very slow and painful
reptation there where there was no measure of slowness or
suffering but where one was reptation and being reptation
was slowness and suffering. Or the other (the other in a condition without comparable ends?), to be fever, going dizzily
through something like pipes or circuits, going through conditions that might be mathematical sets or musical scores,
leaping from point to point or note to note, going in and out of
computer circuits, being set or score or circuit running through
itself and that was given to be fever, given to run furiously
through instantaneous constellations of signs or notes without
form or sound. In some way it was suffering, the fever. To be
the cube state now or be the wave held a difference, it existed
without fever or without reptation, the cube state was not fever
and being fever was not the cube state or the wave state. In
the cube state now—a now suddenly more now—for the first

time (a now where an indication of first time had just been given), Janet ceased being the cube state to be in the cube state, and later (because that first differentiation of the now contained the feeling of later) in the wave state Janet ceased being the wave state to be in the wave state. And all that contained the indications of a temporality, now a first time could be recognized and a second time, a being in wave or in fever that succeeded each other to be pursued by a being in wind or being in foliage or being again in cube, being each time more Janet in, being Janet in time, being what was not Janet but which was passing from the cube state to the fever state or returning to the caterpillar state, because more and more the states were becoming fixed and established and in some way delimited not only in time but in space, there was a passing from one to another, passing from a cube placidity to a fever mathematical circuit or foliage equatorial jungle or interminable crystalline bottles or maelstrom whirlpools in hyaline suspension or painful reptation over double-faced surfaces or faceted polyhedrons.

The appeal was denied and Robert was transferred to the Santé to await execution. Only a pardon by the president of the republic could save him from the guillotine. The condemned man spent his days playing dominoes with the guards, smoking endlessly, sleeping heavily. He dreamed all the time, through the peephole of the cell the guards would see him toss on his cot, lift up an arm, shudder.

In some one of the steps the first rudiments of a memory would be born, slipping among the leaves or at the end of the cube state to be in the fever she learned something of what Janet had been, unconnectedly a memory was trying to enter and be fixed, once it was knowing that she was Janet, remembering Janet in a wood, the bicycle, Constance Myers and some chocolates on a nickel-plated tray. Everything was beginning to cluster together in the cube state, was being sketched out and confusedly defined, Janet and the woods, Janet and the bicycle, and with the gusts of images a feeling of person was becoming clearer, little by little, a first disquiet, the vision of a shed of rotten boards, being face up and held down by a convulsive force, fear of pain, the rubbing of a skin that scratched her mouth and face, something abominable was coming close, something was fighting to be explained, to say it wasn't like that, that it shouldn't have had to be that way, and on the edge of the impossible the memory stopped, a spiral running in acceleration until nausea pulled her out of the cube to sink her into wave or into fever, or the opposite, the asphyxiating slowness of crawling once more with nothing else but that, being in reptation, like being in wave or glass was once more only that until another change. And when she fell back into the cube state and returned to a confused recognition, shed and chocolate and quick visions of belfries and fellow students, the little that she could have done fought above all to the last there in the cubeness, to maintain itself in that state where there was detention and limits, where she would end by thinking and recognizing herself. On occasion she reached the last sensations, the scratch of a bearded skin against her mouth, the resistance under hands that were pulling off her clothes before getting lost again instantaneously in a thunderous careening, leaves or clouds or drops or hurricanes or explosive circuits. In the cube state she could not pass from the limit where everything was horror and revulsion but if will had been given her that will would have become fixed there where a sensitive Janet was blooming, where there was Janet wanting to abolish the recurrence. In full struggle against the weight that was crushing her against the straw of the shed, obstinately saying no, that it didn't have to happen that way with shouts and rotten straw, she slipped once more into the moving state in which everything flowed as if being created in the act of flowing, smoke spinning in its own cocoon that opens and wraps around itself, the being in waves, in the indefinable decanting that already so many times had held her in suspension, alga or cork or jellyfish. With the difference that Janet felt coming from something that was like waking up from a dreamless sleep, falling into the awakening one morning in Kent, being Janet and her body again, a notion of body, of arms and back and hair floating in the hyaline medium, in the total transparency because Janet couldn't see her body, it was her body finally again but without her seeing it, it was consciousness of her body floating among waves or smoke, without seeing her body Janet moved, put out an arm and stretched her legs in an impulse of swimming, differentiating herself for the first time from the undulating mass that enwrapped her, swam in water or smoke, was her body and enjoyed with each stroke what was no longer a passive race, an interminable transfer. She swam and swam, she didn't need to see herself swim and receive the grace of a voluntary movement, of a direction that hands and feet imposed on the course. Falling without transition into the cube state was the shed again, remembering again and suffering, once more up to the limit of the unbearable weight, the slashing pain, and the red nausea covering her face, she found herself on the other side, crawling with a slowness that now she could measure and abominate, passed to be fever, to be a rush of hurricane, to be in waves again and enjoying her body Janet, and when at the end of the indeterminate everything coagulated into the cube state, it wasn't horror but desire that was waiting for her on the other side of the end, with images and words in the cube state, with pleasure of her body in the being in waves. Understanding, reunited with herself, invisibly she Janet desired Robert, desired the shed again, desired Robert who had brought her to what she was there and now, understood the madness under the shed and desired Robert, and in the delight of the swimming amidst liquid crystals or strata of clouds on high she called him, stretched out her body face up to him, called him so that he could really consummate in the pleasure the clumsy consummation on the foul-smelling straw of the shed.

It is difficult for the defense attorney to inform his client that the recourse of a pardon has been denied; Maître Rolland vomited when he came out of the cell where Robert, sitting on the edge of his cot, was staring into space.

From pure sensation to recognition, from the fluidity of the waves to the severe cube, coming together into something that was Janet again, desire was looking for its road, another step among the recurrent steps. Will was coming back to Janet, at first memory and sensations had been given without an axis to modulate them, now along with desire will was coming back to Janet, something in her stretched out an arch like one of skin and tendons and viscera, projected her toward what couldn't be, demanded access inside and outside the states that enveloped her and abandoned her dizzily, her will was desire opening a way in liquids and flashing constellations and very slow dragging, Robert was in some way a kind of end, the goal that was being sketched out now and had a name and a touch in the cube state and that after or before in the now agreeable swimming among waves and crystals was resolved in clamor, in a flame caressing her and throwing her to herself. Incapable of seeing herself, she felt herself; incapable of thinking articulately, her desire was desire and Robert, was Robert in some unreachable state but which Janet will sought to force, a Robert state in which the Janet desire, Janet will, wanted to accede as now once more to the cube state, to solidification and delimitation in which rudimentary mental operations were more and more possible, strings of words and memories, taste of chocolate and pressure of feet on chrome pedals, rape in the midst of convulsions of protest where now desire nested, the will of finally giving in amidst tears of pleasure, of thankful acceptance, of Robert.

His calm was so great, his politeness so extreme, that they left him alone at times, came to spy through the peephole or offer him cigarettes or propose a game of dominoes. Lost in his stupor, which in some way had always been with him, Robert didn't feel the passage of time. He let himself be shaved, he went to the shower with his two guards, once he asked about the weather, if it was raining in the Dordogne.

It was being in waves or crystals that a more vehement stroke, a desperate blow with her heel, launched her into a cold and enclosed space, as if the sea had vomited her up into a grotto of shadows and Gitanes smoke. Sitting on the cot, Robert was looking into the air, the cigarette burning between his fingers. Janet wasn't surprised, surprise had no course there, neither presence nor absence; a transparent partition, a cube of diamond inside the cube of the cell, isolated her from every attempt, from Robert there under the electric light. The bow of herself stretched out to the ultimate had no string or arrow against the diamond cube, the transparency was silence of impenetrable material, not a single time had Robert raised his eyes to look in the direction that only contained the thick air of the cell, the swirling smoke from the tobacco. Janet clamor, Janet will, capable of reaching there, of finding, smashed into an essential difference, Janet desire was a tiger of translucent froth that was changing shape, stretching out white claws of smoke toward the small barred window, threading off and getting lost as she twisted in her inefficacy. Thrown in one last impulse, knowing that at any moment she could once more be crawling or careening among a foliage of grains of sand or atomic formulas, Janet desire demanded the image of Robert, sought to reach his face or his hair, to call him to her side. She saw him look toward the door, scrutinize for an instant the peephole empty of watchful eyes. With an explosive gesture Robert took something out from under the mattress, a vague noose of twisted blanket. With a leap he reached the window, slipped the noose through. Janet was howling, calling him, the silence of her howl smashed against the diamond cube. The investigation showed that the prisoner had hanged himself by letting himself drop down with all his weight. The jerk must have made him lose consciousness and he couldn't fight against asphyxiation; scarcely four minutes had passed from the last visual inspection by the guards. Nothing now, in the full clamor of the break and the passage to the solidification of the cube state, broken by the Janet entry into being fever, run up in a spiral of uncountable alembics, leap to a depth of thick earth where advance was an obstinate biting of resistant substances, a sticky climbing up to levels vaguely sea green, a passage to being in waves, first strokes like a happiness that had a name now, a propeller reversing its spin, a hopelessness become hope, the steps from one state to another didn't matter much now, being in foliage or in sonorous counterpoint, now Janet desire was provoking them, was seeking them with the bending of a bridge sending itself to the other side of a metal leap. In some condition, passing through some state or all of them at once, Robert. At some moment being fever Janet or being in waves Janet it could be waves Robert or fever or cube state in the now without time, not Robert but cubeness or fever because the nows would let him also pass on to be in fever or in waves, would be giving him Robert little by little, would filter him and drag him along and fix him in a simultaneity sometimes entering the successive, Janet desire struggling against every state to sink itself in the other where still not Robert, to be once more in fever without Robert, to be paralyzed in the cube state without Robert, to enter blandly the liquid where the first strokes were Janet, feeling herself whole and knowing herself Janet, but there some time Robert, there surely some time at the end of the warm swaying in crystal waves a hand would reach Janet's hand, it would at last be Robert's hand.

A

CHANGE

OF

LIGHT

AND

OTHER

STORIES

SUMMER

In the late afternoon Florencio went down to the cabin with his little girl, taking the back road full of holes and loose stones that only Mariano and Zulma were up to following in their Jeep. Zulma opened the door for them, and Florencio thought that her eyes looked as if she had been peeling onions. Mariano appeared from the other room; he told them to come in, but Florencio only wanted to ask them to take care of the little girl until the next morning because he had to go to the coast on an urgent matter and there was nobody in the village he could ask to do him this favor. Of course, said Zulma, leave her, don't worry, we'll set up a bed for her here downstairs. Come on in and have a drink, Mariano insisted, it'll only take five minutes, but Florencio had left his car in the village square, he had to take off right away; he thanked them and kissed his little girl, who had already spotted the stack of magazines on the bench. When the door closed, Zulma and Mariano looked at each other almost questioningly, as if everything had happened too fast. Mariano shrugged his shoulders and returned to his workshop, where he was gluing an old chair; Zulma asked the little girl if she was hungry, she suggested she play with the magazines, in the closet there was a ball and a net for catching butterflies; the little girl said thank you and began to look at the magazines; Zulma watched her a moment while she prepared the artichokes for dinner that evening and thought she could let her play by herself.

Dusk fell early in the south now; they barely had a month left before returning to the capital and getting into that other life during the winter which, in any case, was only a continuation of this one, distantly together, amicably friends, respecting and performing the many trivial, delicate, conventional ceremonies of a couple, as now, when Mariano needed one of the burners to heat the glue jar and Zulma took the pot of potatoes off saying she'd finish cooking them later, and Mariano said thanks because the chair was almost ready and it would be better to do all the gluing in one application, but he had to heat the jar first, of course. The little girl was leafing through the magazines at the end of the large room that was used both as a kitchen and as a living room. Mariano looked in the pantry for some candy to give her; it was time to go out into the garden to have a drink as they watched night fall upon the hills. There was never anybody on the road; the first house in the village could barely be seen at the highest point; in front of them the slope kept on descending to the bottom of the valley, which was already in the shadows. Go ahead and pour, I'll be right there, said Zulma. Everything was done in cyclical fashion, each thing in its time and a time for each thing, except for the little girl, who had suddenly disturbed the pattern just a bit; a stool and a glass of milk for her, a stroke of her hair, and praise for how well she was behaving. The cigarettes, the swallows clustering above the cabin; everything went along repeating itself, fitting into the right slot, the chair must be almost dry by now, stuck together like that new day which had nothing new about it. The insignificant difference was the little girl that afternoon, as sometimes the mailman would draw them out of their solitude for a moment at midday with a letter for Mariano or Zulma that the addressee would receive and put away without saying a word. One more month of foreseeable repetitions, like rehearsals, and the Jeep loaded to the top would take them back to the apartment in the capital, to the life that was only different in form, Zulma's group or Mariano's artist friends, afternoons in the stores for her and evenings in the cafés for Mariano, a coming-and-going separately although they always got together to perform the linking ceremonies, the morning kiss, the neutral programs in common, as now when Mariano offered her another drink and Zulma accepted with her eyes lost in the most distant hills, which were tinted already in deep violet.

What would you like to have for supper, little one? Me? Anything you say, ma'am. She probably doesn't like artichokes, said Mariano. Yes, I like them, said the little girl, with oil and vinegar, but only a little salt because it burns. They laughed; they would make a special vinaigrette dressing for her. And boiled eggs, how do you like them? With a teaspoon, said the little girl. And only a little salt, because it burns, teased Mariano. Salt burns a lot, said the little girl, I give my doll her mashed potatoes without salt, today I didn't bring her because my daddy was in a hurry and wouldn't let me. It's going to be a lovely night, thought Zulma out loud, see how clear the air is toward the north. Yes, it won't be too hot, said Mariano, bringing the chairs into the downstairs room and turning on the lamps next to the picture window that faced the valley. Automatically he also turned on the radio. Nixon is going to Peking, how about that, said Mariano. There's nothing sacred, said Zulma, and they both laughed at the same time. The little girl was into the magazines and marking the comic strip pages as though she planned to reread them.

Night arrived in between the insecticide Mariano was spraying in the bedroom upstairs and the fragrance of an onion Zulma cut while humming along with a pop tune on the radio. Midway through supper the little girl began to doze over the boiled egg; they joked with her, they prodded her to finish; Mariano had already prepared the cot for her with an inflatable mattress in the farthest corner of the kitchen so they wouldn't bother her if they stayed a while in the room downstairs listening to records or reading. The little girl ate her peach and admitted she was sleepy. Go to bed, sweetie, said Zulma, don't forget if you have to tinkle, you only have to go upstairs, we'll leave the stairway light on. The little girl, half-asleep, gave them each a kiss on the cheek, but before she lay down she selected a magazine and placed it under the pillow. They're unbelievable, said Mariano, such an unattainable world and to think it once was ours, everybody's. Perhaps it's not so different, said Zulma, clearing the table, you too have your compulsions, the bottle of cologne on the left and the razor on the right, and as for me, forget it. But they weren't compulsions, thought Mariano, rather a response to death and nothingness, fixing things and times, establishing rituals and passages in opposition to chaos, which was full of holes and smudges. Only now he no longer said it aloud, more and more there seemed to be less of a need to talk to Zulma, and Zulma didn't say anything either that might prompt an exchange of ideas. Take the coffeepot, I've already set the cups on the stool by the chimney. Check to see if there's any sugar left in the bowl, there's a new package in the pantry. I can't find the corkscrew, this bottle of rum has a good color, don't you think? Yes, a lovely color. Since you're going up, bring the cigarettes I left on the dresser. This rum is really good stuff. It's hot, don't you think so? Yes, it's stifling, we'd better not open the windows, the place will fill with moths and mosquitoes.

When Zulma heard the first sound, Mariano was looking among the stack of records for a Beethoven sonata which he hadn't listened to that summer. He stood still with his hand in the air, he looked at Zulma. A noise as if on the stone steps of the garden, but nobody came to the cabin at that hour, nobody ever came at night. From the kitchen he switched on the light that illuminated the nearest part of the garden, saw no one and turned it off. Probably a dog looking around for something to eat, said Zulma. It sounded strange, almost like a snort, said Mariano. An enormous white blur lashed against the window. Zulma muffled a scream, Mariano, with his back toward her, turned around too late, the pane reflected only the pictures and furniture in the room. He had no time to ask anything, the snort resounded near the north wall; a whinny that was smothered just like Zulma's scream, her hands up to her mouth and pressing against the back wall, staring at the window. It's a horse, said Mariano, I hear his hooves, he's galloping through the garden. His mane, his lips, almost as if they were bleeding, an enormous white head was grazing the window; the horse barely looked at them, the white blotch was erased on the right, they heard his hooves again, an abrupt silence coming from the side of the stone steps, the neighing, the flight. But there are no horses in these parts, said Mariano, who had grabbed the bottle of rum by the neck before realizing it and now put it back on the stool. He wants to come in, said Zulma, glued to the rear wall. Of course not, what a foolish idea, he probably escaped from some herd in the valley and headed for the light. I tell you, he wants to come in, he's rabid and wants to get inside. Horses don't get rabies, as far as I know, said Mariano, I think he's gone, I'll take a look from the upstairs window. No, please, stay here, I can still hear him, he's on the terrace steps, he's stomping on the plants, he'll be back, and what if he breaks the window and gets in? Don't be silly, what do you mean he'll break the window, said Mariano weakly, maybe if we turn off the lights he'll go away. I don't know, I don't know, said Zulma, sliding down until she was sitting on the stool, I heard how he whinnied, he's there upstairs. They heard the hooves coming down the steps, the irritated heavy snort against the door, Mariano thought he felt something like pressure on the door, a repeated rubbing, and Zulma ran to him screaming hysterically. He cast her off, not violently, extended his hand toward the light switch; in the dark (the only light still on was in the kitchen, where the little girl was sleeping), the neighing and the hooves became louder, but the horse was no longer in front of the door; he could be heard going back and forth in the garden. Mariano ran to turn out the kitchen light without even looking toward the corner where they had put the little girl to bed; he returned to put his arms around Zulma, who was sobbing. He caressed her hair and face, ask-

ing her to be quiet so he could listen better. In the window
the horse rubbed his head against the large pane, not too
forcefully, the white blotch appeared transparent in the darkness; they sensed the horse looking inside, as though searching for something, but he could not see them any longer, and
yet there he still was, whinnying and puffing, bolting
abruptly from side to side. Zulma's body slipped through
Mariano's arms and he helped her sit on the stool again,
propping her up against the wall. Don't move, don't say anything, he's leaving now, you'll see. He wants to come in,
Zulma said feebly, I know he wants to come in, and what if he
breaks the window, what's going to happen if he kicks it in?
Shh, said Mariano, please shut up. He's going to come in,
muttered Zulma. And I don't even have a shotgun, said Mariano, I'd blast five shots into his head, the son of a bitch. He's
not there anymore, said Zulma, rising suddenly, I hear him
up there, if he sees the terrace door he might come in. It's
shut tight, don't be afraid, remember in the dark he's not
about to enter a house where he couldn't even move around,
he's not that dumb. Oh yes, said Zulma, he wants to come in,
he'll crush us against the walls, I know he wants to come in.
Shh, repeated Mariano, who also was thinking about it, and
could do nothing but wait with his back soaked in cold
perspiration. Once again the hooves echoed upon the flag-
stone steps, and suddenly silence, the distant crickets, a bird
high in a walnut tree.

Without turning on the light, now that the window let
the night's vague clarity enter, Mariano filled a glass with
rum and held it against Zulma's lips, forcing her to drink
even though her teeth hit the glass and the liquor spilled on
her blouse; then holding the bottle by the neck he took a long
swig and went to the kitchen to check on the little girl. With
her hand under the pillow as if clutching the precious maga-

zine, incredibly she was asleep and had heard nothing, she hardly seemed to be there, while in the big room Zulma's sobbing broke every so often into a smothered hiccough, almost a shout. It's all over, it's over, said Mariano, sitting up against her and shaking her gently, it was nothing but a scare. He'll be back, said Zulma, her eyes nailed to the window. No, he's probably far off by now, no doubt he escaped from some herd down below. No horse does that, said Zulma, no horse tries to enter a house like that. It's strange, I'll grant you that, said Mariano, maybe we'd better take a look outside, I have the lantern right here. But Zulma had pressed herself against the wall, the idea of opening the door, of going out toward the white shadow that might be near, waiting under the trees, ready to charge. Look, if we don't check to see if he's gone, nobody will sleep tonight, said Mariano. Let's give him a little more time; meanwhile you go to bed, and I'll give you a tranquilizer; an extra dose, poor kid, you've certainly earned it.

Zulma ended up by accepting passively; without turning on the lights, they went toward the stairs and with his hand Mariano motioned toward the little girl asleep, but Zulma scarcely looked at her, she was climbing the stairs reeling, Mariano had to hold her as they entered the bedroom because she was about to bump into the doorframe. From the window that faced the eaves they looked at the stone steps, the highest terrace of the garden. You see, he's gone, said Mariano, fixing Zulma's pillow, watching her undress mechanically, staring at the window. He made her drink the drops, dabbed cologne on her neck and hands, gently lifted the sheet up to Zulma's shoulders as she closed her eyes and trembled. He wiped her cheeks, waited a moment, and went

downstairs to look for the lantern; carrying it unlit in one
hand and an ax in the other, little by little he opened the
door of the large room and went out to the lower terrace,
where he could get full view of the entire side of the house
facing eastward; the night was identical to so many other
summer nights, the crickets chirped in the distance, a frog let
fall two alternating drops of sound. Not needing the lantern,
Mariano saw the trampled lilac bush, the huge prints in the
pansy bed, the flowerpot overturned at the bottom of the
steps; so it wasn't an hallucination, and, of course, it was
better that it not be; in the morning he would go with
Florencio to check on the herds in the valley, they weren't
going to get the upper hand so easily. Before going in he set
the flowerpot straight, went up to the front trees and listened
for a long while to the crickets and the frog; when he looked
toward the house, Zulma was standing at the bedroom window, naked, motionless.

The little girl had not moved; Mariano went upstairs without making any noise and began to smoke a cigarette next to
Zulma. You see, he's gone, now we can sleep in peace, tomorrow we'll see. Little by little he led her toward the bed, undressed, stretched out on his back still smoking. Go to sleep,
everything is all right, it was only an absurd fright. He
stroked her hair, his fingers slid down to her shoulder, grazing her breasts lightly. Zulma turned on her side, her back
toward him, not speaking; this too was like so many other
summer nights.

Getting to sleep should have been difficult, but no sooner had
Mariano put out his cigarette than he dropped off suddenly;

the window was still open and no doubt mosquitoes would enter, but sleep came first, with no dreams, total nothingness from which he emerged at some moment driven by an indescribable panic, the pressure of Zulma's fingers on one shoulder, the panting. Almost without realizing it, he was now listening to the night, the perfect silence punctuated by the crickets. Go to sleep, Zulma, it's nothing, you must have been dreaming. Insisting she agree with him, that she lie down again, her back turned to him now that she had suddenly withdrawn her hand and was sitting up rigid, looking toward the closed door. He got up at the same time as Zulma, helpless to stop her from opening the door and going to the top of the stairs, clinging to her and asking himself vaguely if it wouldn't be better to slap her, to bring her back to bed by force, to break such petrified remoteness. In the middle of the staircase Zulma stopped, taking hold of the banister. You know why the little girl is there? With a voice that must have still belonged to the nightmare. The little girl? Two more steps, now almost in the bend that led to the kitchen. Zulma, please. And her voice cracking, almost in falsetto: she's there to let him in, I tell you she's going to let him in. Zulma, don't make me do something I'll regret. And her voice, almost triumphant, still rising in tone, look, just look if you don't believe me; the bed's empty, the magazine on the floor. With a start Mariano headed for Zulma, he sprang toward the light switch. The little girl looked at them, her pink pajamas against the door that faced the large room, her face drowsy. What are you doing up at this hour, said Mariano wrapping a dish towel around his waist. The little girl looked at Zulma naked, somewhere between being asleep and embarrassed she looked at her as if wanting to go back to bed, on the brink of tears. I got up to tinkle, she said. And you went out to the garden when we had told you to go upstairs to the bathroom.

The little girl began to pout, her hands comically lost in the pockets of her pajamas. It's okay, go to bed, said Mariano, stroking her hair. He covered her, and placed the magazine under the pillow for her; the little girl turned toward the wall, a finger in her mouth as if to console herself. Go ahead up, said Mariano, you see there's nothing wrong, don't stand there like a sleepwalker. He saw Zulma take a couple of steps toward the door of the large room, he blocked her path; everything was fine now, damn it. But don't you realize she's opened the door for him, said Zulma with that voice which wasn't hers. Stop the nonsense, Zulma. Go see if it's not so, or let me go. Mariano's hand closed around her trembling forearm. Get upstairs right now, pushing her till he had led her to the foot of the steps, looking as he went by at the little girl, who hadn't moved, she must be asleep by now. On the first step Zulma screamed and tried to escape, but the stairway was narrow and Mariano kept shoving her with his whole body; the towel unfastened and fell to the bottom of the stairs. Holding on to her by the shoulders, he hurled her upward to the landing and flung her into the bedroom, shutting the door behind him. She's going to let him in, Zulma repeated, the door is open and he'll get in. Lie down, said Mariano. I'm telling you the door is open. It doesn't matter if he comes in or not, let him come in if he wants to, I don't give a damn now whether he comes in or not. He caught Zulma's hands as they tried to repel him, from behind he pushed against the bed, they fell together, Zulma sobbing and begging, powerless to move under the weight of a body that pressed her nearer and nearer, that bent her to a will murmured mouth to mouth, wildly amidst tears and obscenities. I don't want to, I don't want to, I don't want to ever again, I don't want to, but it was too late now, her strength and pride yielding to that leveling weight, returning her to an impossible past, to the summers without letters and without horses. Later in the night—it was beginning to get light—Mariano dressed in silence and went down to the kitchen; the little girl was sleeping with her finger in her mouth, the door of the big room was open. Zulma had been right, the little girl had opened the door but the horse hadn't entered the house. Unless, he thought, lighting his first cigarette and looking at the blue ridge of the hills, unless Zulma had been right about that too and the horse had entered the house, but how could they prove it if they had not heard him, if everything was in order, if the clock would continue to measure the morning and later Florencio would come to get the little girl, probably around twelve the mailman would arrive whistling from afar, leaving for them on the garden table the letters that he or Zulma would pick up without saying anything, shortly before deciding by mutual consent what was best to prepare for lunch.

—*Translated from the Spanish
by Clementine Rabassa*

IN
THE
NAME
OF
BOBBY

Yesterday was his eighth birthday. We had a fine party for him, and Bobby was happy with the windup train, the soccer ball, and the cake with candles. My sister had been afraid that at precisely this time he would come home from school with bad grades, but it was just the opposite; he'd done better in arithmetic and reading, and there was no reason to take his toys away—quite the contrary. We told him to invite his friends, and he had Beto and Juanita; Mario Panzani came, too, but he didn't stay long, because his father was ill. My sister let them play in the yard until dusk, and Bobby broke in the ball, even though we were both afraid that he would knock over our plants in his enthusiasm. When it was time for orangeade and the cake with candles, we all sang "Happy Birthday" to him in a chorus and laughed a lot, because everybody was happy, especially Bobby, and it seemed to me to be a waste of time keeping an eye on what there was nothing to keep an eye on. Just the same, I kept an eye on Bobby when he was distracted, trying to catch sight of the look that my sister doesn't seem to notice but that upsets me so much.

This time he looked at her that way only once, just as my sister was lighting the candles, scarcely a second before he lowered his eyes and, like the well-brought-up child he is, said, "The cake is very nice, Mama," and Juanita approved, too, and Mario Panzani. I had laid out the long knife for Bobby to cut the cake with, and at that moment especially I kept an eye on him from the other end of the table, but Bobby was so happy with the cake that he hardly looked at my sister again and concentrated on the task of cutting small, equal pieces and passing them around. "You first, Mama," Bobby said, giving her a slice, and then Juanita and me, because ladies first. They immediately went out into the yard to continue playing, except for Mario Panzani, but first Bobby told my sister again that the cake was delicious, and he ran over to me and jumped up and put his arms around my neck and gave me one of his wet kisses. "The train is wonderful, Auntie," he said, and that night he climbed up onto my lap to confide his great secret in me: "I'm eight years old now, you know, Auntie."

We went to bed rather late, but it was Saturday and Bobby could loll about like us until late in the morning. I was the last one to go to bed, and first I busied myself tidying up the dining room and putting the chairs in place. The children had played Going to Jerusalem and other games, which had turned the house upside down. I put away the long knife, and before going to bed I saw that my sister was already sleeping the sleep of the just. I went to Bobby's little room and looked at him; he was face down, as he had always liked to be since he was an infant, and had already thrown the blankets to the floor and had one leg buried in the pillow. If I had a son, I would let him sleep that way, too, but why think about such things? I went to bed and didn't feel like reading. I may have done the wrong thing, because sleep didn't come to me and I went through what I usually do at that hour when you lose your will and ideas leap out from all sides and seem to be true—everything you think about is suddenly true and almost always horrible and there's no way to shake it off, not even by praying. I drank some water and sugar and waited, counting down from three hundred, backward, which is harder and makes sleep come. Just as I was about to fall asleep, I was seized by doubts about whether I'd put the knife away or whether it was still on the table. It was silly, because I'd put everything away and I remembered that I'd put the knife in the bottom drawer of the cupboard, but just the same I got up and, of course, it was there in the drawer, mixed in with the other kitchen utensils. I don't know why, but I got a kind of urge to keep it in my bedroom. I even took it out for a moment, but that was already too much. I looked at myself in the mirror and made a face. That didn't make things any better, and then I poured myself a drink of anisette, even though it was imprudent, with my liver and all, and I sipped it in bed to help sleep come. From time to time my sister's snoring could be heard, and Bobby, as always, was talking or moaning.

Just as I was falling asleep everything came back suddenly—the first time Bobby asked my sister why she was mean to him and my sister, who is a saint, everybody says so, stood looking at him as if it were a joke, and even laughed. But I, who was preparing the maté, remember that Bobby hadn't laughed. On the contrary, he was upset, and wanted to know; at that time he must have already been seven and he always asked strange questions, like all children. I remember the day he asked me why trees were different from us and I in turn asked him why and Bobby said, "But, Auntie, they cover themselves in summer and uncover themselves in winter," and I stood there openmouthed, because, really, that child; they're all like that, but after all . . . And now my sister was looking at him puzzled; she had never been mean to him, she told him—just strict a few times when he'd misbehaved or had been ill and had to do things he didn't like. Juanita's mother and Mario Panzani's mother were also strict with their children when it was necessary. But Bobby kept on looking at her sadly and explained that it wasn't during the day—that she was mean at night, when he was asleep. The two of us were flabbergasted, and I think that it was I who began to explain to him that no one is to blame for what happens in dreams, that it must have been a nightmare and that was all, there was no need to worry. That day Bobby didn't insist—he always accepted our explanations and he wasn't a difficult child—but a few days later he awoke weeping and shouting and when I got to his bed he hugged me and wouldn't speak. He just cried and cried, another nightmare surely, but at noontime he suddenly remembered and asked my sister again why she was so mean to him when he was alseep. This time my sister hugged him to her breast, told him that he was too big now not to know the difference, and that if he kept on insisting about that she was going to talk to Dr. Kaplan, because he probably had worms or appendicitis and something would have to be done. I felt that Bobby was going to start crying and hastened to explain to him again about nightmares—he had to realize that nobody loved him as much as his mother, not even I, who loved him so much—

and Bobby listened very seriously, drying a tear, and said of course he knew and got out of his chair to go kiss my sister, who didn't know what to do and remained thoughtful, looking into space. That afternoon I went to look for him in the yard and asked him to tell me, his aunt, because he could confide everything in me the same as with his mother, and if he didn't want to tell her, he could tell me. You could see that he didn't want to talk—it was too much for him—but finally he said something like at night it was all different; he spoke about some sort of black cloth that he couldn't get his hands or feet out of. Anyone can have nightmares like that, but it was a shame that Bobby should only have them about my sister, who made so many sacrifices for him. I told him that, and I repeated it, and he, of course, agreed.

Right after that my sister came down with pleurisy and I had to take care of things. Bobby was no trouble for me, because, small as he was, he could handle almost everything by himself. I remember that he would come in to see my sister and stay by the side of her bed without speaking, waiting for her to smile at him or to stroke his hair, and then he would go quietly out into the yard and play or into the living room to read. I didn't even have to tell him not to play the piano during that time, even though he would have liked to very much. The first time I saw that he was sad I explained to him that his mother was better now and that one of these days she would get up for a while to take some sun. Bobby put on a strange expression and looked at me out of the corner of his eye; I don't know, the idea suddenly came to me and I asked him if he was having his nightmares again. He began to weep very quietly, hiding his face; then he said he was—why was his mother that way with him? That time I realized that he was afraid; when I lowered his hands to dry his face I could see the fear, and it was hard for me to act indifferent and explain to him once more that they were only dreams. "Don't say anything to her," I told him. "Remember, she's still weak and it might have some effect on her." Bobby nodded in silence—he had so much trust in me—but later on I came to think that he had taken me too literally, because not even when my sister was convalescing did he talk about it again. I could sense it in him on some mornings when I would see him come out of his room with that lost expression, and also because he spent all of his time with me, hovering about in the kitchen. One or two times I couldn't take it anymore and spoke to him in the yard or when I was bathing him, and he was always the same, making an effort not to cry, swallowing his words, because his mother was that way with him at night, but he wouldn't go beyond that, he was weeping too much. I explained again to Bobby, who understood quite well, that I didn't want my sister to find out, because she was still weak from the pleurisy and it might affect her too much, but on the other hand he could tell me anything. He would soon see that when he got a little older he'd stop having those nightmares; it would be better, though, if he didn't eat so much bread at night. I was going to ask Dr. Kaplan if he might not need a laxative, so he could sleep without any bad dreams, but I didn't, of course; it was difficult to talk about something like that with Dr. Kaplan, who had such a busy practice and wasn't about to waste his time. I don't know if I did the right thing or not, but little by little Bobby stopped worrying me so much. Sometimes I would see him in the morning with that slightly lost air and I would say to myself, probably again, and then I would wait for him to come and confide in me, but Bobby would start to sketch or go to school without saying anything to me and would come home happy, and he was stronger and healthier each day and got the best grades.

The last time was during the February heat wave; my sister was completely recovered and we lived life as usual. I don't know if she was aware that something was wrong, but I didn't want to say anything to her, because I know her and I know that she's too sensitive, especially when it's a question of Bobby, even though I can remember when Bobby was small and my sister was still suffering from the shock of the divorce and all that—how hard it was for her to bear up when Bobby would cry or do some bit of mischief, and I had to take him out into the yard and wait for everything to calm down; that's what we aunts are for. Actually, I think that my sister didn't realize that sometimes Bobby would get up as if he were re-turning from a long trip, with a lost face that lasted until breakfast; when we were alone I always waited for her to say something, but she didn't, and I thought it was bad to remind her of something that could only make her suffer. I imagined, rather, that one of those times Bobby would ask her again why she was mean to him, but Bobby also must have thought that he didn't have the right to do something like that; it was possible that he remembered my request and thought that he would never have to talk about that to my sister anymore. Occasionally I would get the feeling that I was the one who was inventing it all, and would be certain that Bobby was no longer dreaming anything bad about his mother—he would have told me at once in order to console himself. But after-ward I would see on him that face from certain mornings and start to worry again. I decided it would be better for my sister not to be aware of anything, not even the first time that Bobby gave her the look. I was ironing and from the door of the pantry he looked at my sister in the kitchen, and I don't know how something like that can be explained except that the iron almost put a hole in my blue nightgown—I lifted it off just in time. Bobby was still looking at my sister that way as she rolled dough to make meat tarts. When I asked him what he wanted, just for the sake of saying something to him, he was startled and said he didn't want anything, that it was too hot outside to play ball. I don't know what tone I used to ask the question, but he repeated the explanation as if to convince me and went off to sketch in the parlor. My sister said that Bobby was quite dirty and she was going to give him a bath that afternoon—big as he was, he always forgot to wash his feet and behind his ears. In the end I was the one who bathed him, because my sister still got tired in the afternoon, and while I was soaping him in the bathtub and he was playing with the plastic duck that he refused to let go of, I got up the courage to ask him if he was sleeping better these days.

"More or less," he told me after a moment dedicated to making the duck swim.

"What do you mean, more or less? Are you dreaming ugly things or not?"

"The other night I did," Bobby said, sinking the duck and holding it under the water.

"Did you tell your mother?"

"No, not her. She—"

He didn't give me time for anything; soaped up and all, he threw himself on top of me and hugged me, weeping, trembling, making me miserable while I tried to push him off, and his body slipped between my fingers until be dropped into a sitting position in the bathtub and covered his face with his hands, weeping and shouting. My sister came running and thought Bobby had slipped and hurt himself somewhere, but he said no with his head, stopped crying with an effort that wrinkled up his face, and stood up in the bath-tub so that we could see that nothing had happened to him—refusing to speak, naked, soapy, and so alone with his held-in weeping that neither my sister nor I could calm him down, even though we brought towels and caresses and promises.

After that I always looked for a chance to build up Bobby's confidence without his realizing that I was trying to make him talk, but weeks passed and he never tried to tell me any-thing. When I spotted something in his face now, he would go away immediately or embrace me and ask for some candy or permission to go to the corner with Juanita and Mario Panzani. He never asked my sister for anything; he was very attentive toward her, as she was basically still in rather deli-cate health, and she didn't worry too much about taking care of him, because I was always there first, and Bobby would accept anything from me, even what was most disagreeable, when it was necessary. So my sister never came to be aware of what I had seen immediately—his way of looking at her like that for a moment, of remaining in the doorway looking at her until I became aware of it and then he would quickly lower his eyes or start running or jumping. The business of the knife was just by chance. I was changing the paper on the pantry shelves and had taken all the dishes down; I didn't realize that Bobby had come in until I turned around to cut another strip of paper and saw him looking at the long knife. He became distracted right away or didn't want me to notice, but I already knew that way of looking he had, and, I don't know, it's stupid to think such things, but it all came over me like a chill, almost an icy wind in that overheated pantry. I was unable to say anything to him, but at night I thought of how Bobby had stopped asking my sister why she was mean to him; only at times would he look at her as he had looked at the long knife—that different look. It might have been just chance, of course, but I didn't like it during the following week when I saw the same face on him precisely at the moment I was cutting the bread with the long knife and my sister was explaining to Bobby that it was time now for him to learn to shine his own shoes. "Yes, Mama," Bobby said, paying attention only to what I was doing to the bread, accompanying every movement of the knife with his eyes and swaying in his chair, almost as if he were cutting the bread himself; he was probably thinking about the shoes and moving as if he were shining them—my sister certainly thought that, because Bobby was so obedient and so good.

At night I wondered whether I shouldn't talk to my sister, but what was I going to tell her, since nothing was happening and Bobby was getting the best grades in his class and things like that. Except that I couldn't sleep, because suddenly everything came together again; it was like a mass that grew thicker and then the fear, impossible to know of what, because Bobby and my sister were already asleep and they could be heard moving or sighing from time to time—they were sleeping so well, much better than I, lying there thinking all night long. And, of course, I finally sought out Bobby in the garden after I saw him look at my sister that way again, and I asked him to help me transplant a mastic and we talked about lots of things and he confided in me that Juanita had a sister who was engaged.

"Naturally. She's big now," I told him. "Look, go get me the long knife from the kitchen so we can cut these raffias."

He ran off as always, because there was no one better than he for doing what I wanted, and I remained looking toward the house waiting for him to come back, thinking I really should have asked him about the dreams before send-

ing him for the knife, just to be sure. When he came back,
walking very slowly, as if wading through the siesta-time atmosphere in order to take longer, I saw that he had picked
out one of the short knives, even though I had left the long
one in plain view, because I wanted to be sure that he would
see it as soon as he opened the cupboard drawer.

"This one is no good," I told him. It was hard for me to
speak; it was stupid with someone as small and innocent as
Bobby, but I couldn't look him in the eye. I only felt the
shove when he threw himself into my arms, letting go of the
knife, and pressing himself against me, pressing himself so
much against me and weeping. I think that at that moment I
saw something that must have been his last nightmare. I
couldn't ask him, but I think that I saw what he had dreamt
the last time before he stopped having the nightmares, and
yet there was that way of looking at my sister, of looking at
the long knife.

LILIANA
WEEPING

At least it's better that it's Ramos and not some other doctor; with him there was always a pact, I knew that when the moment arrived he'd tell me or at least would let me understand without telling me everything. It's been hard on the poor guy: fifteen years of friendship and nights of poker and weekends in the country, the usual problem; but that's the way it is, at the moment of truth and between men that's worth more than office lies, colored like the pills or the pink liquid that enters my veins drop by drop.

For three or four days, without his telling me, I know that he's going to see to it that there isn't that thing they call the death agony, letting the dog die slowly, what for; I can trust him, the last pills will still be green or red but inside there'll be something else, the big sleep that I thank him for already while he stays with me, Ramos, looking at me from the foot of the bed, a little lost because the truth has emptied him out, poor guy. Don't say anything to Liliana, why should we make her weep before it's necessary, don't you think? Alfredo, yes, you can tell Alfredo, so he can arrange for time off to take care of Liliana and Mama. Yeah, and tell the nurse not to bug me when I'm writing, it's the only thing that makes me forget the pain, apart from your eminent pharmacopoeia, of course. Oh, and have them bring me coffee when I want it, this hospital takes things so seriously.

It's true that writing calms me from time to time, maybe that's why there's so much correspondence from those condemned to die, who can say. It even amuses me to imagine in writing those things that are only thought of when something is caught in your throat, not to mention the lachrymals; I can see myself through the words as if I were someone else, I can think anything as long as I write it down immediately, a professional deformation or something that begins as a softening in the meninges. I only stop when Liliana comes, I'm not so nice with the others; since they don't want me to talk much, I let them tell me if it's cold outside or if Nixon is going to beat McGovern, with the pencil in my hand I let them talk and even Alfredo realizes it and tells me just to go right on, to act as if he weren't there, he has the newspaper and he'll stay a while longer. But my wife deserves better than that, her I listen to and smile at and it hurts me less, I accept that slightly damp kiss that comes back time and again although it tires me a little more every day when they shave me and I must hurt her mouth, poor dear. It has to be said that Liliana's courage is my greatest consolation, seeing myself dead already in her eyes would take away from me that remnant of strength with which I can talk to her and return some one of her kisses, so that I keep on writing as soon as she's left and the routine of injections and sympathetic little words begins. No one dares get involved with my notebook, I know I can keep it under my pillow or on the night table, it's my whim, we have to let him because of Dr. Ramos, we have to let him, poor thing, it's a distraction for him.

So it means Monday or Tuesday, and the little place in the crypt Wednesday or Thursday. In the middle of summer Chacarita is going to be an oven and the boys are going to have a bad time of it, I can see Pincho with those twill jackets and shoulder pads that are a source of such amusement for Acosta, who, for his part, will have to dude up even if it hurts, the king of the campground putting on a coat and tie in order to go with me, it's going to be wild. And Fernandito, the trio complete, and Ramos too, of course, right to the end, and Alfredo taking Liliana by the arm and Mama, weeping with them. And it will be real, I know how much they love me, how they're going to miss me; they won't go the way we went to Fats Tresa's funeral, partisan obligation and a few shared vacations, doing our duty rapidly with the family and cutting out back to life and forgetting. Of course, they'll have a fierce hunger, especially Acosta, who's got no match as a glutton; even though it pains them and they curse this absurdity of dying young and in the middle of one's career, there's the reaction that we've all known, the pleasure of going back and getting on the subway or into the car, of taking a shower and eating with hunger and shame at the same time, how can we deny the hunger that follows staying up nights, the smell of flowers at the wake and the interminable cigarettes and strolls along the sidewalk, a kind of recovery that's always felt at those moments and which I never denied because it would have been hypocritical. I like to think that Fernandito,. Pincho, and Acosta will go to a barbecue place together, sure that they'll go together because we did it when it was Fats Tresa, friends have to go on for a while, drink a quart of wine, and get rid of some innards; God damn it, I can see them now, Fernandito will be the first to crack a joke and swallow it along the way with half a sausage, sorry but too late already, and Acosta will look at him out of the corner of his eye, but Pincho will already have let out a laugh, it's something that he can't help, and then Acosta, who's as good as gold, will say to himself that there's no reason for him to pass as an example in front of the boys and he'll laugh too before lighting a cigarette. And they'll talk about me for a long time, each one will remember so many things, the life that brought us four together, although, as always, full of gaps, moments that we all didn't share and which will pop up in Acosta's or Pincho's memory, so many years and fights and love affairs, the gang. It's going to be hard for them to separate after lunch because that's when the other thing comes back, the time to go back home, the last, definitive burial. It will be different for Alfredo and not because he doesn't belong to the gang, quite the contrary. Alfredo's going to take care of Liliana and Mama and not even Acosta or the rest can do that, life goes on creating special contacts among friends, they've always come to the house but Alfredo is something else, the closeness that was always good for me, his pleasure in staying for a long time chatting with Mama about plants and medicines, how he liked to take Pocho to the zoo or the circus, the serviceable old bachelor, a package of petits four and gin rummy when Mama wasn't feeling well, his timid and clear confidence with Liliana, the friend of friends who now will have to spend those two days swallowing his tears, probably taking Pocho to his country place and coming back at once to be with Mama and Liliana

until the end. After all, he's going to have to be the man of
the house and bear up under all the complications, starting
with those of the funeral arrangements, this had to happen
just when the old man is traveling in Mexico or Panama, who
knows if he'll get back in time to stand the eleven o'clock heat
in Chacarita, poor old man, so it will be Alfredo who will
take Liliana because I don't think they'll let Mama go, Liliana on his arm, feeling her trembling against his own trembling, whispering to her everything I probably whispered to
Fats Tresa's wife, the useless necessary rhetoric that isn't
consolation or a lie or even coherent phrases, a simple being
there, which is so much.

For them, too, the worst part will be the return, before
that there's the ceremony and the flowers, there's still contact
with that inconceivable thing covered with handles and gilt,
the halt in front of the crypt, the operation neatly executed
by those in the trade, but afterward it's the return automobile and especially the house, entering the house again, knowing that the day is going to stagnate without telephone or
hospital, without the voice of Ramos stretching out hope for
Liliana, Alfredo will make coffee and tell her that Pocho is
happy in the country, that he likes the ponies and plays with
the farmboys, he'll have to look after Mama and Liliana but
Alfredo knows every corner of the house and of course he'll
stay there lying awake on the couch in my study, right there
where once we laid out Fernandito, the victim of a poker
game in which he hadn't had a single good hand, not to mention the five compensatory cognacs. Liliana has been sleeping
alone for so many weeks that maybe the fatigue will get the
better of her, Alfredo won't forget to give Liliana and Mama
sedatives. Aunt Zulema will be there passing out manzanilla
and linden tea, Liliana will let herself slip into sleep little by
little in that silence of the house which Alfredo will have

conscientiously locked up before going to stretch out on the couch and light another of the cigarettes that he doesn't dare smoke in front of Mama because of the smoke that makes her cough.

In the end there's that good part: Liliana and Mama won't be so alone or in that even worse loneliness which is the invasion of the house of mourning by distant relatives; there will be Aunt Zulema, who's always lived on the upper floor, and Alfredo, who also has been among us as if he weren't there, the friend with his own key; during the first hours perhaps it will be less hard to feel the irrevocable absence than to bear up under a troop of embraces and verbal wreaths, Alfredo will take care of maintaining distances, Ramos will come for a while to see Mama and Liliana, he'll help them sleep and will leave some pills with Aunt Zulema. At some moment there will be the silence of the darkened house, only the church clock, a distant horn, because the neighborhood is quiet. It's nice thinking that it's going to be like that, that abandoning herself little by little to a stupor without images Liliana is going to stretch out with her slow cat movements, one hand lost under the pillow wet with tears and cologne, the other beside her mouth in a juvenile recurrence before sleep. Imagining her like that is so good, Liliana sleeping, Liliana at the end of the black tunnel, feeling vaguely that today is ending and becoming yesterday, that the light in the curtains will no longer be the same one that beat full on her breast while Aunt Zulema opened the boxes from which the blackness was emerging in the form of clothing and veils strewn over the bed and mingled with an angry weeping, one last, useless protest against what still had to come. Now the light from the window would arrive before anyone, before the memories dissolved in sleep and which only in confusion would open a path in the final drowsiness. Alone,

knowing that she was really alone in that bed and in that
room, on that day which was beginning in a different direction, Liliana would be able to weep, hugging the pillow
without their coming to calm her, letting herself use up the
weeping until the end, and only much later, with a half-sleep
of deception holding her back in the nest of the sheets, the
hollow of the day would begin to be filled with coffee, with
opened curtains, with Aunt Zulema, with Pocho's voice telephoning from the farm with news about the sunflowers and
the horses, a catfish caught after a fierce struggle, a splinter in
his hand but nothing serious, they had given him one of Don
Contreras' remedies, he was the best for such things. And
Alfredo, waiting in the living room with the newspaper in his
hand, telling her that Mama had slept well and that Ramos
would come at twelve o'clock, proposing that she go see
Pocho in the afternoon, with that sun it would be worth traveling to the farm, and it was one of those times they could
even take Mama, the country air would do her good, maybe
spend the weekend on the farm, and why not everybody, with
Pocho, who would be so happy having them there. Accepting
or not was all the same, they all knew it and waited for the
answers that things and the passage of the morning were giving, going passively in to lunch or commenting on the textile
strike, asking for more coffee and answering the telephone,
which they would have to disconnect some time, the telegram
from the father-in-law abroad, a noisy collision on the corner,
shouts and whistles, the city out there, two thirty, going with
Mama and Alfredo to the farm because one of these times the
splinter in his hand, you never knew with children, Alfredo
behind the wheel, calming them, Don Contreras was better
than a doctor for things like that, the streets of Ramos Mejía
and the sun like boiling syrup until they took refuge in the
great whitewashed rooms, maté at five o'clock, and Pocho

with his catfish that was beginning to smell, but so beautiful, so big, what a fight to get it out of the brook, Mama, it almost cut my line, I swear, look at the teeth. Like leafing through an album or seeing a movie, the images and the words one after the other filling the vacuum, now you'll see what Carmen's roasts are like, ma'am, light and so delicious, a green salad and that's it, that's all we need, with this heat it's best not to eat too much, I brought the insecticide because of the mosquitoes this time of day. And Alfredo silent there, but Pocho, his hand patting Pocho, you're the fishing champ, old boy, tomorrow we'll go out early and one of these times, they told me there was a peasant who caught one weighing five pounds. Here under the eaves it's nice, Mama can sleep a while in the rocker if she wants, Don Contreras was right, you haven't got a thing in your hand anymore, show us how you can ride the piebald pony, look, Mama, look at me when I gallop, why don't you come fishing with us tomorrow, I'll show you how, you'll see, Friday with a red sun and the catfish, the race between Pocho and Don Contreras' boy, the stew at noon and Mama slowly helping husk the corn, telling Carmen's daughter that she had that stubborn cough, siesta in the naked rooms that smelled of summer, the darkness against the rather rough sheets, sunset under the eaves and the bonfire against the mosquitoes, the never manifest nearness of Alfredo, the way of being there and taking care of Pocho, seeing that everything was comfortable, even the silence that his voice always broke in time, his hand offering a soft drink, a handkerchief, turning on the radio to hear the news, the strikes and Nixon, it was foreseeable, what a country.

The weekend and hardly a mark from the splinter on Pocho's hand, they returned to Buenos Aires very early on Monday to avoid the heat, Alfredo dropped them at the house so he could go meet the father-in-law, Ramos was also at the airport in Ezeiza, and Fernandito, who helped during those hours of meeting because it was good to have other friends at the house, Acosta at nine with his daughter who could play with Pocho in Aunt Zulema's apartment, everything was becoming more muffled, going backward but in a different way, with Liliana making herself think more about the old people than about herself, controlling herself, and Alfredo among them with Acosta and Fernandito, turning the straight shots aside, crossing over to help Liliana, to convince the old man to get some rest after a trip like that, friends coming and going until only Alfredo and Aunt Zulema, the house quiet, Liliana accepting a pill, letting herself be put to bed without having faltered one single time, falling asleep almost at once as after something fulfilled to the very last. In the morning it was Pocho running into the living room, the old man dragging his slippers, the first telephone call, almost always Clotilde or Ramos, Mama complaining of the heat or the humidity, talking about lunch with Aunt Zulema, at six o'clock Alfredo, sometimes Pincho with his sister or Acosta so that Pocho could play with his daughter, the colleagues from the lab who scolded Liliana, she had to go back to work and not stay cooped up at home, she should do it for them, they were short of chemists and Liliana was needed, she should come for half a day in any case, until she felt in better spirits; Alfredo took her the first time, Liliana didn't feel like driving, then she didn't want to be a bother and she took out the car, sometimes she went out with Pocho in the afternoon, took him to the zoo or the movies, at the lab they were grateful that she was giving them a hand with the new vaccines, an epidemic on the coast, staying late at work, getting to like it, a team race against the clock, twenty cases of ampuls to Rosario, we did it, a job, Pocho at school and Alfredo protesting, they're teaching these kids a different type of math, he asks me all kinds of questions that turn me off,

and the old folks with their dominoes, everything was different in our day, Alfredo, they taught us penmanship and look
at the handwriting this boy has, where are we going to end
up. The silent recompense of looking at Liliana lost on a
couch, a simple glance over the newspaper and seeing her
smile, a silent accomplice, saying the old folks were right,
smiling at him from afar, almost like a little girl. But for the
first time a real smile, from within, like when they went to
the circus with Pocho, who'd done better at school, and they
took him for some ice cream, for a stroll along the docks. The
big cold was starting, Alfredo came to the house less frequently because there were union problems and he had to go
out to the provinces, sometimes Acosta came with his daughter and on Sundays Pincho or Fernandito, it didn't matter
anymore, everybody had so much to do and the days were
short, Liliana would come back late from the lab and give a
hand to Pocho, lost in decimals and the Amazon basin, in the
end and always Alfredo, the little gifts for the old folks, that
never mentioned tranquillity of sitting down with him by the
now late fire and talking in a low voice about the problems of
the country, Mama's health, Alfredo's hand resting on Liliana's arm, you're getting too tired, your face doesn't look
good, the thankful smile denying it, one day we'll go to the
farm, this cold can't last for our lifetime, nothing could last
for a lifetime even though Liliana would slowly withdraw
her arm and look for the cigarettes on the table, the words
almost without meaning, the eyes meeting in a different way
until the hand again, slipping along the arm, the heads coming together and the long silence, the kiss on the cheek.

There was nothing to say, it had happened that way and
there was nothing to say. Leaning over to light the cigarette
that was trembling between her lips, simply waiting without
speaking, perhaps knowing that there would be no words,

that Liliana would make an effort to swallow the smoke and would let it out with a moan, that she would begin to weep deeply, from another time, without moving her face away from Alfredo's face, without denying and weeping silently, only for him now, because of all the other things that he would understand. It was useless to murmur things so well known, Liliana weeping was the end, the edge from which a different way of life was going to begin. If calming her, if returning her to tranquillity would have been as simple as writing it with the words lining themselves up in a notebook like congealed seconds, small sketches of time to help the interminable passage of the afternoon, if only it were that, but night arrives and so too Ramos, incredibly, Ramos' face looking at the tests just taken, feeling for my pulse, then another Ramos, incapable of hiding, pulling off the sheets to look at me naked, feeling my side, with an incomprehensible order to the nurse, a slow, incredulous recognition at which I am present as if from afar, almost amused, knowing that it can't be, that Ramos is mistaken and that it isn't true, and that the only thing true was the other thing, that the time remaining hadn't been hidden from me, and Ramos' laugh, his way of touching me as if he couldn't admit it, his absurd hope, nobody's going to believe this from me, old man, and I, forcing myself to recognize that it's probably that way, that who can say after all, looking at Ramos, who's getting up and laughing again and giving orders with a voice that I had never heard from him in that drowsy penumbra, having to convince myself little by little, yes, so I'm going to have to ask him, as soon as the nurse leaves, I'll have to ask him to wait a bit, to wait at least until it's daylight before telling Liliana, before pulling her out of that dream in which for the first time she's no longer alone, out of those arms that hold her tight while she sleeps.

A
PLACE
NAMED
KINDBERG

Named Kindberg, ingenuously translated as child mountain
or called gentle mountain, friendly mountain, something or
other like that, a town which they reach at night coming in
out of a rain that washes itself wrathfully against the wind-
shield, an old hotel with deep hallways where everything has
been prepared for forgetting what's still out there beating
and scratching, the place, at last, where one can change, tast-
ing good shelter; and soup in a large silver tureen, white
wine, breaking the bread and giving the first piece to Lina,
who takes it in the palm of her hand as if it were an homage,
and it is, and then she blows on it, who knows why, but in
that way seeing Lina's bangs rise up a little and tremble as if

the blowing on the hand and the bread were about to raise the curtain in a tiny theater, almost as if from that moment on Marcelo could see Lina's thoughts come out onstage, Lina's images and memories as she sips savory soup still smiling.

But no, the smooth animated forehead doesn't change, at first it's just the voice that goes along dropping bits of person that make up a first approximation of Lina: Chilean, for example, and a theme hummed from Archie Shepp, her nails a little chewed but all shiny against clothes that were dirty from hitchhiking and sleeping in barns or youth hostels. Youth, Lina laughs, sipping her soup like a little bear, of course you couldn't imagine: fossils, just imagine, walking corpses like in that horror movie by Romero.

Marcelo is about to ask her what Romero, the first he's heard of such a Romero, but better let her talk, it amuses him to be a witness to that happiness over a hot meal, as over his contentment with a room with a fireplace that waits and crackles, the protective bourgeois bubble of traveler's checks and no problems, the rain exploding outside there against the bubble as that afternoon it had on Lina's white face by the side of the road as she came out of the woods at dusk, what a place to hitchhike but there she was, some more soup, little bear, eat it for me because you have to be saved from an attack of angina, her hair still damp but the fireplace crackling now waiting there in the room with the big Hapsburg bed, with mirrors to the floor, with small tables and decorations and curtains and why were you there in the rain, tell me, your mother would have spanked you.

Corpses, Lina repeats, better to go on alone, of course if it rains but don't worry my raincoat is really rainproof, only my hair and legs a little, that's all, an aspirin just in case. And between the empty bread basket and the nice full new one that the teddy bear is already sacking and what delicious butter, and what do you do, why do you travel around in that great big car, and you why, oh and you're Argentine? A double acceptance that fate does things well, the predictable memory that if Marcelo hadn't stopped twelve miles back to have a drink the little bear settled in a different car now or still in the woods, I sell prefabricated materials, it's something that makes you travel a lot but this time I'm wandering around between two meetings. Teddy bear attentive and almost serious, what's all that prefabricated stuff, a boring subject right off, but what can he do, he can't tell her that he's a lion tamer or movie director or Paul McCartney: the salt. That brusque way of a bird or an insect even though little bear bangs dancing around him, Archie Shepp's recurrent refrain, so you've got the records, but how, oh well. Catching on, Marcelo thinks ironically of how normal it would have been for him not to have had the Archie Shepp records and it's idiotic because in reality of course he has them and sometimes he listens to them with Marlene in Brussels but he just doesn't know how to live them like Lina, who suddenly hums a piece between two bites, her smile full of free jazz and a mouthful of goulash and damp little hitchhiking bear, I never had such good luck, you were good. Good and consequential, Marcelo intones his concertina Gardel revenge, but the ball goes out of bounds, it's a different generation, it's a little Shepp bear, no more tango, eh?

Of course the tickling still remains, almost a kind of bittersweet cramp with the arrival in Kindberg, the hotel parking place in the enormous ancient shed, the old woman lighting their way with a period lantern, Marcelo valise and briefcase, Lina knapsack and slogging, the invitation to dine accepted before Kindberg, so we can talk a little, the night and the rain shrapnel, not good going on, better for us to stop in Kindberg and for me to invite you to dine with me, oh yes great, that way you can dry your clothes, the best thing is to stay over here until morning, it's raining, it's pouring, the old man is snoring, oh yes, Lina said, and then the parking shed, the resonant Gothic galleries to the desk, how nice and warm this hotel, what luck, the last drop of water on her bangs, the knapsack hanging teddy bear girl scout with good uncle, I'm going to get the rooms now so you can dry out a little before dinner. And the tickling, almost a cramp down there, Lina looking at him all bangs, the rooms what foolishness, just ask for one. And he no, looking at her but the tickle disagree-agreeable, so she's a hooker, so she's a delight, so little bear soup fireplace, so another one and what luck, old man, she's quite pretty. But then seeing her take another pair of blue jeans and the black sweater out of her knapsack, turning her back to him gabbling what a fireplace, it smells, perfumed fire, looking for aspirins for her in the bottom of his suitcase among vitamins and deodorants and after-shave and how far are you going, I don't know, I've got a letter to some hippies in Copenhagen, some sketches that Cecilia gave me in Santiago, she told me they're great types, the satin screen and Lina hanging up her wet clothes, indescribably emptying out her knapsack onto the gilded arabesqued franzjosef table: James Baldwin Kleenex buttons dark glasses cardboard boxes Pablo Neruda sanitary napkins map of Germany, I'm hungry, Marcelo, I like your name it sounds good and I'm hungry, so let's go eat, forget the shower you've had enough of a one already, you can arrange that knapsack afterward, Lina raising her head quickly, looking at him: I never arrange anything, what for, the knapsack is like me and this trip and politics, all mixed up and what difference does it make. Snot-nose, Marcelo thought, cramp, almost tickle (give her the aspirins at coffee time, more rapid effect) but she was bothered by those

verbal distances, those you're-so-young-how-can-you-travel-
around-alone-like-thats, in the middle of soup she'd laughed:
youth, fossils, just imagine, walking corpses like in the movie
by Romero. And the goulash and little by little from the heat
and the teddy bear content again and the wine, the tickle in
the stomach giving way to a kind of joy, a peace, she speaking
nonsense, continuing to explain to him her vision of a world
that must have been his some time back although he was no
longer up to remembering, looking at him from the theater
formed by her bangs, suddenly serious and as if worried and
then brusquely Shepp, saying how nice to be like that, feeling
dry and inside the bubble and how once in Avignon hitchhiking in a wind that tore the tiles off the roofs I saw a bird
fly into a tree, fall like a handkerchief just imagine, the pep-
per please.

So (they took away the empty platter) you intend to go
on to Denmark just the same, but have you got any money or
what? Of course I'm going on, aren't you going to eat your
lettuce, give it to me then, I'm still hungry, a way of folding
the leaves with her fork and chewing them slowly humming
Shepp to them from time to time a silvery bubble plop on her
damp lips, pretty well-shaped mouth ending just where it
should, those Renaissance drawings, Florence in autumn
with Marlene, those mouths that pederast geniuses loved so
much, sinuous sensual subtle, etc., this riesling sixty-four is
going to your head, listening to her between bites and humming I don't know how I got through philosophy in Santiago,
I'd like to read a lot of things, it's now that I've got to start
reading. Predictable, poor little bear so content with her lettuce and her plan to swallow Spinoza in six months mixed
with Allen Ginsburg and Shepp again; how many clichés
would she parade out until the coffee came (don't forget to
give her the aspirin, if she starts sneezing on me it'll be a

problem, little snot-nose with wet hair face all sticky bangs the rain lashing her by the side of the road) but parallel between Shepp and the end of the goulash everything was kind of spinning in a short while, changing, they were the same phrases and Spinoza or Copenhagen and at the same time different, Lina there across from him breaking the bread drinking the wine looking at him content, far away and near at the same time, changing with the spinning of the night, although far away and near wasn't an explanation, something else, something like a show, Lina showing him something that wasn't herself but what then, please tell me. And two slices along the grain of the Gruyére, why don't you have some, Marcelo, it's delicious, you didn't eat anything, silly, a fine gentleman like you, because you are a gentleman, right, nothing but cigarettes, rettes, rettes, rettes, without eating anything, listen, and a little more wine, you'd like some, wouldn't you, because with this cheese, you can imagine, you have to wash it down a little, come on, eat some: more bread, it's incredible the way I eat bread, they always predicted that I'd get fat, just what you hear, it's true that I've got a bit of a belly already, it doesn't look it but it's there, I swear, Shepp.

Useless to expect her to talk about anything sensible and why expect it (because you're a gentleman, right?), teddy bear among the flowers of the dessert looking dazzled and at the same time with calculating eyes at the tea cart full of tarts compotes meringues, a bit of a belly, yes, they'd always predicted she'd get fat, *sic*, this one with more cream, and why don't you like Copenhagen, Marcelo? But Marcelo hadn't said that he didn't like Copenhagen, just a little absurd that business of traveling in the middle of a rainstorm and weeks to discover most probably that the hippies were already wandering around California, but you don't realize that it doesn't matter, I told you I don't know them, I'm bringing

them some sketches that Cecilia and Marcos gave me in Santiago and a little record by the Mothers of Invention, do you
think they have a record player here so I can play it for you,
probably too late and too Kindberg, don't forget, still if they
were gypsy violins but those Mothers, wow, the very idea, and
Lina laughing with lots of cream and a bit of a belly under a
black sweater, the two of them laughing thinking about the
Mothers howling in Kindberg, the innkeeper's face and the
heat there that for some time now had replaced the tickling
in the stomach, wondering whether she'd play hard to get,
whether in the end the legendary sword in the bed, in any
case the rolled-up pillow and one on either side moral barrier
modern sword, Shepp, that's it, you're starting to sneeze, take
some aspirin coffee will be right along, I'm going to order
some cognac it activates the salicylic, I learned it from a good
source. And really he hadn't said he didn't like Copenhagen
but the little bear seemed to understand the tone of his voice
more than his words, like him with that teacher he'd fallen in
love with at the age of twelve, what did words matter in the
face of that cooing, that thing that was born out of the voice
like a desire for heat, to be wrapped up and stroked on the
skin, so many years later psychoanalysis: anguish, bah, nostalgia for the primordial uterus, everything since the word go
after all was floating on the waters, read the Bible, fifty thousand pesos to be cured of dizzy spells and now that snot-nosed
girl who in a way was plucking out pieces of him, Shepp, but
of course, if you swallow it dry it's sure to stick in your throat,
silly. And she stirring, suddenly raising a pair of intense eyes
and looking at him with a new respect, of course if she was
beginning to pull his leg she'd pay double for it, but no,
really, Marcelo, I like it when you get so doctor and so papa,
don't be angry, I always say what I shouldn't, don't be angry,
but I'm not angry, silly, yes, you did get a little angry because

I called you doctor and papa, it wasn't in that sense but precisely because it looks so good on you when you talk about aspirin and just think you remembered to get it and bring it, I'd already forgotten, Shepp, you see how I need you, and you're a little comical because you look at me so doctor, don't be angry, Marcelo, how delicious this cognac is with the coffee, how good for sleeping, you know that. And yes, on the highway since seven in the morning, three cars and a truck, pretty good all told except for the storm at the end but then Marcelo and Kindberg and the cognac, Shepp. And to leave her hand very still, palm up on the tablecloth covered with crumbs when he stroked it lightly to tell her no, that he wasn't angry because now he knew that it was true, that he really had moved her with that minimal care, the pill that he'd taken out of his pocket with detailed instructions, plenty of water so it won't stick in her throat, coffee and cognac; friends all of a sudden, but really so, and that fire must have been getting the room even warmer, the maid must have turned down the bed already as no doubt always in Kindberg, a kind of ancient ceremony, welcome to the tired traveler, to foolish teddy bears who wanted to get soaked all the way to Copenhagen and afterward but what did afterward matter, Marcelo, I already told you I don't want to be tied down, donwanna-donwanna, Copenhagen is like a man you find and leave (ah), a day that passes, I don't believe in the future, my balls swell up with the future, and he too his Uncle Roberto transformed into a loving tyrant to take care of Marcelito, who'd lost his father and still so little poor thing, you've got to think about tomorrow, m'boy, Uncle Roberto's ridiculous retirement, what's needed is a strong government, the young people of today only think about having fun, God damn it, in my day on the other hand, and the teddy bear leaving her hand for him on the tablecloth and why that suction, that going back to a Buenos Aires of the thirties or forties, better Copenhagen, yeah, better Copenhagen and the hippies and the rain beside the road, but he'd never hitchhiked, practically never, once or twice before going to the university, then he'd had enough to get by on, for the tailor, and still he could have done it that time the guys were planning to sail on a windjammer that took three months to get to Rotterdam, cargo and stopovers and six hundred pesos in all or something like that, giving the crew a hand, having fun, of course we're going, at the Café Rubí on Plaza Once, of course we're going, Monk, you've got to get up the six hundred clams, it wasn't easy, your salary going for cigarettes and a girl from time to time, one day the get-togethers end, there was no more talk about the windjammer, you've got to think about the future, m'boy, Shepp. Ah, again; come on, you've got to get some rest, Lina. Yes, doctor, but just one more little minute, you don't know how good this supply of warm cognac is for me, taste it, yes, see how nice and warm it is. And something he should have said without knowing what while he remembered the Rubí because Lina again and with that way of guessing his voice, what his voice was really saying more than what it was saying which was always idiotic and aspirin and you have to get some rest or why go on to Copenhagen for example when now, with that little hot white hand under his, everything could be called Copenhagen, everything could have been called windjammer if six hundred pesos, if balls, if poetry. And Lina looking at him and then quickly lowering her eyes as if all that was there on the table, among the crumbs, the trash of time already, as if he had spoken of all that instead of come on, you've got to get some rest, without mustering the courage for the more logical plural, come on, let's go to bed, and Lina, who was licking her chops and remembering some

horses (or were they cows, he only heard her at the end of the
sentence), some horses running across the field as if something had suddenly frightened them: two white horses and
one sorrel, on my aunt and uncle's farm you don't know what
it was like to gallop into the wind in the afternoon, come
back late and tired and of course the scolding, tomboy, right
away, wait till I finish this little drink and then, right away,
looking at him with her bangs all blown as if on horseback at
the farm, snorting because the cognac was so strong, he had to
be an idiot to make problems when it had been she in the
long, dark hallway, she splashing and happy and two rooms
what foolishness, ask for just one, assuming of course all the
meaning of that economizing, knowing and probably used to
it and expecting it at the end of every episode, but and what
if it wasn't like that in the end because it didn't seem like
that, if in the end surprises, the sword in the middle of the
bed, if in the end suddenly on the couch in the corner, of
course then he, a gentleman, don't forget the coverlet, I never
saw such a wide staircase, this certainly must have been a
palace, there were counts who gave parties with candelabra
and things, and the doors, look at that door, but it's ours,
painted with stags and shepherds, it can't be. And the fire, the
red fleeing salamanders and the open white enormous bed
and the curtains smothering the windows, oh how delicious,
how good, Marcelo, what a sleep we're going to have, wait at
least till I show you the record, it's got a wild cover, you're
going to love it, I've got it here at the bottom with my letters
and maps, I can't have lost it, Shepp. You can show it to me
tomorrow, you're really catching cold, get undressed fast, it'll
be better with the lights out, that way we can see the fire, oh
yes, Marcelo, look at the coals, all those cats together, look at
the sparks, it's nice in the dark, it's a pity to go to sleep, and
he hanging his jacket on the back of a chair, going over to the
teddy bear huddled by the fireplace, taking off his shoes be-

side her, crouching down to sit facing the fire, watching the
light and shadows run across her loose hair, helping her take
her blouse off, looking for the catch on her bra, his mouth
against her naked shoulder now, his hands searching among
the sparks, snot-nosed little girl, silly little bear, at some moment both of them naked now standing in front of the fire
and kissing, the bed cold, white and suddenly nothing now, a
total fire running over his skin, Lina's mouth on his hair,
on his chest, her hands on his back, the bodies letting themselves be borne off and known and only a moan, an anxious
breathing and having to ask her because that did have to be
asked, before the fire and sleep he had to ask her, Lina, you're
not doing this out of thanks are you, and the hands lost on his
back coming up like whiplashes to his face, his throat, squeezing it furiously, inoffensively, sweetly and furiously, tiny and
wrathfully dug in, a moan of protest and denial, a rage too in
her voice, how can you, how can you, Marcelo, and if that's it,
then yes, everything fine like that, I'm sorry, love, I'm sorry I
had to ask you, I'm sorry sweet, I'm sorry, the mouths, the
other fire, the caresses with pink edges, the bubble that trem-
bles between the lips, phases of the knowledge, silences in
which everything is skin or the slow running along of hair, a
wave of eyelids, denial and demand, a bottle of mineral water
drunk from the neck which is passed from one mouth to another to quench a single thirst, ending in the fingers that feel
on the night table, that light, there's that gesture of covering
the lampshade with a slip, with anything, of gilding the air
in order to start looking at Lina from behind, at the teddy
bear beside him, the cub face down, Lina's tender skin that
asks him for a cigarette, that sits against the pillows, you're so
bony and hairy, Shepp, wait till I cover you a little if I can
find the bedspread, look at it there by your feet, I think the
edges have been singed, Shepp.

Then the slow, low fire in the fireplace, in them, growing smaller and golden, the water drunk now, the cigarettes, university courses were a pain, it was so boring, I learned the best things in cafés, reading before going to the movies, talking to Cecilia and Perucho, and he hearing her, the Rubí, so likely like the Rubí twenty years earlier, Arlt and Rilke and Eliot and Borges, except that Lina yes, she yes in her hitchhiking windjammer, in her day's sail in Renault or Volkswagen, the teddy bear among dry leaves and rain on the bangs, but why so much windjammer and so much Rubí again, she doesn't know any of it, hadn't even been born, snotnosed little Chilean girl vagabond Copenhagen, why from the beginning, from the soup and white wine going along dragging so many things past and lost out of his face, so many buried dogs, so many windjammers for six hundred pesos, Lina looking at him from half-sleep, slipping down on the pillows with the sigh of a satisfied animal, searching his face with her hands, I like you, bones, you've read every book there is, Shepp, I mean it's nice with you, you're up on everything, you've got those big strong hands, you've got life behind you, you're not old. So the teddy bear felt he was alive in spite of, more alive than people her age, the corpses from the Romero movie and who could that be under the bangs where the little theater damp now slid into sleep, eyes rolling and looking at him, taking her softly one more time, feeling her and letting her go at the same time, listening to her purr of half-protest, I'm sleepy, Marcelo, not like that, yes, my love, yes, her light hard body, the tense thighs, the attack returned duplicated without pause, no longer Marlene in Brussels, the women like him, paused and assured, with all books read, she the teddy bear, her way of receiving his strength and answering it but afterward still on the edge of that wind full of rain and shouts, slipping in turn into half-sleep, realizing that this too was windjammer and Copenhagen, his face sunk between Lina's breasts was the face of the Rubí, the first adolescent nights with Mabel or with Nélida in the apartment borrowed from Monk, the furious and elastic waves and almost immediately why don't we go out and walk around downtown, give me the candy, if Mama ever found out.

Then not even like that, not even in love could he get rid of that rearview mirror, the old portrait of his young self that Lina put in front of him by stroking him and Shepp and let's go to sleep now and a little more water please; like having been her, from her in every thing, unbearably absurd irreversible and finally sleep amidst the last murmured caresses and all the teddy bear's fur brushing his face as if something in her knew, as if she were trying to erase him so that he would wake up Marcelo again, as he woke up at nine o'clock and Lina on the sofa was combing her hair humming, already dressed for another highway and another rainstorm. They didn't talk too much, it was a brief breakfast and the sun was out, several miles from Kindberg they stopped to have some more coffee, Lina four lumps and her face as if washed, absent, a kind of abstract happiness, and then you know, don't get angry, tell me that you're not going to get angry, but of course not, tell me anything, if you need anything, stopping just short of the cliché because the word had been there like the bills in his wallet, waiting to be used and already on the verge of being spoken when Lina's timid hand in his, the bangs covering her eyes and finally asking him if she could go on a little farther with him even if it wasn't the same route, what difference did it make, going on a little more with him because it felt so good, letting it go on a little longer with this sun, we'll sleep in the woods, I'll show you the record and the sketches, only until nighttime if you want, and feeling that yes, that he wanted to, that there was no reason for him not to want to, and slowly pushing her hand away and telling her no, best not to, you know, you'll find it easy here, it's an important crossroads, and the teddy bear accepting as if suddenly beaten and distant, eating the sugar lumps head down, watching him paying and getting up and bringing her the knapsack and kissing her on the hair and turning his back on her and getting lost in a furious shifting of gears, thirty, fifty, sixty, a route wide open for a salesman of prefabricated materials, a route without Copenhagen and full only of rotting windjammers along the curb, of jobs that paid better and better, of the Buenos Aires gossip about the Rubí, of the shadow of the solitary plane tree at the curve, the trunk against which he was squashed at eighty miles an hour with his head bent over the steering wheel the way Lina had lowered her head a few minutes ago because a bear cub always lowers its head like that to eat sugar.

SECOND
TIME
AROUND

We just waited for them, each one had his date and his time, but there was no rush about it, smoking slowly, every so often Nigger López would come by with coffee and then we'd stop working and talk about what was new, almost always the same things, the boss's visit, the changes higher up, the races at San Isidro. They, of course, had no way of knowing that we were waiting for them, what's called waiting, things like that had to happen without making waves, you people go ahead without worrying, the boss's word, he would repeat it every so often just in case, you people just go ahead nice and easy, when you come down to it, it was easy, if there was a slip they wouldn't take it out on us, the ones responsible were higher up and the boss was okay, just rest easy, boys, if there's any trouble here I'll take the responsibility, the only thing I ask is that you don't get your subjects mixed up on me, an investigation first so you don't get involved where you shouldn't, and then you can go right ahead.

Frankly, they weren't any trouble, the boss had picked out functional offices so that there wouldn't be any crowding, and we received them one at a time, as it should be, with all the time necessary. Nobody with better manners than us, eh, the boss would say from time to time, and it was true, everything was synchronized in a way that would put I.B.M. to shame, things worked Vaseline-smooth here, no getting your piss hot or getting ahead of yourself. We had time for coffee and picking Sunday's races, and the boss was the first to come by to get the sure things because in that business Slats Bianchetti was a regular oracle. So the same thing every day, we'd arrive with the newspapers, Nigger López would bring the first round of coffee, and in a little while they would begin to come by for the procedure. The summons said that, a procedure which concerns you, and us, just there waiting. Now this is important, even if it is written on yellow paper, a summons always has a serious look about it; that's why María Elena had looked at it several times at home, the green stamp around the illegible signature and the date and the place. She took it out of her purse again on the bus and wound her watch just to be safe. They were summoning her to an office on the Calle Maza, it was strange that there should be a ministry there but her sister had told her that they were setting up offices all over because the ministries didn't have enough room anymore, and as soon as she got off the bus she saw that it must have been true, the neighborhood was like any other, with three- or four-story houses and most of all a lot of retail stores, even some of the few trees left in the district.

At least it most likely will have a flag, María Elena thought as she approached the seven-hundred block; it was probably like the embassies, which were in residential districts but could be spotted from a distance by the colored piece of cloth over one of the balconies. Although the number stood out quite clearly on the summons, she was surprised not to see the national flag and for a moment she stood on the corner (she was early, there was plenty of time) and for no particular reason she asked the man in the newsstand if the government office was on that block.

"Yes, indeed," the man said, "down there in the middle of the block, but first why don't you keep me company for a little while; see how all alone I am."

"On the way back." María Elena smiled at him, going away in no hurry and consulting the yellow paper once more. There was almost no traffic and not many people, a cat in front of a grocery store and a fat lady with a little girl coming out of a doorway. The few cars were parked by the government office, almost all of them with someone behind the wheel reading the newspaper or smoking. The entrance was narrow, like all those on the block, with a majolica-tile passageway and a stairway in the rear; the plaque on the door looked like one for a doctor or a dentist, that was all, dirty, and with a piece of paper pasted over the bottom part to cover that line of the inscription. It was strange that there was no elevator, a third-floor walkup after that paper which was so serious with its green stamp and signature and everything.

The door on the third floor was closed and she didn't see any bell or plaque. María Elena tried the knob and the door opened noiselessly; the tobacco smoke reached her before she saw the greenish tiles of the hallway and the benches on both sides with people sitting on them. There weren't many, but with that smoke and such a narrow hallway their knees seemed to be touching, the two old ladies, the bald man, and the boy with the green necktie. They obviously had been chatting in order to kill time, for just as she opened the door María Elena caught the tail end of a phrase from one of the ladies, but, as always, they fell silent almost immediately as they looked at the latest arrival, and also as always and feeling so foolish, María Elena blushed and was barely able to raise enough voice for a good-morning as she stood there by the door until the boy signaled to her, pointing to the empty space on the bench next to him. Precisely as she sat down, thanking him, the door at the other end of the corridor opened to let out a redheaded man who made his way between the knees of the others without taking the trouble to excuse himself. The clerk held the door open with his foot, waiting until one of the two ladies got up with difficulty and, begging their pardon, passed between María Elena and the bald man; the exit door and the office door closed at almost the same time, and those left began to chat again, stretching a little and making the benches creak.

Each one had his or her theme as always: the bald man about the slowness of the procedures, since this is my first time, what can I expect, tell me, over half an hour wasted for what in the end will probably be four or five questions and so long, at least that's what I imagine.

"Don't you believe it," said the boy with the green tie, "it's my second time and I can assure you that it's not so short, with everything that has to be typed up and some guy who can't remember a date, things like that, it ends up lasting quite a while."

The bald man and the old lady listened with interest because it was obviously the first time for them, the same as for María Elena, although she didn't feel she had the right to join in the conversation. The bald man wanted to know how

much time there was between the first and the second summons, and the boy explained that in his case it had been three
days. But why two summonses, María Elena wanted to ask,
and once more she felt the color rising to her cheeks and
she waited for someone to talk to her and give her confidence,
let her form part of the group, not be the last one anymore.
The old lady had taken out a small vial with salts or something in it and took a whiff, breathing in deeply. It might
have been all the smoke that was upsetting her, and the boy
offered to put his cigarette out and the bald man said of
course, this hallway was a disgrace, they'd better put out their
cigarettes if she wasn't feeling well, but the woman said no,
just a touch of fatigue that will go away immediately, her
husband and sons smoked all the time at home, I practically
don't notice it anymore. María Elena, who had also had the
urge to take out a cigarette, saw that the men were putting
theirs out, that the boy was crushing his against the sole of his
shoe: people always smoke too much when they have to wait,
the last time it had been worse because there were seven or
eight people then and in the end you couldn't see a thing in
the hallway with so much smoke.

"Life is a waiting room," said the bald man, carefully
stepping on his cigarette and looking at his hands as if he
didn't know what to do with them, and the old lady sighed an
agreement of many years' standing and put away the vial precisely as the door opened and the other lady came out with
that air they all envied, the almost compassionate good-bye as
she reached the exit door. It doesn't take so long after all,
María Elena thought, three people ahead of her, let's say
three-quarters of an hour; of course, in any one of the cases
the procedure might take longer than in the others, the boy
had already been there a first time and had said so. But when
the bald man went into the office, María Elena got up the

courage to ask in order to feel more secure, and the boy thought for a while and then said that the first time some had taken a long time and others less, you never could tell. The old lady called attention to the fact that the other lady had come out almost at once, but that the redheaded gentleman had been in there for an eternity.

"It's good there are only a few of us left," María Elena said. "These places are depressing."

"You have to be philosophical about it," the boy said. "Don't forget that you're going to have to come back, so you might as well relax. When I came the first time there was no one to talk to, there was a whole bunch of us but, I don't know, no one hit it off, and today, on the other hand, the time has passed nicely from the moment I got here because ideas have been exchanged."

María Elena enjoyed chatting with the boy and the lady; she almost didn't feel the time passing until the bald man came out and the lady got up with a rapidity that one wouldn't have expected at her age. The poor thing probably wanted to get the procedure over with quickly.

"Well, just us now," the boy said. "Would it bother you if I smoked a cigarette? I can't take it anymore, but the lady there seemed so upset . . ."

"I feel like a smoke too."

She accepted the cigarette he offered her and they exchanged names, where they worked; it did them good to swap impressions and forget about the hallway, the silence that seemed too heavy at times, as if the streets and people had been left far behind. María Elena had also lived in Floresta, but when she was a child; now she lived in Constitución. Carlos didn't like that section, he preferred the west side; the air is cleaner, there are trees. His ideal would be to live in Villa del Parque; when he got married he'd probably rent an apartment over there, his future father-in-law had promised to help him, he was a man with a lot of connections and he could get something through one of them.

"I don't know why, but something tells me I'm going to spend the rest of my life in Constitución," María Elena said. "It's not so bad, after all. And if sometime . . ."

She saw the door in the rear open and she was almost surprised as she looked at the boy, who smiled at her as he got up, see how time flies when you talk, the lady gave them a friendly nod, she seemed so happy to be leaving, everyone had a younger, more agile look when they left, as if a weight had been lifted from them, the procedure over, one thing less to do and outside the street, the cafés, where they would probably go to have a drink or a cup of tea in order to feel that they were really on the other side of the waiting room and the forms. Now time would drag for María Elena, all alone; although if it kept on like that Carlos would come out fairly soon, but some took longer than others because it was the second time around and who could say what complications there might be.

She almost didn't understand at first when she saw the door open and the clerk looked at her and nodded for her to come in. She thought that's how it is, then, that Carlos would have to stay a while longer filling out forms and in the meantime they would take care of her. She nodded to the clerk and went into the office; scarcely had she gone through the door when another clerk pointed to a chair in front of a black desk. There were several people in the office, only men, but she didn't see Carlos. From the other side of the desk a clerk with a sickly face was looking at a form; without raising his eyes he held out his hand and it took María Elena an instant to realize he was asking for the summons; she suddenly understood and looked for it, a little flustered, murmuring excuses. She took two or three things out of her purse until she found the piece of yellow paper.

"Start filling this out," the clerk said, handing her a form. "Print it in capital letters, nice and clear."

It was the usual nonsense, first and last name, sex, address. In between two words María Elena got the feeling that something was bothering her, something that wasn't completely clear. Not on the form, where it was easy to go along filling in the blanks; something outside it, something that was missing or wasn't in its place. She stopped writing and took a look around, the other desks with the clerks working or talking among themselves, the dirty walls with posters and photographs, the two windows, the door she had come through, the only door in the office. *Profession*, and next to it the dotted line; she automatically filled in the blank. The only door in the office, but Carlos wasn't there. *Length of time in job*. Capital letters, nice and clear.

When she signed at the bottom, the clerk was looking at her as if she had taken too long in filling out the form. He studied the paper for a moment, found no errors, and put it into a folder. The rest consisted of questions, some of them unnecessary because she had answered them on the form, but about her family too, moves over the past years, insurance, whether she took many trips and where to, whether she had taken out a passport or was planning to. No one seemed very interested in the answers; in any case, the clerk didn't write them down. Suddenly he told María Elena that she could leave but to come back in three days at eleven o'clock; there was no need for a written summons, but she wasn't to forget.

"Yes, sir," María Elena said, getting up. "Thursday at eleven, then."

There was no one in the hallway, and going along it was just as it had been for all the others, a haste, a lightness in her breathing, the urge to get out onto the street and leave the other thing behind. María Elena opened the exit door and as she started down the stairs she thought of Carlos again; it was strange that Carlos hadn't come out like the others. It was strange because the office had only one door, of course at some moment she may not have taken a good look because it couldn't be, the clerk had opened the door for her to come in and Carlos hadn't passed her, he hadn't come out first like all the others, the redheaded man, the ladies, everybody except Carlos.

The sun broke against the sidewalk, it was the noise and the smell of the street; María Elena walked a few steps and stopped, standing by a tree at a spot where no cars were parked. She looked back at the door of the building, told herself that she was going to wait for a moment to see Carlos come out. It was impossible for Carlos not to come out, they'd all left after the procedure was over. She thought that he was probably taking longer because he was the only one who had come for a second time; who knows, that must have been it. It seemed so strange not seeing him in the office, although there probably was a door hidden behind the posters, something she'd missed, but just the same it was strange because everybody had gone out through the hallway like her, all those who had come for the first time had left through the hallway.

Before leaving (she had waited a while, but she couldn't stay there any longer), she thought about the fact that she had to come back on Thursday. Maybe things would be different then and they would have her go out through the other side, although she didn't know where or why. Not her, no, of course, but us, yes, we knew, and we'd be waiting for her and the others, smoking slowly and chatting while Nigger López brewed another of the many rounds of morning coffee.

SEVERO'S PHASES

IN MEMORIAM
REMEDIOS VARO

Everything was sort of quiet, sort of frozen in some way into its own movement, odor, and form, which went on and varied along with the smoke and the soft talk between cigarettes and drinks. Bebe Pessoa had already given out three sure things for the track at San Isidro; Severo's sister was sewing the four coins into the corners of the handkerchief for when sleep overcame Severo. There weren't so many of us but suddenly a house becomes small, between two phrases the transparent cube of two or three seconds of suspension appears, and at moments like that some must have felt like me that all of that, necessary as it might have been, was hurting us because of Severo, Severo's wife, and the friends of so many years.

We'd arrived about eleven at night with Ignacio, Bebe Pessoa, and my brother Carlos. We were kind of family, especially Ignacio, who worked in the same office as Severo, and we came in without anyone's paying too much attention to us. Severo's elder son asked us to go into the bedroom, but Ignacio said that we'd stay in the dining room a while; there were people everywhere in the house, friends or relatives who didn't want to be a bother either and were sitting in corners or gathering beside a table or sideboard to talk or look at each other. Every so often Severo's children or sister would bring coffee and glasses of cane liquor, and at those moments everything would almost always quiet down as if it were freezing into its own movement and in one's memory the idiotic phrase "an angel passing over" began to flutter. But even though afterward I'd comment about a double win by Nigger Acosta at Palermo track or Ignacio would stroke the hair of Severo's younger son, we all felt that underneath everything the immobility persisted, that we were sort of waiting for things that had already happened or that all that could happen was something else perhaps or nothing, as in dreams, even though we were awake and from time to time, without wanting to listen, we heard Severo's wife weeping, almost timidly, in a corner of the room where the closest relatives must have been with her.

You go along forgetting what time it is in cases like that, or as Bebe Pessoa said laughing, it's just the opposite and time forgets you, but in a little while Severo's brother came over to say that the sweating was going to start and we stubbed out our butts and began going into the bedroom one by one, where almost all of us fit because the family had taken out the furniture and there was nothing left but the bed and a night table. Severo was sitting up in bed, supported by the pillows, and a blue serge coverlet and a pale blue towel could be seen at his feet. There was no need to be silent and Severo's brothers with cordial gestures (they're all such nice people) invited us to come closer to the bed, to surround Severo, who had his hands crossed on his knees. Even the younger son, so tiny, was now beside the bed looking at his father with a dream face.

The sweat phase was disagreeable because at the end it was necessary to change the sheets and his pajamas; even the pillows were becoming soaked and were heavy, like enormous tears. Unlike others, who tended to become impatient, Severo remained motionless, not even looking at us, and almost at once the sweat covered his face and hands. His knees stood out like two dark splotches; even though his sister kept drying the sweat on his cheeks, the perspiration would break out again and fall onto the sheet.

"Actually, that's very good," insisted Ignacio, who'd stayed near the door. "It would be worse if he moved, the sheets stick something fierce."

"Papa is a calm man," Severo's elder son said. "He's not the kind to cause people trouble."

"It's ending now," said Severo's wife, who'd come in at the end and was carrying clean pajamas and a set of sheets. I think all of us without exception admired her more than ever at that moment because we knew that she'd been weeping a short time before and now she was capable of attending to her husband with a calm and peaceful, even energetic, face. I suppose that some of the relatives said words of encouragement to Severo; I was in the entranceway once more and the younger daughter was offering me a cup of coffee. I would have liked to have engaged her in conversation to take her mind off things, but other people came in and Manuelita is a little timid: she'd probably think I'm interested in her and I prefer to remain neutral. On the other hand, Bebe Pessoa is the kind who comes and goes through the house and among people like nothing, and he, Ignacio, and Severo's brother had already formed a group with some girl cousins and their friends, talking about brewing up some bitter maté, which at that hour would be more than welcome because it would settle the roast. As it turned out they couldn't, because at one of those moments when we suddenly remained motionless (I insist that nothing was changing, we were still talking and gesticulating, but that's how it was and somehow it's necessary to say it and give it a reason or a name) Severo's brother came with an acetylene lantern and from the door advised us that the phase of leaps was going to begin. Ignacio drank down his coffee in one gulp and said that everything that night seemed to be moving faster; he was one of those who placed himself near the bed, with Severo's wife and the smallest child, who was laughing because Severo's right hand was oscillating like a metronome. His wife had dressed him in white pajamas and the bed was impeccable again; we smelled the cologne and Bebe gave an admiring look to Manuelita, who must have thought of it. Severo took the first leap and remained sitting on the edge of the bed, looking at his sister, who was encouraging him with a somewhat stupid and circumstantial smile. What need was there for that, I thought, as one who prefers things neat; and what difference could it make to Severo whether his sister encouraged him or not. The leaps followed each other rhythmically: sitting on the edge of the bed, sitting against the headboard, sitting on the opposite side, standing in the middle of the bed, standing on the floor between Ignacio and Bebe, squatting on the floor between his wife and his brother, sitting in the corner of the doorway, standing in the center of the room, always between two friends or relatives, falling precisely into the empty spaces as nobody moved and only eyes followed him, sitting on the edge of the bed, standing against the headboard, squatting in the middle of the bed, kneeling between his younger son and me, sitting at the foot of the bed. When Severo's wife announced the end of the phase, everyone began to talk at the same time and congratulate Severo, who seemed as though he hadn't been there; I can no longer remember who accompanied him back to the bed because we all went out at the same time, commenting on the phase and looking for something to calm our thirst, and I went out into the courtyard with Bebe to breathe the night air and drink two beers from the bottle.

There was a change in the next phase, I remember, because according to Ignacio it was to be the watch one but we heard Severo's wife weeping again in the living room and almost at once the elder son came to tell us that the moths were already starting to come in. We exchanged slightly puzzled looks with Bebe and Ignacio, but it wasn't impossible for there to be changes and Bebe said the usual thing about the order of factors and things like that; I don't think anybody liked the change but we hid it as we went in again and formed a circle around Severo's bed, which the family had placed in the center of the bedroom.

Severo's brother came last with the acetylene lantern, turned off the spider-legged chandelier on the ceiling and brought the night table over to the foot of the bed; when he put the lantern on the night table we fell silent and motionless, looking at Severo, who had half sat up between the pillows and didn't seem too tired out from the previous phases. The moths began to come in through the door, and the ones that were already on the walls or the ceiling joined the others and began to fly around the acetylene lantern. With his eyes very wide Severo followed the ash-colored whirlwind that kept growing and he seemed to be concentrating all his strength in that unblinking contemplation. One of the moths (it was quite large, I think that it really was a great moth, but in that phase only miller moths were mentioned and no one would have argued over the name) broke away from the others and flew to Severo's face; we saw that it was clinging to his right cheek and that Severo closed his eyes for an instant. One after another the moths abandoned the lantern and flew around Severo, clinging to his hair, his mouth, and his forehead until they had transformed him into an enormous trembling mask in which only the eyes were his and these stared at the acetylene lantern, which one moth insisted on whirling around looking for an entry. I felt Ignacio's fingers digging into my forearm, and only then did I realize that I too was trembling and had a hand sunk into Bebe's shoulder. Someone moaned, a woman, probably Manuelita, who couldn't control herself as well as the others, and at that same instant the last moth flew to Severo's face and was lost in the gray mass. We all shouted at once, embracing and clapping each other on the back while Severo's brother ran to turn on the chandelier; a cloud of moths sluggishly sought the way out and Severo, Severo's face once more, continued looking at the now useless lantern and cautiously moved his lips as if he were afraid of poisoning himself with the silver powder that covered them.

I didn't stay there because they had to wash Severo and somebody was already talking about a bottle of grappa in the kitchen, apart from the fact that in cases like that it's surprising how a sudden falling back into normality, to put it that way, can distract and even deceive a person. I followed Ignacio, who knew all the nooks and crannies, and we latched on to the grappa with Bebe and Severo's elder son. My brother Carlos had lain down on a bench and was smoking with his head tilted to one side, breathing heavily; I brought him a glass and he swallowed it in one gulp. Bebe Pessoa was insisting that Manuelita have a drink, and he was even talking to her about movies and racing; I was putting away one grappa after another, not wanting to think about anything, until I couldn't take it anymore and looked for Ignacio, who seemed to be waiting for me with his arms folded.

"If the last moth had chosen . . ." I began.

Ignacio shook his head negatively. Of course, there was no reason to ask; at least at that moment there was no reason to ask; I don't know if I understood completely, but I had the feeling of a great hollow, something like an empty crypt that was slowly throbbing in some part of my memory with the drip-drip of filtration. In Ignacio's negation (from a distance it had looked to me as if Bebe Pessoa was also shaking his head, and that Manuelita was looking at us anxiously, too timid to say no in turn) there was a kind of suspension of judgment, a not wanting to go further; things were therefore in their absolute present, as they were happening. Then we could go on and when Severo's wife came into the kitchen to tell us that Severo was going to say the numbers, we left our glasses half-finished and made haste, Manuelita between Bebe and me, Ignacio behind, with my brother Carlos, who's always late wherever he goes.

The relatives had already crowded into the bedroom and there wasn't much space to be found. I was just coming in (the acetylene lantern was burning on the floor beside the bed now, but the chandelier was still lighted) when Severo rose up, put his hands in his pajama pockets, and, looking at his elder son, said: "6," looking at his wife, said: "20," looking at Ignacio, said: "23," with a voice that was tranquil and from beneath, without hurrying. To his sister he said 16, to his younger son 28, to other relatives he went along saying numbers that were almost always high, until he told me 2 and

I felt Bebe looking at me out of the corner of his eye and tightening his lips, waiting his turn. But Severo went on to say numbers to other relatives and friends, almost always higher than 5 and without ever repeating them. Almost at the end he said 14 to Bebe, and Bebe opened his mouth and shuddered, as if a great wind had passed between his eyebrows, rubbed his hands, and then was ashamed and hid them in the pockets of his pants precisely as Severo said 1 to a woman with a very ruddy face, probably a distant relative who had come alone and who had spoken to practically no one that night, and suddenly Ignacio and Bebe were looking at each other and Manuelita leaned against the doorframe and it looked to me as if she were trembling, holding back a scream. The rest were no longer paying attention to their numbers, Severo was saying them just the same, but they were beginning to talk, even Manuelita when she recovered and took two steps forward and got 9; no one was interested anymore and the numbers ended with a hollow 24 and a 12 that were for a relative and my brother Carlos; Severo himself seemed less concentrated and with the last one he flung himself backward and let himself be covered by his wife, closing his eyes like a person who is losing interest or forgetting.

"It's a question of time, of course," Ignacio told me as we were leaving the bedroom. "The numbers by themselves have no meaning, you know."

"Do you think so?" I asked him, swallowing the drink that Bebe had brought me.

"But of course," Ignacio said. "Just remember that years can pass between 1 and 2, make it ten or twenty, even more, perhaps, it's a matter of chance."

"Of course," Bebe backed him up. "I wouldn't let it bother me if I were you."

I thought how he had brought me the glass without anyone's asking him, taking the trouble to go to the kitchen with all those people. And he had got 14 and Ignacio 23.

"Not to mention that there's the watch business," my brother Carlos said, having come up beside me and resting his hand on my shoulder. "That's not too easily understood, but it probably has its importance. If it's your turn to fall behind . . ."

"An added advantage," Bebe said, taking the empty glass from my hand as if fearing I would drop it.

We were in the entranceway next to the bedroom and that's how we were among the first to go in when Severo's elder son came to tell us just then that the watch phase was beginning. It seemed to me that Severo's face had suddenly become thin, but his wife had just combed his hair and he smelled of cologne again, which always imparts confidence. I was surrounded by my brother, Ignacio, and Bebe, as if watching over my spirits, and, on the other hand, no one was concerned about the woman relative who had drawn 1 and was at the foot of the bed, her face redder than ever, her mouth and eyelids trembling. Without even looking at her, Severo told his elder son to advance and the kid didn't understand and began to laugh until his mother grabbed him by the arm and took off his wristwatch. We knew that it was a symbolic gesture, all that was necessary was to advance or retard the hands without looking at the hours or minutes, since on leaving the room we would reset our watches to the correct time. Several had already been set ahead or back, Severo was distributing the indications almost mechanically, without taking any interest; when it was my turn to retard, my brother sank his fingers into my shoulder again; this time I thanked him, thinking like Bebe that it might be an added advantage, although nobody could be sure; and also the relative with the red face drew retarding, and the poor woman was drying tears of gratitude, perhaps completely useless after all's said and done, and she was going into the courtyard to have a good nervous attack among the potted plants; something we heard later from the kitchen in the midst of some fresh drinks of grappa and the congratulations of Ignacio and my brother.

"The dream will be soon," Manuelita told us. "Mama says to get ready."

There wasn't much to getting ready: we went slowly back to the bedroom, dragging along the fatigue of the night; soon it would be dawn and it was a working day, our jobs were waiting for most of us at nine or nine thirty; suddenly it was growing colder, the icy breeze in the courtyard coming in through the entranceway, but in the bedroom the lights and the people warmed up the air, there was almost no talking and all we had to do was find room, place ourselves around the bed after putting out our cigarettes. Severo's wife was sitting on the bed, straightening the pillows, but she got up and stood by the head; Severo was looking up, ignoring us, he was looking at the lighted chandelier without blinking, his hands resting on his belly, motionless and indifferent he was looking without blinking at the lighted chandelier and then Manuelita came over to the edge of the bed and we all saw the handkerchief with the coins sewn into the four corners in her hand. There was nothing to do but wait, almost sweating in that close, hot air, thankful for the cologne and thinking about the moment when we would finally be able to leave the house and smoke and talk in the street, discussing or not what happened that night, probably not, but smoking until we were lost at the corner. When Severo's eyelids began to lower slowly, slowly erasing the image of the lighted chandelier, I heard Bebe Pessoa's deep breathing near my ear. There was a sudden change, a loosening, it could be felt as if we were nothing but a single body with countless arms and legs and heads suddenly becoming loose, understanding that it was the end, Severo's dream was beginning, and Manuelita's gesture as she leaned over her father and covered his face with the handkerchief, using the four corners to hold it naturally, without wrinkles or small uncovered spaces, was the same as that contained sigh which enveloped all of us, covered us with the same handkerchief.

"And now he's going to sleep," Severo's wife said. "He's already sleeping, look."

Severo's sister had put a finger to her lips but there was no need, no one would have said anything, we were beginning to move on tiptoe, leaning on one another so as to leave without any noise. Some were still looking back at the handkerchief on Severo's face as if wanting to be sure that Severo was asleep. Against my right hand, I felt stiff and curly hair; it was Severo's younger son, whom a relative had held close to him so that he wouldn't talk or move, and who had come to cling to me now, trying to walk on tiptoe and looking at me from below with questioning and sleepy eyes. I stroked his chin, his cheeks, bringing him along beside me into the entranceway and the courtyard, between Ignacio and Bebe, who were already taking out their packs of cigarettes; the gray of dawn with a rooster out there in the depths was bringing each one of us back to his life, to the future already set up in that grayness and that cold, horribly beautiful. I thought of Severo's wife and Manuelita (maybe the brothers and the elder son), who stayed inside keeping watch over Severo's dream, but we were on our way to the street already, leaving the kitchen and the courtyard behind.

"Aren't you going to play anymore?" Severo's son asked me, dropping with sleepiness but with the obstinacy all kids have.

"No, it's time to get some sleep now," I told him. "Your mother'll put you to bed, get back inside, it's cold."

"It was a game, wasn't it, Julio?"

"Yes, old fellow, it was a game. Go get some sleep now."

With Ignacio, Bebe, and my brother, we reached the first corner, we lighted another cigarette without saying much. Others were already walking far off, some were still standing by the door of the house, talking about trolley cars or taxis; we knew the neighborhood well, we could go on together for the first few blocks, then Bebe and my brother would turn to the left, Ignacio would continue on for a few blocks more, and I would go up to my place and put the kettle on for some maté; after all, it wasn't worth going to bed for such a short time, it would be better to put on my slippers and smoke and drink some maté, things like that, which help.

BUTTERBALL'S NIGHT

It was typical of Peralta, that idea. Generally he would barely
give any explanation to anybody, but this time he opened up
a little more and said it was like the tale of the purloined
letter. Estévez didn't understand at first and stood looking at
him waiting for more; Peralta shrugged his shoulders like
someone giving up something and handed him the ticket to
the fight. Estévez saw a big number 3 in red on a yellow
background and underneath it 235; but then, from the beginning, how could he miss those letters that leaped before
his eyes, MONZÓN vs. NÁPOLES. They'll get the other ticket to
Walter, Peralta said. You'll be there before the fights start
(he never repeated instructions, and Estévez listened so he

could retain each phrase) and Walter will arrive in the middle of the first preliminary, he's got the seat to your right. Watch out for people who get sharp at the last minute and start looking for a better seat, say something in Spanish to him to be sure. He'll come with one of those bags hippies carry, he'll put it down between the two of you if it's a bench or on the floor if they're chairs. Don't talk to him about anything except the fights and take a good look around you, there are sure to be Mexicans or Argentines, have them spotted when you put the package in the bag. Does Walter know that his bag has to be open, Estévez asked. Yes, Peralta said as if brushing a fly from his lapel, only wait till the main bout when nobody will be looking around. It's hard to look around with Monzón, Estévez said. Or with Butterball either, said Peralta. No chatting, remember. Walter will leave first, let the people start leaving, and you go out a different door.

He thought about all that as in a final review while the Métro took him to Défense among passengers who, from their looks, were also going to the fight, men in threes and fours, Frenchmen bearing the scars of the double beating Monzón had given Bouttier, seeking a vicarious revenge or maybe now secretly won over. What a stroke of genius of Peralta's, giving him that mission, which must be critical, coming from him, and at the same time letting him watch a fight that seemed to have been put together for millionaires. Now he understood the allusion to the purloined letter, who would ever have thought that Walter and he could meet at the fights, it really wasn't a question of a meeting because that could have happened in a thousand crannies in Paris, but of the responsibility of Peralta, who weighed everything very slowly. For those who might be following Walter or following him, a movie theater or a café or an apartment was a possible meeting place, but that fight was like an obligation for anyone who had the money, and if they followed him there they'd be fucking well disappointed in the circus tent set up by Alain Delon; no one could get in there without the little yellow piece of paper, and tickets had been sold out a week ahead of time, all the papers said so. Even more in Peralta's favor, if they got there by following him or following Walter, it would be impossible to see them together either going in or coming out, two fans among thousands and thousands pouring like mouthfuls of smoke out of subways and buses, clogging up, bit by bit, as the paths merged and the hour approached.

No fool, Alain Delon: a circus tent set up on a vacant lot that was reached by going over a footbridge and following some walkways improvised out of boards. It had rained the night before and the people didn't leave the boards, guiding themselves from the subway exit by the huge arrows that showed the right direction and MONZÓN-NÁPOLES in bright colors. No fool, Alain Delon, capable of putting up his own arrows in the sacred territory of the Métro even if it cost him money. Estévez didn't like the guy, that overbearing way of organizing the world championship on his own, setting up a tent and paying who knows what and how much dough in advance, but you had to hand it to him, he gave you something in exchange, let's not talk about Monzón and Butterball but also the colored arrows in the subway, that way of receiving people like a lord, pointing the way for the fans who would have been confused at the exits and in those vacant lots all full of puddles.

Estévez arrived as he was supposed to, with the tent half-full, and before showing his ticket he stood for a moment looking at the police vans and the large trailers lighted up outside but with dark curtains on the windows, connected to the tent by covered passages, like the ones used to get onto an airplane. The fighters were there, Estévez thought, the newest white trailer most certainly belongs to Carlitos, you don't mix him in with the others. Nápoles would have his trailer on the other side of the tent, it was all scientific and, in passing, pure improvisation, lots of canvas and trailers on a vacant lot. That's how you make dough, Estévez thought, you've got to have big ideas and balls, by God.

His row, the fifth after the ringside section, was a plank with large numbers on it, Alain Delon's courtesy seemed to have ended there, because outside of the chairs at ringside the rest were circus accommodations and a bad circus, plain boards although there were usherettes in miniskirts who made you forget any complaints as soon as you came in. Estévez found 235 on his ticket, although the girl smiled, showing him the number as if he couldn't read, and he sat down to thumb through the newspaper that he would use later as a cushion. Walter would be on his right, and that's why Estévez had the package with the money and papers in the left pocket of his jacket; when the moment came he would take it out with his right hand, bringing it immediately toward his knees, and he would slip it into the open bag beside him.

The wait was getting long; there was time to think about Marisa and the kid, who were probably finishing dinner, the kid already half-asleep and Marisa watching television. They were probably televising the fight and she would see it, but he wasn't going to tell her where he'd been, at least he couldn't now, maybe someday when things had calmed down. He opened the paper listlessly (Marisa watching the fight, it was comical thinking that he wouldn't be able to tell her anything, with the great urge he had to tell her, especially if she said something to him about Monzón and Nápoles); in the midst of reports from Vietnam and the crime news the tent was filling up, a group of Frenchmen behind him were discussing Nápoles' chances, on his left a snob type was about to settle himself after having studied for a long time and with a kind of horror the bench on which he would have to rest his immaculate blue pants. Farther down there were couples and groups of friends and among them three who were talking in an accent that could have been Mexican; although Estévez wasn't much of an expert on accents, there must have been a lot of Butterball rooters there that night with the challenger aspiring to nothing less than taking Monzón's crown. Besides Walter's there were still a few empty places, but people were piling up at the entrances to the tent and the girls had to work extra hard to get everybody seated. Estévez found that the ring lights were too strong and the music too pop, but now that the first preliminary was starting the crowd didn't waste any time on criticisms and eagerly followed a bad match that was all butting and clinching; at the moment Walter sat down beside him Estévez was reaching the conclusion that this wasn't a real boxing crowd, at least those around him; they'd swallow anything out of snobbism just to see Monzón or Nápoles.

"Excuse me," Walter said, sitting down between Estévez and a fat woman who was following the fight half hugging her husband, who was also fat and had the look of someone who knew what was going on.

"Settle in," Estévez said. "It's not easy, these Frenchmen always calculate on places for skinny people."

Walter laughed as Estévez pushed gently to the left so as not to upset the man in blue pants; finally there was room for Walter to move the blue canvas bag from his knees to the plank. They were already into the second preliminary, which was also bad; the people were mostly amusing themselves with what was going on outside the ring, the arrival of a tight group of Mexicans with sombreros but dressed as what they must have been: big shots able to charter a plane to come from Mexico to root for Butterball, broad and chubby types with prominent asses and Pancho Villa faces, almost too typical when they threw their hats into the air as if Nápoles were already in the ring, shouting and arguing before they encrusted themselves into ringside seats. Alain Delon must have foreseen it all because the loudspeakers immediately blatted out a kind of corrido that the Mexicans didn't seem to recognize too well. Estévez and Walter looked at each other ironically, and at that moment in poured through the farther entrance a swarm of people headed by five or six women broader than they were tall, in white sweaters, with shouts of "Argentina, Argentina!" and brandishing an enormous blue and white flag. The group opened its way through usherettes and chairs, determined to advance to the edge of the ring, where their tickets were most certainly not valid. In the midst of delirious shouts they finally formed a line that the usherettes with the help of some smiling gorillas and many explanations led toward two half-empty planks, and Estévez saw that the women displayed a black MONZÓN on the back of each of their sweaters. It was all enjoyed considerably by an audience that cared little about the nationality of the pugilists since they weren't French, and the third prelim was going hard and fast although Alain Delon didn't seem to have spent much dough on the little fish when the two sharks were probably ready in their trailers and were the only thing the public cared about.

There was a kind of instantaneous charge in the air, something climbed up Estévez's throat; from the loudspeakers came a tango played by an orchestra that could well have been Pugliese's. Only then did Walter look at him face on and in a friendly way, and Estévez wondered if he might be a compatriot. They exchanged barely a word except for some comment having to do with the action in the ring, probably Uruguayan or Chilean, but no questions, Peralta had been quite clear about it, people meeting at the boxing match and chance has it that they both speak Spanish, enough said.

"Well, now's the time," Estévez said. Everybody was standing up in spite of the protests and the whistling, on the left a wild uproar and a flight of Mexican hats in the midst of applause, Butterball climbed into the ring, which suddenly seemed even brighter, people were looking to the right now, where nothing was going on, the applause gave way to a murmur of expectation and from their seats Walter and Estévez couldn't see the entrance to the other side of the ring, the near silence and suddenly clamor as the only signal, the white robe outlined suddenly against the ropes, Monzón showing his back, talking to his people, Nápoles going over to him, a quick greeting in the midst of flashbulbs and the referee waiting for the microphone to be lowered, people sitting back down little by little, one last sombrero flying far off, returned in the opposite direction out of pure fucking around, a tardy boomerang amidst the indifference because now introductions and greetings, Georges Carpentier, Nino Benvenuti, a French champion, Jean-Claude Bouttier, photographs and applause and the ring slowly emptying, the Mexican national anthem with more hats and finally the Argentine flag being unfurled to await its anthem, Estévez and Walter not standing up although it hurt Estévez, but this was no time to bungle anything, in any case it let him find out that he didn't have any compatriots too close by, the group with the flag was singing at the end of the anthem and the blue and white banner was waving in such a way that it made the gorillas run to that side just in case, the voice announcing names and weights, seconds out of the ring.

"Who do you like?" Estévez asked. He was nervous,

childishly worked up now that the gloves were touching in the initial greeting and Monzón, facing him, was using that guard that didn't look like a defense, his arms long and thin, an almost fragile silhouette opposite Butterball, shorter and more muscular, already letting go with two opening punches. "I've always liked challengers," Walter said, and in back a Frenchman explaining that the difference in height was going to favor Monzón, probing punches, Monzón going in and coming out effortlessly, the round almost had to be even. So he liked challengers, then he wasn't Argentine because otherwise; but the accent, he had to be Uruguayan, he'd ask Peralta, who certainly wouldn't answer him. In any case, he couldn't have been in France for long because the fat man embracing his wife had made some comment to him and Walter answered in such an incomprehensible way that the fat man made a gesture of discouragement and started talking to someone below. Nápoles hits hard, Estévez thought restlessly, twice he'd seen Monzón draw back and the response came a little late, he'd probably felt the blows. It was as if Butterball understood that his only chance was close in, sparring with Monzón wouldn't serve him the way it had always served him, his marvelous speed found a kind of emptiness, a torso that dodged and got away while the champion landed once, twice on the face and the Frenchman behind repeated anxiously, you see, you see how his arms are helping him, maybe the second round went to Nápoles, the people were quiet, every shout came out in isolation and was poorly received, in the third round Butterball gave everything he had and then the expected, Estévez thought, now they're going to see what's coming, Monzón against the ropes, a swaying willow, a one-two like a whiplash, the furious clinch to get off the ropes, a close-in hand-to-hand until the end of the round, the Mexicans up on their seats and the people behind hollering-protestsorstandingupinturntosee.

"Some fight, eh," Estévez said. "This is what makes it all worthwhile."

"Aha."

They took out cigarettes at the same time, exchanged them smiling, Walter's lighter was out first, Estévez looked at his profile for a minute, then he looked at him from the front, it wasn't a question of looking for long, Walter had graying hair but he looked rather young, with his blue jeans and brown polo shirt. Student, engineer? Pulling himself out from down there like so many others, getting into the struggle, with dead friends in Montevideo or Buenos Aires, who knows maybe Santiago, he'd have to ask Peralta, although after everything was over he certainly wouldn't see Walter again, each in his own way would remember some time that they'd met on Butterball's night, as he was going strong in the fifth round, with the crowd on its feet and delirious now, the Argentines and the Mexicans swept away by an enormous French wave that saw the fight more than the fighters, that spotted the reactions, the play of legs; finally Estévez realized that almost all of them really understood the thing, only from time to time some idiot applauding a showy punch that had no effect and he lost what was really happening in that ring, where Monzón was going in and coming out, taking advantage of his speed which more and more left Butterball standing, tired, hurt, fighting with everything he had against the long-armed willow who was once more rocking on the ropes to come in and attack again high and low, dry and precise. When the gong sounded Estévez looked at Walter, who took his cigarettes out again.

"Oh, well, that's the way it goes," Walter said, holding out the pack to him. "If it can't be done, it can't."

It was difficult to talk with all the shouting, the public knew that the next round might be the deciding one, Nápoles' fans were urging him on almost as if saying good-bye, Estévez thought with a sympathy that no longer went against his desire now that Monzón was looking for the fight and finding it and for twenty interminable seconds going for the face and the body while Butterball tried to clinch like someone diving into the water, closing his eyes. He can't take any more, Estévez thought, and with effort he took his eyes off the ring to look at the canvas bag on the plank, he would have to do it exactly between rounds when everyone was sitting down, exactly at that moment because afterward they would stand up again and once more the bag would be alone on the board, two lefts in a row to Nápoles' face as he tried to clinch again, Monzón out of range, hardly waiting to come back with an ultra-precise hook to the middle of the face, now the legs, you had to look especially at the legs, Estévez, an expert at that, was watching tired Butterball, throwing himself forward without that precision of his while Monzón's feet slid to the side or backward, the cadence perfect so that his last right would land with all it had full in the stomach. A lot of people didn't hear the bell in the hysterical clamor but Walter and Estévez did, Walter sat down first, straightening up the bag without looking at it and Estévez followed him more slowly, slipped in the package in a fraction of a second and raised his empty hand again to gesticulate his enthusiasm at the guy in the blue pants, who didn't seem to be very aware of what was going on.

"That's a champion," Estévez told him without forcing his voice, because in any case the other one wouldn't have heard him in all that noise. "Carlitos, God damn it."

He looked at Walter, who was peacefully smoking, the man was beginning to give up, what can you do, if it can't be done it can't. Everybody standing, waiting for the bell for the seventh round, a quick, incredulous silence and then the unanimous howl when they saw the towel on the canvas, Nápoles still in his corner and Monzón coming forward with his gloves held up, more champion than ever, waving before he got lost in the whirlwind of congratulations and flash-bulbs. It was an ending without beauty but it was incontest-able, Butterball quitting so he wouldn't be Monzón's punch-ing bag, all hope lost now that he was getting up to go over to the winner and lift his gloves to his face, almost a caress, while Monzón put his on his shoulders and they separated once more, now yes forever, Estévez thought, now never to meet again in a ring.

"It was a beautiful fight," he told Walter, who was sling-ing the bag over his shoulder and working his feet as if he had a cramp.

"It could have gone on longer," Walter said. "I'm sure that Nápoles' seconds wouldn't let him go out."

"What for? You could see he'd had it, eh, too much of a boxer not to realize it."

"Yes, but when you're like him you've got to go on to the end, finally you never know."

"With Monzón you do," Estévez said, and remembering Peralta's orders, he held out his hand cordially. "Well, it's been a pleasure."

"The same here. So long."

"Ciao."

He watched him go out on his side, following the fat man, who was arguing with his wife in shouts, and he stayed behind the guy in the blue pants, who wasn't in a hurry; little by little they headed toward the left to go out between the boards. The Frenchmen behind were arguing about tech-niques, but Estévez was amused to see one of the women embrace her boyfriend or her husband and kiss him on the mouth and on the neck. Unless the guy is an idiot, Estévez thought, he has to realize that she's kissing Monzón. The package no longer weighed in his jacket pocket, it was as if he could breathe better, be interested in what was going on, the girl hugging the guy, the Mexicans leaving with their sombreros, which suddenly seemed smaller, the Argentine flag half furled but still waving, the two fat Italians looking at each other with the air of people who understood, and one of them saying almost solemnly *gliel' a messo in culo*, and the other one approving such a perfect synthesis, the way out jammed, a slow tired exit and the board paths up to the gangplank in the cold and drizzly night, finally the gangplank creaking under a critical load, Peralta and Chaves smoking, leaning on the railing, without making a motion because they knew that Estévez would see them and that he would hide his surprise, would come over the way he came over, taking out a cigarette in turn.

"He clobbered him," Estévez informed them.

"I know," Peralta said. "I was there."

Estévez looked at him with surprise, but they turned around at the same time and went down the gangplank among the people, who were already beginning to thin out. He knew he had to follow them and he saw them leave the avenue that led to the subway and go down a darker street, Chaves turned only once to make sure he hadn't lost sight of them, then they went directly to Chaves' car and got in without haste but without losing any time. Estévez got in back with Peralta, the car started up heading south.

"So you were there," Estévez said. "I didn't know you liked boxing."

"I don't give a shit about it," Peralta said, "although Monzón is worth every penny. I went to watch you from a distance just in case, it wasn't a time to leave you alone if at some moment . . ."

"Well, you saw. You know, poor Walter was rooting for Nápoles."

"It wasn't Walter," Peralta said.

The car continued south, Estévez sensed confusedly that by this route they would never get to the Bastille district, he felt it as if from way behind because the rest was an explosion full in his face, Monzón hitting him and not Butterball. He couldn't even open his mouth, he sat looking at Peralta and waiting.

"It was too late to warn you," Peralta said. "Too bad you left your house so early, when we phoned Marisa told us that you'd already left and weren't coming back."

"I felt like walking a bit before taking the subway," Estévez said. "But, then, tell me."

"Everything went to hell," Peralta said. "Walter telephoned when he got to Orly this morning, we told him what he had to do, he confirmed to us that he'd gotten the ticket for the fight, everything was just right. We agreed that he'd call me from Lucho's hideout before leaving, a matter of being sure. At seven thirty he hadn't called, we telephoned Geneviève and she called back to say Walter hadn't gotten to Lucho's."

"They were waiting for him at the exit from Orly," Chaves' voice said.

"But then who was it who . . ." Estévez began, and left the phrase hanging; suddenly he understood and it was cold sweat running off his neck, slipping down inside his shirt, the knot tightening in his stomach.

"They had seven hours to get the information out of him," Peralta said. "For proof, the guy knew every detail of what he was supposed to do with you. You know how they work, not even Walter could take it."

"Tomorrow or the day after they'll find him in some vacant lot," Chaves' voice said, almost bored.

"What difference does it make to you now," Peralta said. "Before coming to the fight I fixed it so they'd scram out of the hideouts. You know, I still had some hope when I went into that shitty tent, but he'd already arrived and there was nothing to do."

"But then," Estévez said, "when he left with the money . . ."

"I followed him, of course."

"But before, if you already knew . . ."

"Nothing to do," Peralta repeated. "It was all lost, the guy would have put up a fight right there and they would have busted us all, you already know how in they are."

"So what happened?"

"Three more of them were waiting outside, one had a pass or something like that and quicker than I can tell you they were in a car in the parking space for Delon's pals and people with dough, and they took off. Then I went back to the gangplank, where Chaves was waiting for us, and there you have it. I took down the number of the car, of course, but that isn't worth shit."

"We're leaving Paris," Estévez said.

"Yes, we're going to a quiet spot. The problem now is you, you must have realized that."

"Why me?"

"Because now the guy knows you and is going to end up finding you. There aren't any more hideouts after the Walter business."

"I've got to get away then," Estévez said. He thought about Marisa and the kid, how could he take them, how could he leave them alone, everything was getting mixed up with the trees at the beginning of some woods, the buzzing in his ears as if the crowd were still there shouting Monzón's name, the instant in which there'd been a pause of disbelief and the towel fell into the center of the ring, Butterball's night, poor guy. And the fellow had been rooting for Butterball, now that he thought about it, it was strange that he should have been on the side of the loser, he should have been with Monzón, carrying off the money like Monzón, like someone who turns his back and leaves with everything, making it worse by making fun of the loser, of the poor guy with the broken face or with his hand held out saying well, it's been a pleasure. The car put on its brakes among the trees and Chaves turned off the motor. In the darkness the match of another cigarette was lighted, Peralta.

"I've got to get away, then," Estévez repeated. "To Belgium, if you think so, the one you know is there."

"You'd be safe if you got there," Peralta said, "but you already saw with Walter that they've got people everywhere and a lot of pull."

"They won't grab me."

"Like Walter, who was going to grab Walter and make him sing. You know different things from Walter, that's the bad part."

"They won't grab me," Estévez repeated. "Look, it's just that I've got to think of Marisa and the kid, now that everything's turned to shit I can't leave them here, they'll take it out on her. I'll make all the arrangements in one day and take them with me to Belgium, I'll see the one you know and go on alone to somewhere else."

"One day is too much," Chaves said, turning in his seat. His eyes were getting used to the darkness, Estévez saw his profile and Peralta's face when he raised the cigarette to his mouth and dragged on it.

"All right, I'll leave as soon as possible," Estévez said.

"Right now," said Peralta, taking out the pistol.

TRADE
WINDS

Who can say who got the idea, Vera maybe on the night of her birthday, when Mauricio insisted that they open another bottle of champagne and between glasses they danced in the living room, sticky with cigarette smoke and midnight, or maybe Mauricio at the moment when *Blues in Thirds* was bringing back the memory of the earliest times to them from so far back, from the first records, when birthdays were more than a rhythmic and recurring ceremony. Like a game, talking while they danced, smiling accomplices in the gradual lethargy of alcohol and smoke, asking themselves why not, since after all, since they could do it and it would be summer there, together and indifferent they'd looked over the travel agency folder, suddenly the idea, Mauricio or Vera, just a phone call, going to the airport, to see if the game was worthwhile, things like that are done right away or not at all, besides what was it, at worst returning with the same friendly sarcasm that had brought them back from so many boring trips, but proving something in a different way now, playing the game, balancing things, deciding.

Because this time (and that's what's new about it, the idea had occurred to Mauricio but it could just as well have come out of a casual reflection or Vera's pout, twenty years of life in common, the mental symbiosis, sentences started by one and finished at the other end of the table or on the other telephone), this time it might be different, there was nothing to do but lay down the rules, get some fun out of the absolute absurdity of leaving on different planes and arriving at the hotel like strangers, letting chance introduce them in the dining room or on the beach after one or two days, mingling with the new acquaintances of the summer vacation, treating each other courteously, talking about profession and family during the round of cocktails in the midst of so many other professions and other lives that were probably searching like them for the brief contact of vacations. No one would think anything of the coincidence of last names because it was a common name, it would be so much fun to calibrate the slow mutual acquaintance, attuning it to the rhythm of the other guests, each having fun with people individually, leaving meetings to chance and from time to time finding themselves alone and looking at each other as now while they danced to *Blues in Thirds* and stopped every so often to lift their glasses of champagne and clink them softly in exact time to the music, courteous and mannerly and tired and one thirty already in the midst of so much smoke and perfume which Mauricio had tried to place that night on Vera's skin, won-

dering if she hadn't made a mistake in perfumes, if Vera
would lift her nose a little and approve, Vera's difficult and
rare approval.

They had always made love at the end of their birthday
parties, waiting with amiable coolness for the last friends to
leave, and this time there was no one, because they hadn't
invited anyone since being with people bored them more
than being alone; they danced until the record was over and
remained embracing, looking at each other in a mist of half-
sleep, went out of the living room still keeping an imaginary
rhythm, lost and almost happy and barefoot on the bedroom
rug, they lingered in a slow disrobing beside the bed, helping
each other and getting mixed up and kisses and clasps and
once more the encounter with its inevitable preferences, the
adjustment of each to the light of the lamp that was condemning them to the repetition of tired images, known
murmurs, the slow sinking into the unsated drowsiness after
the repetition of the formulas that returned to words and
bodies like a necessary, almost tender duty.

In the morning it was Sunday and rain, they had breakfast in bed and decided on it seriously; now they had to legis-
late, set up each phase of the trip so that it wouldn't turn into
just another departure and, most of all, just another return.
They figured it out by counting on their fingers: they would
travel separately, one; they would stay in different rooms
with nothing to prevent them from taking advantage of the
summer, two; there would be no censuring or looks like the
ones they knew so well, three; a meeting without witnesses
would let them exchange impressions and find out if it had
been worth the trouble, four; the rest was routine, they
would come back on the same plane since the other people
would no longer matter (or they would, but that was to be
seen in accordance with article four), five. What would hap-

pen afterward wasn't numbered, it was going into a zone determined and uncertain at the same time, an aleatory sum in
which anything could happen and about which nothing
should be said. The flights to Nairobi left on Thursdays and
Saturdays, Mauricio took the first one after a lunch at which
they had salmon just in case, declaiming toasts and exchanging talismans, don't forget the quinine, remember, you always leave your shaving cream and sandals behind.

It was amusing to arrive in Mombasa after an hour in a
taxi that took her to the Trade Winds, to a bungalow on the
beach with monkeys cavorting in the coconut palms and smiling African faces, seeing Mauricio from a distance, already
master of his house, playing on the beach with a couple and
an old man with red sideburns. Cocktail hour caught up with
them on the open veranda by the sea talking about reefs and
seashells, Mauricio came along with a woman and two young
men, at some moment he asked where Vera was from and
explained that he had arrived from France and was a geologist. Vera thought it was nice that Mauricio was a geologist
and answered the other tourists' questions, the pediatrics that
every so often demanded a few days' rest so as not to sink
you into depression, the old man with red sideburns was a
retired diplomat, his wife dressed as if she were twenty years
old but it didn't look so bad on her in a place where almost
everything looked like a Technicolor movie, waiters and
monkeys included, and even the name Trade Winds, which
reminded one of Conrad and Somerset Maugham, cocktails
served in coconut shells, shirttails, the beach, where one
could stroll after dinner under a moon so pitiless that the
clouds projected their moving shadows on the sand to the
surprise of the people who had been squashed down by dirty,
misty skies.

The last shall be first, Vera thought when Mauricio said

that they had given him a room in the more modern part of the hotel, comfortable but without the charm of the bunga- lows on the beach. They played cards at night, day was an endless dialogue of sun and shade, sea and refuge under the palm trees, rediscovering the pale and tired body with each lash of the waves, going to the reefs in a dugout to dive with masks and see the blue and red coral, the fish so innocently close by. There was a lot of talk on the second day about the encounter with two starfish, one with red spots and the other violet and covered with triangles, unless it was the third day already, time slipped away like the warm sea on the skin, Vera was swimming with Sandro, who had surfaced between two cocktails and said he was sick of Verona and automobiles, the Englishman with red sideburns had had too much sun and the doctor was coming from Mombasa to have a look at him, the lobsters were incredibly huge in their last dwelling of mayonnaise and lemon slices, vacations. All that had been seen of Anna was a distant and kind of distancing smile, the fourth night she came to get a drink at the bar and took her glass out onto the veranda, where the three-day veterans re- ceived her with information and advice, there were danger- ous sea urchins in the northern part, she should by no means go out in a dugout without a hat and something to cover her shoulders, the poor Englishman was paying dearly for it and the blacks forget to warn tourists because for them, of course, and Anna thanking them quietly, drinking her martini slowly, almost demonstrating that she had come to be alone from some Copenhagen or Stockholm that needed to be for- gotten. Without even thinking about it, Vera decided that Mauricio and Anna, of course, Mauricio and Anna before twenty-four hours were up, she was playing Ping-Pong with Sandro when she saw them go to the beach and lie down on the sand. Sandro was joking about Anna, who didn't seem

very communicative to him, Nordic mists, he was easily win-
ning the games but the Italian gentleman ceded a few points
from time to time and Vera realized it and thanked him in
silence, twenty-one to eighteen, she hadn't been bad, she was
making progress, a matter of applying herself.

At some moment before sleep Mauricio thought that,
after all, they were doing quite well, it was almost comical to
think that Vera was sleeping a hundred yards away from his
room in the enviable bungalow caressed by the palms, you
were lucky, baby. They'd coincided on a trip to the nearby
islands and had had a lot of fun swimming and playing with
the others; Anna's shoulders had been burned and Vera gave
her a cream that never failed, you know that a baby doctor
ends up knowing everything about creams, the hesitant return of the Englishman protected by a pale blue robe, the
radio at night talking about Jomo Kenyatta and tribal problems, somebody knew a lot about the Masai and over many
drinks entertained them with legends and lions, Karen
Blixen and the authenticity of elephant skin amulets, pure
nylon and that's the way everything was going in those countries. Vera didn't know whether it was Wednesday or Thursday when Sandro accompanied her to the bungalow after a
long walk on the beach where they'd kissed as that beach and
that moon had demanded, she let him come in as soon as he
put a hand on her shoulder, let herself be loved all night,
heard strange things, learned some differences, slept slowly,
savoring every minute of the long silence under an almost
inconceivable mosquito netting. For Mauricio it was the siesta, after a lunch during which his knees had found Anna's
thighs, accompanying her to her rooms, murmuring a so-long
by the door, seeing how Anna kept her hand on the latch,
going in with her, losing himself in a pleasure that only released them at nightfall, when some people were already

wondering if they were ill and Vera smiled uncertainly between two drinks, burning her tongue on a mixture of
Campari and Kenyan rum that Sandro had mixed at the bar
to the astonishment of Moto and Nikuku, those Europeans
would all end up crazy.

The rules had set Saturday at seven in the evening, Vera
took advantage of a meeting without witnesses on the beach
and pointed out a propitious palm grove in the distance.
They embraced with an old love, laughing like kids, obeying
article four, good people. There was a soft solitude of sand
and dry branches, cigarettes and those bronzed people on the
fifth or sixth day whose eyes began to glow like new, to whom
talk is a festival. It's going very well for us, Mauricio said
almost at once, and Vera, yes, of course it's going very well for
us, I can see it in your face and in your hair, why in my hair,
because it shines differently, it's the salt, silly, maybe but salt
mats hair together instead, laughter wouldn't let them talk, it
was good not talking while they laughed and looked at each
other, a last sun going down quickly, the Tropics, take a good
look and you'll see the legendary green ray, I already tried
from my balcony and didn't see anything, ah, of course, the
gentleman has a balcony, yes ma'am, a balcony, but you've
got a bungalow for enjoying ukuleles and orgies. Slipping
along the slope without effort, with another cigarette, really,
he's marvelous, he's got a way of. It must be, if you say so.
What about yours, speak. I don't like your saying yours, it's
like a distribution of prizes. It is. All right, but not like that,
not Anna. Oh, my, what a voice, all full of glucose, you say
Anna as if you were sucking on every letter. Not every letter,
but. Pig. What about you, then. In general it's not me who does
the sucking, although. I imagined so, all those Italians are
right out of *The Decameron*. Just a minute, we're not in group
therapy, Mauricio. I'm sorry, it's not jealousy, what right do I

have. Oh, good boy. Yes, then? Yes, then, perfect, slowly, interminably perfect. I congratulate you, I wouldn't have liked
for it to be any less good for you than for me. I don't know
how it's going with you, but article four demands. Agreed,
although it isn't easy to put it into words, Anna is a wave, a
starfish. The red one or the violet one? All of them together, a
golden river, pink coral. This man is a Scandinavian poet.
And you're a Venetian libertine. He isn't from Venice, he's
from Verona. It's the same thing, it always makes you think
of Shakespeare. You're right, I hadn't thought of that. So
that's how we're doing, right? That's how we're doing,
Mauricio, and we've still got five days left. Five nights,
above all, make good use of them. I think I shall, he's
promised me some new things that he calls tricks to reach
reality. You can explain them to me, I'll wait. In detail, you
can be sure, and you'll tell me about your river of gold and
the blue coral. Pink coral, little girl. Well, you can see that
we haven't been wasting our time. That remains to be seen,
in any case, we're not wasting the present and talking about
it, it's no good for us to spend too much time on article four.
Another dip before whisky? Whisky, how common, I get
served Carpano mixed with gin and bitters. Oh, I beg your
pardon. That's all right, refinement takes time, let's go look
for the green ray, one of these times, who can say.

Friday, Robinson Crusoe day, someone remembered between drinks and there was talk for a while about islands and
shipwrecks, there was a brief and violent hot downpour that
silvered the palm trees and brought a new sound of birds
afterward, migrations, the Ancient Mariner and his albatross,
they were people who knew how to live, every whisky came
with its ration of folklore, of old songs from the Hebrides or
Guadeloupe, at the end of the day Vera and Mauricio were
thinking the same thing, the hotel deserved its name, it was

the hour of trade winds for them, Anna the giver of forgotten vertigos, Sandro the maker of subtle machines, trade winds bringing them back to other times without customs, when they too had had a time like that, inventions and enlightenments on the bed-sheet sea, except that now, except that no longer and therefore, therefore the trade winds that would blow till Tuesday, precisely until the end of the interregnum that was the remote past once more, an instantaneous trip to fountains in flower again, bathing them in a present delight but one already known, known sometime before there were rules, before *Blues in Thirds.*

They didn't talk about that when they met on the Boeing in Nairobi, while they lighted the first cigarette of their return together. Looking at each other as before filled them with something for which there were no words and about which they both kept silent in the midst of drinks and anecdotes about the Trade Winds, in some way they had to preserve the Trade Winds, the winds had to keep driving them, that wonderful old sailing before the wind coming back to destroy propellers, to do away with the slow dirty petroleum of every day that contaminated glasses by birthday champagne, the hope of every night. The trade winds of Anna and Sandro, keeping on drinking while they looked at each other between puffs of smoke, why Mauricio now if Sandro was still there, his skin and his hair and his voice sharpening Mauricio's face as Anna's hoarse laugh in full love dissolved that smile that in Vera was an amiable absence. There was no article six, but they could invent one without words, it was so natural that at some moment he would invite Anna to have another whisky, that she, accepting it with a stroke on the cheek, would say yes, would say yes, Sandro, it would be so nice if we had another whisky in order to get rid of the fear of height, playing like that during the whole flight, there was no longer any need for rules to decide that at the airport Sandro would offer to see Anna home, that Anna would accept with a simple respect for gentlemanly duties, that once at the house she would be the one to look for her keys in her purse and invite Sandro to have another drink, have him leave his bag in the foyer and show him the way to the living room, making excuses for the traces of dust and the closed-in air, opening the drapes and getting ice while Sandro with an appreciative air examined the stacks of records and the Friedlander print. It was after eleven o'clock at night, they drank their glasses of friendship and Anna brought a tray with pâté and crackers, Sandro helped her make canapés and they didn't get to taste them, hands and mouths sought each other, rolling around on the bed and getting undressed, clinging already, looking for each other in the midst of belts and clothing, pulling off the last pieces and turning down the bed, lowering the lights and taking each other slowly, searching and murmuring, above all hoping and murmuring the hope.

Who can say when the drinks and cigarettes came back, the pillows to sit up in bed with and smoke by the light of the lamp on the floor. They almost didn't look at each other, the words went to the wall and came back in a slow game of catch for blind people, and she first, wondering as if to herself what could have become of Vera and Mauricio after the Trade Winds, what could have become of them after their return.

"They've probably realized by now," he said. "They've probably understood and after that they won't be able to do anything more."

"Something can always be done," she said. "Vera's not going to stay that way, you only had to look at her."

"Mauricio either," he said. "I barely knew him but it

was so obvious. Neither one is going to stay like that and it's almost easy to imagine what they're going to do."

"Yes, it's easy, it's like seeing it from here."

"They probably haven't gone to sleep, just like us, and now they're probably talking slowly, without looking at each other. They won't have anything more to say to each other, I think it'll be Mauricio who opens the drawer and takes out the blue vial. Like this, see, a blue vial like this."

"Vera will count them and divide them up," she said. "Practical things are always left to her, she'll do it well. Sixteen apiece, not even the problem of an odd number."

"They'll swallow them by twos, with whisky and at the same time, without getting ahead of each other."

"They'll taste a little bitter," she said.

"Mauricio will say no, more acidy."

"Yes, they could be more acidy. And then they'll turn out the light, no one knows why."

"No one ever knows why, but it's true, they'll turn out the light and embrace. That's for sure, I know they'll embrace."

"In the dark," she said, looking for the switch. "Like this, right?"

"Like this," he said.

MANUSCRIPT

FOUND

IN

A

POCKET

Now that I'm writing this, it might seem like roulette or the
racetrack to others, but it wasn't money I was looking for; at
some moment I'd begun to feel, to decide that a Métro
window might give me the answer, the finding of a happiness,
here precisely where everything happens under the sign of
the most implacable break, in a below-ground time that traveling between stations sketches out and limits in that way,
unappealingly under ground. I say break in order to get a
better understanding (I've had to understand so many things
since I've begun to play the game) of that hope of a conver-
gence that I might receive from the reflection on a windowpane. Going beyond the break that people don't seem to

understand even though who knows what those people crammed together getting on and off the Métro cars are thinking, what, besides transportation, are those people getting on sooner or later to get off later or sooner looking for, only coming together in the zone of a car where everything has been decided beforehand, without anyone's knowing whether we'll get off together, whether I'll get off first or that skinny man with a roll of papers, whether the old woman in green will go to the end of the line, whether those children will get off now, it's clear that they'll be getting off because they're picking up their notebooks and rulers and playing by the door while in the corner there's a girl who's settled down to endure, to stay for many stations to come in the seat that's free at last, and that other girl is unpredictable, Ana was unpredictable, she sat very stiffly against the back of the window seat, she was already there when I got on at the Étienne Marcel station and a black man left the seat opposite and it didn't seem to interest anyone and I was able to slip in between the knees of the two passengers sitting on the outside seats with a vague apology and remained opposite Ana and almost immediately, because I'd gone down into the Métro to play the game once more, I looked for Margrit's profile in the reflection on the windowpane and I thought she was pretty, that I liked her black hair cut in a kind of short bob that she combed diagonally across her forehead.

It isn't true that the names Margrit or Ana came later or that it's a way now of differentiating between them in writing, things like that are decided instantaneously by the game, I mean that the reflection in the window could in no way be named Ana, just as the girl sitting opposite me without looking at me couldn't be named Margrit, her eyes lost in the boredom of that interregnum where everybody seems to consult a zone of vision not in his immediate vicinity, except

children, who stare fully at things until the day when they too
are taught to place themselves at the interstices, to look without seeing with that civil ignorance of neighboring appearances, of all sensible contact, each one installed in his bubble,
lined up between parentheses, watching out for the viable
space of the minimal free air between others' knees and elbows, taking refuge in *France-Soir* or paperback books even
though always, like Ana, a pair of eyes fills the gap between
what is really seeable in that neutral and stupid distance that
goes from my face to that of the man concentrating on *Le
Figaro*. But then Margrit, if there was something I could
have foreseen it was that at some time Ana would turn distractedly toward the window and then Margrit would see my
reflection, the crossing of looks in the images of that glass
where the darkness of the tunnel has spread its thin quicksilver, its purple, moving felt which gives faces a life on other
planes, takes away from them that horrible chalk mask of the
municipal car lights and above all, oh yes, you couldn't have
denied it, Margrit, makes them really look at the other face in
the glass, because during the instantaneous time of the double look there's no censure, my reflection on the glass was not
the man sitting opposite Ana, whom Ana couldn't look at
fully in a subway car, and, besides, the one who was looking
at my reflection was no longer Ana but Margrit at the moment in which Ana had quickly averted her eyes from the
man sitting opposite her because it wasn't right to look at him
and on turning toward the window she'd seen my reflection,
which was waiting for that instant to smile slightly, without
insolence or expectation, when Margrit's look landed on his
look like a bird. It must have lasted a second, maybe a little
more, because I felt that Margrit had noticed the smile that
Ana reproved even though it was only by the gesture of lowering her face, of vaguely examining the clasp of her red leather

purse; and it was almost proper to keep on smiling even though Margrit was no longer looking at me because in some way Ana's expression acknowledged my smile, she continued knowing that and it wasn't necessary any longer for her or Margrit to look at me, concentrating with application on the trivial task of testing the clasp on the red purse.

As with Paula (with Ofelia) already and with so many others who had concentrated on the task of checking a clasp, a button, the fold of a magazine, once more it was the pit where hope becomes enmeshed with fear in a deadly cramp of spiders fighting in his stomach, where time begins to throb like a second heart in the pulse of the game; from that moment on every station of the subway was a different plotting of the future because the game had so decided; Margrit's look and my smile, Ana's instantaneous withdrawal to the contemplation of the clasp on her purse were the opening of a ceremony that had begun to be celebrated contrary to everything reasonable, preferring the worst missed meetings to the stupid chains of everyday causality. It isn't hard to explain it but playing it had a lot of blind combat about it, a quivering colloidal suspension in which every path raised a tree of unforeseeable courses. A map of the Paris subway encompasses in its Mondrianesque skeleton, its red, yellow, blue, and black branches, a vast but limited surface of subtended pseudopodia; and that tree is alive twenty out of twenty-four hours, a tormented sap runs through it with precise finalities, the one that gets off at Châtelet or gets on at Vaugirard, the one that changes at Odéon to continue on to La Motte-Picquet, the two hundred, three hundred, who knows how many possible combinations, for each codified and programmed cell enters one sector of the tree and comes to the surface in another, comes out at Galeries Lafayette to deliver a package of towels or a lamp to a third floor on the Rue Gay-Lussac.

My rules for the game were maniacally simple, they were beautiful, stupid, and tyrannical: if I liked a woman, if I liked a woman sitting opposite me, if I liked a woman sitting opposite me beside the window, if her reflection in the window crossed glances with my reflection in the window, if my smile in the reflection in the window disturbed or pleased or repelled the reflection of the woman in the window, if Margrit saw me smile and then Ana lowered her head and began to examine the clasp on her red purse with concentration, then there was a game, it was exactly the same if the smile was respected or answered or ignored, the first time the ceremony didn't go beyond that, a smile registered by one who'd deserved it. Then the combat in the pit began, the spiders in the stomach, the wait, with its pendulum, from station to station. I remember how I awoke that day: now they were Margrit and Ana, but a week before they'd been Paula and Ofelia; the blond girl had gotten off at one of the worst stations, Montparnasse-Bienvenüe, which opens its foul-smelling hydra to the maximum possibilities of failure. My connection was with the Porte de Vanves line and almost at once, in the first passageway, I understood that Paula (that Ofelia) would take the passageway leading to the connection with the Mairie d'Issy line. Impossible to do anything, just look at her for the last time where the passageways cross, see her move away, go down some stairs. Those were the rules of the game, a smile in the window glass and the right to follow a woman and hope desperately that her connection would coincide with the one decided on by me before each trip; and then—always until now—seeing her take another passageway and being unable to follow her, being obliged to return to the upper world and go into a café and continue to live until little by little, hours or days or weeks, the thirst again demanded the possibility that everything would coincide someday, woman and window glass, accepted or rejected smile, train connection, and then finally yes, then the right to go over and say the first word, thick with stagnant time, with endless ravaging at the bottom of the pit among the cramp of spiders.

Now we were coming into the Saint-Sulpice station, someone beside me was getting up; Ana, too, was left alone opposite me, had stopped looking at her purse, and once or twice her eyes swept me distractedly before losing themselves in the ad for the thermal baths that was repeated in the four corners of the car. Margrit hadn't looked at me again in the window but that proved the contact, her stealthy throb; Ana was timid perhaps or it simply seemed absurd to her to accept the reflection of that face which would smile again at Margrit; and, besides, reaching Saint-Sulpice was important because if there were still eight stations left to the end of the line at Porte d'Orléans, only three had connections with other lines, and only if Ana got off at one of those three would the possibility of coinciding be left to me; when the train began to brake at Saint-Placide I looked and I looked at Margrit, looking in her for the eyes that Ana still had resting softly on the things in the car as if admitting that Margrit wouldn't look at me anymore, that it was useless to hope that she'd look at the reflection which was waiting to smile at her again.

She didn't get off at Saint-Placide, I discovered that before the train began to slow down, there's that haste of a passenger, especially the women, who nervously check their packages, button their coats, or look to the side as they get up, avoiding knees at that instant in which the loss of speed make bodies clumsy and confused. Ana vaguely reviewed the ads in the station, Margrit's face was being erased under the platform lights and I couldn't find out if she'd looked at me again; or if my reflection had been visible in that morass of neon and photographic ads, of bodies getting on and off. If Ana got off at Montparnasse-Bienvenüe my possibilities were minimal; how could I forget Paula (Ofelia) there where a possible quadruple combination made all predictions tenuous; and yet on Paula's (Ofelia's) day I had been absurdly certain that we would coincide, until the last minute I'd walked nine feet behind that slow blond woman dressed as if in dry leaves and her turn to the right had caught my face like the lash of a whip. That's why now Margrit no, that's why the fear, it could happen again abominably at Montparnasse-Bienvenüe; the memory of Paula (of Ofelia), the spiders in the pit against the tiny confidence that Ana (that Margrit). But who can do anything against the innocence which goes on letting us live, almost immediately I told myself that maybe Ana (maybe Margrit) wouldn't get off at Montparnasse-Bienvenüe but at one of the other possible stations, that maybe she wouldn't get off at one of the intermediate ones where I wasn't allowed to follow her; that Ana (that Margrit) wouldn't get off at a Montparnesse-Bienvenüe (she didn't), that she wouldn't get off at Vavin, and she didn't, that maybe she'd get off at Raspail, which was the first of the last two possible ones; and when she didn't get off and I knew that only one station was left where I could follow her as against the last three where everything would already be the same, I looked for Margrit's eyes once more in the window glass, I called her from a silence and an immobility that must have reached her like a demand, like a breaking wave, I smiled at her with a smile that Ana could no longer ignore, that Margrit had to admit even though she wasn't looking at my reflection lashed by the half-lights of the tunnel as it came out into Denfert-Rochereau. Maybe the first touch of the brakes had made the smooth purse on Ana's thighs quiver, maybe only boredom moved her hand to the lock of black hair that crossed her forehead; in those three, four seconds in which the train came to a halt at the platform, the spiders sank their claws into the skin of the pit to conquer me once more from inside; when Ana stood up with a single and clean bend of her body, when I saw her from behind between two passengers, I think I still absurdly looked for Margrit's face in the passive shadow of that body that went out onto the platform, until I awoke to what was about to come, the irrevocable fulfillment of the final double choice.

I think it's clear, Ana (Margrit) would take a daily or circumstantial route while I, before getting on that train, had decided that if anyone got into the game and got off at Denfert-Rochereau, my connection would be the Nation-Étoile line, in the same way that if Ana (if Margrit) had got off at Châtelet I could only have followed her if she took the Vincennes-Neuilly connection. In the last moment of the ceremony the game was lost if Ana (if Margrit) took the connection with the Ligne de Sceaux or went directly out onto the street; immediately, right then, because there weren't the endless passageways of other times in that station and the stairs led rapidly to destiny, to what methods of transportation also called destination. I was watching her move among the people, her red purse like a toy pendulum, lifting her head in search of the directional signs, hesitating an instant before going toward the left; but the left was the exit that led to the street.

I don't know how to put it, the spiders were biting too much, I wasn't being dishonest during the first minute, I simply followed her perhaps in order to accept it later, to let her go off in one of her directions up there; halfway up the stairs I understood that it wasn't that, that maybe the only way to get rid of them was to deny, one time, the law, the code. The cramp that had gripped me during the second in which Ana (in which Margrit) had begun to climb the forbidden stairs gave way suddenly to a dreamy lassitude, to a slow-moving golem; I refused to think, it was enough knowing that I could still see her, that the red purse was going up onto the street, that the black hair trembled on her shoulders with every step. It was already night and the air was icy, with a few snowflakes among the gusts of wind and the drizzle; I know that Ana (that Margrit) wasn't afraid when I moved alongside her and said: "We just can't separate like this before we meet."

In the café later on, now only Ana as the reflection of Margrit gave way to a reality of Cinzano and words, she told me that she didn't understand anything, that her name was Marie-Claude, my smile in the reflection had annoyed her, that for a moment she'd thought of getting up and changing her seat, that she hadn't seen me follow her and that on the street she hadn't been afraid, contradictorily, looking into my eyes, drinking her Cinzano, smiling without being ashamed to smile, of having accepted my harassment right on the street almost immediately. At that moment of happiness, like the one when you let yourself go in the waves, or the one you get in a timber-drift between poplar trees, I couldn't tell her what she would have taken for madness or a mania, which it was, but in another way, as seen from other shores of life; I spoke to her about her lock of hair, her red purse, her way of looking at the ad for the thermal baths, said that I hadn't smiled at her as a Don Juan or out of boredom but to give her a flower I didn't have, a sign that I liked her, that she did me good, that riding across from her, that another cigarette and another Cinzano. At no moment were we emphatic, we spoke as if from a known and accepted already, looking at each other without doing harm; I think that Marie-Claude was letting me come and be in her present as perhaps Margrit would have answered my smile in the glass if so much previous molding hadn't intervened, so much you don't have to answer if you're spoken to on the street or offered candy and invited to the movies, until Marie-Claude, freed now from my smile to Margrit, Marie-Claude on the street and in the café had thought that it was a good smile, that the stranger down there hadn't smiled at Margrit in order to test new terrain, and my absurd way of coming up to her had been the only comprehensible thing, the only reason to say yes, we could have a drink and a chat in a café.

I don't remember what I was able to tell her about me, maybe everything except the game but so little then, at some moment we laughed, someone cracked the first joke, we discovered that we liked the same cigarettes and Catherine Deneuve, she let me see her to the door of her building, shook hands simply, and consented to the same café at the same time on Tuesday. I took a taxi back to my neighborhood, in myself for the first time as if in an incredible foreign country, repeating to myself yes, Marie-Claude, Denfert-Rochereau, closing my eyes tightly to hold on better to her black hair, to that way of tilting her head before speaking, of smiling. We were punctual and we told each other about movies, work, we verified partial ideological differences, she continued accepting me as if miraculously that present without reasons, without interrogation was enough; she didn't even seem to realize that any imbecile would have thought her easy or foolish; observing that I didn't so much as try to share the same bench in the café, that going along the Rue Froidevaux I didn't put my arm around her shoulder in the first gesture of intimacy, that knowing she was practically alone—a younger sister, often absent from the apartment on the fourth floor—I didn't ask her to let me come up. If there was something she couldn't suspect it was the spiders, we'd met three or four times without their biting, motionless in the pit and waiting until the day when I found out, as if I hadn't known it all the time, but Tuesdays, arriving at the café, imagining that Marie-Claude was probably there already or watching her come in with her agile steps, the dark revival that had fool-ishly fought against the spiders who were awake again, against the betrayal of the game that only she had been able to defend with nothing more than giving me a brief, warm handclasp, with nothing but that lock of hair that strolled across her forehead. At some moment she must have realized, she sat looking at me, silent, waiting; it was impossible now for me not to be given away by the effort of making the truce last, not to admit that they were coming back little by little in spite of Marie-Claude, against Marie-Claude, who couldn't understand, who sat looking at me, silent, waiting; drinking and smoking and talking to her, defending the sweet inter-regnum without spiders until the last, learning about her simple life and schedule and student sister and allergies, de-siring so much that black lock which was combed across her forehead, desiring her as something terminal, as really the last station on the last subway of life, and then the pit, the distance from my chair to that bench where we could have kissed, where my mouth could have drunk in Marie-Claude's first whiff of perfume before taking her home in an embrace, going up the stairs, freeing ourselves finally from so much clothing and so much waiting.

Then I told her, I remember the cemetery wall and that Marie-Claude leaned on it and let me talk with her face hid-den in the warm moss of her overcoat, who knows if my voice reached her with all of its words, if it was possible for her to understand; I told her everything, every detail of the game, the confirmed improbabilities after so many Paulas (so many Ofelias) lost at the end of a passageway, the spiders in every ending. She was weeping, I felt her tremble against me although she continued sheltering me, sustaining me with all of her body leaning against the wall of the dead; she didn't ask me anything, she didn't want to know why or how long, it didn't occur to her to fight against a machine put together by a whole life against its own grain, against the city and its countersigns, just that weeping there like a wounded little animal, resisting without effort the triumph of the game, the exasperated dance of the spiders in the pit.

At the door of her building I told her that everything wasn't lost, that an attempt at a legitimate meeting depended on both of us; she knew the rules of the game now, maybe they'd be favorable to us since all we had to do was look for each other. She told me that she could ask for two weeks off, ride carrying a book so that time would be less damp and hostile in the world below, going from one connection to another, waiting for me, reading, looking at the ads. We refused to think about the improbability, the fact that maybe we would meet on a train but that it wouldn't be enough, that this time the pre-established would have to be followed; I asked her not to think, to let the subway run, never to cry during those two weeks while I searched for her; it was understood without words that if the time limit ended without our seeing each other again or only seeing each other until two passageways separated us, it wouldn't make any more sense to go back to the café, to the door of her building. At the foot of that neighborhood stairway where an orange light stretched softly upward, toward the image of Marie-Claude in her apartment, among her furniture, naked and asleep, I kissed her on the hair, stroked her hands; she didn't seek my mouth, she drifted off and I saw her from behind, going up one more of the innumerable stairs that took them away without my being able to follow them; I walked back to my place, without spiders, empty and washed by the new wait; now they couldn't do anything to me, the game was going to begin again like so many other times but only with Marie-Claude, Monday going into the Couronnes station in the morning, coming out at Marx Dormoy at night, Tuesday going in at Crimée, Wednesday at Philippe Auguste, the precise rules of the game, fifteen stations in which four had connections, and then at the first of the four knowing that it was up to me to follow the Sèvres-Montreuil line as at the second she would have to make the Clichy-Porte Dauphine connection, each itinerary chosen without any special reason because there could be no reason, maybe Marie-Claude would come out near her place, at Denfert-Rochereau or at Corvisart, she would be changing at Pasteur to continue on to Falguière, the Mondrianesque tree with all of its dry branches, the chance of the red, blue, white, dotted temptations; Thursday, Friday, Saturday. Watching the trains come in on some platform or other, the seven or eight cars, letting myself look while they passed slower and slower, running to the last one and getting on a car without Marie-Claude, getting off at the next station and waiting for another train, going on to the first station to get another line, watching the cars arrive without Marie-Claude, letting a train or two pass, getting on the third, going to the end of the line, returning to a station from where I could get another line, deciding that I'd only take the fourth train, abandoning the search and going up to eat, returning almost immediately with a bitter cigarette and sitting on a bench until the second, until the fifth train. Monday, Tuesday, Wednesday, Thursday, without spiders because I was still hoping, because I still am hoping on this bench in the Chemin Vert station, with this notebook where a hand writes in order to invent a time that won't just be that interminable gust of wind that flings me toward the Saturday when everything will perhaps have ended, when

I'll return alone and feel them wake up and bite, their raven-
ous pincers demanding a new game from me, other Marie-
Claudes, other Paulas, the repetition after each defeat, the
cancerous beginning all over again. But it's Thursday, the
station is Chemin Vert, night is falling outside, it's still possible to imagine something, it doesn't even seem too incredible that in the second train, that in the fourth car, that Marie-
Claude in a window seat, that she's seen and stands up with a
shout that nobody but me can hear full in the face like that,
at a full run to jump into the loaded car, pushing indignant
passengers, muttering excuses that no one expects or accepts,
standing against the double seat occupied by legs and umbrellas and packages, by Marie-Claude with her gray coat by
the window, the black lock, which the sudden lurch of the
train barely agitates as her hands tremble on her thighs in a
call that has no name, that's all that's going to happen now.
There's no need to talk, nothing could be said about that
impassable and mistrusting wall of faces and umbrellas between Marie-Claude and me; there are three stations left that
connect with other lines, Marie-Claude will have to choose
one of them, cross the platform, follow one of the passageways
or look for the exit stairs, alien to my choice, which I can't
betray this time. The train enters the Bastille station and
Marie-Claude sits there, the people get off and get on, someone leaves the seat next to her empty but I don't go over, I
can't sit there, I can't tremble next to her as she is probably trembling. Now come Ledru-Rollin and Faidherbe-
Chaligny, Marie-Claude knows I can't follow her at those stations with no connections and she doesn't move, the game has
to be played out at Reuilly-Diderot or Daumesnil; while the
train is entering Reuilly-Diderot I turn my eyes away, I don't
want her to know, I don't want her to be able to understand
that it's not there. When the train starts up I see that she

hasn't moved, that we have one last hope left, at Daumesnil there's only one connection and the exit to the street, red or black, yes or no. Then we look at each other, Marie-Claude has lifted her face to look at me directly, clinging to the handle of the seat, I'm the thing she's looking at, something as pale as what I'm looking at, the bloodless face of Marie-Claude who squeezes her red purse, who's going to make the first gesture toward getting up as the train enters the Daumesnil station.

APOCALYPSE AT SOLENTINAME

Ticos, Costa Ricans, are always like that, rather quiet but full of surprises; you land in San José and waiting for you there are Carmen Naranjo and Samuel Rovinski and Sergio Ramírez (who's from Nicaragua and not a Tico, but what difference does that make since it's all the same after all, what difference does it make that I'm Argentine although out of niceness I should say Tino, and the rest of them Nicas or Ticos). It was one of those hot spells and to make things even worse it all got started right away, a press conference with the usual business, why don't you live in your own country, why was *Blow Up* so different from your short story, do you think a writer must be involved? With things going like that I can see that my final interview will be at the gates of hell and there're sure to be the same questions, and if by chance it's chez St. Peter it won't be any different: don't you think that you're writing over the heads of the people down there?

Afterward the Hotel Europa and that shower which caps trips with a long monologue of soap and silence. Except that at seven o'clock it was already time to take a stroll through San José and see if it was as simple and smooth as they had told me, a hand tugged at my jacket and there was Ernesto Cardenal behind me and such an embrace, poet, how wonderful for you to be there after our meeting in Rome, after so many meetings on paper over the years. It always surprises me, always moves me that someone like Ernesto should come to see me and seek me out, you're probably saying what a crock of false modesty, but you just go right on saying it, old man, the jackal howls, but the bus passes, I'll always be an amateur, someone who from way down loves some people so much that one day it turns out that they love him too, those are things that are beyond me, we'd better get on to the next line.

The next line was that Ernesto found out I was coming to Costa Rica and zip, he'd come by plane from his island because the little bird that brings him news had told him that the Ticos were planning a trip to Solentiname for me and the idea of coming to pick me up seemed irresistible to him, so two days later Sergio and Oscar and Ernesto and I were filling up the all too fillable capacity of a little Piper Aztec, the name of which will always be a mystery to me, but which flew with hiccoughs and bowel rumblings while the blond pilot hummed some countervailing calypso songs and seemed completely unconcerned by my notion that the Aztec was taking us straight to the sacrificial pyramid. It didn't turn out that way, as can be seen, we came down at Los Chiles and from there an equally bouncy Jeep brought us to the farm of the poet José Coronel Urteche, whom more people would do well to read and at whose house we rested, talking about so many other poet friends, Roque Dalton and Gertrude Stein and Carlos Martínez Rivas, until Luis Coronel arrived and we left for Nicaragua in his Jeep and his outboard of frightening speed. But first there were souvenir photographs with one of those cameras that let the little piece of sky-blue paper pop out right there and little by little and miraculously and Polaroid it fills up little by little with images, first disturbing ectoplasms and little by little a nose, some curly hair, Ernesto's smile and his Nazarene headband, Doña María and Don José outlined against the porch. That seemed quite normal to all because, of course, they were accustomed to using that camera, but not to me, I was filled with amazement as I saw those faces and those good-bye smiles coming out of nothing and I told them so, I remember asking Oscar what would happen if sometime after a family snapshot the sky-blue paper started to fill up with Napoleon on horseback, and Don José Coronel's laugh, listening to everything as always, the Jeep, let's go to the lake now.

We got to Solentiname late at night, waiting there were Teresa and William and a gringo poet and the other young people from the community; we went to bed almost immediately but first I looked at the paintings in a corner, Ernesto was talking to his people and was taking the provisions and gifts he was bringing from San José out of a bag, someone was asleep in a hammock and I saw the paintings in a corner, I began to look at them. I don't remember who explained to me that they were the work of peasants from the region, this one was painted by Vicente, this is by Ramona, some signed and others not, but all so beautiful, once more the first vision of the world, the clean look of a person who describes what's around him like a song of praise: midget cows in poppy fields, the sugar-making shed with people coming out like ants, the horse with green eyes against a background of cane fields, a baptism in a church that doesn't believe in perspective and climbs up or falls down on top of itself, the lake with little boats like shoes and in the background an enormous fish laughing with turquoise teeth. Then Ernesto came over to explain to me that the sale of the paintings helped things along, in the morning he would show me some work in wood and stone done by the peasants and also some of their own sculptures; we were falling asleep but I kept on looking at the little pictures piled up in a corner, taking out the great piles of canvases with little cows and flowers and that mother with two children on her knees, one in white, the other in red, under a sky so full of stars that the single cloud hung in a corner as if in humiliation, squeezing up against the frame of the picture, already pushing out of the canvas from pure fear.

The next day was Sunday and eleven o'clock mass, the Solentiname mass in which the peasants and Ernesto and the visiting friends comment together on a chapter of Scripture which that day was Jesus' arrest in the garden, a theme that the people of Solentiname treated as if they were talking about themselves, about the threat of being pounced on at night or in broad daylight, that life of permanent uncertainty on the islands and on the mainland and in all of Nicaragua and, yes, almost all of Latin America, a life surrounded by fear and death, life in Guatemala and life in El Salvador, life in Argentina and Bolivia, life in Chile and Santo Domingo, life in Paraguay, life in Brazil and Colombia.

A while later we had to think about going back and it was then that I thought about the paintings again; I went to the community hall and began to look at them in the dazzling light of noon, the bright colors, the acrylics or oils facing each other out of their ponies and sunflowers and fiestas in the symmetrical fields and palm groves. I remembered that I had a roll of color film in my camera and I went out onto the porch with an armful of paintings; Sergio, who was coming up, helped me stand them up in a good light, and I went along photographing them carefully one by one, centering them so that each painting filled the viewer completely. Chance is like that: I had just the number of exposures as there were paintings, not one was left out and when Ernesto came to tell us that the outboard was ready, I told him what I'd done and he laughed, art thief, image smuggler. Yes, I told him, I'm taking all of them, I'll show them on my screen back there and they'll be bigger and brighter than these, screw yourself.

I returned to San José, I was in Havana and I did some things there, back in Paris with a weariness that was full of nostalgia, Claudine silently waiting for me at Orly, once more the life of wristwatch and *merci, monsieur, bonjour, madame*, committees, movies, red wine and Claudine, Mozart quartets and Claudine. In among so many things the toad suitcases had spat out onto the bed and rug, magazines, clippings, handkerchiefs and books by Central American poets, the gray plastic tubes with the rolls of film, so many things over two months, the sequence of the Lenin School in Havana, the streets of Trinidad, the outline of the Irazú volcano and its vat of boiling green water, where Samuel and I and Sarita had imagined ourselves already roasted and floating in the midst of sulfur smoke gases. Claudine took the rolls to be developed; one afternoon while walking through the Latin Quarter I remembered and since I had the stub in my pocket I picked them up and there were eight of them. I immediately thought about the little paintings from Solentiname and when I got home I opened the boxes and looked at the first slides in each series, I remembered that before I had photographed the paintings I'd been shooting Ernesto's mass, some children playing among the palm trees, just as in the paintings, children and palms and cows against a brilliantly blue sky and a lake that was just a touch greener, or maybe just the opposite, I wasn't sure about it anymore. I put the slides of the children and the mass into the projector; I was aware that the paintings began afterward and I went on to them.

It was growing dark and I was alone, Claudine would come by after work to listen to some music and stay with me; I fixed the screen and some rum with lots of ice, the projector and its carrousel and its remote-control button all ready; there was no need to draw the curtains, the cooperative night was there already, lighting up the lamps and the aroma of the rum; it was pleasant thinking that everything would be revealed to me again little by little, after the paintings from Solentiname I would go through the boxes with the Cuban photographs, but why the paintings first, why the professional deformation, art before life, and why not, the one said to the other in their eternal unresolvable fraternal and rancorous dialogue, why not look at the Solentiname paintings first since they're life too, since it's all the same.

The photographs of the mass went by first, rather poor because of errors of exposure, the children, on the other hand, playing in full light and with such white teeth. I was unwillingly pushing the change button, I would have lingered a while longer looking at each photograph that was sticky with memory, the small fragile world of Solentiname, surrounded by water and police, the same way the boy I was looking at was surrounded and didn't understand, I'd pushed the button and the boy was there very clearly in the background, a broad, smooth face, as if full of incredulous surprise as his body pitched forward, the neat hole in the middle of his forehead, the officer's pistol still marking the trajectory of the bullet, the others on the side with their submachine guns, a confused background of houses and trees.

You think what you think, it always gets ahead of you and leaves you so far behind; I stupidly told myself that they must have made a mistake at the camera place and given me some other customer's pictures, but the mass then, the children playing on the grass, how then. Nor did my hand obey when I pushed the button and it was an endless sand flat at noon with two or three rusty-roofed sheds, people gathered on the left looking at the bodies laid out face up, their arms open to a naked gray sky; you had to look closely to make out a uniformed group in the background with their backs turned and going away, the Jeep waiting at the top of a rise.

I know that I continued on, in the face of what resisted all sanity the only thing I could do was keep on pressing the button, seeing the corner of Corrientes and San Martín in Buenos Aires and the black car with the four guys taking aim at someone on the sidewalk in a white shirt and loafers who was running, two women trying to take cover behind a parked truck, someone looking straight out, a face of horrified disbelief, raising a hand to his chin as if to touch himself and feel that he's still alive, and suddenly the room that's almost in darkness, a dirty light falling from the barred little window up high, the table with the naked girl on her back, her hair hanging down to the floor, the shadow of shoulders putting a wire between her open legs, the two guys in front talking to each other, a blue necktie and a green sweater. I never knew if I kept on pushing the button or not, I saw a clearing in the jungle, a cabin with a thatched roof and trees in the foreground, against the trunk of the nearest one a thin fellow looking to the left where a confused group, five or six of them close together, were aiming rifles and pistols at him; the fellow with a long face and a lock of hair falling down over his dark forehead was looking at them, one hand half-raised, the other probably in his pants pocket, it was as if he were saying something to them unhurriedly, almost listlessly, and even though the photograph was hazy I sensed and I knew that the fellow was Roque Dalton, and then I did press the button as if with that I could save him from the infamy of that death and I managed to see an automobile flying into pieces right in the heart of a city that could have been Buenos Aires or São Paulo, I kept on pressing and pressing through the waves of bloody faces and parts of bodies and women running and children on a Bolivian or Guatemalan hillside, suddenly the screen filled with mercury and with nothing and with Claudine, who was coming in silently, casting her shadow on the screen before she bent over and kissed me on the hair and asked me if they came out well, if I was pleased with the pictures, if I felt like showing them.

I clicked the carrousel and put it back to zero, you don't know how or why you do things when you've gone beyond a limit that you don't understand either. Without looking at her, because she might have understood or would simply be afraid of what my face must have looked like, without explaining anything because everything was one single knot from my throat down to my toenails, I got up and slowly sat her down in my chair and I must have said something to her about going to get her a drink. In the bathroom I think I threw up or I didn't do anything and just sat on the edge of the bathtub letting time pass until I could go to the kitchen and fix Claudine her favorite drink, fill it with ice, and then feel the silence, realize that Claudine wasn't shouting or running to ask me, silence, nothing else and for a moment the sugary bolero that filtered in from the apartment next door. I don't know how long it took me to cover the distance between the kitchen and the living room, to see the back part of the screen precisely as she was coming to the end and the room filled up with the instantaneous mercury reflection and then the shadows, Claudine turning off the projector and settling back in the chair to take the glass and smile at me slowly, happy and cat and so content.

"They came out so well, that one with the smiling fish and the mother with the two children and the cows in the field; wait, and that other one with the baptism in the church, tell me who painted them, you couldn't see the signatures."

Sitting on the floor, not looking at her, I reached for my glass and drank it down in one swallow. I wasn't going to tell her anything, what could I tell her now, but I do remember that I vaguely thought about asking her something idiotic, asking her if at some moment she'd seen a photograph of Napoleon on horseback. But I didn't, of course.

San José, Havana,
April 1976

FOOTSTEPS

IN

THE

FOOTPRINTS

*A rather tedious chronicle, more in
the style of an exercise than in the
exercise of a style, say that of a
Henry James who might have sipped
maté in some Buenos Aires or Mar
del Plata courtyard in the twenties*

Jorge Fraga had just turned forty when he decided to study
the life and works of the poet Claudio Romero.

The whole thing was born out of a café conversation in
which Fraga and his friends were forced to admit once more
the uncertainty that surrounded Romero's person. The author of three books passionately read and envied and which
had brought him an ephemeral fame during the years following the Centenary, Romero had an image that was confused
with his creations. He suffered from the lack of a systematic
criticism and even a satisfactory iconography. Aside from par-
simoniously laudatory articles in the magazines of the period
and a book committed by an enthusiastic professor from

Santa Fe, for whom lyricism replaced ideas, not even the slightest investigation into the life or work of the poet had been attempted. A few anecdotes, some hazy photographs; the rest was legends for café talk and panegyrics in anthologies put out by obscure publishers. But Fraga's attention had been called to the fact that a lot of people were still reading Romero's poetry with the same fervor as that of Carriego or Alfonsina Storni. He had discovered it himself during his high school years and in spite of the lower-class tone and the images that had been worn out by his followers, the poems by the Bard of the River Plate had been one of the decisive experiences of his youth, like Almafuerte or Carlos de la Púa. Only later on, when he had become known as a critic and essayist, did it occur to him to think seriously about Romero's work and he didn't take long to realize that almost nothing was known of its more personal and perhaps deeper meaning. Compared to the poetry of other good turn-of-the-century poets, that of Claudio Romero was distinguished by a special quality, a less emphatic resonance that immediately earned him the trust of the young, tired of high-sounding tropes and padded evocations. When he spoke to students or friends about the poems, Fraga came to wonder whether or not underneath it all the mystery might be what lent prestige to that poetry of obscure keys, evasive intent. He ended up being irritated by the facility with which ignorance favors admiration; after all, Claudio Romero's poetry stood too high to have a better knowledge of its origins bring it down. On leaving one of those café get-togethers where Romero had been discussed with the usual admiring vagueness, he felt a kind of obligation to get down to serious work on the poet. He felt, too, that it shouldn't be a mere essay with philological or stylistic intent, as were almost all of those that had been written. The notion of a biography in the highest sense of the word imposed itself upon him from the beginning: man, land, and work must rise up out of a single act of living, even though the undertaking seemed impossible in all that mist of time. When the period of note taking was over, he would have to arrive at the synthesis, to provoke, unthinkably, the encounter of the poet with his pursuer; only that contact would reinvest Romero's work with its deepest reason.

When he decided to undertake the study, Fraga was entering a critical segment of his life. A certain academic prestige had earned him an adjunct professorship at the university and the respect of a small group of readers and students. At the same time, a recent attempt to attain the official backing that would have allowed him to work in certain libraries in Europe had failed for reasons of bureaucratic politics. His publications were not those that open the doors of ministries without knocking. The novelist in vogue, the literary columnist received more than he. Fraga was not unaware that if his book on Romero was a success, the basest problems would be solved all by themselves. He wasn't ambitious, but it irritated him to see himself left behind by the scribes of the moment. Also, Claudio Romero, in his day, had complained haughtily that the poetaster of elegant salons had gotten the diplomatic post denied him.

For two and a half years he gathered material for the book. The task wasn't difficult, but it was lengthy and, in some respects, boring. It included trips to Pergamino, Santa Cruz, and Mendoza, correspondence with librarians and archivists, the examination of collections of newspapers and magazines, the collation of texts, parallel studies of the literary currents of the period. Toward the end of 1954, the central elements of the book were collected and evaluated, although Fraga had still not written a word of text.

While he was inserting a new card into his black cardboard file one September night, he wondered if he was in shape to undertake the task. He wasn't worried about obstacles, but, quite the contrary, rather about how easy it would be to run across a field so well known. The information was there and nothing important would come out of the files or memories of Argentines of the time anymore. He'd collected news items and events, apparently unknown, that would perfect the image of Claudio Romero and his poetry. The only problem was that of making a mistake in the central focus, the lines of flight, and the composition of the whole.

"But is that image clear enough for me?" Fraga would wonder, looking at the glow of his cigarette. "The affinities between Romero and me, our common preference for certain aesthetic and poetic values, the thing that makes the choice of theme inevitable for the biographer, won't that make me fall into a disguised autobiography more than once?"

He could answer that with the fact that he hadn't been endowed with any creative capacity, that he wasn't a poet but one who enjoyed poetry, and that his faculties had been affirmed in criticism, in the pleasure that accompanies knowledge. An alert attitude would be sufficient, a watchfulness as he faced submersion in the work of the poet so as to avoid any unwarranted transfusion. He had no reason not to trust his sympathy for Claudio Romero and his fascination with his poems. As with good photographic equipment, the necessary adjustment would have to be made so that the subject would remain precisely framed without the shadow of the photographer treading on his toes.

Now that the first blank page was awaiting him like a door that it would be necessary to start opening from one moment to the next, he went back to wondering whether or not he would be capable of writing the book as he had imagined it. The biography and criticism could verge dangerously on the facile, being oriented only toward that type of reader who expects a book that is the equivalent of a movie or of André Maurois. The problem consisted in not sacrificing that anonymous and multitudinous consumer whom his socialist friends called the people to the erudite satisfaction of a handful of colleagues. To find the angle that would permit him to write a book of impassioned reading without falling into the recipes of a best seller; to earn simultaneously the respect of the academic world and the enthusiasm of the man on the street who wants to be entertained in his easy chair on Saturday night.

It had a touch of Faust's moment, the time of the pact. Almost at dawn, the cigarette consumed, the glass of wine in his indecisive hand. *Wine, like a glove of time*, Claudio Romero had written somewhere.

"Why not?" Fraga said to himself, lighting another cigarette. "With everything I know about him now, it would be stupid for me to stick with a mere essay, in an edition of three hundred copies. Juárez or Ricardi could do that just as well. But nobody knows anything about Susana Márquez."

An allusion by the justice of the peace in Bragado, the younger brother of a deceased friend of Claudio Romero's, had put him on the track. Someone who worked in the civil registry in La Plata had gotten an address in Pilar for him after much searching. Susana Márquez's daughter was a woman of some thirty years, small and sweet. She had refused to talk at first, under the pretext that she had to take care of the business (a vegetable store); then she allowed Fraga to come into the parlor, sit in a dusty chair, and ask her questions. In the beginning she looked at him without answering; then she wept a little, put her handkerchief to her eyes, and spoke about her poor mother. It was hard for Fraga to make her understand that he already knew something about the relationship between Claudio Romero and Susana, but he ended up telling himself that the love of a poet was just as good as a marriage license, and he hinted at it with the necessary delicacy. After a few minutes of strewing flowers along the way, he saw her come toward him, totally convinced and even moved. A moment later he had in his hands an extraordinary photograph of Romero, never published, and another one, smaller and yellowed, where next to the poet was seen a woman as small as her daughter and with just as sweet a look.

"I have some letters too," Raquel Márquez said. "If they can be of any help to you, since you say you're going to write about him . . ."

She searched for a long time, selecting from a pile of papers that she had taken out of a music cabinet, and finally she handed him three letters that Fraga put away without reading, after ascertaining that they were in Romero's handwriting. At this point in the conversation he was already sure that Raquel wasn't the poet's daughter, because with the first insinuation he saw her lower her head and fall silent for a moment, as if thinking. Then she explained that her mother later on had married a military man from Balcarce ("Fangio's town," she said, almost as if it were proof), and that they had both died when she was only eight years old. She remembered her mother very well, but didn't remember much about her father. He was a strict man, that he was.

When Fraga returned to Buenos Aires and read Claudio Romero's three letters to Susana, the final fragments of the

mosaic seemed to fall into place quickly, revealing a completely unexpected composition, a drama that the ignorance
and prudery of the poet's generation hadn't even suspected.
In 1917 Romero had published the series of poems dedicated
to Irene Paz, among which the famous "Ode to Your Double
Name" figured, the one that critics had proclaimed the most
beautiful love poem ever written in Argentina. And, nevertheless, a year before the appearance of the book, another
woman had received those three letters where the tone that
defined the best poetry of Romero reigned, a mixture of exaltation and disengagement, like that of a person who was
simultaneously the motive and the subject of the action,
protagonist and chorus. Before reading the letters, Fraga had
suspected the usual amorous correspondence, the mirrors
face to face, isolating and petrifying their reflection, important only to them. In every paragraph, on the contrary, he
discovered the reiteration of Romero's world, the richness of
a totalizing vision of love. Not only had his passion for Susana
Márquez not cut him off from the world, but with every line
one could feel throbbing a reality that amplified the beloved,
the justification and demand of a poetry that was doing life-
size battle.

The story itself was simple. Romero had met Susana at a
dull literary salon in La Plata and the beginning of their
relationship coincided with an almost total eclipse of the
poet, one which his few biographers had not explained or
attributed to the first attacks of the tuberculosis that was to
kill him two years later. The story of Susana Márquez had
escaped everybody, as befitted her hazy image, the great
frightened eyes that stared fixedly from the old photograph.
She was an unemployed schoolteacher, the only daughter of
old and poor parents, lacking friends who might take an interest in her, and their simultaneous disappearance from literary
gatherings in La Plata had coincided with the most dramatic

period of the European war, other public interests, new literary voices. Fraga could consider himself fortunate in having
heard the casual allusion by a country justice of the peace;
with that thread between his fingers he managed to locate the
gloomy house in Burzaco where Romero and Susana had
lived for almost two years; the letters that Raquel Márquez
had entrusted to him corresponded with the end of that
period. The first, postmarked La Plata, referred to a previous
piece of correspondence in which he had dealt with his marriage to Susana. The poet confessed his anguish at feeling ill,
and his scruples about marrying someone who would have to
be a nurse rather than a wife. The second letter was admirable, the passion gave ground to a feeling of almost unbearable purity, as if Romero were struggling to awaken in his
beloved an analogous lucidity that would make the necessary
break less painful. One sentence summed it all up: "No one
has any reason to know about our life and I offer you freedom with silence. Free, you will be even more for eternity. If
we were to marry, I would feel like your executioner every
time you came into my room with a flower in your hand."
And he added harshly: "I don't want to cough in your face, I
don't want you to dry my sweat. You've known a different
body, I've given you different roses. I need the night for myself alone, I won't let you see me weep." The third letter was
more serene, as if Susana had begun to accept the poet's sacrifice. Somewhere it said: "You insist I magnetize you, oblige
you to do my will. . . . But my will is your future, let me sow
these seeds that will be the consolation of a stupid death."

In the chronology established by Fraga, the life of
Claudio Romero from that moment entered a monotonous
stage, one of almost continuous reclusiveness in his parents'
home. No other testimony led one to suppose that the poet
and Susana Márquez had ever met again, although it was also

impossible to state the contrary; nevertheless, the best proof that Romero's renunciation had been consummated and that Susana must finally have preferred freedom to condemning herself to the side of the sick man was the ascendancy of the new and resplendent planet in the heavens of Romero's poetry. One year after that correspondence and that renunciation, a magazine in Buenos Aires published "Ode to Your Double Name," dedicated to Irene Paz. Romero's health seemed to have improved and the poem, which he himself had read in some salons, suddenly brought him the glory that his previous work had paved the way for almost secretly. Like Byron, he could say that one morning he had awakened to discover that he was famous, and, like Byron, he never stopped saying so. But, contrary to what one might have hoped for, the poet's passion for Irene Paz was not returned, and, judging from a series of mundane episodes related by the wits of the period in a contradictory way, the personal prestige of the poet plunged suddenly, obliging him to retreat once more into his parents' home, removed from friends and admirers. His last book of poems was from that period. A brutal hemoptysis caught Romero in the street a few months after, and three weeks later he was dead. His funeral brought together a group of writers, but from the tone of the funeral orations and the chronicles it was obvious that the world to which Irene Paz belonged had not been present, nor had it rendered the homage that might have been expected under those circumstances.

It wasn't difficult for Fraga to understand that Romero's passion for Irene Paz must have flattered and scandalized the aristocratic world of La Plata and Buenos Aires in equal measure. He hadn't been able to get a clear idea of Irene; the photos of her at twenty .attested to her beauty, but the rest was nothing but society news. The true heiress to the traditions of the Pazes, she had an attitude toward Romero that was easy to imagine; she must have met him at some gathering that her people gave from time to time to listen to those they called, stressing the quotation marks with their inflection, the "artists" and "poets" of the moment. If the ode flattered her, if the admirable initial invocation revealed to her like a flash of lightning the truth of a passion that demanded her in the face of all obstacles, only Romero, perhaps, could have known it, and even that wasn't certain. But at that point Fraga understood that the problem ceased being such and that it had lost all importance. Claudio Romero had been too lucid to have imagined for a single instant that his passion was returned. The distance, the barriers of all kinds, Irene's complete inaccessibility, sequestered within the double prison of her family and herself, faithful mirror of her caste, had made her unattainable from the beginning. The tone of the ode was unmistakable and went well beyond the current images of love poetry. Romero called himself "the Icarus of your honeyed feet"—an image that earned him the mockery of an Aristarchus from *Caras y Caretas*—and the poem was nothing more than a supreme leap in quest of the impossible and therefore most beautiful ideal, the ascent through verse of a desperate flight toward the sun that would burn him and fling him to his death. Even the poet's final withdrawal and silence poignantly resembled the phases of a fall, of a lamentable return to the earth he had dared abandon for a dream beyond his forces.

Yes, Fraga thought, pouring himself another glass of wine, everything coincides, everything falls into place; now all I have to do is write it.

The success of *Life of an Argentine Poet* went beyond anything the author and publishers could have imagined.

Though the book was barely commented on during the first
weeks, an unexpected article in *La Razón* awoke the people
of Buenos Aires from their cautious drowsiness and incited
them to taking a position that few refused to assume. *Sur, La
Nación*, the best provincial newspapers took over the theme
of the moment, which immediately invaded café conversations and after-dinner talk. Two violent polemics (about the
influence of Darío on Romero and a chronological question)
converged to interest the public. The first edition of the *Life*
was sold out in two months—the second in a month and a
half. Obliged by the circumstances and the advantages
offered him, Fraga consented to do a dramatic adaptation and
another for radio. The time had arrived when the interest
and the novelty of a work reach the fearful apex behind
which the unknown successor is already lurking; inevitably,
and as if it were meant to redress an injustice, the National
Prize cleared a way for itself to Fraga through the interven-
tion of two friends who had preceded the telephone calls
and the shrill chorus of the first congratulations. Laughing,
Fraga recalled that being awarded the Nobel Prize hadn't
stopped Gide from going to see a Fernandel movie the same
night; maybe that's why he enjoyed seeking refuge at a
friend's place and avoiding the first avalanche of collective
enthusiasm with a tranquillity which even his accomplice in
that friendly kidnapping found excessive and almost hypocritical. But, during those days, Fraga had his doubts, without any explanation, as to why a kind of desire for solitude
was taking root in him, a wish to be on the margin of his
public figure, which by means of photography and radio was
breaching walls, reaching provincial circles, and appearing in
the foreign media. The National Prize wasn't a surprise,
merely a reparation. Now the rest would come, what underneath it all had driven him to write the *Life*. He wasn't

wrong: a week later the Minister of Foreign Relations received him at home ("we diplomats know that good writers aren't interested in the official apparatus") and offered him the post of cultural attaché in Europe. Everything had an almost oneiric air about it: it all went so much against the current that Fraga had to make an effort to accept fully the ascent up the stairway of honors; step by step, starting with the first reviews, the smiles and embraces of his publishers, invitations from literary societies, he had reached the landing from which, by just leaning over, he would be able to take in the whole of the fashionable salon world, dominate it allegorically, and scrutinize it to its last corner, to the last white tie and last chinchilla of the protectors of literature, between mouthfuls of foie gras and Dylan Thomas. Further off—or closer by, it depended on the angle of vision, the momentary state of mind—he also saw the humble and sheeplike multitude of magazine devourers, of televiewers and radio listeners, the many who on a certain day, without knowing how or why, submit to the imperative of buying a washing machine or a novel, an object of thirty cubic feet or three hundred eighteen pages, and they buy it, buy it immediately, making some kind of sacrifice, and take it home where madam and the children are waiting anxiously because the neighbor woman already has one, because the commentator in vogue on Radio El Mundo has praised it again on his eleven fifty-five broadcast. The startling thing had been that his book had entered the catalogue of things that must be bought and read, after so many years during which the life and works of Claudio Romero had been nothing more than a mania of intellectuals—which is to say, of almost no one. But when, time and again, he felt the necessity of remaining alone once more and thinking about what was happening (it was the week of contacts with movie producers now), the initial surprise gave

way to a nervous expectation of he didn't know what. Nothing
could come that wasn't another step on the stairway of honor,
except the inevitable day when, as on garden bridges, the last
rising step is followed by the first descending one, the re-
spectable path toward public satiety and a turn in search of
new emotions. When he had to isolate himself in order to
prepare his acceptance speech for the National Prize, the synthesis of the dizzying experiences of those weeks was summed
up in an ironic satisfaction with what his triumph had of
retaliation about it, softened by that inexplicable restlessness
which at moments rose to the surface and tried to project
itself toward a territory to which his sense of balance and
humor were resolutely denied. He thought that the prepa-
ration of the lecture would bring the pleasure of work back to
him, and he went to Ofelia Fernández's country place to
write it, a place where he would have peace and quiet. It was
the end of summer, the woods were already taking on the
colors of autumn, which he liked to look at from the porch
while he chatted with Ofelia and petted the dogs. In a room
on the second floor his working materials were waiting; when
he lifted the cover of his main file box, running through it
distractedly like a pianist warming up, Fraga told himself
that all was well, that in spite of the inevitable vulgarity of all
literary triumphs on a grand scale, the *Life* was an act of
justice, an homage to the race and to the nation. He could sit
down and write his speech, receive the prize, get ready for his
trip to Europe. Dates and notes were mingled in his mind
with the clauses of contracts and dinner invitations. Soon
Ofelia would come in with a decanter of sherry, she would
come over, silent and attentive, would watch him work. Yes,
everything was fine. There was nothing to do but take a sheet
of paper, adjust the lamp, light up a Havana cigar listening to
the distant call of a tero bird.

He never knew exactly whether the revelation had come at that moment or later, after making love to Ofelia, while they were smoking, lying in bed and looking at a small green star high up on the window. The invasion, if one were to call it that (but its true name or nature didn't matter), might have coincided with the first sentence of his speech, drawn up swiftly to a point at which it had been interrupted suddenly, replaced, swept by something like a wind that took all meaning from it. The rest had been a long silence, but perhaps everything was already known when he came down out of the hall, known and formulated, weighing like a headache or the beginning of the flu. Ungraspable, at some indefinable moment, the confused weight, the black wind had been resolved in certainty: the *Life* was false, the story of Claudio Romero had nothing to do with what he had written. No reasons, no proofs: everything false. After years of work, of gathering facts, of following tracks, of avoiding personal excesses: everything false. Claudio Romero had not sacrificed himself for Susana Márquez, nor had he given her back her freedom at the cost of his renunciation, he had not been the Icarus at the honeyed feet of Irene Paz. As if he were swimming underwater, unable to return to the surface, lashed by the roar of the current in his ears, he knew the truth. And it was not sufficient torture; behind it, still lower in the water that was mud and filth now, dragging him along was the certainty that he'd known it from the first moment. It was useless to light another cigarette, plead neurosis, kiss the thin lips that Ofelia offered him in the shadows. Useless to argue that the excessive dedication to his hero might have provoked that momentary hallucination, that rejection, because of an excess of energy. He felt Ofelia's hand stroking his chest, the intermittent warmth of her breathing. Inexplicably, he fell asleep.

In the morning he looked at the open file, the papers, and they were more alien than the feelings of the night before. Downstairs Ofelia was busy telephoning the station to get the train connections. He got Pilar around eleven thirty and went directly to the vegetable store. Susana's daughter received him with a curious air of simultaneous resentment and adulation, like a dog after a kick. Fraga asked her to give him five minutes and once more went into the dusty parlor and sat down in the same white-bottomed chair. He didn't have to talk much because Susana's daughter, after drying a few tears, began to approve, with her head tilted, leaning more and more forward.

"Yes, sir, that's how it was. Yes, sir."

"Why didn't you tell me the first time?"

It was difficult to explain why she hadn't said so the first time. Her mother had made her swear that she would never mention certain things and she'd married the non-commissioned officer from Balcarce later on, so . . . She'd almost thought of writing him when they'd begun to talk so much about the book on Romero because . . .

She looked at him perplexed, and from time to time a tear fell down to her mouth.

"How did you find out?" she asked him then.

"Don't worry about that," Fraga said. "Everything comes out in the end."

"But you wrote it so differently in the book. I read it, you know. I have it and everything."

"The blame for its being so different is on you. There are other letters from Romero to your mother. You gave me the ones that fitted, the ones that flattered Romero and, by ricochet, your mother. I need the others right now. Give them to me."

"There's only one," Raquel Márquez said. "But Mama made me swear, sir."

"If she kept it without burning it, it's because it wasn't so important. Let me have it. I'll buy it from you."

"Mr. Fraga, that's not why I won't give it to you . . ."

"Here," Fraga said brutally. "You won't get money like this selling pumpkins."

While he watched her bending over the music case, going through papers, he thought that what he knew now he'd already known (in a different way, perhaps, but he'd known it) the day of his first visit with Raquel Márquez. The truth didn't take him completely by surprise, and now he could judge himself in retrospect and wonder, for example, why he'd abbreviated his first interview with Susana's daughter in such a way, why he'd accepted Romero's letters as if they were the only ones, without insisting, without offering something in exchange, without getting to the bottom of what Raquel knew and was keeping quiet. It's absurd, he thought. At that moment I had no way of knowing that Susana had prostituted herself and the fault was Romero's. But why, then, had he deliberately abbreviated his conversation with Raquel, appearing satisfied with the photographs and the three letters. Oh, yes, I knew it, who knows how, but I knew it, and I wrote the book knowing it, and maybe the readers know it too, and the critics, and it's all an immense lie in which we're all caught up . . . But it was easy to get out of it by way of generalizations, accepting only a small part of the blame. Also a lie: there was only one guilty party, he.

The reading of the letter was a mere superimposition of words on something that Fraga already knew from a different angle and which the epistolary proof could only reinforce in case of a polemic. The mask fallen, an almost ferocious Claudio Romero appeared in those phrases, so cutting and having an unanswerable logic. Condemning Susana to the filthy profession in which she was to drag herself along during her last years and which was alluded to in two passages, he imposed silence, distance, and hate on her forever. He pushed her with sarcasm and threats toward a downhill course that he himself must have prepared in two years of slow and minute corruption. The man who weeks before had taken pleasure in writing: "I need the night for myself alone, I won't let you see me weep" now finished off a paragraph with a filthy allusion whose effect he must have malignantly foreseen, and he piled up sarcastic recommendations and advice, light farewells interrupted by explicit threats in case Susana tried to see him again. Nothing of that surprised Fraga anymore, but he remained for a long time with his shoulder leaning against the window of the train, the letter in his hand, as if something in him were struggling to awaken from a slow, unbearable nightmare. And that explains the rest, he heard himself think. The rest was Irene Paz, "Ode to Your Double Name," Claudio Romero's final failure. Without proof or reasons, but with a certainty much deeper than could emanate from just any letter or testimony, the last two years of Romero's life were ordered day by day in the memory—if there was some name you could give it—of a person who, in the eyes of the passengers on the train from Pilar, must have been a gentleman who had drunk one vermouth too many. When he got off at the station it was four o'clock in the afternoon and starting to rain. The gig that took him to the farm was cold and smelled of rancid leather. How much good sense had dwelt under the haughty brow of Irene Paz, from how much long aristocratic experience had the negative of her world been born. Romero had been capable of magnetizing a poor woman, but he didn't have the wings of Icarus that his poem claimed. Irene, or not even she, her mother or her brothers, had immediately guessed the attempt of the arriviste, the grotesque leap of the social climber who begins by denying his origins, killing them if that failed (and the crime was called Susana Márquez, schoolteacher). All they had needed was a smile, the refusal of an invitation, a retreat to their ranch, the sharp weapons of money and butlers with instructions. They hadn't even bothered to attend the poet's funeral.

Ofelia was waiting on the porch. Fraga told her that he had to get to work right away. When with a cigarette between his lips and an enormous fatigue that sank his shoulders he faced the page begun the night before, he told himself that nobody knew anything. It was like the time before he'd written the *Life* and he was still the master of the keys. He just smiled and began to write his speech. Much later he realized that at some point on the trip he'd lost Romero's letter.

Anyone can read in the files of Buenos Aires newspapers the comments aroused by the National Prize award ceremony in which Jorge Fraga had deliberately provoked the upset and wrath of sound minds when from the platform he presented an absolutely wild version of the life of the poet Claudio Romero. One reporter pointed out that Fraga had given the impression of being indisposed (but the euphemism was clear), among other things because several times he had spoken as if he were Romero himself, correcting himself immediately only to fall back into the absurd aberration a moment later. Another reporter called attention to the fact that Fraga had a few scribbled pages that he scarcely looked at during the course of the speech, giving the feeling of his being his own audience, approving or disapproving certain phrases that were scarcely spoken, until he produced a growing and an ultimately unbearable irritation in the vast audience that had gathered together with the express intention of applauding him. Another writer reported the violent altercation between Fraga and Dr. Jovellanos after the lecture, when a large part of the audience had abandoned the hall with exclamations of chagrin, and reported with grief that in reply to Dr. Jovellanos' intimation that he present convincing proof of the fearful affirmations of calumny to the sacred memory of Claudio Romero, the lecturer had shrugged his shoulders and ended by raising a hand to his forehead as if the required proof had not gone beyond his imagination; and, lastly, he had remained motionless, looking into the air, as aloof from the tumultuous departure of the audience as to the provocative applause and congratulations of a small group of youths and humorists who seemed to find that particular manner of accepting a National Prize admirable.

When Fraga reached the farm two hours later, Ofelia silently handed him a long list of telephone calls, one from the Foreign Ministry to another from a brother with whom he had broken. He looked distractedly at the series of names, some underlined, others poorly written. The piece of paper fell from his hand and onto the rug. Without picking it up, he began to climb the stairs that led to his workroom.

Much later Ofelia heard him walking about the room. She went to bed and tried not to think. Fraga's steps came and went, halting at times as if he had stopped by the desk for a moment, to look something up. An hour later she heard him come downstairs, come into the bedroom. Without opening her eyes she felt the weight of his body as he slipped in beside her and lay on his back. A cold hand squeezed hers. In the darkness Ofelia kissed him on the cheek.

"The only thing I don't understand," Fraga said as if he weren't talking to her, "is why it took me so long to know that I'd always known it all. It's idiotic to suppose that I'm a medium, I've had absolutely nothing to do with him. Even up to a week ago I had nothing to do with him."

"If you could only get a bit of sleep," Ofelia said.

"No, I've got to find it. There are two things: what I don't understand and what's going to start tomorrow, what's already started this afternoon. I'm finished, you understand, they'll never forgive me for having put the idol into their arms and then making it fly into pieces. Just look how absolutely imbecilic it all is, Romero will go on being the author of the best poems of the twenties. But idols can't have feet of clay and, using the same banality, my dear colleagues are going to tell me that tomorrow."

"But if you thought that your duty was to proclaim the truth . . ."

"I didn't think it, Ofelia, I did it. That's all. Or someone did it for me. Suddenly there wasn't any other way after that night. It was the only thing that could have been done."

"It probably would have been better if you'd waited a bit," Ofelia said timidly. "All of a sudden, just like that, in front of . . ."

She was going to say "of the Minister," and Fraga heard the words as clearly as if she'd said them. He smiled, stroked her hand. Little by little the waters began to recede; something still obscure was trying to bring itself into view, define itself. Ofelia's long, anguished silence helped him grasp things better, looking into the darkness with his eyes wide open. He would never understand why he hadn't known before that everything was known, why he kept denying that he, too, was a swine, as much a swine as Romero himself. The idea of writing the book had already taken on the aim of a social revenge, of a facile triumph, of the vindication of everything he deserved and which other opportunists were taking away from him. Apparently rigorous, the *Life* had been born armed with all the resourses to open a way into the show windows of bookstores. Every step of the triumph was waiting, minutely prepared in every chapter, in every phrase. His ironical, almost disenchanted progressive acceptance of those stages didn't go beyond one of the many masks of infamy. Behind the anodyne cover of the *Life*, radio, TV, movies, the National Prize, the diplomatic post in Europe, the money, and the lionizing had been lurking. Except that something unforeseen had been waiting until the last moment to land on the painstakingly constructed machine and blow it up. It was useless to want to think about that, useless to be afraid, to feel possessed by the succubus.

"I've had nothing to do with him," Fraga repeated, closing his eyes. "I don't know how it happened, Ofelia, but I've had nothing to do with him."

He could hear her weeping in silence.

"But then it's even worse. Like an infection under the skin, hidden for so long and suddenly bursting and spattering you with rotten blood. Every time it was my turn to choose, to decide on the conduct of that man, I chose the reverse, what he tried to make people believe while he was alive. My choices were his, when anyone could have been able to decipher a different truth in his life, in his letters, in that last year when death was hemming him in and stripping him. I didn't want to see it, I refused to show the truth because, then, Ofelia, then, Romero wouldn't have been the famous person who needed me as I needed him to put together the legend, in order to . . ."

He fell silent, but everything kept on taking shape and falling into place. Now, from out of the depths, he was arriving at his identity with Claudio Romero, and it had nothing to do with the supernatural. Brothers in the farce, in the lie and the hope of a blazing ascent, brothers in the brutal fall that struck them down and destroyed them. Clearly and simply, Fraga felt that anyone like him would always be Claudio Romero, that the Romeros of yesterday and tomorrow would always be Jorge Fraga. Just as he had been afraid one distant September night, he had hypocritically written his autobiography. It gave him an urge to laugh and at the same time he thought of the pistol he kept in the desk.

He never knew whether it had been at that moment or later that Ofelia had said: "The only thing that counts is that today you showed them the truth." She hadn't meant to make him think about that, to bring back the almost incredible hour in which he had spoken, facing looks that passed progressively from the admiring or courteous smile to the wrinkled brow, the disdainful grimace, the arm rising in a sign of protest. But that was the only thing that counted, the only certain and solid thing in the whole story; no one could take that hour when he had really triumphed away from him, beyond the simulacra and his avid supporters. When he leaned over Ofelia to stroke her hair it seemed to him that she was a little like Susana Márquez and that his caress was saving her and keeping her close to him. And at the same time the National Prize, the post in Europe, and the honors were Irene Paz, something that had to be rejected and abolished if he didn't want to sink completely into Romero, miserably identified until the end with a false hero of the printed word and soap operas.

Later on—the night spun slowly in its heaven boiling with stars—other decks of cards became mingled in the interminable insomnia solitaire. Morning would bring the telephone calls, the newspapers, the scandal well tailored to fit into two columns. It seemed mad to him to have thought for a moment that everything was lost when a minute of assurance and skill was all that was needed to win the game, point by point. Everything depended on a few hours, a few interviews. If he felt like it, the cancellation of the prize, the refusal of the Foreign Ministry to confirm its proposal could be converted into news that would throw him into the international world of vast printings and translations. But he could also stay on his back in bed, refusing to see anyone, shutting himself up for months on the farm, picking up and continuing with his old philological studies, his best and now hazy friendships. In six months he would be forgotten, admirably replaced by the most stolid newspaperman of the moment in the listings of success. Both paths were equally simple, equally secure. It was all a matter of choosing. And even though he'd already decided, he still thought, just for something to think about, choosing and giving reasons for his choice until dawn began to brush against the window, against the hair of Ofelia asleep and the silk-cotton tree in the garden, imprecisely outlined like a future that takes shape as present, hardens little by little, enters into its everyday form, accepts it and defends it and condemns it in the morning light.

ENCOUNTER
WITHIN
A
RED
CIRCLE

FOR BORGES

It seems to me, Jacobo, that you must have been very cold
that night and that the persistent Wiesbaden rain was closing
in to make you decide to go into the Zagreb. Maybe your
appetite was the dominant reason, you'd worked all day and
now it was time to have dinner in some quiet, peaceful spot;
if the Zagreb lacked other qualities, it did combine those two
and you, shrugging your shoulders, I think, as if teasing
yourself a little, decided to dine there. In any case, there were
plenty of tables in the shadows of the vaguely Balkan dining
room and it was nice to be able to hang your soaked raincoat

This tale was included in the catalogue of an exhibit by the Venezuelan painter
Jacobo Borges.

on the old rack and search out that corner where the green candle on the table softly moved the shadows and let ancient silverware and a very tall glass show through where the light took refuge like a bird.

First there was the usual feeling in an empty restaurant, something between annoyance and relief; from its looks it shouldn't be bad, but the absence of customers at that hour gave cause for thought. In a foreign city meditations like that don't last long: what does a person know about customs and schedules, what counts is the warmth, the menu where surprises or reappearances are proposed, the tiny woman with large eyes and black hair who arrived as if out of nowhere, suddenly outlined against the white tablecloth, a slight fixed smile as she waited. You thought that perhaps it was already too late in the routine of the city, but you almost didn't have time to raise a look of touristic interrogation; a small, pale hand deposited a napkin and lined up the saltshaker that had been out of rhythm. As was logical, you chose shish kebab with onions and red peppers, and a thick and fragrant wine that had nothing Western about it; like me on other occasions, you liked to escape from hotel meals where the fear of the too typical or exotic is resolved with insipidness, and you even ordered black bread, which might not have been the thing to go with shish kebab, but which the woman brought immediately. Only then, smoking a first cigarette, did you look somewhat intently at the Transylvanian enclave that was protecting you from the rain and a not excessively interesting German city. The silence, the absences, and the vague light from the wicks were already almost your friends; in any case, they put you at a distance from the rest and left you beautifully alone with your cigarette and your weariness.

The hand that poured the wine into the tall glass was covered with hair, and it took you a startled second to break

the absurd logical chain and understand that the pale woman
was no longer by your side and in her place a swarthy and
silent waiter was inviting you to taste the wine with a gesture
that seemed to be only an automatic expectation. It's rare for
anyone to find the wine bad, and the waiter finally filled the
glass as if the interruption had been but a minor part of the
ceremony. Almost at the same time another waiter, curiously
resembling the first (but the native costumes, the black sideburns made them uniform), put the steaming platter on the
table and with a rapid movement pushed the meat off the
skewers. The few necessary words had been exchanged in the
bad German foreseen in the guest and those serving him; he
was surrounded once more by the calm of the shadows in the
room and the weariness, but now you heard the rain beating
more strongly on the street. That too ceased almost immediately and you, barely turning, saw that the entrance door had
been opened to let in another customer, a woman who must
have been myopic, not only because of the thickness of her
glasses, but also because of the senseless assuredness with
which she advanced among the tables to sit down in the opposite corner of the room, lighted only by one or two candles
that flickered as she passed and mingled her uncertain figure
with the furnishings and the walls and the thick-curtained
red of the background, there where the restaurant seemed to
lean against the rest of an unpredictable house.

   While you ate you were vaguely amused that the English
tourist (she couldn't have been anything else with that raincoat and a peep of blouse that was between mauve and to-
mato) was concentrating her myopia on a menu that must
have been totally beyond her, and that the woman with the
large black eyes had remained in the third corner of the
room, where there was a counter with mirrors and wreaths
of dry flowers, letting the tourist finish not understanding

before she went over. The waiters had placed themselves behind the counter, on both sides of the woman, and were also waiting with their arms folded, so similar to each other that the reflection of their backs in the aged quicksilver had something false about it, like a difficult or tricky quadruplication. They were all looking at the English tourist, who didn't seem to realize the passage of time and still had her face glued to the menu. There was still a wait while you took out another cigarette, and the woman finally came over to your table and asked if you wanted some soup, perhaps some Greek goat cheese, continued the questions with each polite negative, the cheeses were quite good, well, then, perhaps some regional pastries. You wanted only some Turkish coffee because the dinner had been abundant and you were starting to feel sleepy. The woman seemed indecisive, as if giving you an opportunity to change your mind and order a platter of cheeses, and when you didn't, she repeated mechanically, Turkish coffee, and you said yes, Turkish coffee, and the woman took a kind of short, quick breath, raised her hand to the waiters, and went on to the English tourist's table.

The coffee was a long time coming, in contrast to the quick start of the dinner, and you had time to smoke another cigarette and slowly finish the bottle of wine while you amused yourself watching the English tourist let a thick-lensed look stroll all about the room without stopping on anything particular. There was something stupid or timid in her, she went through a rather long set of vague movements until she decided to take off the raincoat that was glistening with rain and hang it on the nearest rack; when she sat down again she naturally must have wet her behind, but that didn't seem to worry her as she finished her uncertain observation of the room and remained quite still looking at the tablecloth. The waiters had gone back to their positions behind the

counter, and the woman was waiting beside the small window
to the kitchen; the three were looking at the English tourist,
looking at her as if expecting something, for her to call to
complete an order or maybe change it or leave, they were
looking at her in a way that seemed to you too intense, un-
justified in any case. They had stopped paying attention to
you, the two waiters had their arms folded again, and the
woman had her head a bit tilted and her long hair covered
her eyes, but it was she, perhaps, who was staring hardest at
the tourist and that seemed disagreeable and discourteous to
you, even though the poor myopic mole couldn't have been
aware of anything now that she was digging in her purse and
pulling out something that couldn't be seen in the shadows
but which could be identified by the noise the mole made as
she blew her nose. One of the waiters brought her meal (it
looked like goulash) and returned immediately to his post as
sentinel; the double mania of folding their arms as soon as
they finished their work should have been amusing but in
some way it wasn't, nor was the woman's placing herself in
the most distant angle of the counter and from there continuing to concentrate her attention on the operation of drinking
coffee that you were bringing to a conclusion with all the
slowness that its good quality and aroma demanded. Suddenly the center of attention seemed to have changed, because the two waiters were also watching you drink your
coffee, and before you finished the woman came over to ask if
you wanted another, and you accepted, almost perplexed because in all that, which wasn't anything, there was something
that was escaping you and which you would have liked to
have understood better. The English tourist, for example,
why was it that the waiters suddenly seemed to be in such a
hurry for the tourist to finish eating and leave and they took
away her plate right after her last mouthful and gave her

the menu opened up in her face as one of them went off with the empty plate while the other waited as if urging her to decide.

You, as happens so many times, couldn't have been able to identify the precise moment in which you thought you understood; in chess and in love, too, there are those moments when the mist breaks and it is then that plays or acts are performed which would have been inconceivable one second before. Without even an idea you could articulate you smelled the danger and said to yourself that no matter how long the English tourist dragged out her dinner it was necessary for you to remain there smoking and drinking until the defenseless mole decided to encase herself in her plastic bubble and go out onto the street once more. Since you had always enjoyed sport and absurdity, you found it amusing to consider as such something that at gut level was far from being so; you made a signal and ordered another coffee and a glass of barack, which was advisable in the enclave. You had three cigarettes left and you thought they would last until the English tourist decided on some Balkan dessert; naturally, she wouldn't have any coffee, it was something that could be seen in her eyeglasses and blouse; nor would she ask for tea because there are things one doesn't do outside the mother country. With a little luck she would pay the bill and leave after some fifteen more minutes.

They served you the coffee but not the barack, the woman took her eyes out of her mat of hair to put on the expression that fitted the delay; they were looking for a new bottle in the wine cellar, if the gentleman would be so kind as to wait a few minutes. The voice articulated the words clearly even if they were mispronounced, but you noticed that the woman remained intent on the other table, where one of the waiters was presenting the bill with the gesture of a robot, stretching out his arm and remaining motionless within a perfectly respectful discourtesy. As if she finally understood, the tourist set about digging into her purse; everything about her was clumsy, she was probably running into a comb or a mirror instead of the money that finally must have come to the surface because the waiter brusquely left the table at the moment the woman arrived with the glass of barack. Nor did you know too well why you simultaneously asked her for the check, now that you were sure the tourist would leave first and you could dedicate yourself to savoring the barack and smoking the last cigarette. Maybe the idea of remaining alone once more in the place that had been so agreeable on arriving and was different now, things like the double image of the waiters behind the counter and the woman who seemed to hesitate at the request, as if it were indolence to be in such a hurry, and then turned her back and returned to the counter to close the trio and the wait again. After all, it must have been depressing to work in such an empty restaurant, so far from light and fresh air; those people had begun to wither, their paleness and their mechanical gestures were the only possible response to so many interminable nights. And the tourist gesticulated around her raincoat, went back to the table as if she thought she had forgotten something, looked under the chair, and then you got up slowly, incapable of staying a second longer, and halfway there you ran into one of the waiters, who held out the silver tray on which you put a bill without looking at the check. The gust of wind coincided with the gesture of the waiter as he looked in the pockets of his red vest for the change, but you knew that the tourist had just opened the door and you didn't wait any longer, you raised your hand in a good-bye that took in the waiter and those who continued looking from the counter, and calculating the distance exactly, you picked up your raincoat as you went by and went out into the street, where it was no longer raining. Only there did you really breathe, as if until then and without realizing it you had been holding your breath; only there did you really feel fear and relief at the same time.

The tourist was a few steps ahead, walking slowly in the direction of your hotel, and you followed her with the vague suspicion that suddenly she would remember that she had forgotten something and it would occur to her to return to the restaurant. It was no longer a question of understanding anything, everything was a simple block, evidence with no reason: you had saved her and you had to be sure that she wouldn't return, that the clumsy mole stuck in her damp bubble would arrive with a total, happy unawareness at the shelter of her hotel, at a room where no one would look at her the way they had been looking at her.

When she turned the corner, and even though there was no longer any reason to hurry, you wondered whether or not it wouldn't be better to follow her closely in order to be sure that she wouldn't go around the block in her erratic myopic clumsiness; you hastened to reach the corner and saw the poorly lighted and empty alleyway. The two long stone walls showed in the distance nothing but a doorway, which the tourist could not have reached; only a toad, enlivened by the rain, was hopping across from one sidewalk to the other.

For a moment it was rage, how could that stupid . . . Then you leaned against one of the walls and waited, but it was almost as if you were waiting for yourself, for something that had to open and function in the deepest part so that all of it would come to some meaning. The toad had found a hole at the base of the wall and was also waiting, perhaps for some insect that had nested in the hole or for a passageway to get into a garden. You never knew how long you had stayed there or why you went back to the street where the restaurant was. The windows were dark but the narrow door was still ajar; it almost didn't startle you that the woman was there as if waiting for you without surprise.

"We thought you'd come back," she said. "You see now that there was no reason for you to have left so soon."

She opened the door a little more and stood aside; now it would have been so easy to turn your back and go away without even answering, but the street with the walls and the toad was like a denial of everything you had imagined, of every-thing you had believed to be an inexplicable obligation. In some way it was all the same to you to go in as to go away, even though you felt the twitching that was pushing you back; you went in before deciding to on that level where nothing had been decided that night, and you heard the sound of the door and the lock behind you. The two waiters were very near, and there were only a few lighted wicks in the room.

"Come," said the voice of the woman from some corner, "everything is prepared."

Her voice sounded as if it were distant, something com-ing from the other side of the mirror at the counter.

"I don't understand," you managed to say, "she was there and suddenly . . ."

One of the waiters laughed, just the beginning of a dry laugh.

"Oh, that's the way she is," the woman said, coming toward you. "She did what she could for you, she always tries, poor thing. But they haven't got the strength, they can only do certain things and they always do them poorly, it's so dif-ferent from how people imagine them."

You felt the two waiters by your side, the rub of their vests against your raincoat.

"We almost feel sorry," the woman said, "it's already been twice that she's come and has had to leave because nothing comes out right for her. Nothing ever works out, all you have to do is take a look at her."

"But, she . . ."

"Jenny," the woman said. "That's all we could find out about her when we first met her, she managed to say that her name was Jenny, unless she was calling to someone else, then there was nothing but the screams, it's absurd how they scream so much."

You looked at them without speaking, knowing that even looking at them was useless, and I felt so sorry for you, Jacobo, how could I know that you were going to think what you thought of me and that you were going to try to protect me, I who was there for that reason, to get them to let you go. There were too many distances, too many impossibilities between you and me; we'd played the same game, but you were still alive and there was no way to make you understand. From now on it would be different if you wanted it that way, from now on we would be two coming in on rainy nights, maybe it would turn out better that way, or at least it would be that, we would be two on rainy nights.

THE
FACES
OF
THE
MEDAL

*TO THE WOMAN
WHO WILL ONE DAY
READ THIS, TOO LATE,
AS ALWAYS*

The offices of CERN opened onto a gloomy hallway, and Javier liked to leave his office and smoke a cigarette, walking back and forth, imagining Mireille behind the door on the left. It was the fourth time in three years that he'd gone to work as a temporary in Geneva, and every time he returned Mireille would greet him cordially, invite him to have tea at five o'clock with two other engineers, a female secretary, and a male stenographer, poet and Yugoslavian. We liked the little ritual because it wasn't daily and therefore mechanical; every three or four days, when we would come together in an elevator or in the hall, Mireille would invite him to join his colleagues over tea, which would be improvised on her desk.

Maybe she liked Javier because he didn't disguise his boredom and his desire to get the contract over with and return to
London. It was difficult to know why they hired him; in any
case, Mireille's colleagues were surprised at his disdain for
the work and the soft music from the Japanese transistor with
which he accompanied his calculations and designs. Nothing
seemed to bring us closer in those days, Mireille remained in
her office for hours on end and it was useless for Javier to
invent absurd cabals to see her come out after thirty-three
turns up and down the hall; but if she had come out, they
would only have exchanged a couple of ordinary phrases
without Mireille's imagining that he was strolling with the
hope of seeing her come out, just as he was making a game
out of his stroll, to see if before thirty-three it was Mireille or
defeat once more. We almost didn't know each other, at CERN
almost no one really knows anyone else, the obligation of
coexistence for so many hours a week weaves spiderwebs of
friendship or enmity that any wind of vacation or retirement
can send to the devil. We played at that for those two weeks
which came back every year, but for Javier the return to
London was also Eileen and a slow, irresistible degradation of
something that at one time had had the grace of desire and
pleasure, Eileen a cat up on a barrel, a pole dancer above
boredom and habit. With her he had lived out a safari in the
middle of the city, Eileen had gone with him to hunt ante-
lope in Piccadilly Circus, to light campfires in Hampstead
Heath, everything had speeded up as in silent movies until
one last love race in Denmark, or had it been Romania, suddenly the differences, always known and denied, the cards
that changed position in the deck and modified fortunes, Eileen preferring the movies to concerts or vice versa, Javier
going alone to look for records because Eileen had to wash
her hair, she who had only washed it when there had really

been nothing else to do, protesting against hygiene and please dry my face I've got shampoo in my eyes. The first contract with CERN had arrived when there was already nothing to be said except that the apartment in Earl's Court was still there with the morning routine, love like soup or the *Times*, like Aunt Rosa and her birthday at the country place in Bath, the gas bills. All that was now a muddy emptiness, a past present of contradictory recurrences filled with Javier's back and forth along the hallway by the offices, twenty-five, twenty-six, twenty-seven, perhaps before thirty the door and Mireille and hi, Mireille, who would be going to pee or to check a fact with the English statistician with white sideburns, Mireille dark and silent, blouse up to her neck where something must have been slowly throbbing, a little bird of life without too many ups and downs, a distant mother, some love affair that was unfortunate and had no sequels, Mireille already a little bit old maid, a little bit office worker but sometimes whistling a theme from Mahler on the elevator, dressed without fantasy almost always in gray or a tailored suit, an age too settled, a discretion too withdrawn.

Only one of the two is writing this but it's all the same, it's as if we were writing it together, even though we're never going to be together anymore, Mireille will stay on at her little house on the outskirts of Geneva, Javier will travel about the world and return to his apartment in London with the obstinacy of the fly that alights a hundred times on an arm, on Eileen. We write it in the same way that a medal is obverse and reverse at the same time in the double play of the mirrors of life. We'll never really know which of us two is more sensitive to this way of not being that each had for the other. Both on their own side, Mireille weeps sometimes as she listens to a certain Brahms quintet, alone at dusk in her living room of dark beams and rustic furniture, where at moments the scent from the roses in the garden reaches. Javier doesn't know how to weep, his tears choose to condense into nightmares which awaken him brutally alongside Eileen, which are gotten rid of by drinking cognac and writing texts that inevitably don't contain the nightmares although sometimes they do; sometimes he pours them out in useless words and for a while is the master, the one who decides what will be said or what will slip little by little into the false oblivion of a new day.

In our way we both knew that a mistake had been made, a reparable error, but no one was capable of repairing it. We were certain that we had never judged ourselves, had simply accepted the fact that things were that way and nothing more could be done beyond what we did. I'm not sure if at that time we thought about things like pride, renunciation, deception, whether only Mireille or only Javier thought about them while the other one accepted them as something fateful, submitting to a system that took them in and submitted them; it's too easy now to say to oneself that everything could have depended on some instantaneous rebellion, lighting the lamp by the side of the bed when Mireille refused, keeping Javier by her side all night when he was already looking for his clothes to get dressed again; it's too easy to put the blame on delicacy, on the impossibility of being brutal or obstinate or generous. Between simpler or more ignorant beings it wouldn't have happened like that, maybe a slap or an insult would have contained the charity and the right road that decorum courteously forbade us. Our respect came from a way of life that brought us close together like the two faces of a medal; we accepted it each on his own side, Mireille in a silence of distance and renunciation, Javier murmuring his now ridiculous hope to her, finally falling silent in the middle of a phrase, in the middle of a last letter. And in the end all we had left, have left is the mournful task of still being worthy, still living with the vain hope that forgetfulness will not forget us too much.

One noon we came together at Mireille's house, almost by obligation she had invited him to have lunch with some other colleagues, she couldn't leave him out when Gabriela and Tom mentioned the lunch while they were having tea in her office, and Javier had thought that it was sad that Mireille had invited him because of simple social pressures but he'd bought a bottle of Jack Daniel's and gotten to know the cabin on the outskirts of Geneva, the small rose garden and the barbecue where Tom officiated among cocktails and a Beatles record that didn't belong to Mireille, that certainly wasn't part of Mireille's stern collection, but which Gabriela had put on the turntable because for her and Tom and half of CERN the air was unbreathable without that music. We didn't talk much, at some moment Mireille took him through the rose garden and he asked her if she liked Geneva and she answered him by just looking at him and shrugging her shoulders, he watched her busy herself with plates and glasses, heard her curse because of a spark on her hand, the fragments were coming together and perhaps it was then that he desired her for the first time, the lock of hair falling over her dark forehead, the blue jeans marking her waist, the somewhat grave voice that must have known how to sing lieder, say important things in a simple murmur. He returned to London at the end of the week and Eileen was in Helsinki, a piece of paper on the table told about a well-paying job, three weeks, there was a chicken in the freezer, kisses.

The next time CERN was aglow with a high-level conference, Javier really had to work and Mireille seemed to feel sorry for him when he mournfully told her between the fifth floor and the street; she suggested going to a piano concert, they went, they coincided on Schubert but not on Bartók, they had some drinks in an almost deserted little café, she had an old English car and dropped him off at his hotel, he'd brought her a record of some madrigals and it was good to know that she didn't know it, that he wouldn't have to exchange it. Sunday and the country, the transparency of an afternoon that was almost too Swiss, we left the car in a village and walked through the wheat fields, at some moment Javier told her about Eileen, just for something to tell her, without any precise necessity, and Mireille listened to him in silence, she held back the pity and the comments that he might have wanted in some way because he was expecting something from her that would begin to resemble what he felt, his desire to kiss her softly, lean her against the trunk of a tree and know her lips, her whole mouth. We almost didn't talk about ourselves on the way back, we let ourselves go along through the paths that proposed their themes at every turn, the hedges, the cows, a sky with silvered clouds, the postcard of a good Sunday. But when we ran down a hill between fences, Javier felt Mireille's hand near his and he squeezed it and they kept on running as if they were drawn along and back in the car Mireille invited him to have tea at her cabin, she liked to call it cabin because it wasn't a cabin but it had so much of a cabin about it, and listen to records. It was a halt in time, a line that suddenly ceases in the rhythm of the sketch before starting up again on some other part of the paper, seeking a new direction.

We made a very clear balance that afternoon: Mahler yes, Brahms yes, the Middle Ages in toto yes, jazz no (Mireille), jazz yes (Javier). We didn't talk about the rest, left to explore were the Renaissance, baroque, Pierre Boulez, John

Cage (but Mireille Cage certainly not, even if they hadn't mentioned him, and probably Boulez the musician no, although the conductor yes, those important nuances). Three days later we went to a concert, had dinner in the old city, there was a postcard from Eileen and a letter from Mireille's mother but we didn't talk about them, everything was still Brahms and a white wine that Brahms would have liked. Mireille dropped him at the hotel and they kissed on the cheek. That night Javier answered Eileen's card, and Mireille watered her roses in the moonlight, not because of any romanticism because there was nothing romantic about her, but because sleep was slow in coming.

Politics was missing, except for isolated comments that little by little showed our partial differences. Maybe we hadn't wanted to face it, maybe in a cowardly way; tea in the office unleashed it, the poet stenographer came down hard on the Israelis, Gabriela found them wonderful, Mireille only said that they were in the right and what the hell, Javier smiled without sarcasm and observed that the same exact thing might be said of the Palestinians. Tom was for an international arrangement with blue helmets and the rest of the show, otherwise it was tea and forecasts of the week's work. We would talk seriously about all that some time, now we just liked to look at each other and feel good, tell each other that soon we would have a Beethoven night at Victoria Hall; we talked about it at the cabin, Javier had brought cognac and an absurd toy that according to him had to please Mireille but that she found exceedingly silly, which didn't stop her from putting it on a shelf after having wound it up and watching in a pleasant way its contortions. That afternoon was Bach, Rostropovich's cello, and a light that descended slowly like the cognac in the bubbles of the glasses. Nothing could have been more ours than that agreement on silence, we had never needed to raise a finger or hush a comment; only afterward, with the gesture of changing the record, did the first words come. Javier said them, looking at the floor; he asked simply if sometime he would be able to know what she already knew about him, her London and her Eileen.

Yes, of course he could, but no, in any case, not now. Sometime, when young, nothing to tell except that, well, there were days when everything weighed so much. In the shadows Javier felt that the words were reaching him as if wet, an instantaneous giving in but drying her eyes with the back of her sleeve now, without giving him time to ask anything more or beg her pardon. Confused, he put an arm around her, sought the face that she didn't refuse but which was as if somewhere else, in some other time. He tried to kiss her and she slipped away, murmuring a bland excuse, a little more cognac, there was no need to pay any attention to her, no reason to insist.

Everything mixes in little by little, we wouldn't remember in detail the before or after of those weeks, the order of the walks or the concerts, the meetings in museums. Perhaps Mireille might have ordered the sequence of things better, all Javier did was lay his few cards down face up, the return to London was drawing near, Eileen, the concerts, discovering Mireille's religion through a simple phrase, her faith and her precise values, what in him was nothing more than the hope of a present that was almost always repealed. In a café, after a laughing dispute over the question of who was going to pay, we looked at each other like old friends, comrades suddenly, we called ourselves dirty words that were deprived of meaning, the claws of bears at play. When we listened to music in the cabin again there was a different way of talking between us, a different familiarity of the hand that helped a waist through the door, Javier's right to get a glass by himself or request Telemann no, first Lotte Lehmann and lots, lots of ice in the whisky. Everything was all as if it had been subtly reversed, Javier felt it and something, he didn't know what, was disturbing him, a having arrived before arriving, a key to the city that no one had given him. We never looked at each other during music time, it was enough being there on the old leather couch and letting the sun set and Lotte Lehmann. When he searched for her mouth and his fingers brushed the curve of her breasts, Mireille remained motionless and let herself be kissed and answered his kiss and ceded her tongue and her saliva to him for a second, but still without moving, without answering his gesture of raising her up from her seat, silent while he babbled his request to her, he was calling her to everything that was waiting for them on the first step of the stairs, in the whole night.

He waited too, thinking that he understood, he begged her pardon but first, with his mouth still close to her face, he asked her why, he asked her if she was a virgin, and Mireille said no, tilting her head, smiling at him a little as if asking, it was foolish, useless. They listened to another record, eating crackers and drinking, night had fallen and he would have to leave. We got up at the same time, Mireille let herself be hugged as if she'd lost her strength, she didn't say anything when he murmured his desire again; they went up the narrow staircase and on the landing they separated, there was that pause in which doors are opened and lights turned on, a request to wait and a disappearance which was prolonged while in the bedroom Javier felt beside himself, incapable of thinking that he shouldn't have let that happen, that it couldn't be that way, the intervening wait, the probable precautions, the almost debasing routine. He saw her come back wrapped in a white terrycloth bathrobe, go over to the bed and reach her hand out to the lamp. "Don't put the light out," he asked her; Mireille refused with a nod and turned it off, leaving him to get undressed in total darkness, feel for the edge of the bed, slide up against her motionless body in the shadows.

We didn't make love. We were one step away after Javier knew with hands and lips the silent body that awaited him in the darkness. His desire was different, seeing her in the light of the lamp, her breasts and her stomach, stroking a defined back, seeing Mireille's hands on his own body, detail in a thousand fragments, the pleasure that precedes pleasure. In the total silence and darkness, in the distance and timidity that fell over him from Mireille, invisible and mute, everything gave way to an unreality of half-sleep and at the same time he was incapable of standing up to her, of leaping from the bed and turning on the light and imposing a necessary and beautiful will once more. He thought confusedly that afterward, after she had known him, when true intimacy would begin, but the silence and the shadows and the ticking of that clock on the dresser were more powerful. He babbled an excuse that she muted with a friendly kiss, squeezed himself against her body, felt unbearably tired, perhaps slept for a moment.

Perhaps we slept, yes, perhaps at that moment we were left to ourselves and were lost. Mireille got up first and turned on the light, wrapped in her robe she went back to the bathroom while Javier got dressed mechanically, incapable of thought, his mouth as if dirty and the residue of the cognac biting his stomach. They scarcely spoke, they scarcely looked at each other, Mireille said it was nothing, that there were always taxis on the corner, she'd go down with him. He couldn't break the rigid chain of causes and consequences,

the obligatory routine that from long before them had demanded that he lower his head and leave the cabin in the
middle of the night; his only thought was that the next day
they would talk more calmly, that he would try to make her
understand, but understand what. And it's true that they
talked in the usual café and that Mireille once again said it
was nothing, it wasn't important, maybe it would be better
another time, you mustn't think about it. He would be going
back to London three days later, when he asked her to let him
go to the cabin she said no, better not. We didn't know what
to do or what else to say, we didn't even know how to be
silent, embrace at some corner, find each other in some look.
It was as if Mireille were waiting for something from Javier
that he was waiting for from Mireille, a question of initiatives
or priorities, of the gestures of a man and the compliance of a
woman, the immutability of sequences decided by others, received from without; we had advanced along a road where no
one had wanted to face the march, break the harmonious
parity; not even now, after knowing that we'd taken the
wrong road, were we capable of a shout, a hand reaching for
the lamp, the impulse above useless ceremonies, bathrobes
and it's nothing, don't worry about it, it'll be better another
time. It would have been preferable to accept it then, at once.
It would have been preferable to repeat together: we lose our
life because of niceties; the poet would have pardoned us if
we were also talking for ourselves.

We didn't see each other for months. Javier wrote, of course,
and a few words from Mireille, cordial and distant, reached
him punctually. Then he began to telephone her at night,
almost always on Saturdays when he imagined her alone in
the cabin, begging her pardon if he was interrupting a quar-

tet or a sonata, but Mireille would always answer that she'd been reading or working in the garden, that it was fine to call at that time. When she traveled to London six months later to visit a sick aunt, Javier got her a hotel room, they met at the station and went to visit the museums, King's Road, enjoyed a film by Milos Forman. That time, as in the past, in a small restaurant in Whitechapel, their hands met with a confidence that wiped out memory, and Javier felt better and told her so, he told her that he wanted her more than ever but that he'd never talk to her about that again, that it all depended on her, on the day she decided to return to the first step of the first night and simply held out her arms to him. She nodded without looking at him, without agreement or negation, she just found it absurd that he kept turning down the contracts they offered him in Geneva. Javier went back to the hotel with her and Mireille said good-bye in the lobby, she didn't ask him up but she smiled when she kissed him softly on the cheek, murmuring a see-you-soon.

We know so many things, that arithmetic is false, that one and one aren't always one but two or zero; we have more than enough time to thumb through the album of holes, of closed windows, of letters without voice or scent. The daily office, Eileen convinced and lavishing happiness, weeks and months. Geneva in summer again, the first stroll along the lake shore, a concert by Isaac Stern. Left in London now was the tiny shadow of María Elena, whom Javier had met at a cocktail party and who had given him three weeks of light games, pleasure for its own sake where everything else was an amiable daily emptiness with María Elena becoming tireless at tennis and at the Rolling Stones, a good-bye without melancholy after a last weekend enjoyed like that, like a good-bye without melancholy. He told Mireille, and without need of asking her he knew that she no, that she the office and girl-friends, that she always the cabin and the records. He thanked her without words that Mireille listened to with her grave, attentive, comprehensive silence, leaving his hand in hers while they watched sunset over the lake and decided on a place for dinner.

Afterward it was work, a week of isolated meetings, night in the Romanian restaurant, tenderness. They'd never spoken of what was once again there in the gesture of pouring the wine or looking at each other slowly at the end of a con-versation. True to his word, Javier was waiting for a time he didn't think he had the right to wait for. But the tenderness, then, something present there among so many other things, a gesture of Mireille's as she lowered her head and passed her hand over her eyes, her simple phrase to tell him that she would go with him to his hotel. In the car they kissed again as on the night in the cabin, he held her body and felt her thighs open under the hand that was rising and caressing. When they went into the room Javier couldn't wait and embraced her standing up, losing himself in her mouth and her hair, leading her step by step to the bed. He heard her murmur a muffled no, ask him to wait a moment, felt her break away from him and look for the bathroom door, close it and time, silence and water and time while he pulled down the bed-spread and left only a light in a corner, took off his shoes and shirt, wondering whether to get completely undressed or to wait because his robe was in the bathroom and if the light was on, if Mireille on coming back found him naked and stand-ing, his erection grotesque, or if he turned his back even more grotesquely so that she wouldn't see him like that as she would really have to see him now that she was coming out with a bath towel wrapped around her, going over to the bed with her eyes lowered and he had his pants on, they'd have to be taken off and he'd have to take off his shorts and then yes embrace her, pull away the towel and lay her down on the bed and see her golden and dark and kiss her again to the deepest and caress her with fingers that hurt her perhaps because she moaned, threw herself back, stretching out on the farthest part of the bed and blinking at the light, asking once more for a darkness that he wouldn't give her because he wouldn't give her anything, his suddenly useless sex searching for a passage that she was offering him and that would not be crossed, the exasperated hands trying to excite him and excite himself, the mechanics of gestures and words that Mireille would slowly reject, rigid and distant, understanding that not now either, that tenderness and all of that had become unreconcilable, that her acceptance and her desire had only served to leave her once more beside a body that had ceased to struggle, that was clinging to her without moving, that wasn't even trying to begin again.

It might be that we slept, we were too distant and alone and dirty, the repetition had been fulfilled as in a mirror, except that now it was Mireille who was getting dressed to leave and he went with her to the car, he heard her say goodbye without looking at him and the soft kiss on the cheek, the car that started up in the silence of the late night, the return to the hotel and not even knowing how to cry, not even knowing how to kill himself, only the couch and the alcohol and the ticking of the night and the dawn, the office at nine o'clock, Eileen's card and the telephone waiting, the inside number that he would have to dial at some moment because at some moment he would have to say something. Because yes, don't worry, all right, in the café at seven o'clock. But telling him that, telling him don't worry, in the café at seven o'clock was coming after that interminable trip to the cabin,

getting into a cold bed and taking a useless sleeping pill, seeing every scene of that progression toward nothingness once
more, repeating in the midst of nausea the instant they had
stood up in the restaurant and she had said she would go to
the hotel with him, the rapid operations in the bathroom, the
towel to drape around her loins, the hot strength of the arms
that were leading her and laying her down, the murmuring
shadow stretching out on top of her, the caresses and that
flaming feeling of a hardness against her stomach, between
her thighs, the useless protest about the lighted lamp and
suddenly the absence, the hands slipping away lost, the voice
murmuring delays, the useless waiting, the drowsiness, all
again, all why, why tenderness, why acquiescence, why the
hotel, and the innocuous sleeping pill, the office at nine
o'clock, a special meeting of the council, impossible to be
absent, everything impossible except the impossible.

We won't have spoken of this, imagination brings us together
today as uselessly as reality then. Together we'll never seek
blame or responsibility or the maybe not unimaginable new
beginning. There is only a feeling of punishment in Javier,
but what does punishment mean when one loves and desires,
what grotesque atavism is unleashed there where happiness
was waiting, why before and after this present Eileen or
María Elena or Doris in which a past Mireille will plunge her
knife of silence and disdain to the hilt. Of silence only even
though he thinks disdain with every nauseous moment of
memory, because there isn't any disdain in Mireille, silence
yes, and sadness, telling herself that she or he but also she and
he, telling herself that not every man fulfills the moment of
love and not every woman knows how to find a man in him.
The mediations remain, the last recourses, Javier's invitation

to take a trip together, spend two weeks in some distant corner to break the curse, vary the formula, find each other finally in a different way without towels or waits or summonses. Mireille said yes, later on, he should phone her from London, maybe she could get two weeks' leave. They were saying good-bye at the railroad station, she was taking the train back to the cabin because there was something wrong with her car. Javier could no longer kiss her on the mouth but he held her against him, he asked her again to accept the trip, he looked at her until it hurt her, until she lowered her eyes and repeated yes, that everything would come out all right, that he should go to London in peace, that everything would end up turning out well. We also talk to children like that before taking them to the doctor or doing something that hurts them, Mireille from her side of the medal probably no longer expected anything, she wouldn't come to believe in anything, she would simply go back to the cabin and the records, without even imagining another way of running toward what they hadn't reached. When he phoned her from London proposing the Dalmatian coast, giving her dates and directions with a detail that barely hid the fear of a negative answer, Mireille answered that she'd write him. From his side of the medal Javier was only able to say yes, that he'd keep on waiting, as if in some way he already knew that the letter would be brief and gracious and no, it was useless to begin something lost again, better to be just friends; in scarcely eight lines a hug from Mireille. Each on his and her side, incapable of turning over the medal with a push, Javier wrote a letter that might have tried to show the only path left to them by inventing together, the only one that hadn't already been traced by others, by usage and acceptance, that would not of needs pass through a staircase or an elevator to arrive at a bedroom or a hotel, that would not demand his taking off his clothes at the very same moment in which she was taking off hers; but his letter was only a wet handkerchief, he couldn't even finish it and he signed it in the middle of a sentence, he buried it in the envelope without rereading it. From Mireille there was no reply, the offers of work in Geneva were courteously turned down, the medal was there between us, we live at a distance from each other and we will never write each other again, Mireille in her little house in the suburbs, Javier traveling about the world and returning to his apartment with the obstinacy of the fly that alights on an arm a hundred times. One day at dusk Mireille wept while she listened to a certain Brahms quintet, but Javier doesn't know how to cry, he only has nightmares from which he frees himself by writing texts that try to be like nightmares, there where no one has his true name but perhaps his truth, there where there is no medal standing on edge with obverse and reverse, where there are no consecrated steps to climb; but, of course, they're only texts.

SOMEONE
WALKING
AROUND

TO ESPERANZA MACHADO,
CUBAN PIANIST

Jiménez had been put ashore as soon as night fell, accepting all the risks of the cove's being so close to the docks. They made use of an electric launch, of course, capable of slipping along as silent as a ray and losing itself in the distance again while Jiménez waited in the underbrush for a moment until his eyes got used to the dark, until every sense adjusted to the hot breeze and the sounds from inland. Two days before it had all been a plague of hot asphalt and city sizzle, the barely disguised disinfectant in the lobby of the Atlantic, the almost pathetic camouflage of bourbon with which they all tried to cover the memory of rum; now, although tense and on guard and barely letting himself think, the smell of Oriente was penetrating him, the single unmistakable call of the night bird that might have been welcoming him: it was better to think of it that way, like an incantation.

At first York had thought it mad for Jiménez to go ashore so close to Santiago, it was against all principles; for that very reason and because Jiménez knew the terrain like no one else, York accepted the risk and arranged for the electric launch. The problem was not to get his shoes dirty, to arrive at the motel with the look of a tourist from the provinces who was traveling around his country; there Alfonso would take charge of getting him set up, the rest was a matter of a few hours, the plastic charge in the place agreed upon and back to the shore where the launch and Alfonso would be waiting; the remote control was on board and once they were at sea the reverberation from the explosion and the first flames from the factory would send them off with full honors. For the moment it was necessary to go to the motel using the old road, abandoned since they'd built the new highway farther to the north, resting a bit before the last leg so that no one would suspect the weight of the suitcase when Jiménez met Alfonso and the latter would take it with the gesture of a friend, avoiding the solicitous bellboy and taking Jiménez to one of the better-located rooms in the motel. It was the dangerous part of the whole thing, but the only possible access was through the motel garden; with luck, with Alfonso, everything would turn out well.

Of course there was no one on the road that had been invaded by underbrush and disuse, only the smell of Oriente and the complaint of the bird that bothered Jiménez for a moment, as if his nerves needed some pretext to relax a little, so that against his will he could accept the fact that he was defenseless there, without a pistol in his pocket because York had been firm about that, the mission would be accomplished or would fail, but a pistol was of no use in either case and, in fact, it could ruin everything. York had his ideas about Cuban character and Jiménez knew it and cursed him from deep inside while he climbed up the road and the lights of the few houses and the motel were opening up like yellow eyes in the last part of the underbrush. But there was no need for cursing, everything was going according to schedule, as that fairy York would have said, and Alfonso in the garden of the motel yelling out—if you can believe it!—and where the hell did you leave the car, fellow, the two bellboys watching and listening, I've been waiting for you a quarter of an hour, yes but we got here late and I left the car with a comrade who needed it to go to her family's, she dropped me off at the bend, hey, you're always the perfect gentleman, cut it out, Alfonso, it's nice walking around here, the suitcase going from one hand to the other with perfect lightness, the muscles tense but the gesture muffled, nothing, let's go get your key and then we can have a drink, how did you leave Choli and the kids, a little sad, old man, they wanted to come but you know school and work, this time we didn't coincide, tough luck.

The quick shower, checking that the door locked well, the suitcase open on the other bed and the green bundle in the dresser drawer among shirts and newspapers. At the bar Alfonso had already asked for some extra-drys with plenty of ice; they smoked and talked about Camagüey and Stevenson's last fight, the piano reached them as if from far away although the piano player was right there at the end of the bar, playing something very softly, a habanera and then something by Chopin, going on to a danzón and an old song from the movies, something that in the good old days must have been sung by Irene Dunne. They had another rum and Alfonso said that he'd come by for him in the morning to take him around and show him the new parts of town, there was so much to see in Santiago, they were working hard to finish the plans and go beyond them, the microbrigades were wild, Almeida would come to open two factories, one of those times out there even Fidel dropped by, the comrades were putting their shoulders to the wheel in a way that was a sheer delight.

"Santiagans don't sleep," the bartender said, and they laughed in approval, there were few people in the dining room and Jiménez had already been assigned a table near a window. Alfonso said good night after repeating that he'd come by the next morning; at the table, stretching out his legs, Jiménez began to study the menu. A fatigue that wasn't just in his body obliged him to be careful about every movement. Everything there was placid and cordial and calm and Chopin, who was returning now with that prelude that the pianist was playing very slowly, but Jiménez felt the threat like an ambush, the slightest slip and those smiling faces would turn into masks of hate. He knew those feelings and he knew how to control them; he ordered a mojito in order to pass the time and let himself by advised on the meal, fish rather than meat that night. The dining room was almost empty, a young couple at the bar and farther on a man who looked foreign and was drinking without looking at his glass, his eyes lost on the piano player who was repeating the Irene Dunne theme, now Jiménez recognized "Smoke Gets in Your Eyes," that Havana of times gone by, the piano went back to Chopin, one of the études Jiménez had also played when before the big panic, as a boy, he had taken piano lessons, a slow and melancholy étude that brought back the living room of his house, his dead grandmother, and almost against his will the image of his brother who'd stayed behind in spite of the paternal curse, Robertico who was killed like an imbecile at the Bay of Pigs instead of helping to reconquer the true freedom.

He was almost surprised to find himself eating with a
good appetite, savoring what his memory hadn't forgotten,
admitting ironically that it was the only good thing after the
soggy food they swallowed on the other side. He wasn't sleepy
and he liked the music, the piano player was a woman still
young and pretty, she played as if for herself without ever
looking at the bar, where the foreign-appearing man continued to fiddle with his hands, and began another rum and
another cigarette. After coffee Jiménez thought that it was
going to be a long time waiting for the moment in his room
and he went over to the bar to have another drink. The bartender wanted to chat but he did so with respect for the pianist, almost a murmur as if he understood that the foreigner
and Jiménez liked that music, now it was one of the waltzes,
the simple melody into which Chopin had put something like
slow rain, like talcum powder or pressed flowers in an album.
The bartender didn't pay any attention to the foreigner,
maybe he couldn't speak Spanish well or was a man of silence,
the dining room was closing now and he would have to go
sleep, but the pianist went on playing a Cuban melody that
Jiménez was leaving behind as he lighted a cigarette and with
a sweeping good-night headed for the door and entered what
was waiting for him as soon as four a.m. sharp synchronized
on his watch and the one on the launch.

Before going into his room he let his eyes become accustomed to the darkness of the garden to be sure of what Alfonso had explained to him, he follows the path about three
hundred feet away, goes off it toward the new highway,
crosses the highway carefully and continues on toward the
west. From the motel he could only see the shadowy place
where the path began, but it was useful to detect the lights in
the background, two or three toward the left, in order to have
a notion of the distance. The factory area began several hundred yards to the west, next to the third concrete post he

would find the hole in the fence. Normally it was rare for the sentries to be on that side, they made a round every fifteen minutes, but they preferred chatting with each other on the other side, where there were light and coffee; in any case, getting his clothes dirty no longer mattered, he would have to crawl through the bushes up to the place that Alfonso had described in detail to him. The return would be easy without the green bundle, without all those faces that had surrounded him until now.

He stretched out on his bed almost at once and turned out the light to smoke peacefully; he would even sleep for a while in order to relax his body, he had the habit of waking up on time. But first he made sure that the door locked tightly from the inside and that his things were as he had left them. He hummed a little waltz that had stuck in his memory, mixing up past and present for him, he made an effort to exchange it for "Smoke Gets in Your Eyes," but the little waltz came back or the prelude; he dozed off without being able to get rid of them, still seeing the very white hands of the piano player, her head leaning over to listen attentively to herself. The night bird sang again in some bush or in the palm grove to the north.

Something darker than the darkness of the room woke him, darker and heavier, vaguely at the foot of the bed. He'd been dreaming about Phyllis and the pop music festival, with such intense lights and sounds that opening his eyes was like falling into pure space without barriers, a pit filled with nothing, and at the same time his stomach told him it wasn't like that, that part of it was different, had a different consistency and blackness. He found the light switch with his hand; the foreigner from the bar was sitting at the foot of his bed and looking at him unhurriedly, as if until that moment he'd been watching over his sleep.

Doing something and thinking something were equally inconceivable. Viscera, pure horror, an interminable and perhaps instantaneous silence, the double bridge of gazes. The pistol, the first useless thought; if at least the pistol. A panting that restaged time, rejection of the last possibility that it was still the dream where Phyllis, where the music and the lights and the drinks.

"Yes, that's the way it is," the foreigner said, and Jiménez felt the thick accent as if on his skin, the proof that he wasn't from there, like something about his head and his shoulders already when he'd seen him for the first time at the bar.

Inching himself up, seeking an equality of height at least, a total disadvantage of position, the only thing possible was surprise, but even in that he would be completely lost, broken ahead of time; his muscles weren't going to respond for him, he wouldn't have the leverage in his legs for the desperate shove, and the other one knew it, he was quiet and almost lax at the foot of the bed. When Jiménez saw him take out a cigarette and lose the other hand, sinking it into his pants pocket to get the matches, he knew that he would be wasting his time if he leaped on him; there was too much disdain in his way of paying no attention to him, of not being on the defensive. And something even worse, his own precautions, the door locked, the bolt thrown.

"Who are you?" he heard being asked absurdly from what couldn't be dream or wakefulness.

"What difference does it make?" the foreigner said.

"But Alfonso . . ."

He saw himself watched by something that had a kind of different time, a hollow distance. The flame of the match was reflected in a pair of hazel eyes. The foreigner blew out the match and looked at his hands for a moment.

"Poor Alfonso," he said. "Poor, poor Alfonso."

There was no pity in his words, only a kind of indifferent verification.

"But who the hell are you?" Jiménez shouted, knowing that it was hysteria, the loss of his last control.

"Oh, someone walking around," the foreigner said. "I always come by when they play my music, especially here, you know. I like to hear it played here, on these pitiful little pianos. In my time it was different, I've always had to listen to it away from my own land. That's why I like to come by, it's a kind of reconciliation, justice."

Clenching his teeth in order to control the trembling that gripped him from head to foot, Jiménez managed to think that the only sane thing to do was to decide that the man was mad. It no longer mattered how he'd gotten in, how he knew, because he did know of course, but he was crazy and that was the only possible advantage. To gain time, then, drift with the current, ask him about the piano, the music.

"She plays well," the foreigner said, "but, of course, only what you heard, the easy things. Tonight I would have liked for her to have played that étude they call the Revolutionary, I really would have liked it very much. But she can't, poor thing, she hasn't got the fingers for it. For that you need fingers like these."

His hands raised to shoulder level, he showed Jiménez his separated fingers, long and tense. Jiménez saw them only a second before he felt them on his throat.

Cuba, 1976

THE
FERRY,
OR
ANOTHER
TRIP
TO
VENICE

Ever since I was young I've been tempted by the idea of rewriting literary texts that have moved me but the making of which seemed to me to be inferior to their internal possibilities; I think some stories by Horacio Quiroga brought this temptation to a limit that dissolved, as is preferable, into silence and abandonment. What might have been attempted through love would only be received as insolent pedantry; I accepted the fact of having to deplore in my heart of hearts that certain texts had come to me at a lower level than what something in them and in me had demanded in vain.

Fate and a pile of old papers give me today an

analogous opening into that unrealized desire, but the temptation is legitimate in this case since it deals with a text of my own, a long tale entitled The Ferry. On the last page of the rough draft I find this notation: "How awful! I wrote this in Venice in 1954; I reread it ten years later and I like it, and it's so bad."

The text and the marginal note were forgotten; twelve more years have been added to the first ten, and rereading these pages now I agree with my note, except that perhaps I'd like to know better why the tale seemed and still seems bad to me and why I liked it and still like it.

What follows is an attempt to show myself that the text of The Ferry is poorly written because it's false, because it takes place alongside a truth that I was unable to grasp at the time and that has become obvious to me now. Rewriting it would be wearisome and, in some hazy way, disloyal, almost as if it were some other author's tale and then I would be falling into the pedantry I mentioned earlier. I can, on the other hand, leave it just as it was born, and at the same time show what I can now manage to see in it. That's where Dora comes on the scene.

If Dora had thought of Pirandello, she would have immediately sought out the author to reproach him for his ignorance and his persistent hypocrisy. But I'm the one who's going in her direction now so that in the end she'll lay down the cards face up. Dora can't know who the author of the tale is and her criticism is directed only at what happens in it as seen from within, there where she exists; but the fact that these events happen to be a text and she a character in the writing of it has no effect at all on her equally textual right to rebel at a chronicle she judges insufficient or insidious.

Therefore, from time to time today, Dora's voice will interrupt the original text, which, apart from corrections that are nothing but details and the elimination of short repetitious passages, is the same that I wrote by hand in the Pensione dei Dogi in 1954. In it the reader will find all that seems bad to me as writing and bad to Dora as content, and which, perhaps once again, is the reciprocal effect of a cause that is one and the same.

Tourism plays games with its adepts: it inserts them into a deceptive temporality, it fixes it so that leftover English coins emerge from a pocket in France, one searches in vain in Holland for a taste that only Poitiers can give. For Valentina, the small Roman bar on the Via Quattro Fontane was reduced to Adriano, to the taste of a lingering martini and Adriano's face, which had begged her pardon for having pushed her against the bar. She almost couldn't remember if Dora had been with her that morning, she most likely had been because they were "doing" Rome together, organizing a camaraderie that, like so many, had begun in a silly way at Cook's and American Express.

Of course I was. Right from the start she pretends not to see me, reducing me to the role of an extra who is sometimes a comfort and sometimes an annoyance.

In any case, that bar near the Piazza Barberini was Adriano, another traveler, another idle person circulating the way all tourists circulate in cities, a phantom among men who come and go to and from work, have families, speak the same language, and know what's happening at that moment and not in the archeology of the Blue Guide.

The parts of Adriano that faded away immediately were

his eyes, his hair, his clothing; all that remained was his large and sensuous mouth, the lips that trembled a little after he spoke, while he listened. He listens with his mouth, Valentina had thought when out of the first dialogue there was born an invitation to have one of the bar's famous cocktails, which Adriano recommended and which Beppo, shaking it in a chrome container, proclaimed the jewel of Rome, the whole Tyrrhenian Sea distilled into a glass along with its tritons and sea horses. That day Dora and Valentina found Adriano nice;

Hm.

he didn't look like a tourist (he considered himself a traveler and emphasized the distinction with a smile) and the noontime dialogue was one more enchantment of Rome in April. Dora forgot him immediately,

Not true. Distinguishing between savoir faire and silliness. No one like me (or Valentina, of course) could forget someone like Adriano just like that; but it so happens that I'm intelligent and from the word go I could feel that my wavelength wasn't his. I'm talking about friendship, not about something else because you can't even talk about waves in that. And since nothing was possible, why waste time?

so busy visiting the Lateran, St. Clement's, everything in one afternoon because they were leaving two days later, Cook's had ended up selling them a complicated itinerary; for her part, Valentina found the pretext of some shopping in order to return to Beppo's bar the following morning. When she saw Adriano, who was staying at a nearby hotel, neither of the two pretended surprise. Adriano was going to Florence a week later and they discussed itineraries, exchange, hotels, guidebooks. Valentina believed in buses but Adriano was pro-train; they went to argue the problem at a trattoria on the Suburra where one could eat fish in an atmosphere that was picturesque for those who were only going there once.

From guidebooks they went on to personal information; Adriano learned about Valentina's divorce in Montevideo and she about his family life on a country estate near Osorno in Chile. They swapped impressions of London, Paris, Naples. Valentina kept looking at Adriano's mouth, she looked at it nakedly at the moment his fork brought the food to the lips that opened to receive it, when one shouldn't look. And he was aware of it and tightened his mouth on the piece of fried octopus as if it were a woman's tongue, as if he were already kissing Valentina.

Not true because of omission: Valentina didn't look at just Adriano that way, she looked at everybody who attracted her; she'd done it to me the moment we met at the counter of American Express, and I know that I wondered if she wasn't probably like me; the way she had of fixing her always somewhat dilated eyes on me . . . Almost at once I found out she wasn't, it wouldn't have bothered me personally to get close to her as part of the no man's land of the trip, but when we decided to share the hotel room I knew that there was something else, that the look came from something that could have been fear or the need to forget. Exaggerated words in that time of simple laughter, shampoo, and touristic happiness; but afterward . . . In any case, Adriano must have taken as a mark of courtesy what a friendly bartender or a woman selling wallets would have received too. By the by, there's also some before-the-fact plagiarism from a famous scene in the movie Tom Jones.

He kissed her that afternoon in his hotel on the Via Nazionale after Valentina telephoned Dora to tell her that she wouldn't be going with her to the Baths of Caracalla.

Wasting a phone call like that!

Adriano had some chilled wine sent up and in his room there were English magazines and a large window facing the western sky. Only the bed was uncomfortable, too narrow for them, but men like Adriano almost always make love on small beds, and Valentina had too many bad memories of her double bed not to enjoy the change.

If Dora suspected anything, she didn't say so.

Not true: I already knew. True: I didn't say anything.

Valentina told her that night that she'd happened to run into Adriano, and that maybe they'd see him again in Florence; when they met him coming out of Orsanmichele three days later, Dora seemed to be the happiest of the three.

In cases like that you have to play dumb so they don't think you are dumb.

Adriano had found the separation unexpectedly exasperating. Suddenly he realized that he missed Valentina, that the promise of meeting again, the hours they would spend together hadn't been enough for him. He was jealous of Dora, he could barely hide it while she—more ugly, more common —carefully repeated to him what she'd read in the guidebook of the Touring Club Italiano.

I've never used Touring Club Italiano guidebooks because they were incomprehensible to me; the Michelin in French is more than adequate for me. Passons sur le reste.

When they met at Adriano's hotel at dusk, Valentina measured the difference between that date and the first one in Rome; preparations had been made now, the bed was perfect and on a curiously inlaid table a little box wrapped in blue paper awaited her, inside it an admirable Florentine cameo that she—much later, when they were drinking by the window—pinned to her breast with the easy, almost familiar gesture of one turning a key in the everyday lock.

I have no way of knowing what Valentina's gestures were like at that moment, but, in any case, they could never have been easy; everything in her was knot, chain, and whip. At night, from my bed, I would look at her walking around before going to bed, time and again picking up and putting down a vial of perfume, a bottle of pills, going to the window as if she heard strange noises; or, later on, while she was sleeping, that way of sobbing in the middle of a dream, waking me up suddenly, making me come over to her bed, get her a glass of water, stroke her forehead until, calmed down, she went back to sleep. And her challenges that first night in Rome when she came to sit down beside me: you don't know me, Dora, you haven't the slightest idea of what's going on inside me, this emptiness full of mirrors that show me a street in Punta del Este, a child who's crying because I'm not there. Easy, her gestures? For my part, at least, they'd shown me from the beginning that I had nothing to expect from her on an affectionate level, apart from camaraderie. It's hard for me to imagine that Adriano, masculinely blind as he might have been, wouldn't come to suspect that Valentina was kissing nothingness on his mouth, that before and after love Valentina would keep on crying in her sleep.

Until then he hadn't fallen in love with the ones he made love to; something in him made him take them too quickly, as if to create the aura, the necessary zone of mystery and desire, to organize the mental hunt that sometimes might be called love. With Valentina it had been the same, but during the days they were separated, during those last sunsets in Rome and the trip to Florence, something different had burst forth in Adriano. Without surprise, without humility, almost without marvel, he saw her rise up in the golden shadows of Orsanmichele, emerging out of Orcagna's tabernacle as if one of the innumerable small stone figures had broken away from the monument to come to meet him. Only then perhaps did he realize that he was falling in love with her. Or perhaps afterward, in the hotel, when Valentina had wept as she embraced him without giving any reasons, letting herself go like a child who gives in to a long-contained necessity and finds relief mingled with shame, with disapproval.

As for what was immediate and superficial, Valentina was weeping over the precariousness of the meeting. Adriano would go on his way a few days later; they wouldn't meet again because the episode was going into a vulgar calendar of vacations, a framework of hotels and cocktails and ritual phrases. Only their bodies would emerge sated, as always, for a while they would have the filled-up feeling of a dog who finishes his chewing and flops down in the sun with a grunt of contentment. In itself the meeting was perfect, bodies brought to press together, entwine, hold back or provoke delight. But when she looked at Adriano sitting on the edge of the bed (and he looked at her with his thick-lipped mouth) Valentina felt that the rite just fulfilled had no real content, that the instruments of passion were hollow, that there was no spirit in them. All of that had been tolerable and even favorable in other situations during that hour, and yet this time she would have wanted to have held Adriano, delayed the moment of getting dressed and leaving, those gestures that in some way were already announcing a farewell.

Something was meant to be said here without being said, without understanding anything but an uncertain rumor. Valentina had also looked at me while we bathed and got dressed in Rome, before Adriano; I too had felt that those breaks in the continuum were doing her harm, were pulling her toward the future. The first time I made the mistake of implying it, of going over and stroking her hair and suggesting we have some drinks sent up and watch the sunset from the window. Her answer was dry, she hadn't come out of Uruguay to spend her time in a hotel. I thought simply that she still didn't trust me, that she attributed a precise meaning to that hint of a caress, just as I had misunderstood her first look in the travel agency. Valentina looked, without knowing exactly why; it was the rest of us who gave in to that obscure interrogation that had something of a pursuit about it, but a pursuit that didn't concern us.

Dora was waiting for them in one of the cafés on the Signoria, she had just discovered Donatello and explained him much too emphatically, as if her enthusiasm were serving her as a cape to help hide some irritation.

"Of course we're going to see the statues," Valentina said, "but we couldn't go into museums this afternoon, there was too much sun to go to museums."

"You won't be here long enough to afford to sacrifice all that for the sun."

Adriano made a vague gesture, waiting for Valentina's words. It was hard to tell what Dora represented for Valentina, whether the pair's trip was already laid out and wouldn't allow any changes. Dora returned to Donatello, piling up the useless references one makes in the absence of a work. Valentina was looking at the tower of the Signoria, mechanically taking out her cigarettes.

I think it happened exactly like that, and for the first time Adriano really suffered, he was afraid that I represented the sacred trip, culture as a duty, train and hotel reservations. But if someone had asked him about the other possible solution, he would only have been able to think about something like that beside Valentina, with no precise goal.

The next day they went to the Uffizi. As if hiding from the necessity of a decision, Valentina clung obstinately to Dora's presence so as not to leave any opening for Adriano. Only for one fleeting moment, when Dora hung back looking at a portrait, was he able to speak to her intimately.

"Will you come this afternoon?"

"Yes," Valentina said without looking at him, "at four o'clock."

"I love you so much," Adriano murmured, stroking her shoulder with fingers that were almost timid. "Valentina, I love you so much."

A group of American tourists entered, preceded by the nasal voice of their guide. Their faces drew apart, avidly empty, falsely interested in the painting they would forget an hour later with spaghetti and wine at the Castelli Romani.

Dora was also coming along thumbing through her guide-book, lost because the numbers in the catalogue didn't correspond with those on the pictures.

> *On purpose, of course. In order to let them talk, make a date, get fed up. Not him, I already knew that, but her. And not to get fed up, but, rather, to get back to the ever-present impulse to flee, which might bring her back to my way of accompanying her without badgering her, waiting simply by her side, even though it did no good.*

"I love you so much," Adriano repeated that afternoon as he leaned over Valentina, who was resting on her back. "You can feel it, can't you? It's not in the words, it's got nothing to do with saying it, with looking for names for it. Tell me you can feel it, that you can't explain it but that you can feel it now that . . ."

He sank his head between her breasts, kissing her for a long time, as if he were drinking in the fever that throbbed in Valentina's flesh as she stroked his hair with a distant, distracted gesture.

> *D'Annunzio lived in Venice, didn't he? Unless it was Hollywood scriptwriters . . .*

"Yes, you love me," she said. "But it's as if you were also afraid of something, not of loving me, but . . . Not afraid, maybe, anxious, rather. You're worried about what's going to happen now."

"I don't know what's going to happen; I haven't got the slightest idea. How could I be afraid of so much emptiness? My fear is you, it's a concrete fear, here and now. You don't love me as much as I love you, Valentina, or you love me in a different way, limited or held back, who knows for what reason."

Valentina was listening to him, closing her eyes. Slowly, coinciding with what he had just said, she glimpsed something behind, something that at first was only an empty space, a restlessness. She felt too happy at that moment to let the slightest fault mingle with that pure and perfect hour in which both had made love with no thought other than that of not wanting to think. At the same time, however, she couldn't help understanding Adriano's words. She was suddenly measuring the fragility of that touristic situation under a borrowed roof, between alien sheets, threatened by railroad timetables, itineraries that carried them into different lives, motives that were unknown and probably antagonistic as always.

"You don't love me the way I love you," Adriano said again, rancorously. "I'm useful to you, I'm useful to you, like a knife or a waiter, nothing else."

"Please," Valentina said. *"Je t'en prie."*

It was so hard to realize why they were no longer happy so few minutes after something that had been like happiness.

"I know very well I'll have to go back," Valentina said without taking her fingers away from Adriano's anxious face. "My son, my job, so many obligations. My son's quite small, quite defenseless."

"I have to go back too," Adriano said, averting his eyes. "I've got a job too, a thousand things."

"So you see."

"No, I don't see. How do you expect me to see? If you make me consider this as just an episode on a trip, you'll take everything away from it, you'll squash it like a bug. I love you, Valentina. Loving is more than remembering or preparing yourself to remember."

"I'm not the one you have to tell that to. No, not me. I'm afraid of time, time is death, its horrible disguise. Don't you realize that we love each other against time, that we have to deny time?"

"Yes," Adriano said, dropping down on his back beside her, "and it so happens that you're leaving for Bologna the day after tomorrow, and a day later I'm going to Lucca."

"Be quiet."

"Why? Your time is Cook's time, even though you try to fill it up with metaphysics. Mine, on the other hand, is decided by my whim, my pleasure, the railroad timetables I accept or reject."

"So you see," Valentina murmured. "You see how we have to give in to the evidence. What else is there?"

"Coming with me. Leaving your famous excursion, let Dora talk about what she doesn't know. Let's leave together."

He's referring to my pictorial enthusiasm; we won't discuss whether he's right or not. In any case, both of them are talking with a mirror in front, a perfect dialogue for a best seller, meant to fill up two pages with nothing in particular. Yes, no, that time . . . Everything was so clear to me, Valentina piuma al vento, neurosis and depression and a double dose of Valium at night, the same old picture of our youthful period. A wager with myself (at this moment I remember it well): of the two evils, Valentina would choose the lesser, me. No problem with me (if she chose me); at the end of the trip good-bye, my dear, it was all so nice and so beautiful, good-bye, good-bye. On the other hand, Adriano . . . Both of us sensed the same thing: you don't fool with Adriano's mouth. Those lips . . . (To think that she let them know every inch of her skin; there are things that are beyond me, of course it's a question of libido, we know we know we know.)

And yet it was easier to kiss him, give in to his strength, slip blandly under the wave of the body that held her; it was easier to give in than to refuse the assent that he, lost in pleasure again, was already forgetting.

Valentina was the first to get up. The water in the shower lashed her for a long time. Putting on a bathrobe, she went back into the bedroom, where Adriano was still on the bed, half sitting up and smiling at her as if from an Etruscan tomb, smoking slowly.

"I want to see night coming on from the balcony."

On the banks of the Arno, the hotel received the last light. The streetlights on the Ponte Vecchio still hadn't gone on, and the river was a purple ribbon with lighter fringes, flown over by small bats hunting invisible insects; higher up the swallows' scissors squeaked. Valentina stretched out in the rocker, breathing in the now cool air. A sweet fatigue overcame her, she could have fallen asleep; maybe she did sleep for a few seconds. But in that hiatus of abandonment she continued thinking about Adriano and time, the monotonous words came back like the chorus of a silly song, time is death, a disguise of death, time is death. She looked at the sky, the swallows playing their neat games, squeaking briefly as if they were shattering the deep blue pottery of sunset. And Adriano was also death.

Curious. After so many false premises suddenly he touches bottom. It might be simpler that way (thinking about it some other day, in other contexts). It's surprising that beings who are so far removed from their own truth (Valentina more than Adriano, that's for sure) hit the mark at times; they don't realize it, of course, and it's

better that way: what follows proves it. (I mean it's
better for me, if you take a good look at it.)

She straightened up, rigid. Adriano was also death. Had she
thought that? Adriano was also death. It didn't make the least
bit of sense, she'd threaded the words together as in a childish
refrain and that absurdity had emerged. She stretched out
once more, relaxing, and she looked at the swallows again.
Maybe it wasn't so absurd; in any case, having thought it was
only good as a metaphor, since denying Adriano would kill
something in her, would pull her out of a momentary part of
herself, would leave her alone with a different Valentina, a
Valentina without Adriano, with Adriano's love, if that babbling for so few days was love, if in herself that furious surrender to a body that dissolved her and returned her as if
exhausted to the abandonment of the sunset was love. In that
way, yes, seen in that way Adriano was death. Everything one
possesses is death because it presages dispossession, it sets up
the emptiness to come. Childish refrains, tra-la-la, but she
couldn't give up her itinerary, remain with Adriano. The
accomplice of death, then, she would let him go to Lucca
simply because it was inevitable sooner or later, there in the
distance Buenos Aires and her son were like the swallows
over the Arno, twittering weakly, plaintive in the nightfall
that was spreading like black wine.

"I'll stay," Valentina murmured. "I love him, I love
him. I'll stay and I'll take him away with me someday."

She knew quite well that it wouldn't be that way, that
Adriano wouldn't change his life for her, Osorno for Buenos
Aires.

How could she know? Everything points in the opposite
direction; it's Valentina who will never exchange Buenos
Aires for Osorno, her established life, her River Plate

routines. Underneath I don't think she was thinking what she's being made to think; it's also certain that cowardice tends to project one's own responsibility into others, etc.

She felt as if she were floating in the air, almost alien to her body, only fear and something like anxiety. She saw a flock of swallows that had bunched together over the middle of the river, flying in great circles. One of the swallows broke away from the rest, losing altitude, coming closer. When it seemed as if it were going to fly up again, something in that marvelous mechanism failed. Like a dull piece of lead, spinning about by itself, it plunged diagonally and with an opaque thud landed on the balcony at Valentina's feet.

Adriano heard the scream and came running. Valentina was covering her face and trembling horribly, taking refuge at the other end of the balcony. Adriano saw the dead swallow and pushed it with his foot. The swallow fell to the street.

"Come inside," he said, taking Valentina by the shoulders. "It's nothing, it's all over. You were scared, poor thing."

Valentina was silent, but when he took her hands away and saw her face he was frightened. He was only reflecting her fear, perhaps the final fear of the swallow as it plunged down out of air that, unfriendly and cruel, had suddenly ceased to sustain it.

Dora liked to chat before going to sleep and she spent half an hour on items about Fiesole and the Piazzale Michelangelo. Valentina listened to her as if from far away, lost in an internal sound that couldn't be confused with meditation. The swallow was dead; it had died in full flight. A presage, an intimation. As if in a strangely lucid half-dream Adriano and the swallow had begun to be confused in her, turning into an almost ferocious desire to escape, break away. She didn't feel guilty of anything but she felt the fault itself, the swallow landing dully at her feet like a fault.

She told Dora in a few words that she was going to change her plans, that she was going directly to Venice.

"You'll meet me there in any case. I'm only moving up two days, I really prefer being alone for a few days."

Dora didn't seem too surprised. Too bad that Valentina would miss Ravenna, Ferrara. In any case, she understood that she preferred going directly and alone to Venice; better to see one city well than two or three badly . . . Valentina was no longer listening to her, lost in her mental flight, in the race that was to take her away from the present, away from a balcony over the Arno.

> *Here it's almost all true, starting with the mistake, which is ironical and amusing. I accept the business of my not being too surprised and that I performed the necessary lip service to tranquilize Valentina. What isn't known is that my lack of surprise had other roots, Valentina's voice and face as she told me about the balcony episode, so out of proportion unless one felt it as she felt it, a presage beyond all logic and therefore irresistible. And also a delightful, cruel suspicion that Valentina was confusing the reasons for her fear, confusing me with Adriano. Her polite distance that night, her rapid way of getting ready and going to bed without giving me the opportunity of sharing the bathroom mirror, the rites of the shower, le temps d'un sein nu entre deux chemises. Adriano, yes, let's say yes, that Adriano. But why that way of going to bed and turning her back to me, cover-*

*ing her face with an arm to suggest that I turn out the
light as soon as possible, that I let her sleep without any
more words, without even a soft good-night kiss between
the two traveling companions?*

On the train she thought about it in a better way, but the fear
was still there. What was she escaping from? It wasn't easy
accepting the solutions of prudence, praising herself for having broken the bond in time. There remained the enigma of
fear, as if Adriano, poor Adriano, were the devil, as if the
temptation of really falling in love with him were the balcony
that opened onto emptiness, the invitation to the irresistible
leap.

Valentina vaguely thought that she was fleeing from herself more than from Adriano. Even the rapidity with which
she'd surrendered in Rome proved her resistance to all seri-
ousness, to all basic new beginnings. The basic had remained
on the other side of the ocean, torn to shreds forever, and
now it was the time of adventure without ties, as with others
already, before and during the trip, the acceptance of circum-
stance without any moral or logical analysis, Dora's episodic
company as the product of a counter at a travel agency,
Adriano at another counter, the time for a cocktail or a city,
moments and pleasures as hazy as the furniture in the hotel
rooms that were being left behind.

*Episodic company, yes. But I would like to believe that
there's more in that reference which would at least equate
Adriano and me as two sides of a triangle where the
third is a counter.*

And yet, Adriano in Florence had advanced toward her with
the demands of the possessor, no longer the fugitive lover

from Rome; worse still, demanding reciprocity, waiting for her and urging her. Maybe the fear was born of that, it was nothing but a dirty, base fear of mundane complications, Buenos Aires/Osorno, people, children, reality installing itself in such a different way in the calendar of that shared life. And maybe not: something else always behind, ungraspable like a swallow in flight. Something that could suddenly have plunged down on her, a dead body hitting her.

> *Hm. Why did nothing go right for her with men? While she thinks the way she's made to think, there's a kind of image of something penned up, besieged: the profound truth, encircled by the lies of an undeniable conformism. Poor thing. Poor thing.*

The first days in Venice were gray and almost cold, but on the third the sun burst through early and it warmed up immediately and with the heat came the tourists who were enthusiastically leaving the hotels and filling the Piazza San Marco and the Merceria in a merry disorder of colors and tongues.

Valentina found it pleasant to let herself be borne along by the rhythmical serpent that went up the Merceria in the direction of the Rialto. Every bend, the Ponte dei Baretieri, San Salvatore, the dark postcard space of the Fondamento dei Tedeschi, received her with that impersonal calm Venice offers its tourists, so different from the convulsive expectation of Naples or the broad opening of the panoramas of Rome. Withdrawn, always secretive, Venice was playing at hiding its true face once more, smiling impersonally at the hope that on a propitious day and hour it will show its real self to the good traveler as recompense for his faithfulness. From the Rialto Valentina looked at the splendors of the Grand Canal and she was surprised at the unexpected distance between her and that luxury of water and gondolas. She penetrated into the alleyways that from *campo* to *campo* led her to churches and museums, went out onto the docks from which she could face the façades of the great palaces corroded by a green and leaden time. She saw everything, she admired everything, knowing, nevertheless, that her reactions were conventional and almost forced, like the repeated praise for the pictures shown us in family albums. Something—blood, anxiety, or just an urge to live—seemed to have remained behind. Valentina suddenly hated the memory of Adriano, found repugnant the petulance of Adriano, who had made the mistake of falling in love with her. His absence made him all the more hateful because his mistake was of the kind that is only punished or pardoned in person. Venice

> *Having taken a choice, he makes Valentina think the way he wants, but other choices are possible if one keeps in mind the fact that she opted to go to Venice alone. Can exaggerated terms like hate and repugnance really be applied to Adriano? A mere change in the prism and it's not Adriano that Valentina is thinking about as she wanders through Venice. That's why my friendly Florentine faithlessness was necessary: it was necessary to keep on projecting Adriano into the center of an action, which, perhaps in that way, perhaps toward the end of the trip, would return me to that beginning where I had hoped, as I was still capable of hoping.*

presented itself to her like an admirable stage without actors, without the sap of participation. Better that way, but also much worse; walking through the alleyways, lingering on the little bridges that cover the dreams of the canals like eyelids, began to seem like a nightmare. To awake, to be awakened by any means, but Valentina felt that only something resembling a whiplash could awaken her. She accepted the offer of a gondolier who proposed taking her to San Marco through the interior canals; sitting in the old easy chair with red cushions, she felt that Venice was beginning to move delicately, to pass by her as she looked at it like an immobile eye obstinately fixed on itself.

"Ca' d'Oro," said the gondolier, breaking a long silence, and he pointed to the façade of the palace. Then, entering the Rio di San Felice, the gondola was swallowed up in a dark and silent labyrinth, smelling of mildew. Like all tourists, Valentina admired the impeccable skill of the oarsman, his way of calculating the bends and avoiding obstacles. She sensed him behind her, invisible but alive, plunging in his oar almost noiselessly, sometimes exchanging a brief phrase in dialect with someone on the bank. She had hardly looked at him when she got in; he seemed to her to be like the majority of gondoliers, tall and thin, his body held in by tight black pants, his jacket vaguely Spanish, his hat made of yellow straw, with a red band. She remembered, rather, his voice, sweet but not low, offering: "Gondola, signorina, gondola, gondola." She had accepted the price and the itinerary, distractedly, but now, when the man called her attention to the Ca' d'Oro and she had to turn to look at him, she noticed the strength of his features, the almost imperious nose and the small, astute eyes; a mixture of pride and calculation, also present in the unexaggerated vigor of his torso and the relative smallness of his head, with something of a viper at the joining with the neck, perhaps in the movements imposed by the rhythmic rowing.

Looking toward the prow again, Valentina saw a small bridge coming up. Already before she had said to herself how delightful the instant of passing under the bridges must be, losing oneself for a moment in the concavity that reeked with mildew, imagining the pedestrians up above, but now she watched the bridge coming up with a vague anguish, as if it were the gigantic cover of a large chest that was going to close over her. She made herself keep her eyes open during the brief transit, but she suffered, and when the narrow strip of bright sky rose up above her again, she made a confused gesture of thanks. The gondolier was pointing out another palace, one of those which only let themselves be seen from the inner canals and which pedestrians have no suspicion of since they only see the service entrances, exactly like so many others. Valentina would have liked to have made a comment, to have become interested in the simple information the gondolier was giving her; suddenly she had to be close to something alive and alien at the same time, to get caught up in a dialogue which would take her away from that absence, from that nothingness which was vitiating the day and things for her. She rose and went to seat herself on a small crosspiece closer to the prow. The gondola wobbled for a moment

> *If the "absence" was Adriano, I can find no proportion between the preceding conduct on the part of Valentina and this angst that is ruining a ride in a gondola for her, which was not at all cheap. I will never know what her Venetian nights in the hotel were like, the bedroom without words or the day's recounting; maybe Adriano's absence was gaining weight in Valentina, but once again, like the mask of another distance, of another lack she didn't want to or couldn't look in the face. (Wishful thinking, perhaps; but what about that vaunted female intuition? The night we reached for a jar of cream at the same time and my hand came to rest on hers and we*

*looked at each other . . . Why didn't I complete the
caress that chance had begun? In some way everything
remained as if suspended in the air between us, and
gondola rides, it is well known, are the exhumers of half-
dreams, nostalgias, and repentant tallies.)*

but the oarsman didn't seem to be surprised at the conduct of
his passenger. And when she asked him, smiling, what he had
said, he repeated his information in greater detail, satisfied
with the interest he was arousing.

"What's on the other side of the island?" Valentina
wanted to know in her rudimentary Italian.

"On the other side, signorina? On the Fondamente
Nuove?"

"If that's what it's called . . . I mean the other side,
where the tourists don't go."

"Yes, the Fondamente Nuove," the gondolier said, rowing very slowly now. "Well, the boats for Burano and Torcello
leave from there."

"I still haven't been to those islands."

"It's very interesting, signorina. The lace factories. But
this side isn't so interesting, because the Fondamente
Nuove—"

"I like to know places that aren't tourist spots," Valentina said, diligently repeating the desire of all tourists. "What
else is there on the Fondamente Nuove?"

"The cemetery is across the way," the gondolier said.
"It's not interesting."

"On an island?"

"Yes, across from the Fondamente Nuove. Look, signorina, ecco Santi Giovanni e Paolo. Bella chiesa, bellissima
. . . Ecco il Colleoni, capolavoro dal Verrocchio . . ."

Tourists, Valentina thought. They and we, the ones to

explain and the others to think we understand. In the end, let's look at your church, let's look at your monument, molto interessante, vero . . .

So many cheap tricks, after all. Valentina is made to speak and think when it's a matter of foolishness; otherwise, silence or attributions almost always aimed in the wrong direction. Why don't we hear more of what Valentina might have murmured before falling asleep, why don't we know more about her body in her solitude, about her look when she opened the hotel window every morning?

The gondola came alongside the Riva degli Schiavoni, by the Piazzetta crowded with strollers. Valentina was hungry and was getting bored in advance thinking that she was going to eat alone. The gondolier helped her ashore, received his payment and tip with a flashing smile.

"If the signorina would like to take another ride, I'm always over there." He pointed to a distant mooring, marked by four poles with lanterns. "My name is Dino," he added, touching the brim of his hat.

"Thank you," Valentina said. She was about to go off, plunge into the human tide of shouts and photographs. There behind her back would remain the only living creature with whom she had exchanged a few words.

"Dino."

"Signorina?"

"Dino . . . where can a person get a good meal?"

The gondolier gave an open laugh, but he was looking at Valentina as if at the same time he understood that the question wasn't a tourist stupidity.

"Does the signorina know the ristoranti over the Canal?" he asked a little by chance, testing.

"Yes," said Valentina, who didn't know them. "I mean a quiet place, without many people."

"Without many people . . . like the signorina?" the man said brutally.

Valentina smiled at him, amused. Dino wasn't stupid at least.

"Without tourists, yes. A place like . . ."

The one where you and your friends eat, she was thinking, but she didn't say it. She felt the man rest his fingers on her elbow, smiling, and he invited her to get into the gondola. She let herself be taken, almost intimidated, but the shadow of boredom was erased immediately, as if dragged away by Dino's gesture as he drove the blade of the oar to the bottom of the lagoon and pushed the gondola along with a clean movement in which one barely noticed the effort.

It was impossible to remember the route. They'd passed under the Ponte dei Sospiri, but then everything became confused. Valentina would close her eyes at times and let herself be carried along by other vague images that paraded by parallel to what she refused to see. The midday sun was raising a foul-smelling vapor off the canals and everything was being repeated, the shouts in the distance, the accepted signals at corners. There were few people on the streets and bridges in that section; Venice was now having lunch. Dino was sculling forcefully and finally he put the gondola into a narrow, straight canal at the end of which the greenish gray of the lagoon could be glimpsed. Valentina said to herself that the Fondamente Nuove must be there, the other bank, the place that wasn't interesting. She was going to turn around and ask when she felt the boat stop alongside some mossy steps. Dino gave a long whistle and a window on the second floor opened noiselessly.

"It's my sister," he said. "We live here. Would you like to eat with us, signorina?"

Valentina's acceptance came ahead of her surprise, her almost irritation. The man's confidence was of the kind that allowed no middle way; Valentina could have refused with the same strength with which she had just accepted. Dino helped her up the steps and left her waiting while he moored the gondola. She heard him singing softly in dialect, in a rather muted voice. She felt a presence behind her and turned; a woman of indeterminate age, poorly dressed in faded pink, was peeping out the door. Dino spoke some unintelligible phrases to her.

"The signorina is a nice lady," he added in Tuscan. "Let her in, Rosa."

And she's going to go in, of course. Anything so long as she can keep on escaping, keep on lying to herself. Life, lie, wasn't it a character in O'Neill who pointed out that life and lie are only separated by one single innocent letter?

They ate in a room with a low ceiling, which surprised Valentina, already used to grand Italian spaces. At the black wooden table there was room for six people. Dino, who had changed his shirt without getting rid of that smell of perspiration, was sitting across from Valentina. Rosa was to her left. On the right the pet cat who, with his dignified beauty, helped them break the ice of the first moments. There was pasta *asciutta*, a large bottle of wine, and fish. Valentina found everything excellent and was almost happy with what her drowsing good sense continued to consider a folly.

"The signorina has a good appetite," said Rosa, who barely spoke. "Have a little cheese."

"Yes, thank you."

Dino was eating avidly, looking more at his plate than at Valentina, but she had the impression that he was observing her in some way, without asking her questions; not even asking her what nationality she was, just the opposite of almost all Italians. In the end, Valentina thought, such an absurd situation has got to explode. What could they say to each other when the last mouthful had been consumed? That terrible moment after a meal among strangers. She petted the cat, gave him a little piece of cheese to taste. Dino was laughing now, his cat ate only fish.

"Have you been a gondolier long?" Valentina asked, looking for an opening.

"Five years, signorina."

"Do you like it?"

"Non si sta male."

"In any case, it doesn't seem to be such hard work."

"No . . . that it isn't."

Then he does other things too, she thought. Rosa served her some more wine, and although she didn't want to have any more, the brother and sister insisted, smiling, and filled the glasses. "The cat doesn't drink," Dino said, looking into her eyes for the first time in a long while. The three laughed.

Rosa left and came back with a plate of small fruits. Then Dino accepted a Camel and said that Italian tobacco was no good. He smoked leaning backward, rolling his eyes; sweat was running down his muscular bronzed neck.

"Is my hotel very far from here?" Valentina asked. "I don't want to bother you any longer."

I really should pay for this lunch, she was thinking, debating the problem and not knowing how to solve it. She named her hotel and Dino said he would take her there. Rosa had left the dining room a moment before. The cat, stretched out in a corner, was dozing in the heat of siesta time. It smelled of canal, old houses.

"Well, you people certainly have been kind," Valentina said, pushing back the rough chair and rising. "I'm sorry I can't say it in good Italian . . . In any case, you understand me."

"Oh, of course," Dino said without moving.

"I'd like to say good-bye to your sister, and . . ."

"Oh, Rosa. She's probably gone out. She always goes out at this time."

Valentina remembered a brief, incomprehensible dialogue in the middle of the lunch. It was the only time they'd spoken in dialect, and Dino had apologized. Without knowing why, she thought that Rosa's leaving had come out of that conversation and she felt a little afraid, and also ashamed at being afraid.

Dino in turn got up. Only then did she notice how tall he was. The little eyes were looking toward the door, the only door. The door opened into a bedroom (the sister had made excuses for having to go through it on their way to the dining room). Valentina picked up her straw hat and purse. He has beautiful hair, she thought. She felt uneasy and at the same time sure of herself, occupied. It was better than the bitter emptiness of that whole morning; now there was something, she was confidently facing somebody.

"I'm so sorry," she said, "I would have liked to have said good-bye to your sister. Thank you for everything."

She held out her hand and he shook it without squeezing, letting go of it immediately. Valentina felt her vague uneasiness disappearing before this unpolished gesture full of timidity. She went toward the door, followed by Dino. She

went into the other room, barely making out the furniture in
the shadows. Wasn't the door that led to the hallway on the
right? Behind her she heard Dino close the dining room door.
Now the room seemed much darker. With an involuntary
gesture she turned to wait for him to precede her. An exhala-
tion of sweat enveloped her a second before Dino's arms enwrapped her brutally. She closed her eyes, barely resisting.
If she could have, she would have killed him right there,
beating him until she caved in his face, breaking that mouth
that was kissing her throat while a hand ran along her contracted body. She tried to get loose and fell suddenly backward onto the shadow of a bed. Dino let himself slip on top of
her, holding down her legs, kissing her full on the mouth
with lips that were damp from wine. Valentina closed her
eyes again. If he'd taken a bath at least, she thought, ceasing
to resist. Dino held her prisoner for a moment, as if aston-
ished at that surrender. Then, murmuring and kissing her,
he got on top of her and with clumsy fingers looked for the
buttons of her blouse.

> *Perfect, Valentina. As Anglo-Saxon* sagesse *teaches, hav-
> ing prevented many deaths by strangulation in that way,
> the only thing to do in such circumstances was the in-
> telligent relax-and-enjoy-it.*

At four o'clock, with the sun still high, the gondola docked by
San Marco. As he did the first time, Dino offered his forearm
for Valentina to lean on, and he stood as if waiting, looking
into her eyes.

"Arrivederci," Valentina said, and started to walk.

"I'll be there tonight," Dino said pointing to the mooring poles. "At ten o'clock."

Valentina went directly·to the hotel in search of a hot

bath. Nothing could be more important than that, getting rid of Dino's smell, the contamination of the sweat, the saliva that stained her. With a moan of pleasure she slipped into the steaming tub and for a long time was incapable of reaching out her hand toward the cake of green soap. Afterward, diligently, to the rhythm of her thoughts as they returned little by little, she began to wash.

The memory wasn't painful. Everything sordid about its preparations seemed to be erased by the thing itself. She'd been tricked, drawn into a stupid trap, but she was too smart not to understand that she herself had woven the net. In that confused skein of memories she found Rosa especially repugnant, the evasive figure of the accomplice who now, in light of what had happened, was hard to think of as Dino's sister. His slave, rather, his mistress, willing, out of necessity, in order to keep him for a while longer.

She stretched out in the bath, aching. Dino had conducted himself like what he was, furiously demanding his pleasures with no consideration of any kind. He had possessed her like an animal, over and over, demanding ugly things of her that wouldn't have been ugly if he'd had a minimum of gentleness. And Valentina didn't regret it, didn't regret the stuffy smell of the unmade bed, Dino's panting like a dog, the vague attempt at reconciliation afterward (because Dino was afraid, he was already weighing the possible consequences of his rape of a foreign woman). In reality she regretted nothing except the lack of grace in the adventure. And maybe she didn't even regret that, the brutality had been there like the garlic in common people's stew, the indispensable and tasty requisite.

It amused her, a little hysterically,

No, no. Not hysteria. Only I could see Valentina's expression here the night I told her the story of my fellow

THE FERRY, OR ANOTHER TRIP TO VENICE   365

*student Nancy in Morocco, an identical situation but
much uglier, with her rapist Islamically frustrated when
he found out that Nancy was in full menstruation, and
with blows and whipping making her render him the
other route. (I didn't find what I was looking for when
I told her, but I saw that her eyes were like a wolf's for
an instant before she rejected the theme and sought as
always the pretext of fatigue and sleep.) Maybe if Adriano had proceeded like Dino, without the garlic and the
sweat, skillful and beautiful. Maybe if I, instead of
letting her go to sleep . . .*

to think that Dino, while he tried to help her dress with absurdly clumsy hands, had attempted the tenderness of a lover,
too grotesque even for himself to believe. Making the date,
for example, when he said good-bye to her at San Marco, was
ridiculous. Imagining that she could come back to his house,
cold-bloodedly give herself to him . . . It didn't make her the
least bit upset, she was certain that Dino was an excellent
individual in his way, he hadn't added robbery to rape, which
would have been easy, and she even admitted that there was a
more normal, more logical tone in what had happened than
in her encounter with Adriano.

You see, Dora, you see, stupid?

The terrible thing was to realize to what point Dino was far
away from her, without the slightest possibility of communi-
cation. With the last gesture of pleasure, silence began, upset,
the ridiculous comedy. There was one advantage after all:
she didn't have to run away from Dino as she did from Adriano. No danger of falling in love; not even he would fall in
love, of course. What freedom! With all his filth, the adven-

ture didn't disgust her, especially after she had soaped herself.

Dora arrived from Padua at dinnertime bubbling over with news of Giotto and Altichiero. She found that Valentina was very well and said that Adriano had spoken vaguely about giving up his trip to Lucca, but that afterward she'd lost sight of him. "I'd say that he's fallen in love with you," she dropped in passing, with her oblique laugh. She was enchanted with Venice, of which she hadn't even seen anything, and boasted of being able to guess how wonderful the city was just by the conduct of the waiters and the *facchini*. "Everything so refined, so refined," she repeated, savoring her shrimp.

> *If you'll excuse the word, never in my fucking life have I said a phrase like that. What kind of unknown vengeance lies in this? Or rather (yes, I'm beginning to sense it, believe it), everything is born of a subconscious that has also made Valentina be born, that not knowing her on the surface and being mistaken all the time about her conduct and her motives, hitting the mark without knowing it in deeper waters, there where Valentina hasn't forgotten Rome, the counter at the agency, the acceptance of sharing a room and a trip. In those flashes that are made by fish out of the abyss as they appear for a second over the water, I am deliberately deformed and offended, I become what they make me say.*

There was talk of Venice by night, but Dora was done in by the beaux-arts and returned to the hotel after two turns about the square. Valentina performed the ritual of drinking port at the Florian, and waited for it to be ten o'clock. Mingling with the people who were eating ice cream and taking flash pictures, she spied the quay. There were only two gondolas on that side, with their lanterns lighted. Dino was on the dock, next to a pole. He was waiting.

He really thinks I'm going to go, she thought, almost with surprise. An English-looking couple went over to the gondolier. Valentina saw him take off his hat and offer the gondola. The couple got in almost at once; the small lantern trembled in the night of the lagoon.

Vaguely upset, Valentina returned to the hotel.

The morning light washed away her bad dreams, but without removing a certain feeling of nausea, the pressure at the mouth of the stomach. Dora was waiting for her in the salon for breakfast, and Valentina was pouring herself some tea when a waiter came to the table.

"The signorina's gondolier is outside."

"Gondolier? I haven't asked for any gondola."

"The man indicated the signorina."

Dora was looking at her with curiosity and Valentina felt herself suddenly naked. She made an effort to swallow some tea and got up after hesitating a moment. Amused, Dora thought it would be fun to watch the scene from the window. She saw the gondolier, Valentina going to meet him, the man's curt but decisive greeting. Valentina was speaking to him almost without gestures, but she saw her raise a hand as if begging—of course it couldn't be—for something that the other refused to grant. Then it was he who spoke, moving his arms Italian fashion. Valentina seemed to be waiting for him to go away, but the man insisted, and Dora stayed there long enough to see Valentina look at her wristwatch and make a sign of assent.

"I'd forgotten completely," she explained on returning, "but a gondolier doesn't forget his customers. Aren't you going out?"

"Yes, of course," Dora said. "Are they all as good-looking as the ones you see in the movies?"

"All of them, naturally," Valentina said without smiling. Dino's boldness had left her so stupefied that she was having trouble controlling herself. For a moment she was bothered by the idea that Dora would propose joining the outing; so logical and so Dora. But that would be the solution precisely, she said to herself. Brute that he is, he's not going to feel like raising a row. He's hysterical, that's obvious, but not stupid.

Dora didn't say anything although she was smiling at her with an amiability that seemed vaguely repugnant to Valentina. Without really knowing why, she didn't propose their taking the gondola together. It was extraordinary how during those weeks they did all the important things without knowing why.

Tu parles, ma fille. What had seemed incredible to me became simple evidence as soon as they left me out of that little ride. That couldn't have had any importance, of course, just a parenthesis of cheap and energetic consolation without the slightest future risk. But it was the recurrence at a low level of the same verification: Adriano or a gondolier, and I the outsider once more. All that was worth another cup of tea and asking oneself if there still wasn't something to do to perfect the small clockwork I had set in motion—oh, with complete innocence—before leaving Florence.

Dino took her along the Grand Canal to beyond the Rialto, amiably choosing the longest route. At the Valmarana Palace they went into the Rio dei Santi Apostoli and Valentina, looking obstinately ahead, saw once more, coming one after another, the small, black, swarming bridges. It was hard for her to convince herself that she was in that gondola again, leaning her back against the ancient red cushion. A thread of water ran along the bottom, canal water, Venice water. The famous carnivals. The doge marrying the sea. The famous palaces and carnivals of Venice. I came to look for you because you didn't come to look for me last night. I want to take you out in the gondola. The doge marrying the sea. With perfect cheek. Cheek. And now he was taking her in the gondola, from time to time giving a cry that was somewhere between melancholic and unsociable before turning down an inner canal. In the distance, still very far off, Valentina glimpsed the open, green strip. The Fondamente Nuove again. It was foreseeable, the four mossy steps, she recognized the place. Now he was going to whistle and Rosa would appear at the window.

> *Lyrical and obvious. Missing are the Aspern papers, Baron Corvo, and Tadzio, beautiful Tadzio and the plague. Missing too is a certain telephone call to a hotel near the Teatro La Fenice, although it's nobody's fault (I mean the absence of the detail, not the telephone call).*

But Dino was docking the gondola in silence and waiting. Valentina turned for the first time since she'd gotten in and looked at him. Dino was smiling beautifully. He had stupendous teeth, which, with a little toothpaste, would have been perfect.

I'm lost, Valentina thought, and leaped out onto the first step without taking the forearm he was offering her.

*Did she really think that? One must be careful with met-
aphors, rhetorical figures, or whatever they're called.
That's touching bottom too; if I'd known it at that moment, maybe there wouldn't . . . But I wasn't allowed to
go into time's beyond either.*

When she came down to dinner, Dora was waiting with the
news (although she wasn't completely sure) that she'd seen
Adriano among the tourists on the Piazza.

"Very far off, in one of the arcades, you know. I think it
was him because of that light-colored suit, a bit tight. He
probably got in this afternoon . . . Pursuing you, I imagine."

"Oh, come on."

"Why not? This wasn't on his itinerary."

"You're not even sure it's him either," Valentina said
with hostility. The news hadn't shocked her too much, but it
did start up the lamentable machinery of ideas. That again,
she thought. Again. She would run into him, that was certain,
in Venice it's like living in a bottle, everybody ends up meeting on the Piazza or the Rialto. Fleeing again, but why? She
was sick of fleeing from nothing, of not knowing what she was
fleeing from and if she really was fleeing or doing the same
thing as the pigeons there before her eyes, the female pigeons
pretending to avoid the conceited attack of the males, the
better in the end to consent blindly with a leaden ruffling of
feathers.

"Let's have coffee at the Florian," Dora proposed.
"We'll probably meet him, he's such a good boy."

They saw him almost at once, he had his back to the
square under the arches of the arcade, withdrawn in the contemplation of some horrendous Murano crystal. When
Dora's greeting made him turn around, his surprise was so
minimal, so civil, that Valentina felt relieved. Nothing the-

atrical, at least. Adriano greeted Dora with his distant courtesy and shook Valentina's hand.

"Well, this certainly is a small world. No one can escape the Blue Guide, one day or another."

"Not us, at least."

"Or the ice cream of Venice. May I invite you?"

Dora took over the conversation almost at once. She had in her possession two or three more cities than they, and naturally she was trying to wrap them up in the catalogue of everything they'd missed. Valentina might have been wishing that her themes would never end or that Adriano would finally decide to look straight at her, make her the worst of reproaches, the eyes that fasten themselves on the face with something that's always more than an accusation or a reproach. But he was diligently eating his ice cream or smoking with his head tilted forward—his beautiful South American head—attentive to every word from Dora. Only Valentina was observing the slight trembling of the fingers that held the cigarette.

Me too, my dear girl, me too. And I didn't like it at all because that calm hid something that hadn't seemed so violent to me until now, that tight spring, as if waiting for the trigger that would release it. So different from his glacial and matter-of-fact tone on the telephone. For the moment I was out of the game, I could do nothing to make things happen as I had hoped they would. Warn Valentina . . . But it meant revealing everything to her, going back to the Rome of those nights when she'd slipped away, going off and leaving the shower and soap free for me, going to sleep with her back toward me, murmuring that she was so sleepy, that she was already half asleep.

The conversation became circular, along came the comparison of museums and small touristic misfortunes, more ice cream and tobacco. There was talk of covering the city together the next morning.

"Maybe," Adriano said, "we'll annoy Valentina, who likes to go alone."

"Why are you including me?" Dora laughed. "Valentina and I understand each other by dint of not understanding each other. She won't share her gondola with anyone, and I've got some little canals that are mine alone. Try reaching an understanding like that with her."

"You can always try," Adriano said. "Well, in any case, I'll come by the hotel at ten thirty, and you people will have decided or will decide."

When they went up (they had rooms on the same floor), Valentina rested a hand on Dora's arm.

It was the last time you touched me. Like that, as always, lightly.

"I want to ask a favor of you."

"Of course."

"Let me go out alone with Adriano tomorrow morning. It will be the only time."

Dora was looking for the key that she'd dropped into the bottom of her purse. It took her a while to find it.

"It would be too long to explain now," Valentina added, "but you'll be doing me a favor."

"Yes, of course," Dora said, opening her door. "You don't want to share him either."

"Him either? If you think . . ."

"Oh, I was only joking. Have a good night's sleep."

*It doesn't matter now, but when I closed the door I could
have dug my nails into my face. No, it doesn't matter
now; but if Valentina had tied the ends together . . .
That "him either" was the end of the skein; she didn't
entirely realize, she let it slip out in the confusion in
which she was living. So much the better for me, naturally, but maybe . . . Finally it really doesn't matter
anymore now; sometimes Valium is enough.*

Valentina waited for him in the lobby and it didn't even
occur to Adriano to ask about Dora's absence; as in Florence
or Rome, he didn't seem too sensitive to her presence. They
walked along Orsolo, scarcely looking at the little inside lake
where the gondolas slept at night, and they headed in the
direction of the Rialto. Valentina went on a little ahead,
wearing a light-colored dress. They hadn't exchanged more
than two or three ritual phrases, but when they went into an
alleyway (they were lost, neither of them had looked at, the
map), Adriano went forward and took her by the arm.

"It's too cruel, you know. There's something swinish
about what you've done."

"Yes, I know. I use worse words."

"Going off like that, shabby. Just because a swallow died
on a balcony. Hysterical."

"You have to recognize," Valentina said, "that the reason, if that's what it is, was poetic."

"Valentina—"

"Oh, enough," she said. "Let's go to some quiet spot and
talk it out once and for all."

"Let's go to my hotel."

"No, not your hotel."

"To a café, then."

"They're full of tourists, you know that. A quiet place

that won't be interesting . . ." She hesitated because the phrase brought out a name. "Let's go to the Fondamente Nuove."

"What's that?"

"The other shore, to the north. Have you got a map? Around here, there it is. Let's go."

Beyond the Malibran theater, alleys without shops, with rows of doors that were always closed, an occasional poorly dressed child playing in a doorway, they reached Fumo and close by now they could see the glimmer of the lagoon. Suddenly they came out of the gray shadows onto a rise dazzling with sunlight, peopled with workers and street vendors. A few evil-looking cafés clung like barnacles to the floating shacks from which the vaporetti left for Burano and the cemetery. Valentina had spotted the cemetery immediately; she remembered Dino's explanation. The small island, its parallelogram surrounded as far as one could see by a reddish wall. The tops of the funereal trees stood out above it like a dark festoon. The landing dock could be seen very clearly, but at that moment the island seemed to contain only the dead; not a ferry, nobody on the marble steps of the landing. And everything was sharply ablaze under the eleven o'clock sun.

Indecisive, Valentina started walking to the right. Adriano followed her morosely, almost without looking around. They crossed a bridge under which one of the inner canals connected with the lagoon. The heat was making itself felt, its invisible flies landing on the face. Another bridge of white stone came up and Valentina stopped at the top of the arch, leaning on the balustrade, looking toward the inner part of the city. If they had to talk someplace, let it be there, so neutral, so devoid of interest, with the cemetery behind and the canal that penetrated deep into Venice, separating the graceless, almost deserted banks.

"I left," Valentina said, "because none of that made any sense. Let me talk. I left because one of us had to leave in any case, and you're making things difficult, knowing quite well that one of us had to leave. What difference does it make except in time? One week sooner or later . . ."

"There's no difference for you," Adriano said. "For you it's exactly the same."

"If I could only explain to you . . . But we'd be left with the words. Why did you follow me? What sense does this make?"

If she really said those things, at least I know she didn't think I had anything to do with Adriano's presence in Venice. Behind it, of course, the usual bitterness: that tendency to ignore me, not even to suspect that there was a third hand shuffling the cards.

"I know it doesn't make any sense," Adriano said. "That's the way it is, that's all."

"You shouldn't have come."

"And you shouldn't have left like that, abandoning me like—"

"No fancy words, please. How can you call something that was nothing but normal after all abandonment? The return to normality, if you prefer."

"Everything is so normal for you," he said furiously. His lips were trembling and he grasped the railing as if to calm himself by the blank and indifferent contact with stone.

Valentina was looking toward the end of the canal, watching a larger than ordinary gondola approaching, still imprecise in the distance. She was afraid to meet Adriano's eyes and her only wish was for him to leave, to shower her with insults if necessary and then leave. But Adriano was still there in the perfect voluptuousness of his suffering, prolonging what they had meant to be an explanation and which didn't go beyond a pair of monologues.

"It's absurd," Valentina finally murmured, still looking at the gondola that was slowly approaching. "Why do I have to be like you? Wasn't it clear that I didn't want to see you anymore?"

"Underneath it all you love me," Adriano said grotesquely. "It can't be that you don't love me."

"Why can't it be?"

"Because you're different from all the others. You didn't give in just like anyone, like a hysterical woman who doesn't know what to do on a trip."

"You're imagining that I gave in, but I could say that it was you who gave in. The same old ideas about women, when . . .

Etc.

But we're not getting anywhere with this, Adriano; it's all so useless. Either leave me alone today, right now, or I'm leaving Venice."

"I'll follow you," he said, almost petulantly.

"We're both being ridiculous. Wouldn't it be better if . . . ?"

Every word of that senseless talk was growing painful to the point of nausea. The façade of a dialogue, a painted hand under which something useless and rotten was stagnating like the waters of the canal. Halfway through the question Valentina realized that the gondola was different from the rest. Broader, like a barge, with four oarsmen standing over the crossbars, where something seemed to rise up like a black and gold catafalque. But it *was* a catafalque, and the oarsmen were dressed in black, without the merry straw hats. The boat had reached the landing alongside a heavy grayish building. There was a dock in front of something that looked like a chapel. The hospital, she thought. The hospital chapel. People were coming out, a man carrying wreaths that he threw carelessly into the boat of death. Others were appearing now with the coffin, and the maneuver of putting it on board began. Even Adriano seemed absorbed by the clear horror of what was taking place under the morning sun in the Venice that wasn't interesting, where tourists weren't supposed to go. Valentina heard him murmur something, or perhaps it was a muffled sob. But she couldn't take her eyes off the boat, the four oarsmen who were waiting with their oars dug in so that the others could put the coffin into the niche with black curtains. In the prow she saw a shiny mass instead of the familiar toothed cutout usually seen on gondolas. It looked like a huge silver owl, a figurehead with something live about it, but when the gondola went forward along the canal (the family of the dead man was on the dock and two boys were supporting an old woman) it could be seen that the owl was a silvery sphere and cross, the only bright and shiny thing on the whole boat. It came toward them; it was going to pass under the bridge, right under their feet. All that was needed was a leap to land in the bow, on top of the coffin. The bridge seemed to be moving slightly toward the boat. ("Then you won't come with me?") Valentina was staring very hard at the gondola, which the oarsmen were slowly moving.

"No, I won't go. Leave me alone, leave me in peace."

She couldn't say anything else among all the things she could have said or not said, now that she felt the trembling of Adriano's arm against hers; she heard him repeat the question and breathe heavily, as if he were panting. But she couldn't look at anything but the boat either, closer and closer to the bridge. It was going to pass under the bridge, almost up against them; it would come out the other side into the open lagoon and cross over like a slow black fish to the isle of the dead, bearing another coffin, piling one more dead body into the silent village behind the red walls. It almost didn't surprise her to see that one of the oarsmen was Dino,

> *Can that have been for sure, isn't it an abuse of too gratuitous a chance? It's impossible to know now, just as it's impossible to know why Adriano didn't reproach her for her cheap adventure. I think he did, that this dialogue of pure nothing that sustains the scene wasn't the real one, the one that was born of other deeds and led to something that seems inconceivable without it because it's so extreme, so horrible. After all, maybe he kept quiet what he knew so he wouldn't give me away; yes, but what did his giving me away matter if immediately after . . . ? Valentina, Valentina, Valentina, the delight of your reproaching me, insulting me, being here cursing me, being you shouting at me, the consolation of seeing you again, Valentina, of feeling your slaps, your saliva on my face . . . (A whole pill this time. Right away, my girl.)*

the tallest one, in the stern, and that Dino had seen her and had seen Adriano beside her, and that he'd stopped rowing to look at her, lifting his astute little eyes to her, full of questions and probably ("Please don't insist") jealous rage. The gondola was a few feet away, every silver-headed nail could be seen, every flower, and the modest iron fittings on the coffin ("You're hurting me, let go"). On her elbow she felt the unbearable pressure of Adriano's fingers and closed her eyes for a second, thinking he was going to hit her. The boat seemed to flee under their feet, and Dino's face (startled, above all, it was comical to think that the poor imbecile had also given himself illusions) slid away suddenly, was lost under the bridge. There I go, Valentina managed to say to herself, there she went in that coffin, beyond Dino, beyond the hand that was brutally squeezing her arm. She felt Adriano making a movement as if taking something out, maybe his cigarettes, with the gesture of someone trying to gain time, to prolong the moment at all cost. Cigarette or whatever it might be, what did it matter since she was already on the black gondola, going toward her island without fear, finally accepting the swallow.

THERE
BUT
WHERE,
HOW

A painting by René Magritte shows a pipe that occupies the center of the canvas. At the bottom of the picture its title: This is not a pipe.

TO PACO,
WHO LIKED MY TALES
(*Dedication of* Bestiario,
1951)

it doesn't depend on will

it's he all of a sudden: now (before beginning to write; the reason for having begun to write) or yesterday, tomorrow, there's no previous indication, he's there or he's not; I can't even say that he's come, there's neither arrival nor departure; he's like a pure presence that manifests itself or doesn't in this dirty present, full of echoes of past and obligations of future

Those of you reading me, hasn't it happened to you, that thing that starts as a dream and turns into many dreams but isn't that, isn't just a dream? Something that's there but where, how; something that happens in dreaming, of course, nothing but a dream but afterward there too, in a different way because soft and full of holes but there while you brush your teeth, in the bottom of the bathroom glass you keep on seeing it while you spit out the toothpaste or put your face in the cold water, and thinning out already but still sticking to your pajamas, to the root of the tongue while you warm the coffee, there but where, how, stuck to the morning, with its silence that the sounds of the day are already entering, the news on the radio that we turn on because we're awake and up and the world goes on. God damn it, God damn it, how can it be, what's that thing that was, that we were in a dream but is something else, comes back every so often and is there but where, how is it there and where is there? Why tonight again, Paco, now that I'm writing in this same room, beside this same bed where the sheets show the hollow of my body? Doesn't it happen the same way to you as to me with someone who died thirty-one years ago, whom we buried one sunny noon in Chacarita, carrying the coffin on our shoulders with friends from our crowd, with Paco's brothers?

> his small, pale face, his tight jai alai player's body, his eyes like limpid water, his blond hair combed with brilliantine, the part on the side, his gray suit, his black loafers, almost always a blue tie but sometimes in shirt sleeves or in a white terry cloth robe (when he waits for me in his room on the Calle Rivadavia, getting up with effort so I won't realize that he's so sick, sitting on the edge of the bed wrapped in the white bathrobe, asking me for the cigarette he's been forbidden)

I know that what I'm writing can't be written, certain that it's another of the day's ways of ending the dream's weak operations; now I'll go to work, I'll find myself among translators and editors at the conference in Geneva where I've been for four weeks, I'll read the news from Chile, that other nightmare that no toothpaste can loosen from my teeth; why jump from my bed to the typewriter, then, from the house on the Calle Rivadavia in Buenos Aires where I've just been with Paco to this typewriter that won't be good for anything now that I'm awake and know that thirty-one years have gone by since that October morning, that niche in a cemetery, the few flowers that almost nobody brought because damn it if flowers mattered to us while we were burying Paco. I tell you, those thirty-one years are not what matter, this passage from dream to words is much worse, the gap between, what still goes on here but is giving itself over more and more to the neat rows of things on this side, to the knife blade of the words I keep writing and which are no longer what follow there, but when, how. And if I insist it's because I can't help it, I've known so many times that Paco is alive or that he's going to die, that he's alive in a different way from our way of being alive or going to die, that in writing it at least I can fight against what I can't grasp, I can run the fingers of the words over the holes of that very slim plot that still binds me to the bathroom, the toaster, the first cigarette, still there but where, how; repeating, reiterating formulas of enchantment, really, probably you who are reading me also sometimes try to fix what is getting away from you with some psalmody, you stupidly repeat a childhood verse, along came a spider, along came a spider, closing your eyes in order to concentrate on the capital scene of the frayed dream, rejecting the spider, shrugging off the along-came, the newsboy knocks on the door, your wife looks at you with a smile and tells you, Pedrito, you've got cobwebs on your eyes and she's so right you think, along came a spider, cobwebs, naturally.

> when I dream about Alfredo, about other dead people, it can be any one of so many images. options of time and life; I can see Alfredo driving his black Ford, playing poker, marrying Zulema, leaving the Mariano Acosta Normal School with me to go have a vermouth at the Perla del Once; afterward, finally, before, any one of the days in any one of the years, but not Paco, Paco is only the naked and cold room of his house, the iron bed, the white terry cloth robe, and if we meet at the café and he's wearing his gray suit and blue tie, his face is the same, the earthen final mask, the silences of an irreparable weariness

I'm not going to waste any more time; if I write it's because I know, even if I can't explain what it is I know and can barely manage to separate the thickest parts, to put the dreams to one side and Paco to the other, but it has to be done if one day, if right now at some moment I can manage to grapple beyond. I know that I dream about Paco because of logic, because dead people don't walk the streets and there's an ocean of water and time between this hotel in Geneva and his house on the Calle Rivadavia, between his house on the Calle Rivadavia and him dead thirty-one years ago. So it's obvious that Paco is alive (in what useless, horrible way do I have to say it so I can get closer, so I can gain some ground) while I sleep; what's called dreaming. Every so often, weeks can pass and even years, I know again while I sleep that he's alive and is going to die; there's nothing extraordinary in dreaming about him and seeing him alive, it happens with so many others in everybody's dreams, I too sometimes find my grandmother alive in my dreams, or Alfredo alive in my dreams, Alfredo, who was one of Paco's friends and died before him. Anybody can dream about his dead and see them alive, that's not why I'm writing; if I write it's because I know, even though I can't explain what it is I know. Look, when I dream about Alfredo the toothpaste does its job well; the melancholy is left, the recurrence of timeworn memories, then the day without Alfredo begins. But with Paco it's as if he too were waking up with me, he can allow himself the luxury of dissolving the vivid sequences of the night almost immediately and continue on in the present and out of the dream, denying with a strength that Alfredo, that nobody has in broad daylight, after shower and newspaper. What does he care if I can only remember that moment when his brother Claudio came to get me, to tell me that Paco was very ill, and that the succeeding scenes, frayed now but still rigorous and coherent in lack of memory, a little like the hollow of my body still marked on the sheets, are diluted like all dreams. What I know, then, is that having dreamed is only a part of something different, a kind of superimposition, a different zone, even though the expression might not be right, but I also have to superimpose or violate words if I want to get close, if I hope to be there sometime. Broadly, as I feel it now, Paco is alive even though he's going to die and if I know one thing it's that there's nothing supernatural in that; I have my own ideas about ghosts, but Paco isn't a ghost. Paco is a man, the man he was until thirty-one years ago, my classmate, my best friend. He hasn't had to come back to my side now and then, the first dream was enough for me to know that he's alive on this side or beyond the dream and for sadness to come over me again as it did those nights on the Calle Rivadavia when I saw him giving ground to an illness that was eating him up inside, consuming him without haste in the most perfect of tortures. Every night that I've dreamt about him again it's been the same, the variations on the theme; it isn't the recurrence that could be fooling me, what I know now I already knew the first time, in Paris in the fifties, I think, fifteen years after his death in Buenos Aires. It's true that at that time I tried to be healthy, brush my teeth better; I rejected you, Paco, even though something in me already knew that you weren't there like Alfredo, like my other dead; facing dreams one can be a swine and a coward too, and maybe that's why you came back, not out of vengeance but to prove to me that it was useless, that you were alive and so ill, that you were going to die, that some night or other Claudio would come looking for me in dreams to weep on my shoulder, to tell me that Paco is in bad shape, what can we do, Paco is in such bad shape.

> his earthen and sunless face, not even the moon over the cafés on Eleventh, student night life, a bloodless triangular face, the sky blue water of the eyes, the lips peeled by fever, the sweet smell of Bright's disease, his delicate smile, the voice reduced to a minimum, having to breathe between each phrase, replacing words with a gesture or ironic grimace

You see, that's what I know, it isn't much but it changes everything. Time-space hypotheses bore me, n dimensions, not to mention occultist jargon, astral life, and Gustav Meyrink. I'm not going out searching because I know I'm incapable of illusion or maybe, in the best of cases, of the capacity to enter different territories. I'm simply here and ready, Paco, writing about what one more time we've lived together while I was asleep; if I can help you in anything, it's in knowing that you're not just my dream that there but where, how,

that there you're alive and suffering. About that there I can't
say anything, except what comes to me dreaming and awake,
that it's a there without a handle; because when I see you I'm
sleeping and I don't know how to think, and when I think
I'm awake but I can only think; image or idea, they're always
that there but where, that there but how.

> rereading this means lowering my head, cursing and
> lighting a new cigarette, wondering about the meaning of
> typing on this machine, who for, just tell me, who for
> who won't shrug his shoulders and quickly wrap it up,
> put on a label, and go on to something else, another story

And besides, Paco, why. I leave it for the end but it's the
hardest, it's this rebellion and this disgust at what's happened
to you. You can imagine that I can't think of you in hell, we
would've found that so funny if we could have talked about
it. But there's got to be a why, it isn't true, you yourself have
got to ask yourself why you're alive there where you are since
you're going to die again, since Claudio has to come and get
me again, since, as just a moment ago I'm going to climb the
stairs on the Calle Rivadavia to find you in your sickroom,
with that bloodless face and eyes like water, smiling with
stained, parched lips, giving me a hand that's like a piece of
paper. And your voice, Paco, the voice that I finally recognized in you, precariously articulating the few words of a
greeting or a joke. You're not in the house on the Calle Rivadavia, of course, and I, in Geneva, haven't climbed the stairs
of your house in Buenos Aires, those are the props of the
dream and, as always, on awakening the images become un-
tied and only you are still on this side, you who aren't a
dream, who've been waiting for me in so many dreams but
like someone who makes a date in a neutral place, a station or

a café, the other props that we forget as soon as we've used them.

> how can I say it, how can I go on, tearing up reason re-
> peating that it isn't just a dream, that if I see him in
> dreams, like any of my dead, he's something else, he's
> there, inside and out, alive although

> what I see of him, what I hear of him: the illness en-
> circling him, fixes him in that last appearance that's my
> memory of him thirty-one years ago; that's what he's
> like now, that's what he is

Why are you alive if you've gotten sick again, if you're going to die again? And when you die, Paco, what's going to happen between the two of us? Am I going to find out that you've died, am I going to dream, since dream is the only zone where I can meet you, that we're burying you again? And after that, am I going to stop dreaming, will I really know that you're dead? Because it's been many years now, Paco, that you've been living there where we meet, but with a useless and withered life, this time your illness lasts interminably longer than the other, weeks or months pass, Paris passes or Quito or Geneva and then Claudio comes and embraces me, Claudio, so young and such a puppy, weeping silently on my shoulder, telling me that you're in bad shape, to go up and see you, sometimes it's a café but almost always you have to go up the narrow staircase of that house that they've already torn down, a year ago from a taxi I looked at that block on Rivadavia and Once and I found out that the house was no longer there or that they'd remodeled it, that the door was missing and the narrow staircase that went up to the second floor, the rooms with high ceilings and yellow stucco, weeks or months pass and I know again that I have to go see you, or I just find you me and it's then that Claudio comes or suddenly I find you in the café where we used to shoot pool or in the room on the first floor where we played Ravel records and read Federico and Rilke, and the dazzling happiness it gives me to know that you're alive is stronger than the paleness of your face and the cold weakness of your hand; because in the middle of the dream I'm not fooled the way I'm fooled sometimes when I see Alfredo or Juan Carlos, the happiness isn't that horrible deception on awakening and understanding that it had been dreamed, with you I awaken and nothing changes except that I've stopped seeing you, I know that you're alive there where you are, in a land that isn't this land and not an astral sphere or an abominable limbo; and it's a hard happiness and it's here while I write and doesn't contradict the sadness of having seen you once more so ill, it's still hope, Paco, if I write it's because I'm waiting even though it's the same every time, the stair that leads to your room, the café where between two pool shots you'll tell me that you'd been sick but that you're already getting over it, lying to me with a poor smile; the hope that sometime it will be different, that Claudio won't have to come and get me and weep embracing me, asking me to go see you.

> even though it's to be near him again when he's dying, as on that October night, the four friends, the cold bulb hanging from the ceiling, the last injection of Coramine, the bare and frozen chest, the open eyes that one of us closed, weeping

And you who read me will think that I'm inventing; it doesn't matter much, for a long time now people have credited my imagination for what I've really lived or vice versa. Look, I have never met Paco in the city I've spoken about sometimes, a city about which I dream every so often, and like the chamber of an infinitely postponed death, of muddied searches and impossible dates. Nothing could have been more natural than to have seen him there, but I haven't found him there nor do I think I'll find him. He has his own territory, a cat in his marked-out and precise world, the house on the Calle Rivadavia, the poolroom café, some corner on Once. Maybe if I'd found him in the city with the arcades and the canal to the north I would have added him to the machinery of the searches, the interminable rooms in the hotel, the elevators that go off horizontally, the elastic nightmare that returns every so often; it would have been easier to explain the presence, imagine it as part of that scenery which would have impoverished it by polishing it, incorporating it into its clumsy games. But Paco stays in his territory, a solitary cat emerging from a zone all his own and unalloyed; the ones who come to get me are only from his family, it's Claudio or his father, sometimes his older brother. When I awaken after having found him at home or the café, seeing death in his eyes like water, the rest is lost in the noise of awakening, only he remains with me while I brush my teeth and listen to the news before going out; his image no longer perceived with the cruel lenticular precision of the dream (the gray suit, the blue tie, the black loafers) but the certainty that without thinking he's still there and he's suffering.

> not even hope in the absurd, knowing him happy again, seeing him in a ball game, in love with those girls he danced with at the club

> small gray larva, animula vagula blandula, little monkey trembling with the cold under blankets, holding out a puppet hand to me, why, to what end

I can't have been able to make you live this, I write it just the same for you who read me because it's a way of breaking the encirclement, of asking you to look into yourselves to see if you don't also have one of those cats, those dead you loved and who are in that there which it exasperates me to name with words on paper. I do it for Paco, because this or any other thing might be worth something, might help him be cured or to die, so that Claudio won't come back to get me, simply to feel at last that everything was a trick, that I only dream about Paco and that he, who knows why, grasps my ankles a little tighter than Alfredo, than my other dead. It's what you're probably thinking, what else could you be thinking unless it's happened to you with somebody, but nobody has ever talked to me about things like this, I don't expect it from you either, I simply had to tell it and wait, tell it and go to bed once more like anybody else, doing whatever possible to forget that Paco is still there, that nothing ends because tomorrow or next year I'll wake up knowing as now that Paco is still alive, that he called me because he expected something from me, and that I can't help him because he's ill, because he's dying.

A

CHANGE

OF

LIGHT

On those Thursdays, at dusk, when Lemos would call to me after the rehearsal at Radio Belgrano, I would be forced over two Cinzanos to listen to the projects for new plays with a great urge to go out onto the street and forget all about the radio theater for two or three centuries, but Lemos was the author of the moment and he paid me well for the little I had to do on his programs, rather secondary and generally unsympathetic roles. You've got just the voice, Lemos would say in a friendly way, the listener hears you and hates you, you don't have to betray anybody or kill your mama with strychnine, you just open your mouth and half of Argentina would like to roast your soul over a slow fire.

Not Luciana. On the very same day that our hero, Jorge Fuentes, at the end of *Roses of Infamy*, received two baskets of love letters and a little white lamb sent by a romantic ranch wife from the Tandil region, Shorty Mazza handed me Luciana's first lilac envelope. Used to nothing in so many of its forms, I put it in my pocket before going to the café (we had a week off between the triumph of *Roses* and the beginning of *Bird in the Storm*) and only on the second martini with Juárez Celman and Olive did I remember the color of the envelope and realize that I hadn't read the letter; I didn't want to do it in front of them because bored people are always looking for something to talk about and a lilac envelope is a gold mine. I waited to get to my apartment, where the cat, at least, didn't notice such things. I gave her her milk and her ration of affection; I found Luciana.

I don't need to see a picture of you, Luciana said, I don't care if *Sintonía* and *Antena* publish pictures of Míguez and Jorge Fuentes but never one of you, I don't care because I have your voice, and I don't care either if they say you're unpleasant and a villain, I don't care if your roles fool half the world, just the opposite, because I give myself the illusion of being the only one who knows the truth: you suffer when you play those parts, you put your talent into it but I can tell that you're not really there like Míguez or Raquelita Bailey, you're so different from the cruel prince in *Roses of Infamy*. Thinking that they're hating the prince, they hate you, people get things mixed up and I realized it just last year with my Aunt Poli and other people when you were Vassilis, the murdering smuggler. I felt a little lonely this afternoon and I wanted to tell you this, maybe I'm not the only one who's told you this and I wanted it for you in some way, for you to know that you've got company in spite of everything, but at the same time I'd like to be the only one who knows how to cross over to the other side of your parts and your voice, the one who's sure that she really knows you and admires you more than the ones with the easy parts. It's like with Shakespeare, I never told anybody, but when you played the part, I liked Iago better than Othello. Don't feel obliged to answer me, I'm putting down my address just in case you really want to, but if you don't I'll feel just as happy having written you all this.

Night was falling, the hand was thin and flowing, the cat had fallen asleep after playing with the lilac envelope on the sofa pillow. Since Bruna's irreversible absence there'd been no more dining in my apartment, cans were enough for the cat and me, and cognac and pipe for me especially. During the time off (later I would have to work on the role in *Bird in the Storm*) I reread Luciana's letter with no intention of answering it because in things like that an actor, even if he only receives one letter every three years; my dear Luciana, I answered her before going to the movies Friday night, your words move me and I am not saying this out of courtesy. Of course I wasn't, I was writing as if that woman who I imagined to be rather small and sad and with chestnut hair and blue eyes were sitting right there and I was telling her that her words moved me. The rest came out more conventional because I couldn't find anything to tell her beyond the truth, all that was left was filling up the sheet of paper, two or three phrases of friendship and gratitude, your friend Tito Balcárcel. But there was another piece of truth in the postscript: I am glad that you gave me your address, it would have been sad not to have been able to tell you how I feel.

No one likes to admit it, but when a person's not working he ends up getting a little bored, someone like me, at least. As a youth I used to have a lot of sentimental adventures, during free moments I could cast my line and the fishing was almost always good, but then Bruna arrived and that lasted four years, at the age of thirty-five life in Buenos Aires begins to fade and seems to get smaller, at least for someone who lives alone with a cat and isn't a great reader and doesn't like to walk much. Not that I feel old, quite the contrary; it would seem rather that it's the others, things themselves that are growing old and getting wrinkled; maybe that's why I'd rather spend my afternoons in the apartment, rehearsing *Bird in the Storm* by myself with the cat looking at me, getting my vengeance on those unpleasant parts by raising them to perfection, making them mine and not Lemos', transforming the simplest sentences into a play of mirrors that multiplies the dangerous and fascinating side of the character. And so at the moment of reading the part on the radio everything was foreseen, every comma and every inflection of the voice, slowly increasing the degree of hatred (again it was one of those characters with certain pardonable traits but who slowly fell into infamy until there was a chase epilogue up to the edge of a cliff and a final leap, to the great satisfaction of the radio audience). When, between two matés, I found Luciana's letter forgotten in the magazine stand and I reread it out of sheer boredom, it happened that I saw her again; I have always been visual and it's easy for me to fabricate anything, in the beginning I had seen Luciana as rather small and my age or near it, most of all with light, almost transparent eyes, and once more I imagined her like that, I saw her pensive once more before writing me each sentence and then deciding. Of one thing I was sure, Luciana was not a woman for rough drafts, certain that she had hesitated before writing me, but after hearing me in *Roses of Infamy* the sentences had started coming to her, you felt that the letter was spontaneous and at the same time—maybe because of the lilac paper—it gave me the sensation of a liqueur that has slept in its flask for a long time.

I even imagined her house by just casting my eyes about; her house must have been one of those with a covered courtyard or at least an inner gallery with plants. Every time I thought about Luciana I would see her in the same place, the gallery finally replacing the courtyard, a closed gallery with skylights of colored glass and screens that let the light pass through, turning it gray, Luciana sitting in a large wicker chair and writing me, you're so different from the cruel prince in *Roses of Infamy*, lifting the pen to her mouth before going on, nobody knows it because you've got so much talent that people hate you, the chestnut hair as if covered by the light of an old photograph, that ash-colored and at the same time clear air of the closed gallery, I would like to be the only one who knows how to cross over to the other side of your parts and your voice.

That evening, before the first performance of *Bird*, it was necessary to eat with Lemos and the others; we rehearsed some of those scenes that Lemos called core and we called bore, a clash of temperaments and theatrical fireworks, Raquelita Bailey fine in the role of Josefina, the haughty girl whom I slowly enveloped in my well-known web of evil, for which Lemos knew no limits. The others fit their parts perfectly, so damn the difference between this one and the eighteen soap operas we had behind us. If I remember the rehearsal it's Shorty Mazza who brought me the second letter from Luciana and this time I had the urge to read it right away and went to the bathroom for a spell while Angelita and Jorge Fuentes were swearing eternal love at a Fencing Academy ball, those scenarios by Lemos that unchained the enthusiasm of the fans and gave more strength to the psychological identification with the characters, at least according to Lemos and Freud.

I accepted the simple, beautiful invitation to meet her at a sweet shop on Almagro. There was the monotonous detail of recognition, she in red and I carrying a newspaper folded in four; it could be no other way and the rest was Luciana writing me again in the covered gallery, alone with her mother or perhaps her father, from the beginning I had seen an old man with her in a house meant for a larger family and now full of hollow spaces and inhabited by the mother's melancholy for another daughter dead or absent, because maybe death had passed through the house not so long ago, and if you don't want to or can't I'll understand, it's not my place to take the initiative but I also know—she'd underlined it without emphasis—that someone like you is above so many things. And she added something that I hadn't thought about and which fascinated me, you don't know me except for that other letter, but I've been living your life for three years now, I can sense what you're really like in every new character, I take you out of the play and you're always the same for me when you're not wearing the mask of your role anymore. (That second letter got lost on me, but that's what the phrases were like, that's what they said; on the other hand, I can remember putting the first letter in a book by Moravia I was reading, it must still be there in the bookcase.)

If I had told Lemos about it, it would have given him an idea for another play, certainly the meeting, which would take place, naturally, after a few alternatives of suspense, and then the fellow would discover that Luciana was exactly as he had imagined, a proof of how love precedes love and sight sight, theories that always work at Radio Belgrano. But Luciana was a woman over thirty, years she carried quite well, of course, not quite so small as the woman writing letters in the gallery and with delightful black hair that had a life of its own when she moved her head. I hadn't created a precise image of Luciana's face for myself except for the blue eyes and the sadness; the ones that greeted me with a smile now were brown and not at all sad under that moving hair. I thought it was nice that she liked whisky, on the Lemos side almost all romantic meetings started with tea (and with Bruna it had been café au lait in a railroad car). She didn't make any excuses for the invitation and I, who sometimes overreact because I basically don't believe too much in anything that happens to me, felt quite natural and the whisky wasn't watered for once. We really enjoyed ourselves very much and it was as if we'd been introduced by chance and without any implications, the way good relationships begin, ones where no one has anything to exhibit or cover up; it was logical that the talk was mainly about me because I was the one who was known and she was only two letters and Luciana; therefore, without seeming vain, I let her recall me in so many soap operas, that one where I was tortured to death, the one about the workers buried in the mine, a few other parts. Little by little I was readjusting her face and voice, making an effort to break away from the letters, the closed gallery, the wicker chair; before we went our separate ways I learned that she lived in a rather small apartment on the ground floor and with her Aunt Poli, who had played piano in Pergamino back in the thirties. Luciana was making her adjustments too, as always happened with blind dates like that, just about at the end she told me that she'd imagined me to be taller, with curly hair and gray eyes; the part about the curly hair surprised me because I'd never thought of myself with curly hair in any of my parts, but maybe her notion was like a summation, a piling up of all the villainies and betrayals in Lemos' plays. I joked about it and Luciana said no, she'd seen the characters just the way Lemos had painted them but she was able to ignore them at the same time, to be beautifully alone with me, with my voice and who knows why with an image of someone taller, someone with curly hair.

If Bruna had still been in my life, I don't think I would have fallen in love with Luciana; her absence was still too present, a hollow in the air that Luciana began to fill without knowing it, probably without expecting it. With her, on the other hand, everything was quicker, it was going from my voice to that other Tito Balcárcel with straight hair and less personality than Lemos' monsters; all those operations lasted barely a month, they took place in two meetings in cafés, a third at my apartment, the cat accepted Luciana's perfume and skin, she fell asleep on her lap, she didn't seem to be in accord with a late afternoon in which suddenly she was in the way, when she had to leap mewing onto the floor. Aunt Poli went to live in Pergamino with a sister, her mission fulfilled, and Luciana moved to my place that week; when I helped her get her things ready I was pained by the lack of the covered gallery, the ash-colored light, I knew that I wasn't going to find them and yet there was something like a lack, a flaw. The afternoon of the move Aunt Poli told me the modest family saga in a sweet way, Luciana's childhood, the fiancé drawn away forever by an offer from the packing plants in Chicago, marriage to a hotel man from Primera Junta, and the breakup six years ago, things I had learned from Luciana but in a different way, as if she hadn't really been speaking about herself now that she seemed to be starting to live because of the presence of someone else, my body against hers, the saucers of milk for the cat, the movies at every moment, love.

I remember that it was more or less around the time of *Blood in the Cornfield* when I asked Luciana to tint her hair a lighter color. At first it seemed to be an actor's whim, I'll buy a wig if you want, she told me laughing, and, by the way, you'd look so nice in one with curly hair, since we're on the subject. But when I insisted a few days later, she said fine, black or chestnut hair didn't really matter to her, it was almost as if she'd realized that in my case change had nothing

to do with my actor's manias but with other things, a covered
gallery, a wicker chair. I didn't have to ask her a second time;
I was pleased that she'd done it for me and I told her so
several times while we made love, while I got lost in her hair
and her breasts and let myself slide with her into another
long sleep mouth to mouth. (Maybe the following morning,
or was it before going out shopping, I don't have it too clear,
I drew her hair together with both hands and tied it at the
back of her neck, I assured her that it looked better that way.
She looked at herself in the mirror and didn't say anything,
although I sensed that she didn't agree and she was right, she
wasn't the kind of woman to tie up her hair, it was impossible
to deny that it looked better on her when she wore it loose
before she lightened it, but I didn't tell her because I liked to
see her that way, to see her in a better way than that afternoon when she'd come into the sweet shop for the first time.)

I'd never liked hearing myself act, I did my job and that
was enough, my colleagues were puzzled by the lack of vanity,
which was so visible in them; they must have thought, maybe
correctly, that the nature of my roles didn't induce me to
remember them too much, and that's why Lemos looked at
me with raised eyebrows when I asked him for the file records
of *Roses of Infamy*, he asked me what I wanted them for and
I gave him some answer or other, problems of diction that I
wanted to solve or something like that. When I got home
with the album of records, Luciana was also a little surprised
because I never talked to her about my work, it was she who
would give me her impressions every so often, would listen to
me on certain afternoons with the cat on her lap. I repeated
what I'd told Lemos but instead of listening to the records in
another room I brought the phonograph into the living room
and asked Luciana to stay with me a while, I made the tea
myself and fixed the lights so she would be comfortable. Why

are you moving that lamp, Luciana asked, it's fine there. It was fine as an object but it gave off a crude, hot light onto the couch where Luciana was sitting, it would be better if only the half-light of the afternoon reached her from the window, a light that was a bit ash-colored and wrapped itself around her skin, her hands, as they busied themselves with the tea. You spoil me too much, Luciana said, everything for me, and you there in a corner without even sitting down.

Naturally, I only put on a few passages from *Roses*, just the time for two cups of tea, a cigarette. It did me good to watch Luciana, intent on the play, raising her head from time to time when she recognized my voice and smiling as if it didn't bother her knowing that poor Carmencita's miserable brother-in-law was beginning his intrigues in order to get hold of the Pardos' fortune, and that the sinister task would continue all through the many episodes until the inevitable triumph of love and justice according to Lemos. In my corner (I had accepted a cup of tea beside her but then I had returned to the back of the room as if I could hear better from there) I felt good, for a moment I was rediscovering something that I had been lacking; I would have liked everything to have been prolonged, for the light of dusk to have kept on resembling that of the covered gallery. It couldn't be, of course, and I turned off the phonograph and we went out onto the balcony after Luciana had put the lamp back in its place, because it really didn't look right where I'd moved it. Did listening to yourself do you any good, she asked me, stroking my hand. Yes, a lot; I talked about breathing problems, vowels, anything that she would accept with respect; the only thing I didn't tell her was that at that perfect moment all that was lacking was the wicker chair and maybe, also, for her to have been sad, like someone looking into space before continuing the paragraph of a letter.

We were coming to the end of *Blood in the Cornfield;* three more weeks and I'd have a vacation. When I got back from the station I would find Luciana reading or playing with the cat in the easy chair I had given her for her birthday along with the matching wicker table. They don't fit this decor at all, Luciana had said half-amused and half-perplexed, but if you like them I do too, it's a beautiful set and so comfortable. It'll be better for you if you have to write letters, I told her. Yes, Luciana admitted, as a matter of fact, I owe Aunt Poli, poor thing. There wasn't much light on the chair in the afternoon (I don't think she'd noticed that I'd changed the bulb in the lamp), so she ended up putting the little table and the chair near the window to knit or to look at magazines, and maybe it was on one of those autumn days, or a little later, that I spent a long time by her side one afternoon; I kissed her for a long time and I told her that never had I loved her as much as at that moment, just as I was seeing her, as I would have wanted to see her forever. She didn't say anything, her hands ran through my hair, mussing it, her head hung over my shoulder and she was quiet, as if absent. Why expect anything else from Luciana, on the edge of dusk like that? She was like the lilac envelopes, like the simple, almost timid phrases of her letters. From now on it would be hard for me to imagine that I'd met her in a sweet shop, that her black hair had swung like a whip at the moment of greeting me, of overcoming the first confusion of the meeting. In the memory of my love there was the covered gallery, the figure in a wicker chair that moved her away from the taller and more vital image that walked about the house in the morning or played with the cat, the image that at dusk would now and then enter into what I had wanted, into what made me love her so much.

Tell her, perhaps. I didn't have time, I think I hesitated

because I preferred keeping her like that, the fulfillment was so great that I didn't want to think about her vague silence, a distraction I hadn't known in her before, a way of looking at me for moments as if searching, something, a quiver of a glance returned immediately to the immediate, to the cat or to a book. That, too, entered into my way of preferring her, it was the melancholy climate of the covered gallery, the lilac envelopes. I know that awakening in the middle of the night sometimes, watching her sleeping against me, I could feel that the time had come to tell her about it, to make her mine again once and for all through a total acceptance of my slowly woven web of love. I didn't do it because Luciana was sleeping, because Luciana was awake, because that Tuesday we were going to the movies, because we were looking for a car for our vacation, because life came in great screenings before and after the dusks where the grayish light seemed to condense her perfection in the pause in the wicker chair. Because she spoke to me so little now, because sometimes she would look at me again as if searching for some lost thing, I held back the obscure necessity to confide the truth to her, to explain at last the chestnut hair, the light in the gallery. I didn't have time, a chance change in schedules brought me downtown one forenoon and I saw her coming out of a hotel, I didn't recognize her when I recognized her, I didn't understand when I understood that she was coming out holding tightly onto the arm of a man who was taller than I, a man who leaned over a little to kiss her on the ear, to brush his curly hair against Luciana's chestnut hair.

anywhere or I know that you're anywhere even though I can't see you, and nothing ends, nothing begins or ends while I sleep or afterward at the office or here writing, you alive for what, you alive why, Paco, there but where, old man, where and until when.

adducing proofs of air, little piles of ash as proofs, securities of a hole; the worst with words, words incapable of vertigo, labels before the reading, that other final label

notion of continuous territory, a room next door; time next door, and at the same time none of that, too easy to take refuge in the binary; as if everything depended on me, on a simple key that a gesture or a leap would give me, and knowing no, that my life locks me up in what I am, on the very edge but

trying to say it in another way, insisting: out of hope, looking for the midnight laboratory, an unthinkable alchemy, a transmutation

I'm no good for going beyond, trying any of the routes that others follow in search of their dead, faith or mushrooms or metaphysics. I know that you're not dead, that three-legged tables are useless; I won't go consult clairvoyants because they have their codes too, they'd look at me as if I were demented. I can only believe in what I know, going along my path like you along yours made small and ill there where you are, without bothering me, without asking me for anything but leaning on me in some way so I know you're alive in that link which ties you to this zone to which you don't belong but which sustains you who knows why, who knows for what. And that's why I think, there are moments when you need

THROAT
OF
A
BLACK
KITTEN

Otherwise it was not the first time it had happened to him, but, in any case, it had always been Lucho who took the initiative, resting his hand almost casually to stroke that of a blonde or a redhead who pleased him, taking advantage of the rocking on the curves in the subway, and then there would be an answer there, a conquest, a small finger that stayed caught a moment before the look of annoyance or indignation, everything depended on so many things, sometimes it turned out well, ran right along, the rest coming into play as the stations appeared through the windows of the car, but that afternoon it was happening in a different way. First, Lucho was frozen and his hair had been covered with snow that melted on the platform and slid down his scarf in icy drops; he'd gotten on the subway at the Rue du Bac station without thinking about anything, one body stuck in among a lot of others waiting for the moment of being by the fireplace, the glass of cognac, the reading of the newspaper before settling down to study German between seven thirty and nine, the usual thing except for that little black glove on the handrail, among piles of hands and elbows and coats a little black glove lost on the metal bar and he with his wet brown glove firmly on the bar so as not to fall on top of the lady with the packages and the weepy little girl, suddenly the awareness that a tiny finger was kind of riding horseback on his glove, that it was coming from a rather worn rabbit-skin sleeve. The mulatto girl seemed quite young and she was looking down as if out of it all, one more person swaying in the midst of the swaying of so many bodies crushed together; to Lucho it seemed like a rather amusing breaking of the rules, he released his hand, without responding, imagining that the girl was distracted, that she hadn't been aware of that gentle mounting of the damp and quiet horse. He wished he'd had enough room to take the newspaper out of his pocket and read the headlines that talked about Biafra, Israel, and soccer games, but the paper was in his right-hand pocket and in order to get it out he would have had to let go of the bar, losing the support necessary for the curves, so that the best thing to do was hold tight, opening up a small precarious space in the midst of overcoats and packages so that the little girl would be less sad and her mother wouldn't keep on talking to her in that tax collector's tone.

He had scarcely looked at the mulatto girl. Now he pictured her mat of curly hair under the hood of her coat and thought critically that with the heat of the car she might just as well have thrown the hood back, precisely when the finger stroked his glove again, first one finger and then two climbing onto the damp horse. The curve before Montparnasse-Bienvenüe pushed the girl against Lucho, her hand slipped off the horse to grasp the bar, so small and silly beside the big stallion who naturally was looking for the tickling with a two-fingered snout, without forcing, amused and still distant and damp. The girl seemed to be suddenly aware (but her previous distraction had also had something sudden and brusque about it), and she moved her hand a little farther away, looking at Lucho from the dark hollow that the hood afforded her to look at her own hand then as if she didn't agree or was studying the distances of good breeding. A lot of people had gotten off at Montparnasse-Bienvenüe and Lucho could now take his newspaper out, except that instead of taking it out he'd remained studying the behavior of the gloved little hand with a somewhat mocking attention, without looking at the girl, who once again had her eyes fixed on her shoes, quite visible now on the dirty floor, where suddenly the crying girl and so many people getting off at the Falguière station were missing. The starting jolt made the two gloves tighten on the bar, separated and each working in its own way, but the train was halted at the Pasteur station when Lucho's fingers sought the black glove, which didn't withdraw as the first time but seemed to loosen on the bar, become even smaller and softer under the pressure of two, three fingers, of the whole hand that was moving along in a slow, delicate possession, without resting on it too much, taking and leaving at the same time, and in the now almost empty car, which was opening its doors at the Volontaires station, the girl, turning little by little on one foot, faced Lucho without raising her face, as if looking at him from the little glove that was covered by Lucho's whole hand, and when she finally looked at him, the pair of them shaken by a hard jolt between Volontaires and Vaugirard, her large eyes in the shadows of the hood were there as if waiting, fixed and grave, without the slightest smile or reproach, with nothing but an interminable waiting that made Lucho vaguely uncomfortable.

"It's always like that," the girl said. "There's just no way with them."

"Ah," Lucho said, accepting the game but wondering why it wasn't funny, why it didn't feel like a game even though it couldn't be anything else, there was no reason to imagine that it was anything else.

"Nothing can be done," the girl repeated. "They don't understand or they don't want to, who can say, but nothing can be done to stop them."

She was talking to the glove, looking at Lucho without seeing him, she was talking to the little black glove that was almost invisible under the large brown glove.

"The same thing happens to me," Lucho said. "They're incorrigible, that's for sure."

"It's not the same thing," the girl said.

"Oh, yes, you saw."

"It's no use talking," she said, lowering her head. "I'm sorry, it was my fault."

It was the game, of course, but why wasn't it funny, why didn't it feel like a game even though it couldn't be anything else, there was no reason to imagine that it was anything else.

"Let's say it was their fault," Lucho said, taking his hand away to mark the plural, to denounce the ones to blame on the bar, the silent distant gloved ones on the bar.

"It's different," the girl said. "It looks the same to you, but it's so different."

"Well, there's always one who starts."

"Yes, there's always one."

It was the game, it was only necessary to follow the rules without imagining that there was anything else, a kind of truth or desperation. Why play dumb instead of following the current if it carried him in that direction.

"You're right," Lucho said. "Something would have to be done about them, not let them have their way."

"It's no use," the girl said.

"That's true, it's just a distraction, you can see."

"Yes," she said. "Even if you're saying it as a joke."

"Oh, no, I'm speaking just as seriously as you. Look at them."

The brown glove was playing at brushing against the motionless little black glove, it passed a finger around its waist, let go of it, went to the other end of the bar and stayed looking at it, waiting. The girl lowered her head all the more and Lucho wondered again why all that wasn't funny now that there was nothing to do but keep on playing.

"If only it were serious," the girl said, but she wasn't speaking to him, she wasn't speaking to anyone in the almost empty car. "If it were serious then probably."

"It is serious," Lucho said, "and nothing can really be done about it."

Now she looked at him in the face, as if waking up; the train was coming into the Convention station.

"People don't understand," the girl said. "When it's the case of a man, of course, he immediately imagines that . . ."

Vulgar, of course, and besides he would have to hurry because there were only three stations left.

"And even worse if it's a woman," the girl was saying. "It's already happened to me and that's why I keep a close watch on them from the moment I get on, all the time, but you can see."

"Of course," Lucho accepted. "That minute when a person is distracted arrives, it's so natural, and then they take advantage."

"Speak for yourself," the girl said. "It's not the same

thing. I'm sorry, it was my fault, I'm getting off at Corentin Celton."

"Of course it's your fault," Lucho mocked. "I should have got off at Vaugirard and look, you've made me go two stations beyond."

The curve threw them against the door, their hands slipped until they came together at the end of the bar. The girl went on saying something, foolishly excusing herself; Lucho again felt the fingers of the black glove as they climbed onto his hand, encircling it. When she let go of him, suddenly murmuring a confused good-bye, there was only one thing to do, follow her along the station platform, come up beside her and look for her hand, which was hanging kind of head down at the end of the sleeve, swaying without any reason.

"No," the girl said. "Please, no. Let me go on alone."

"Of course," Lucho said, without releasing her hand. "But I don't like your going away like that now. If only we'd had more time on the subway . . ."

"What for? What purpose would be served by having more time?"

"We probably would have ended up finding something, together. Something against it, I mean."

"But you don't understand," she said. "You're thinking that . . ."

"Who knows what I'm thinking," Lucho said honestly. "Who knows whether they have good coffee in the café on the corner, or if there is a café on the corner, because I barely know this district."

"There's a café," she said, "but the coffee's no good."

"You can't deny to me that you smiled."

"I don't deny it, but the coffee's no good."

"In any case, there's a café on the corner."

"Yes," she said, and this time she smiled, looking at him.

"There's a café but the coffee's no good, and you believe that
I—"

"I don't believe anything," he said, and he was accurs-
edly correct.

"Thank you," the girl said, incredibly. She was breathing as if the stairs had tired her out, and it seemed to Lucho
that she was trembling, but once more the little black glove
hanging warm inoffensive absent, once more he felt it living
between his fingers, twisting, tightening curling bubbling
being well being warm being content caressing black little
glove fingers two three four five one, fingers seeking fingers
and glove on glove, black on brown, finger between finger, one
between one and three, two between two and four. It was
happening, it was swinging there near their knees, nothing
could be done, it was pleasant and nothing could be done or
it was unpleasant but, in the same way, nothing could be
done, it was happening there and it wasn't Lucho who was
playing with the hand that was sticking its fingers between his
and curling and wriggling nor was it in any way the girl who
was panting as she reached the top of the stairs and was lifting
her face up against the drizzle as if she wanted to wash away
the stale, hot air of the subway passages.

"I live there," the girl said, pointing to a high window
among so many windows among so many identical high
buildings across the street. "We could make some Nescafé;
it's better than going to a bar, I think."

"Oh, yes," Lucho said, and it was his fingers that were
closing slowly over the glove as one squeezes the throat of a
black kitten. The apartment was rather large and very hot,
with an azalea and a floor lamp and Nina Simone records and
a messy bed that the girl embarrassedly and excusing herself
made up with some tugs. Lucho helped her set out the cups
and spoons on the table near the window, they made some

strong and sugary Nescafé, her name was Dina and his was Lucho. Happy, as if relieved, Dina talked about Martinique, Nina Simone, for moments she gave an impression of being barely nubile inside that plain wax-colored dress, the mini-skirt was becoming to her, she worked in a notary's office, broken ankles were painful but skiing in February in the Haute-Savoie, ah. Twice she'd remained looking at him, she'd started to say something with the tone from the subway handrest, but Lucho had cracked a joke, having decided enough now, something else, it was useless to insist and admitting at the same time that Dina was suffering, that it was probably harmful to her to give up the comedy so soon, as if it had the slightest importance. And the third time, when Dina had leaned over to pour the hot water into his cup, murmuring again that it wasn't her fault, that it only happened to her at certain times, that now he could see how it was all different this time, the water and the spoon, the obedience of every gesture, then Lucho understood but who knows what, he had suddenly understood and it was different, it was from the other side, the handrest had its purpose, the game hadn't been a game, broken ankles and skis could go to the devil now that Dina was talking again without his interrupting her or getting her off the track, leaving her alone, sensing her, almost waiting for her, believing because it was absurd, unless it was only because Dina with her sad little face, her small breasts that gave the lie to the Tropics, simply because Dina. I'll probably have to be locked up, Dina had said without emphasis, it happens at any moment, you're you, but other times. Other times what. Other times insults, a slap on the behind, right off to bed, baby, why waste time. But then. Then what. But then, Dina.

"I thought you'd understood," Dina said sullenly. "When I told you that I'd probably have to be locked up."

"Nonsense. But I, at first—"

"I know. It couldn't help happening to you at first. That's just it, at first everybody makes a mistake, it's so logical. So logical, so logical. And locking me up would be logical too."

"No, Dina."

"Yes it would, God damn it. I'm sorry. But it would. It would be better than the other thing, which so many times. Nympho I don't know how many times. Hooker, tart. It would be a lot better in the long run. Or if I cut them off myself with a meat cleaver. But I haven't got a cleaver," Dina said, smiling as if he would therefore forgive her again, so absurd reclining in the easy chair, slipping down fatigued, lost, with her miniskirt higher and higher, forgetting about herself, watching them only taking a cup, putting in the Nescafé, obeying hypocritical industrious tarts hookers nympho I don't know how many times.

"Don't talk nonsense," Lucho repeated, lost in something that he thought could be anything now, desire, mistrust, protection. "I know it isn't normal, you'd have to find the causes, you'd have to. In any case, why go so far? Locking-up or the cleaver, I mean."

"Who knows?" she said. "I'd probably have to go far, right to the very end. It would probably be the only way of getting out."

"What does far mean?" Lucho asked, fatigued. "And what's the very end?"

"I don't know, I don't know anything. I'm only afraid. I'd be impatient too if someone else spoke to me like that, but there are days when. Yes, days. And nights."

"Ah," Lucho said, bringing his match to his cigarette. "Because at night too, of course."

"Yes."

"But not when you're alone."

"When I'm alone too."

"When you're alone too. Ah."

"Understand, I mean that."

"It's fine," Lucho said, drinking his coffee. "It's fine, nice and hot. Just what we needed on a day like this."

"Thanks," she said simply, and Lucho looked at her not because he wanted to please her in anything; he simply felt the recompense of that moment of rest, that the handrest was finally finished.

"And it wasn't bad or disagreeable," Dina said as if guessing. "I don't care if you don't believe me, but for me it wasn't bad or disagreeable, the first time."

"The first time for what?"

"That, that it wasn't bad or disagreeable."

"That they put themselves . . . ?"

"Yes, they put themselves once more and it wasn't bad or disagreeable."

"Were you ever arrested because of it?" Lucho asked, lowering his cup to the saucer with a slow and deliberate movement, guiding his hand so that the cup would land exactly in the middle of the saucer. Contagious, by God.

"No, never, but on the other hand . . . There are other things. I already told you, people who think that it's a proposition and also people who begin, just like you. Or they get furious, like the women, and you have to get off at the first station or run out of the store or the café."

"Don't cry," Lucho said, switching to the familiar form. "We're not going to get anywhere if you start crying."

"I don't want to cry," Dina said. "But I've never been able to talk to anybody like this, after . . . No one believes me, no one can believe me, you yourself don't believe me, you're just good and you don't want to hurt me."

"I believe you now," Lucho said. "Up until two minutes ago I was just like the rest of them. You probably should have laughed instead of crying."

"You see," Dina said, closing her eyes. "You see how useless it is. Not even you, even though you say so, even though you believe. It's too idiotic."

"Have you seen somebody?"

"Yes. You know," she said, going into the familiar form, "tranquilizers and a change of air. You fool yourself for a few days, you think that . . ."

"Yes," Lucho said, offering her a cigarette. "Wait. Like this. Let's see what it does."

Dina's hand took the cigarette with thumb and forefinger, and at the same time the ring finger and the pinky tried to coil around Lucho's fingers as he held his arm out, watching. Free of the cigarette, his five fingers came down until they enwrapped the small dark hand, barely encircling it, beginning a slow caress that slid alone until it was left free, trembling in the air; the cigarette fell into the cup. The hands quickly went up to Dina's face as she doubled over the table, breaking out into a hiccoughing as if she were throwing up.

"Please," Lucho said, lifting up the cup. "Please, no. Don't cry like that, it's so absurd."

"I don't want to cry," Dina said. "There is nothing to cry about, on the contrary, but you can see."

"Drink it, it'll do you good, it's hot; I'll make myself another one, wait till I wash the cup."

"No, let me do it."

They got up at the same time, came together at the edge of the table. Lucho put the dirty cup back down on the table-cloth; their hands hung loose against their bodies; only their lips touched. Lucho looking at her full in the face and Dina with her eyes closed, tears.

"Maybe," Lucho murmured, "maybe this is what we have to do, the only thing we can do, and then."

"No, no, please," Dina said, motionless and without

opening her eyes. "You don't know what . . . No, better not, better not."

Lucho had encircled her shoulders, was slowly squeezing her against him, he felt her breathing against his mouth, a hot breath with the smell of coffee and dark skin. He kissed her fully on the mouth, sinking into her, looking for her teeth and tongue; Dina's body went soft in his arms, forty minutes before her hand had stroked his on the handrail of a subway, forty minutes before a small black glove on a brown glove. He barely heard her resist, repeat the negative in which there had been the beginning of a warning, but everything gave way in her, in the two of them; now Dina's fingers were climbing slowly up Lucho's back, her hair was getting in his eyes, her smell was a smell without words or warnings, the blue blanket against their bodies, the obedient fingers looking for the zippers, scattering clothes, obeying orders, his and Dina's against the skin, between the thighs, the hands like the mouths and knees and now stomachs and waists, a murmured plea, a resisted pressure, a moving back, an instantaneous movement to transfer from the mouth to the fingers and from the fingers to the sexes that hot froth that leveled everything, that in a single movement united their bodies and threw them into the game. When they lighted cigarettes in the darkness (Lucho had tried to put out the lamp and the lamp had fallen onto the floor with a noise of broken glass, Dina had started up as if in terror, refusing the darkness, she'd spoken about lighting a candle at least and going down to buy another bulb, but he'd embraced her again in the darkness and now they were smoking and catching sight of each other every time they inhaled, and they kissed again), it was stubbornly raining outside, the warmed-up room held them naked and lax, rubbing each other with hands and waists and hair they relaxed, they stroked each other interminably, they saw each other with a repeated and damp touch, they smelled each other in the darkness murmuring a happiness of monosyllables and diastoles. At some moment the questions would return, the ones chased away that the darkness was hiding in the corners or under the bed, but when Lucho wanted to know, she leaped on top of him with her wet skin and shut his mouth with kisses, soft bites, only much later, with new cigarettes between their fingers, did she tell him that she lived alone, that nobody lasted long with her, that it was useless, that they never loved her, that there was that illness, everything as if it didn't really matter underneath or was too important for words to be worth anything, or maybe as if it all wasn't going to go beyond that night and didn't need any explanations, something barely started on a subway handrail, something that most of all they had to have some light.

"There's a candle somewhere," she'd insisted monotonously, rejecting his caresses. "It's too late to go down to buy a bulb. Let me look for it, it must be in some drawer. Give me the matches."

"Don't light it yet," Lucho said. "It's so nice like this, not seeing each other."

"I don't want to. It's nice but you know, you know. Sometimes."

"Please," Lucho said, feeling on the floor to find the cigarettes. "For a while we'd forgotten . . . Why are you starting up again? We were fine like this."

"Let me get the candle," Dina repeated.

"Go get it, what difference does it make?" Lucho said, handing her the matches. The flame floated in the stagnant air of the room, outlining the body that was only a little less dark than the shadows, a glow of eyes and nails, darkness again, scratching another match, darkness, scratching another match, the quick movement of the flame that was going out in the back of the room, a short, as if suffocated, run, the weight of the naked body falling across his, hurting his ribs, her panting. He hugged her tightly, kissing her without knowing from what or why he had to calm her down, he murmured words of relief to her, held her against him, under him, possessed her gently and almost without desire from a long fatigue, entered her and rode her feeling her curl and give way and open and now, now, already, now, like that, already, and the ebb tide returning them to a rest face up looking at nothingness, hearing the night throb with the blood of rain outside, the interminable great womb of night guarding them from fears, from subway handrails and broken lamps and matches that Dina's hand had refused to hold, that had folded under to burn itself and burn her, almost like an accident because in the dark space and positions change and a person is clumsy like a child but after the second match was squashed between two fingers, wrathful crab burning itself just so long as the light was destroyed, then Dina had tried to light one last match with the other hand and it had been worse, she couldn't even tell Lucho, who was listening to her out of a vague fear, a dirty cigarette in her hand. Can't you see that they're refusing, there it is again. What again? That. What again? No, nothing, I've got to find the candle. I'll look for it, give me the matches. I dropped them over there, in the corner. Don't move, wait. No, don't go, please don't go. Let go, I'll find them. Let's go together, it's better. No, let me, I'll find them, tell me where the damned candle could be. Over there, in the cupboard, if you lighted a match probably. You can't see anything, let me go. Rejecting her slowly, unknotting the hands that held his waist, getting up little by little. The tug on his sex made him cry out more from surprise than from pain; like a whip he grabbed the fist that bound him to Dina, who was stretched out on her back and moaning, he opened its fingers and pushed it away violently. He heard her call him, ask him to come back, that it wouldn't happen again, that it was his fault for being stubborn. Guiding himself to what he thought was the corner, he crouched beside the thing that might have been the table and felt around for the matches, he seemed to find one but it was too long, maybe a toothpick, and the box wasn't there, the palms of his hands ran over the old rug, he crawled on his knees under the table; he found one match, then another, but not the box; down on the floor it seemed even darker, it smelled of enclosure and of time. He felt the claws running over his back, coming up to the nape of his neck and his hair, he straightened himself with a leap, pushing Dina away as she shouted against him and said something about the light on the landing of the stairs, open the door and the light from the stairs, but of course, why hadn't they thought of that before, where was the door, there opposite, surely not since the table was on that side, under the window, I tell you over there, then you go since you know, let's both go, I don't want to be left alone now, let go of me, you'll hurt me, I can't, I tell you I can't, let go of me or I'll hit you, no, no, let me go. The shove left him alone facing something panting, something that was trembling there alongside, very close; stretching out his arms he went forward looking for a wall, imagining the door; he touched something hot that evaded him with a shout, his other hand closed on Dina's neck as if it were squeezing a glove or the throat of a black kitten, the burning tore his cheek and lips, grazing an eye; he threw himself back to free himself from what was still clutching Dina's throat, fell back onto the rug, dragged himself aside knowing what was going to happen, a hot wind over him, the scratch of nails against his stomach and ribs, I told you, I told you it couldn't be, light the candle, find the door right now, the door. Crawling away from the voice that hung somewhere in the black air, in a hiccough of asphyxia that was repeated and repeated, he came to the wall, moved along it standing up until he felt a frame, a curtain, the other frame, the latch; an icy wind mingled with the blood that filled his lips, he felt for the light switch, behind he heard Dina's running and shriek, her blow against the half-open door, she must have hit her forehead or her nose on the edge, the door closing behind his back just as he pushed the light button. The neighbor who was spying from the door across the way looked at him and with a muffled exclamation went back inside and bolted the door. Lucho naked on the landing cursed him and ran his fingers over his face, which was burning, while everything else was the cold of the landing, the footsteps running up from the first floor, open up, open up at once, for God's sake open up, there's light now, open up there's light now. Inside the silence and a kind of waiting, the old woman wrapped in the purple robe looking from below, a shriek, shameful, at this time of night, pervert, police, they're all the same, Madame Roger, Madame Roger! She's not going to open up for me, Lucho thought, sitting on the first step, wiping the blood from his mouth and eyes; she's been knocked out by the blow and is lying there on the floor, she's not going to open up, always the same, it's cold, it's cold. He began to pound on the door while he heard the voices in the apartment opposite, the running of the old woman going down and calling Madame Roger, the building waking up below him, questions and noises, a moment of waiting, naked and covered with blood, a madman, Madame Roger, open up, Dina, open up, it doesn't matter that it's always been like this but open up, we were something else, Dina, we could have found it together, why are you there on the floor, what did I do to you, why did you bump into the door, Madame

Roger, if you opened up we could find the way out, you've already seen, you saw how everything was going so well, just turning on the light and the two of us continuing to look, but you won't open up for me, you're crying, mewing like an injured cat, I hear you, I hear you, I hear Madame Roger, the police, and you son of a thousand bitches why are you spying on me from that door, open up, Dina, we can still find the candle, we'll wash up, I'm cold, Dina, there they come with a bedspread, it's typical, a naked man is wrapped in a bedspread, I'll have to tell them that you're stretched out there, to bring another bedspread, to knock the door down, to clean up your face, to take care of you and protect you because I won't be there, they'll separate us immediately, you'll see, they'll take us down separately and carry us off far from each other, what hand will you look for, Dina, what face will you scratch while they carry you off so many of them and Madame Roger.